Hearts of Glass

Hearts of Glass

A NOVEL BY

Nicole Jeffords

CROWN PUBLISHERS, INC.
NEW YORK

Published by Crown Publishers, Inc.,
201 East 50th Street, New York, New York, 10022.
Member of the Crown Publishing Group.

CROWN is a trademark of Crown Publishers, Inc.

Manufactured in the United States of America

ISBN 0-517-58638-X

Book design by Shari deMiskey

In memory of my father,
Gustave Schindler

*C*harlie Gallagher's biggest fear was that someone she knew would see her entering the church. She wore an old shearling coat, sunglasses, and a head scarf; but still, as she crossed Second Avenue and walked the final block to Saint Hilda's, she felt painfully visible, the largest thing on the horizon. The church, thank God, was one she had never frequented before since she was an Episcopalian and this place was Lutheran. It was small and not very grand-looking; as her friend Tanya Hendricks hustled her in the door, she caught the distinct soup-kitchen smell of lunch cooking in a basement cafeteria, and she felt, for a moment, as if she herself were a homeless person relying on charity, with no other place to go for food.

"I'm not sure I want to do this," she whispered.

"Of course you don't," agreed Tanya. "What sane woman would want to give up booze unless she had to? But in your case, sweetheart, believe me, you have to."

At that moment Charlie hated Tanya more than she had ever hated anyone in her life. But she followed her friend up a narrow flight of steps and into a room that, at quick first glance, reminded her of a second-rate doctor's waiting room. Not that she had ever been to a second-rate doctor, but she imagined it so: two or three shabby couches and some worn armchairs arranged in a circle, a threadbare carpet, a grimy oil portrait of some unrecognizable person. Only the magazines were missing. And people were smoking, which nowadays would never happen in a doctor's office. Behind the circle of couches was a second circle of metal auditorium chairs. "Oh good, there're still some comfortable seats left," said Tanya. "Sit down here and I'll get coffee." She more or less pushed Charlie into an old armchair, throwing her mink coat down on the one beside it to save her place. "Back in a tick, sweetie," she said, patting Charlie's shoulder with a small freckled hand whose nails were bitten down to the quick.

Although it was warm in the room, Charlie did not remove her own coat. Nor did she remove her dark wraparound sunglasses. This was not so much because she wanted to hide, as because her eyes hurt like hell. Her eyes, and the inside of her skull, which felt as if someone were dragging sharp fingernails across it. Last night she had gotten drunk, and this morning, as on most mornings of her life, she was paying for it.

A woman sat down on the other side of her. "I haven't seen you here before, have I?" she asked Charlie.

Charlie shook her head, not daring to open her mouth because she knew her breath, beneath the Listerine with which she had gargled an hour ago, smelled of stale scotch.

"Well, welcome," said the woman, reaching into a shopping bag and taking out some knitting needles and a ball of yarn. "This is one of the best meetings in the city." She winked at Charlie. "Not that they aren't all good."

Charlie was relieved when the woman, who looked like an aging debutante in pearls and a cashmere twin set, didn't continue talking, but concentrated on her knitting with a small dim smile of pleasure on her lips. The room was getting crowded. Suddenly there were no more seats, and people coming in had to sit on the floor or lean in at the doorway. The air was heavy with cigarette smoke, and it was a relief when someone opened a window, and a burst of fresh—or at least fresher—Manhattan air entered the room.

"Here, darling, take this," said Tanya, handing her coffee in a paper cup.

Charlie took a grateful sip, shrugged out of her coat, and began to rummage in her purse for a cigarette. She crossed her long legs tightly and smoothed the hem of her tweed skirt as far down over her knees as it would go. She felt terribly self-conscious. All around her she sensed expectancy, as if something wonderful were about to happen, something that could not, and perhaps should not, include her. The feeling made her unaccountably angry; pressing her sunglasses more firmly into place, she decided to ignore it. Except for a few coughs, the room had grown quiet, and she was reminded of the moment before a concert begins, when the pianist is already seated and the audience strains its ears for the first few chords of music. Suddenly a thin young man in a shirt and tie and blue jeans began to speak. "Hello everyone, I'm Ted and I'm an alcoholic. Welcome to the lunchtime meeting of the Yorkville Group. We have nine meetings here a week..."

Charlie's mind wandered as the young man went into detail about when the meetings were. On the wall behind Ted's shoulder she had noticed a big white chart that looked like instructions for unruly school children. "What's that thing?" she whispered, nudging Tanya. At the top of the chart, in red letters, was written THE TWELVE STEPS.

"Those are guides to recovery," Tanya whispered back. "Don't worry about them now."

More out of boredom than curiosity, Charlie squinted behind her dark glasses to read the first step. "We admitted we were powerless over alcohol—that our lives had become unmanageable." Well, that was true enough in her case: she couldn't stop drinking, and her life was a mess—Neil, her husband, could barely contain his impatience with her; and in the last weeks, Petra and Colin, her children, seemed to shrink from her touch. And terrible things had happened to her. She had secrets she could talk to no one about, certainly not Tanya, or any of the people in this room.

She tried to read the next few steps, but her vision blurred; she couldn't concentrate. Ken or Ted or whatever his name was had just said, "Is there anyone here who's new to the meeting, or here for the first time?" Charlie blushed wildly as Tanya jabbed her in the ribs with a sharp elbow. She felt as if every single person in the room were staring at her. Her skin was

3

clammy, last night's scotch oozing out of her pores. She opened her mouth and closed it, knowing that never in a million years could she publicly identify herself—and as an alcoholic!—in this hot, crowded room.

But already the moment had passed. Ted or Ken was asking for day counts, and, to much clapping, people were raising their hands and announcing how many days, up to ninety, they had sober. A black woman, who wore a dozen golden bangles that made a tinkling sound as she waved her arm in the air, said she had thirty days sober, and Charlie wondered who she was. Somewhere she had seen that face before. She began to look around her. The people here, as types, were familiar: a lot of older, well-groomed ladies who would have fit in perfectly at one of her mother's bridge parties, several extremely handsome gay men who were probably actors or interior designers, one or two nondescript girls who might have been secretaries or housewives, a few businessmen in suits and ties. Nobody looked like a drunk. At least not her picture of a drunk, which was a red-nosed, broken-down, whiskey-smelling person from off the street. Someone shabby and malodorous. Who probably didn't have a home.

The clapping subsided, and now Ted or Ken introduced the speaker. This was a small, fine, brown-haired woman in her mid-thirties who sat in a chair just across the circle from Charlie's. Her name was Felicity, and she wore a tight little minidress that fit her skinny body perfectly, emphasizing an easy, loose-jointed athleticism. She had kicked off one of her shoes, and for the next few minutes, as she spoke, she kept searching for it with her stockinged foot; somehow this small sign of awkwardness pleased Charlie. The woman had a soft southern accent and she told her story slowly, a story about being blind drunk night after night. Then she hesitated. Even the matron beside Charlie stopped knitting to listen, rapt. This small, somewhat demure-looking woman was talking about how drunk she had been the first time she experienced sexual intercourse. "Didn't even feel it," she said. "Guy pulled off my panties, and I was so sloshed that the only thing I remembered in the morning was him lying on top of me, and then sending me home in a cab."

Charlie couldn't believe that anybody could be so candid.

4

There must have been thirty or forty people in the room, all with their attention focused on her. With pain in her voice, Felicity went on to describe the rest of the experience. "It never occurred to me that the episode would have consequences. In those days I didn't bother to keep track of my menstrual periods, and by the time I realized I was pregnant, it was too late to do anything about it. Eighteen years ago, this week, I had a little baby girl whom I gave up for adoption." Her voice caught in her throat as she said this. Someone handed her a tissue, and she blew her nose softly. Staring at her, Charlie thought, Jesus, how can anyone go and cry like that in public? But secretly she was impressed; if Felicity could be this brave and forthright, maybe Charlie could, too. She lit another cigarette, her third since coming to the meeting, and leaned forward in her chair to hear the rest of Felicity's story.

Gwendolyn Thomas didn't mind being the only black person at the meeting. Like an expatriate long accustomed to speaking a foreign language, she had grown so used to the brainy white intellectual circles in which she traveled that she no longer thought of herself in terms of her blackness. She was a writer, a novelist whose books had managed to occupy the niche on the bestseller list reserved for quality fiction. Although she didn't like to, she often appeared on TV talk shows, and so it wasn't surprising that she looked familiar to people. Gwen Thomas was pointed out in restaurants and approached on the street, and she was so used to the attention that the glamour of it had almost worn off. In AA rooms it was different. Here people had a policy of leaving celebrities alone, ignoring them after a glance or two, and so Gwen, after the first few weeks, had grown to feel very comfortable and anonymous at meetings. It didn't matter who she was. She was just another drunk getting sober, and that, for her, was a wonderful feeling.

Felicity Rettinger, the young woman speaking, was her editor. Totally unaware that Felicity had ever had a problem with alcohol, Gwen had been shocked when she ran into her at an AA meeting a week ago. "Well, it's about time," Felicity had said, hugging her and laughing.

"What's that supposed to mean?" Gwen scowled.

But she knew. Her drunkenness wasn't exactly a secret in the publishing industry. At a dinner for recipients of the Mendelsohn Award, which Gwen had won the year before, she had been too drunk to give a thank-you speech. Her husband, the poet Walter Rudin, had had to do that for her, jokingly saying that his wife had been celebrating for hours and could not come to the podium. Two years ago, at a Christmas party at "21," she had made an enemy of her managing editor, Norman Shultis, by throwing wine in his face and calling him a fat racist pig. And last May, at Thornton College, where she had been invited to give the commencement address, she had lost control of herself and, with a liquor-thickened tongue, begun to hurl abuse at the audience.

So it was no surprise to anyone that she might end up in AA. With Felicity, on the other hand, it was a different story. Gwen could not imagine her editor ever making a fool of herself because of alcohol. Felicity was a smart, even-tempered, peaceful sort of person, happily married to an architect, with a beautiful four-year-old daughter, lots of friends, and a job she loved. She had a brownstone in Brooklyn, gave excellent dinner parties, gardened, sewed her own clothes, was faithful to her husband. As much as Gwen liked her, she had always been vaguely annoyed with Felicity, who seemed as if she'd been perfect from birth. Now Gwen listened with shock as Felicity described one of the more dangerous aspects of her life as an alcoholic: running out to bars and picking up strange men. "I'd get dressed for the evening, saying to myself, 'Tonight you'll be a good girl; you'll have one drink and come straight home without talking to anyone.' But of course I could never just have one drink. I'd have three or four, and then start flirting with some guy, and the next thing I knew I was in bed with him. I never remembered what the sex was like. I never even knew the guy's name or anything about him, and some mornings the only way I knew I'd been with someone was that my diaphragm was in."

Whoa! thought Gwen. She'd never heard that story. The only compulsive behavior she'd ever connected with Felicity was that she worked nonstop, cutting out a pattern for a dress, washing her windows, or weeding her garden when she wasn't driving herself crazy over a manuscript.

"I got sober nine years ago kind of by fluke. My boss, who knew nothing about my private life, had given me a book about women alcoholics. Well, let me tell you, I read through that manuscript with a sinking feeling in my stomach because I saw myself on every page. After that... well, I drank a few more weeks, but not very happily because now I was wise to what I was doing. I had a name for it: alcoholism."

Gwen shifted in her chair. She had a quick mental picture of herself lying shrunken and gray on a hospital bed a month ago. Her own way of getting sober had been much more terrible than Felicity's. But she didn't want to think about that now. She was here and she was safe, and she never, even in her mind, wanted to go back to those last few hours of drinking again. As Felicity's story ended people began to applaud, and Gwen found herself clapping longer and harder than anyone else, her golden bangles making a wild, desperate, metallic sound in the smoky air.

After the applause, there was a secretary's break: announcements were made, and a basket was passed. Standing in the doorway, Musette Hawley, known to the world and herself only as Musette, pulled a dollar from her purse and slipped it into the basket. She was a tall, thin, extremely beautiful woman in tight black jeans and a loose-fitting crimson sweater. In her arms she carried a silvery fox fur jacket. Anyone looking at her—and there were quite a few who did—might have remembered that in the late seventies she had had a big career as a model, her face blossoming onto the covers of all the leading magazines. More recently, eight or nine months ago, that same face had been downgraded to the covers of the sleazoid press. MUSETTE KICKS OUT PHILANDERING HUBBY screamed one headline. ACTRESS ATTACKS MATE WITH KNIFE blared another. After that there was relative silence until, just around Thanksgiving, *People* magazine ran a piece about Musette entering the Betty Ford Center, "to take care of herself after the public ordeal of her divorce from movie director husband, Miroslav Vlk." That had been two months ago, and now, on her agent's orders, she was here in New York where she knew fewer people than in L.A., and thus ran less risk of succumbing, once again, to pills and alcohol.

She had arrived at the meeting late, leaving her little red Porsche around the corner in a no-parking zone. All she heard of Felicity's story was the sober part of it: that Felicity had found a husband in AA and was happy as a lark. Well, ain't she lucky, thought Musette. Most of the men she had met so far in AA were creeps. Take this room for example. No one exciting. She handed the basket on to the next person, stepped carefully over the legs of three people sitting on the floor, and went to get a cup of coffee from a table at the side of the room. Out of habit she ignored the cookies, and used artificial sweetener instead of sugar. The first sip was awful, but she didn't care. Since getting sober she had gotten hooked on caffeine. Coffee and cigarettes, the only drugs she was allowed, and boy did she make use of them! With an amused smile, she turned away from the table, her topaz-colored eyes narrowing to play over the crowd. The usual assortment of out-of-work actors, businesspeople, ladies with their knitting. But when she came to a person in the front row, her heart skipped a beat. Her hand twitched, and she felt scalding coffee on her wrist. There, unbelievably, in a gray cocoon of smoke, was Charlie Gallagher.

Although she had never seen Charlie in person before, Musette was sure it was she. She grabbed a napkin to wipe her wrist, and moved to a spot where she could get a better view. The woman in question wore a string of lustrous pearls, a cream-colored cashmere sweater, a skirt of thick herringbone tweed. On her feet were dark brown Ferragamos, low-heeled because she was so tall. Her chestnut hair was up in a French twist; a wing of it had fallen into her face and, as Musette watched, she pushed it impatiently backward. Of course one couldn't see the eyes because Charlie, probably afraid of being recognized, wore those silly wraparound glasses. But how could Musette not know the elegant, slightly upturned nose, the thickish brows, the freckles, the sharply angular and coolly beautiful New England face?

It was a face that in its own realm—society—was as celebrated as her own, and Musette remembered the first time she had seen it, on a Sunday afternoon nearly sixteen years ago. She had been sitting on the floor of her Lower East Side apartment with the papers spread out around her. For the middle of September it had been hot, and she remembered blowing air down the front of her tank top, and then gasping as a headline caught her eye. CHARLOTTE VANDERMARK WEDS NEIL BYERS GAL-

8

LAGHER. She fell into a crouch over the paper and squinted. Above the headline was a picture of a radiantly smiling dark-haired girl in pearls and a strapless evening gown—a girl with just the same thick brows and uptilted nose as the woman who sat across the room from her now. Quickly she had read the announcement and learned that on her father's side, Charlotte Vandermark was from an old Dutch banking family (her mother's family was from Boston), and that she had attended the best schools: Brearley, Ethel Walker, and Vassar. She had graduated three months before, in June of 1975. She was twenty-two years old. Fighting tears, Musette had raised herself to a sitting position and tossed the paper aside. She didn't need to read about the groom, Neil Byers Gallagher. Until the previous May he had been her lover, the only man she had ever slept with, the man she had dreamed of marrying.

That hot September day, in her fury, she had sworn off Neil Gallagher like a bad drug. But her vow to forget him—and to erase that photo of Charlie from her mind—was one she could never sustain. Even as she re-created from scratch the girl she had been when Neil had known her, changing her looks, her name, her whole persona in her struggle to become a top fashion model, Neil Gallagher was always in the news. He went into politics shortly after his marriage, winning an important congressional seat in his home state, Pennsylvania; and with his Irish good looks, his sharp intelligence, his appealing manner, it was a sure thing that he would one day run for the presidency. And Charlie? According to the society columns, Charlie had borne her husband two children, and was constantly involved in raising funds for such organizations as Planned Parenthood, Meals on Wheels, and the Juvenile Diabetes Foundation. Musette saw pictures of her hosting a party or benefit, chicly dressed, always taller than anyone else, in *Vogue* and *Town & Country*. Musette read about how she was handling her son's dyslexia; Musette saw her choice of clothes for a weekend in the country and the excellent cuisine she had provided for a visiting dignitary. Musette learned that she disliked flashy jewelry, and that, except for when she went riding, she almost never wore pants. Over more than a decade and a half, for reasons she had no wish to explore, Musette had followed Charlie Gallagher's career closely. Sometimes she had the uneasy sense that her own life, filled with drama and chaos, and including three broken marriages, held a ghost in one corner: Charlie Gallagher, the splendid society woman she herself could never become.

As she stared across the room at this woman who had now appeared before her in the flesh, she felt hot flashes of jealousy and recognition. How long had Charlie been sober? She hadn't read anything about it in the society press. Was her marriage still in one piece? She hadn't read anything about that either. And why was she in New York? What was she doing here?

The meeting was coming to an end. People stood and joined hands to say the Serenity Prayer, and Musette noticed that Charlie's hands were shaking badly as she tentatively held them out to the women on either side of her. Even with her head ducked between her shoulders, she was the tallest woman in the room. Keeping her eyes on Charlie, Musette felt the weight of her past life make a decision for her. As people filed from the church, she would follow Charlie, even if only a little way. Perhaps Charlie would go into a coffee shop with the mop-headed, lively-looking woman who was now giving her a hug, and Musette could slip into the booth behind them, and hear at last what this woman's voice and tone were like. She put on her fox fur jacket and began to move toward Charlie in preparation.

C harlie desperately wanted to get away, to disappear into the gritty, anonymous throng on the street. But on the sidewalk in front of Saint Hilda's, Tanya threaded her arm through Charlie's and said, "Come on, we'll go get a cappuccino. I know a terrific place right near here. They make these wonderful Brie sandwiches too—you know, with real baguettes?"

"I don't want to go," said Charlie.

"But you must be hungry. One of the things they say in AA is not to let yourself get hungry, angry, lonely, or tired. Any of those could lead you back to a drink."

"I want to go home."

"Oh. Well, I'll go with you then."

Charlie shook her head. "I want to go by myself."

"I don't think that's a very good idea," said Tanya.

"Why the hell not?"

"Because you've just been to your first meeting. You're withdrawing from alcohol. You need to be with someone who understands about that."

"I need to be by myself," insisted Charlie. "Now if you'll let go of my arm..."

Tanya disengaged herself reluctantly. "I'll call you tonight," she said.

"Yes," said Charlie. "That would be nice." She pulled her silk scarf tightly around her head. The January sun was shining, but it was chilly. "Thanks for taking me to the meeting. I appreciate it."

"Anytime," said Tanya. "I'm there if you need me. Remember that."

As she walked away, Charlie felt Tanya's eyes boring into the soft spot between her shoulders, and she quickened her pace, sighing with relief as she rounded the corner of First Avenue. She wasn't sure where she was going, but already in her mind a faint picture was forming of a gleaming bartop, a row of shining bottles, and her own face smiling back at her from a mirror as she raised a glass of something cool and refreshing to her lips.

Musette, who had stood as close to the two women as she could without being obvious, left the small group of people saying good-bye in front of the church and took off after Charlie. She had heard every word of their conversation, relishing the knowledge that it was Charlie's first day sober, and the fact that she had an abrupt way of dealing with people that bordered on imperial rudeness. But perhaps—in fact, very likely—it was because she was hung over. Musette remembered the incredible irritability and rawness of nerves that accompanied a hangover, and was glad, not for the first time since joining AA, that she didn't have to go through that anymore.

Ahead of her Charlie turned the corner, making a left onto First Avenue, and Musette broke into a run to catch up with her. The woman moved like some kind of weird African bird, her long bowlegs in pale tights catching the light as she strode intently up the avenue. But suddenly, for no apparent reason, she stopped in the middle of the sidewalk and stood looking dazedly around her. She was at Seventy-seventh Street, three blocks from where she had started, and a full minute passed before she got herself in motion again, turning sharply and ducking into the doorway of a restaurant.

Musette, lagging behind, caught up and stared cautiously into the window of the restaurant. It was a bistro, clean and European-looking, with small round wooden tables set close to one another, and a zinc bar in front. At a quarter to two the place was filled with people eating lunch. Charlie stood at the bar, still in her coat, scarf, and sunglasses. She placed her purse on the bar, and when the bartender poured a glass of wine for her, she grabbed it with gloved fingers, raised her aristocratic chin, and drank thirstily. The glass was nearly empty when she put it down.

Well, she's no sipper, thought Musette, a certain mean satisfaction rising in her breast as she watched Charlie finish off the rest of the drink. She considered going in there and engaging Charlie in conversation, but decided against it—she didn't want to be near all that liquor. Anyway, she had a hairdresser appointment in fifteen minutes. Even in the dark plate glass of the window she could see that her roots were showing. She pushed at her hair, and noticed that, beyond her reflection, Charlie had taken off her gloves and was lighting a cigarette. The sunglasses were still on, but now she removed the scarf and unbuttoned her coat, and with a practiced swing, hoisted herself up onto a barstool that had just come empty. Perhaps she felt Musette's eyes digging into her, because she turned for a second toward the window, and Musette jumped back, afraid Charlie would recognize her—not just from the meeting, but somehow, impossibly, from her long-ago affair with Neil.

She felt like a fool hovering outside a restaurant, nose pressed to the window as if she were hungry but couldn't afford to eat. She glanced once more at Charlie: the bartender was pouring her another drink. Then she turned and started back in the direction she had come. Her hairdresser was on Fifty-seventh Street and she'd have to hurry if she were to get there on time. As she walked, she thought of Charlie sitting at the bar, getting sloshed. How amusing that Charlie, who had grown up with all that money, didn't have the couth to remove her gloves before drinking. She herself, who had grown up poor, would never do a thing like that. She was, moreover, proud of her hands: sixteen and a half years ago she had been working as a typist in the front office of a trucking company in Allentown, Pennsylvania, and the bright young lawyer whose Philadelphia firm represented the company had stopped by her desk. "You've got great hands," he had said, watching her fingers fly over the keys.

What a line! But she had fallen for it, and who wouldn't—Neil Gallagher was gorgeous, with blue eyes, darkly tanned skin, and longish brown-black curly hair. That night he had taken her out to dinner, and she still remembered the jolt that had gone through her as he took the wineglass out of her hand and kissed her fingers.

At Seventy-fourth and Second, where her car was parked, her musings were instantly transformed into supreme irritation. A goddamn cop had given her a ticket. She saw the white rectangle of paper fluttering in the wind as she rounded the corner, and all thoughts of Neil Gallagher and his socialite wife went out of her head. "Goddamn fuck!" she said aloud, grabbing the thing from beneath the windshield wiper and ripping it up. She stuffed the pieces into her handbag. Her secretary would tape them together and pay the fine.

Sitting on her barstool, Charlie Gallagher was also filled with annoyance. She had been having such a good time. After the second glass of wine, the awful tension in her stomach and shoulders had begun to lift: there was that click in her head that meant she was in harmony with the world, nothing could get at her. And then a man had come over to her and said, "Don't I know you from somewhere?"

"No," said Charlie rudely, not even looking at him.

"Oh, but I'm sure I do," said the man. He sat down on the stool next to hers. He was well dressed, but a little thick and ruined, probably drunk himself. "Didn't we meet at Peggy Hirsh's party a week ago?"

"I don't know a Peggy Hirsh," said Charlie.

"Oh. Well then, it must have been somewhere else. I'm sure I know you."

Charlie didn't say anything. Despite the liquor in her, she was trembling with rage. She hated strange men approaching her.

"Anyway, supposing I buy you a drink?"

"Supposing you don't," said Charlie, enunciating the words very clearly through clenched teeth. She gestured to the bartender for the check, placed two tens on the cool metal of the bar, and waited for the change. During the whole transaction she didn't once look at the man, though she could sense his mood changing from hopefulness and bravado to surly anger.

"Who cares? You drink like a goddamn camel, and you're so snotty you look like one too," he called after her as she left the bar.

In the street, her open coat flapping around her legs, she hailed a cab. "Take me to Ninety-fourth and Madison," she told the driver, slamming the door and sliding to the middle of the sunken vinyl seat. She was anxious to get home—home being the apartment she was temporarily borrowing from her friend, Rita Rutherford, who was away on an extended business trip in London. In Rita's pantry was a bottle of Dewar's White Label, and she could already see herself putting her keys and purse down on the kitchen table, taking a tall water glass from the shelf, and filling it to the brim with scotch. That man approaching her in the bar a few minutes ago had brought back a memory of another man in another bar, and she wanted to do what she could to get rid of it.

But as the cab crawled through the heavy midafternoon traffic, today's man, coarse as he was, turned into a man she once had thought she loved. Ten months ago she had gone by herself on a trip to Barbados. The trip had been Neil's idea. He had hoped that in easier surroundings, on a white beach, reading her beloved Jane Austen and digging sun-browned toes into the sand, she would ease up on the drinking. But being alone had unnerved her, and on her second afternoon she had wandered into the hotel's poolside bar, telling herself she deserved a treat after a solitary lunch and several hours of looking around the shops of Bridgetown. It was sunset and the bar, with its blue-and-white striped awning, was empty. She was wearing a white linen skirt and a pink cotton blouse, and she thought to herself how nice it was to have bare legs after months of winter clothing. Up above, on several of the balconies, she could see people coming out to watch the huge red ball of the sun drop into the ocean. There was a lone swimmer in the pool behind her, and the regular *snick snick snick* of his arms cutting into the water combined with the rattling of the palms to provide a comforting music. She ordered a planter's punch, lit a cigarette, and opened her book. Heaven! The first drink went down fast, and so she ordered a second one, and as she was savoring its taste, a man's voice said, "What's that book you're reading?"

She didn't particularly feel like conversation. "Just a book," she said.

"Doesn't look like beach reading to me. All that mannered prose."

She looked up. The bar was horseshoe-shaped, and just across from her, in tennis clothes, sat a blond-haired man of about forty. He had faded blue eyes, a Boston accent, and his skin was leathery brown from the sun. "I don't think Jane Austen's all that mannered. Anyway, if you knew what I was reading, why'd you ask?"

He laughed. "To get your attention."

"Ah. And now that you've gotten it, I suppose you're going to ask if you can buy me a drink?"

He laughed again, a pleasant, easy, rumbling sound. "You must be psychic. Johnny," he called to the bartender, who stood to the side polishing glasses, "get this beautiful lady a drink."

It wasn't that he called her beautiful. She wasn't, and she knew it, having no false ideas about her looks. It was something else, a breeziness about him, that made her accept the drink, and then an invitation to dinner. He was so different from Neil, and that, after fourteen years of marriage, appealed to her. He had an honest, big-featured, sensuous face, and a crudely blunt way of expressing himself that she found amusing. Neil always kept himself in athletic trim, but this man had let himself go a little, his body as soft and cuddly-looking as a blond teddy bear's. His name was Gil Hoffeld. He was a commodities broker from—as she had guessed—Boston, and he was in Barbados because he had chartered a boat and intended to spend the next week sailing around the islands.

"It would be nice if you came with me," he said much later that night as they were lying together in the bow of his boat.

"Well, I can't," she said, laughing. "My poor husband would have a fit."

"The hell with your husband. He let you come here on your own. What does he care?"

That got Charlie thinking. She had never been unfaithful to Neil before, but somehow, because she was so far away, and this man was so foreign to her, and the atmosphere was so dreamy, so filled with the heavy scents of fruits and flowers, it didn't seem to matter. Neil, with his crisp executive manner, seemed as remote from the islands as if he were in the Arctic. She liked Gil. He drank as much as she did, if not more, and he was an exciting lover. Their first time together he put his mouth all over her body, licking her and telling her how good she tasted, and the second time, in a hoarse voice, he said: "Baby, I want to put it up your ass." Words Neil would never, in a million years, have used—and not, in any case, something they had ever done. In the morning, exhausted from the night's activities, she went to her hotel room and took a nap. When she awoke two hours later, she ordered an early lunch, made herself a martini from her own private stock of liquor, and put in a call to Neil.

"Darling," she said when she heard his voice, "a most wonderful thing has happened." She paused, hoping the gin coarsing through her veins would water down her sudden, tremendous sense of guilt. "I've been invited by some charming people I've met here, the Reginald Wilsons, to travel with them on their boat. We'll be going to Saint Vincent, Saint Lucia, and Martinique. Isn't that a hoot? You know how much I've always wanted to do that."

"Oh Charlie, I don't know. Who are these people?"

"He does something with insurance. Investments, I think. And she's a sweetheart. Her first cousin, Mary Wyndham, was at Vassar with me, and I know her aunt, too, from a weekend we once spent skiing in Vermont. The whole family comes from Seattle. You'd love them." That last part, at least, was true. She *had* known a Mary Wyndham at college.

"What if there's some sort of trouble? Whose boat is it, anyway?"

Carefully, so he wouldn't hear the ice tinkling in the glass, she took a sip of her martini. "It's a charter. One of those luxury things that comes with a captain and crew. And there won't be trouble. Look, I'll call you every evening at about seven. How're Colin and Petra?"

And so, with those easy lies on her tongue, each tale exquisitely constructed from the social fabric of her life, she had gone off with Gil on a week of adventure. What a week it had been! Hours of happy lovemaking in the V-shaped bow of the yacht, the wide, secret berth rocking like a cradle to the music of the waves. Walking around small port towns with the scent of sex on their fingers. Swimming in waters so still and warm she could feel the tickle of fish on her legs, and then making love on a sea-splashed deck, with only the sun as witness. Gil had introduced her to cocaine, and her senses were constantly heightened—his skin had tasted sweet as she had licked the salt off it, and his cock inside her had made her scream "Yes! Yes! Jesus, yes!" so loudly that she was sure her voice could be heard all over the Caribbean. It was a good thing there *wasn't* a captain and crew; the boat Gil had chartered was small enough for him to manage on his own.

After a weepy parting from Gil, she had returned to Washington utterly worn out from the booze and the coke and the sex and the constant, nerve-wearing excitement—and that, she thought now, taking her wallet from her purse, was when all the trouble had started. The cab pulled up in front of Rita's building, and she quickly paid the driver and got out. Neil had been far too clever for her. Or perhaps, looking at it in hindsight, not quite clever enough. In the elevator her hands fumbled with the keys, and she flushed as a young woman carrying a briefcase and a bag of groceries gave her a funny look. She could already taste the smooth fire of the scotch in her mouth. The hell with AA! And the hell with her old friend, Tanya Hendricks, who was so desperate to help her. Once she was in the apartment and had poured herself a glass of scotch, she would take the phone off the hook so that Tanya, who had said she'd call, would get a busy signal. Then she'd have hours and hours of uninterrupted drinking time, and if the bottle ran out, she'd phone down to the liquor store on the corner for another. She hadn't been in this neighborhood long enough to care what liquor store owners thought of her, and that, after her fishbowl life in Washington, was very liberating.

*L*ater that afternoon, Gwendolyn Thomas stood at the front door of her large, airy apartment on the tenth floor of a Chelsea building that had views over the Hudson just two blocks away, waiting for her husband to let her in. As happened frequently with her, she had forgotten her keys.

"There you are!" said Walter, sliding back the lock and throwing open the door. "Jesus, where were you? You've been gone for hours."

"At an AA meeting. Like I told you." She pushed past him, putting several large shopping bags down on a chair, then slipping out of her coat and hanging it in the foyer closet.

Walter made an elaborate show of looking at his watch. He was a slightly built white man of about forty-five with jet-black eyes set in a pale, bearded face. In faded jeans and a gray sweatshirt he looked like one of his students at New York University. "But it's six o'clock," he said. "The meeting was over at one-thirty."

"I had lunch with Felicity and then I went shopping," said Gwen. "When did you get home?"

"About an hour ago. I got kind of nervous when there wasn't a message from you on the machine."

"Why?" said Gwen, annoyed. "Look Walt, I'm gonna be all right. You don't have to watch over me like a mother hen."

He was standing close to her, breathing slowly, long white fingers rooted in the dark curls of his beard, a gesture that worried her since it usually signaled the beginning of an argument. "I just don't like not knowing where you are. It gets me crazy."

"So it'll get you crazy," she said, cutting him off. "Surely you don't expect me to report back about every single thing I do?" She glanced at him. His dark eyes wore an uncomfortable expression. "I see. You'd like that. Okay, well right now I'm gonna go into my study for a few minutes. When I come out, maybe I'll go to the bedroom to hang up the clothes I bought this afternoon. Or maybe I'll go to the kitchen and make dinner. I'm not sure which yet. But when I decide, I'll let you know. That all right with you?" She threw him a look of mild contempt, picked up her shopping bags, and marched down the hall to her study, aware of the angry tap of her heels on the parquet floor.

In her study she closed the door, leaning against it and breathing deeply. Already she felt a little pang of guilt for snapping at him. But she was so sick of his overbearing concern for her. They had been married for twelve years, and it was only in recent weeks, since she had gotten sober, that he had been this way. Up until then he had been the stronger one, the one who had made all the arrangements, dealt with friends and family, declined or accepted invitations, kept the world at bay. Now that she was more independent, he didn't like it. Sighing, she moved from the door and went to sit down on a big soft chintz-covered armchair, throwing her feet up on the hassock and dropping her bags to the floor. She kept her eyes averted from her desk.

Her study was a small, austere room whose one window looked out over the gardens of London Terrace on Twenty-fourth Street. It was quiet and peaceful; the walls, painted a pale almond beige, were bare of anything that would distract her as she worked. On the desk, beside the telephone and the keyboard of her computer, were three little Japanese animal carvings, ivory netsuke she liked to play with when she was trying to figure something out. But it was weeks since she had touched them, weeks since she had sat down at her desk and, in a ritual that was as familiar as brushing her teeth, removed her golden bangles, taken a pack of cigarettes from the carton in her drawer, and switched on the computer.

Which was why she hated to look at her desk now. In the year and a half that had passed since she had won the Mendelsohn Award she had been unable to write. Not what she considered writing, which in her case meant an open connection with her muse, the words flowing out of her so fast she could hardly move her fingers quickly enough to get them into the memory of her computer. Instead she had been blank. As dry inside as a dead tree.

To get back the connection with her muse, she had begun drinking heavily during writing sessions. And she had gone wailing to her editor, Felicity, who had advised her to stop working on her novel for a while, and try something else. "I'm sure *Ebony* would love a piece about your childhood in Harlem. Or about what it's like for a black woman to marry a Jewish poet-slash-college-professor. They really go for stuff like that."

She had not heeded Felicity's advice. Instead she had distanced herself from Felicity, forcing herself to sit for hours each day at her desk, a constant glass of brandy in her hand as she studied the blank screen of her computer. This had been pure torture; she would get one or two acceptable sentences, and then her mind would freeze over, and in despair she would spend the rest of the day drinking. After several months, she was left with the sense that she, who had lectured all over the country, who had appeared on TV, who was always being quoted as "that notable black author, Gwendolyn Thomas," was an impostor and a fraud. And then in December, two weeks before Christmas, all hell had broken loose.

Walter owned a cottage in the Berkshires, and when a neighbor phoned to say that a window had been shattered in a storm, and the pipes had frozen and burst, he had gone rushing up there. That had been on a Friday. The next day, Saturday, they had plans to go to a tree-trimming party at a colleague of Walter's on the Upper West Side, but early that morning he had phoned to say he wouldn't make it back on time. "The place is a mess, Gwen."

"Sorry, baby." She hated the house in the country and didn't feel all that sympathetic.

"Water everywhere. Plumber says it'll cost a shitload to put in new pipes."

She made a clucking sound with her tongue. "Well, we've got the money. Don't fret."

"It's not the money. It's . . . I don't know, everything. Look Gwennie, would you mind if I stayed up here till tomorrow night? I want to get this place cleaned up, and I'm going to miss the Teasdales' party anyway."

She felt a slight hollowness at the pit of her stomach, but she said, "No, that's all right. You stay up there and do what you have to."

She almost decided against going to the Teasdales' party, too, but then thought it would be good for her to be among people. She had kept to herself so much lately. At the party there was a sizable crowd. Nancy Teasdale, a food writer for the *New York Times,* ran around in a red caftan, talking loudly about an island she had just discovered in the Caribbean. Uniformed waiters passed trays of drinks and fussy, difficult-to-eat hors d'oeuvres, and at the piano little Joey Herman, who had once interviewed Gwen on his radio program, made a great ruckus playing all the Christmas tunes he had ever heard. Gwen wished she hadn't come. She stood at a window overlooking Central Park West, her back to the room, and when someone poked her in the shoulder she jumped skittishly.

"Nervous, hunh?"

It was Walter's colleague, Alfred Teasdale, tall and skinny and peculiarly old-fashioned in a bow tie and glittering rimless glasses.

"Not really."

"Where's Walter?"

"He had to go up to Egremont. There was a problem at the cottage. The pipes froze."

"Oh. Too bad." He stood for a moment, fiddling with an olive pit. Then he said, "How's the novel coming along?"

"Fine," Gwen lied.

"You must be nearly finished by now."

"Yes, just a few chapters to go."

"Good. Listen, Gwen, I wish you'd send me the manuscript. If it's anything like the last one, it'll be a joy to read."

The last one, *Hey Look at Me Mister,* had won the Mendelsohn Award. Gwen knew that Alfred was after the privilege of reviewing her current novel for the *New York Times,* and so she smiled at him and said carefully, "My editor has to read it first."

"Oh, Felicity hasn't seen it yet?"

"Not a word." Gwen forced a laugh. "Well, I think I'll go hang this on the tree." She drew a small gilded angel from her bag, smiled again at Alfred, and pushed her way through the crowd toward the tree, which stood at the other end of the apartment. When she had looped the ornament on the highest branch she could reach, she got her coat from the rented coatrack in the hall and left the party.

It was eight-thirty when she arrived home, early. She hadn't had a lot to drink at the party, and so she poured herself a stiff scotch now. What she wanted more than anything was peace of mind. She took the glass and went into the bedroom, where she sat down in front of the mirror and removed her jewelry. Staring at herself, she thought that it was very hard to be Gwendolyn Thomas. This was not a thought she pursued. Instead she creamed her hands, face, and neck, and morosely lit a cigarette. She was certain that everyone at the party knew she was a failure, that she would never write a word again. Even Alfred hadn't been fooled; it showed in her face that she was dead inside. The phone rang just then, and she clicked off the machine so it rang till the caller gave up; when the ringing had stopped, she took the receiver off the hook. She didn't want to hear from anyone in this sullen, awful mood.

But the mood continued. She thought another drink would help, but this time there was none of the warmth and secret conviviality that the liquor usually brought; no swift turning around of things so that what had seemed bad or frightening suddenly lost impact. Alarmed, she wondered if she should go to bed, although she knew it would be hours before she fell asleep. If she stayed up, on the other hand, she would have to face the fact of her emptiness, her failure, and that was the last thing she wanted to do. Gwendolyn Thomas, whose bleak eyes she had seen in the mirror, was a person she wanted to forget.

In the end she did what came most naturally to her. She finished the bottle of scotch, and opened another. She smoked her way through half a pack of cigarettes. She listened to some music. She wandered around the apartment, touching things. She stared out the window. Eventually she went into the bathroom and emptied Walter's bottle of sleeping pills into the palm of her hand. She didn't bother to count them. She didn't even really look at them. Instead she filled a glass with water, and took the pills one at a time. When she had finished, she went into the bedroom and lay down. The last thing she remembered thinking was that she should put the phone back on the hook. But she no longer had the strength to do so.

What she knew next was pain—pain, mistiness, confusion. She was in a hospital. It was deathly cold. They had forced a tube down her nose and that meant they were pumping her stomach. Later she learned that Walter had come back early from the country because of a threatened snowstorm, had walked into the apartment knowing already something was wrong because of the eerie stillness of the place, and the fact that all the lights were on. It was not quite two in the morning. She lay uncovered on the bed, her body cold and stiff and her pulse so feeble that Walter thought he had lost her.

She spent the next week at Saint Vincent's Hospital, was evaluated by a psychiatric team, and released with the warning that she must, along with weekly therapy, attend AA meetings. "Every day," said the doctor who discharged her. "Your problem is alcoholism and AA is the only place I know that can take care of that."

It was a relief to know that alcohol was at the root of her depression, and not just writer's block. If she held back from drinking, perhaps the words would start to flow. Perhaps, perhaps, she prayed, knowing now that this was a matter of life and death. She went to her first meeting like a drowning person grabbing at a rope flying through the air. She was desperately afraid, and she stared around the room without seeing very much, trying her best to concentrate on an elderly man who stood up in front, telling his story. The man looked like a bum, but his story was wonderful, and once she realized that was what they did in AA—tell stories—she was hooked.

She walked out of there knowing she would not drink again. She couldn't have said why, what had happened in that brief hour to change her, but from the first day she did not miss a meeting. They said that newcomers should go to ninety meetings in ninety days, and she was determined to do that. She was determined to do anything that would keep her from drinking again.

But recently Walter had become annoyed with her growing involvement in AA. "I didn't know you'd have to be out of the house so much," he complained.

She had begun going to coffee shops with people after meetings, and she knew that this was what was getting to him. "I can't help it," she said. "I have to be with other recovering alcoholics if I want to stay sober."

"Well, you should think about me sometimes, too."

"I do think about you. A lot."

"Yeah? Well, you have a weird way of showing it."

"Come on, Walter. Lay off."

"I hate to remind you, Gwennie, but if it weren't for me, you wouldn't be here, remember? If I'd walked into this apartment half an hour later than I did, it would have been curtains, *finito,* one more writer to bite the dust."

He was constantly saying things like that, and she was sick of it, sick of having to feel grateful to him, sick of being reminded that in a moment of drunken despair she had attempted to take her life.

She sighed and for the first time glanced at her desk. Another thing she was sick of was a life that did not include writing. Felicity had warned her that it might take a good six months before she was able to work again. "You're getting sober, Gwen. That's what you have to concentrate on right now, not the book. If I were you, I'd do fun things like shop or go to the movies. The first ninety days are a blur anyway, so you might as well enjoy them."

Gwen gave one of the shopping bags at her feet a kick. She had done plenty of shopping in the past few weeks. She had also gone to plenty of movies, and she had eaten so many dinners with so many old friends that she was now a size fourteen instead of a twelve. She didn't need a vacation. What she needed was a return to her old life, the life of her soul, the words that came through her like whispered music. The fog of alcohol was slowly lifting, departing, and one day soon she would have to go back to her desk to see if the big block of emptiness had been lifted along with the booze.

She was dead scared of finding out.

---

*C*harlie!"

"Hmm...what?"

Fingers grasped her shoulder and shook her roughly.

"Time to get up."

"Hunh?" She opened eyes that felt as if they had been glued together, and saw the big dark form of her husband hovering over her like an angel of retribution. Where was she?

"Time to get up," he repeated.

She lay very still for a moment, looking around with dull, fuzzy eyes, not moving her head, which ached tremendously. Now she remembered where she was: Rita's apartment. Painfully she inched her body up against the pillows, and there was a thudding sound as a bottle rolled from the bed onto the carpeted floor. "How'd you get in here?" she said, the words sounding foreign and leathery on her dry tongue.

"The maid."

"Why didn't you call first?"

Neil laughed bitterly. "I tried. You must have taken the phone off the hook."

"Oh. Yeah. Right." She swung her long legs to the floor and walked shakily over to the the window, pulling open the curtains as if it were an ordinary morning in the life of an ordinary couple. The bedroom, in daylight, was pale blue and pretty— one could sense a decorator's touch in the flowered wallpaper, the frilly sheets, the thick pale carpeting. Not the typical room for a drunken binge, she thought ironically. Behind her she heard Neil grope around for the phone and replace the receiver. While he sat on the bed with the phone on his lap, punching the numbers of his Washington office, Charlie quickly kicked another bottle, this one empty, behind the curtain. A fresh smell of scotch wafted up from the floor. Jesus, she'd gone through a bottle and a half last night. No wonder she felt like death.

She went to the bathroom, and by the time she came out he had finished his call and was standing at the bureau with a big pitcher of orange juice. "I've asked the maid to make coffee," he told Charlie, whose face, after a long hot shower, still felt swollen and baggy. She had wrapped a towel around her head, turban fashion, and was wearing, in a gesture of reconciliation, an almond silk robe he had bought for her in Paris a year ago. He handed her a glass of juice. "How long's this going to go on, Charlie?"

"What do you mean?" She sat down at the dressing table and lit a cigarette. She could see Neil's face in the mirror. His blue eyes looked tired, but otherwise he was, as usual, perfectly groomed, every hair in place, his handsome cheeks freshly shaven, his shirt collar crisp and white, his silk tie expensive, his cuff links—a present from her on their tenth anniversary— shining discreetly, muted against the soft gray of his suit.

"I mean your staying here in New York, drinking yourself silly every goddamn night."

"Oh, that."

"Yes, that."

She laid her cigarette in an ashtray and began to take large gulps of juice. "I'm not sure," she said, putting the glass down. "When I'm ready, I'll come home."

"When will that be?" She had been in New York since New Year's, more than two weeks ago. If she was away for much longer, ugly rumors would start to circulate among the political and social cognoscenti of Philadelphia and Washington.

"I'm not sure, I said." Her eyes met his in the mirror. She

felt angry at being pressured like this. "I need time on my own. That's not going to hurt anyone, is it?"

"As long as you're this way," he said slowly, "I can't let you see the children."

Charlie had put her hands up to remove the towel, and now they dropped to her lap. "But they're coming here this weekend, Neil—you promised!"

"Well, now I'm breaking my promise."

There was a knock on the door. Before either of them could answer, the maid came in and placed a tray of coffee on the bureau next to the orange juice. Neil got up from the bed and thanked her. He poured Charlie a cup, and as he handed it to her, he said, "I can't let them be alone with you while you're drinking."

"Well, I won't drink then." She stirred sugar into her coffee with a loud rattle, took a sip, and made a face because it still tasted bitter.

"Yeah, I've heard that one before."

"This time I mean it. I won't drink. I'll even go to AA meetings."

He laughed as if this were a preposterous idea. "You can see Colin and Petra in Washington. I'm not letting them come up here. That's final."

"Oh, so now you're trying to push me into coming home. Well, you can't. I won't let you. I'm not coming home until I'm good and goddamn ready. *That's* what's final."

"Well, I guess we're at a stalemate then." He put his cup down on the tray and went to stand behind her. "Where are you doing most of your drinking, Charlie? Here in the apartment, or in bars?"

She glanced up at him in the mirror, her eyes filled with bitter amusement. "What's it to you? Afraid someone might see the good congressman's wife pickled, and start all sorts of rumors?"

"I'm afraid," he said tersely, "you'll lose control of your tongue, and start talking about what happened to Gil."

The amusement vanished from her eyes. "I'd never do that," she said. "You know I'd never do that."

"Well, I'd feel a whole lot better if you confined your drinking to the apartment. Will you at least do that for me, Charlie?"

She nodded, the towel slipping from her head a little so he could see her wet hair.

"Good. Well, I'd better go then. I have to speak up at Columbia in half an hour. I'll talk to you tonight...that is, if you can manage to keep the phone on the hook."

He smiled and touched her shoulder before he left the room. When he was gone, she pulled the towel from her hair and gave a deep shuddering sigh. Her life was awful, an open wound, and she wasn't sure what to do with it next.

Neil's visit scared her, and that night she went to another AA meeting, looking up the nearest one—which was in a church on Fifth Avenue and Ninety-second Street—in the little directory Tanya had left with her. To give herself courage, she had a few gulps of scotch before leaving the apartment.

The entrance to the church was filled with a fashionable-looking throng of men and women. Ducking her head and wishing she had thought to bring her sunglasses, Charlie tried to make a pathway through the crowd. She felt a vague floating sensation from the scotch, and was afraid that she might stumble and fall. Voices echoed and rang off the stone walls of the large vaulted entryway, and just in her ear she heard someone say, "Goodness, why it's Charlotte!"

Turning, she saw the bulging, froglike face of Theo Hammond, her mother's interior designer, thrust up into her own. He was an ebullient little man of sixty who loved to talk and gossip and poke his nose into everyone else's business. "Theo— what are you doing here?" she muttered with a sinking heart. The last time she had seen him had been a few weeks ago at her mother's Christmas luncheon, an event she preferred not to remember since she had clumsily managed to overturn her wineglass, sending big red drops flying all over Theo's face and shirtfront.

"Same thing you are. This your first time?"

Peering down at him, she saw that he was stylishly dressed in a navy blue blazer and red silk tie, and that on one of his lapels was a white label that had his name, THEO H., printed on it.

His eyes followed hers. "I'm a greeter," he explained. "I welcome newcomers to AA. Come on, let's go inside and I'll introduce you to some people."

"I just want to sit down," she said quickly, hoping he wouldn't smell the scotch on her breath.

"Fine. We'll get you settled, and I'll go find you a cup of coffee. How's that sound?" He took her firmly by the arm, leading her into a room that seemed very large and bright after the dim hallway. There were rows and rows of auditorium chairs, and in front of a low stage was a tall wooden podium with a mike.

"That seat there," said Charlie, not wanting to walk all the way up the aisle with him. Shaking off his arm, she headed for a chair in the second-to-last row, clambering over the legs of the people who were already seated.

"How about that cup of coffee?" Theo called out in his well-bred nasal voice, watching her with his head thrown back, his feet in their shiny loafers planted twelve inches apart.

"Don't want any," said Charlie, feeling around in the pocket of her mink for her cigarettes before she sat down. "Stuff makes me sick. Why don't you go and greet people like you're supposed to?"

Musette, who had come in just after Charlie, watched from a few feet away as Charlie sat down heavily, putting an ashtray in her lap and fumbling around in her purse for a lighter. She's going to set herself and that coat of hers on fire, thought the actress, choosing a seat just behind Charlie's. She removed her own sleek black mink, ran her fingers through her bright blond curls, and then, taking a deep and cautious breath, leaned forward, tapping Charlie on the shoulder. "Excuse me," she said. "Do you happen to have an extra cigarette?"

"Hunh?" said Charlie, turning.

"I've misplaced my cigarettes. Could I bum one off you?"

Charlie glanced at her suspiciously out of smudged blue eyes. With too much blush and not enough lipstick, the freckles standing out darkly on the thin bridge of her nose, she looked sloppy and ill, a notion that made Musette want to applaud. "I suppose so," she said grudgingly, taking a pack of Winstons from her lap, shaking one out, and handing it to Musette.

"Thanks," said Musette.

Charlie, who had turned back in her seat, didn't bother to reply.

Nice, thought Musette in spite of herself, studying Charlie's long neck and the emerald clasp of her pearl choker. The woman had pushed off her coat, and half of it was lying on the floor. On a whim, Musette leaned forward and touched the velvety fur with her fingers, knowing instinctively that it was of a better quality than her own, softer, denser, more expensive. Up in the front of the room, the speaker had begun his story, but Musette's thoughts wandered and she couldn't concentrate. Instead, she was a girl of eighteen who had just gotten off a train and was taking a cab to a strange man's apartment. The man was Neil Gallagher. She had been out to dinner with him once, in Allentown, the week before, and on this early September Saturday, dressed in her best clothes and more nervous than she had ever been in her life, she was to have lunch with him in his "flat," as he called it, on Chestnut Street in Philadelphia. Chestnut Street was so grand! What wouldn't she have given to have on real pearls, like those worn by the woman in front of her, instead of the cheap strand she had bought at Woolworth's especially for the occasion.

His apartment had been a disappointment, she remembered that, the whole place, except for his bedroom, practically empty of furniture. He had met her at the door, wearing faded jeans and an old blue work shirt, clothes that gave him a look of easy self-assurance. And she in her best dress! "Maggie," he had said softly. She hadn't become Musette until a few years later, when her agent, Harry, chose the name for her. "I'm glad to see you. Come on in." They had gone to the kitchen, where he had poured her a beer. A Bob Dylan album was playing on the stereo. The room smelled of coffee and burned toast, and dirty breakfast dishes still lay in the sink.

They had had a five-minute conversation about how long he had lived in the apartment (two years, but he hardly ever ate there), before he took her to the bedroom. This, she could see, was where he spent most of his time. Through half-closed eyes, she noted the clutter of books, shoes, clothing, newspapers, laundry. On the bureau was a small silver trophy surrounded by several framed photographs. She could still hear Bob Dylan moaning in the background, and inside her was a moan, too, as he ran his fingers through her teased hair and down her neck, making her skin go all shivery. After that she kept her eyes closed. She was too small to have to wear a bra, and she felt the pinch of his fingers at her breasts, and several quick tugs as he pulled down the top of her dress.

"God, you're beautiful!" he said, taking a step back to admire her.

Her cheeks went scarlet. She didn't want to look at him. Unconsciously, she backed up until she felt the bed against her legs and quickly sat down, shivering as if she had a fever. He sat down beside her and, frightened as she was, she let him take off the rest of her dress. When he had removed everything, and she lay in her skimpy, mock-silk Woolworth's panties, she said, "What about you?" in a tiny voice. "Aren't you going to undress?"

"Don't worry about me," he said. He kept staring at her, and his eyes, which had been such a mild friendly blue, were densely focused, almost hostile. Then, in one smooth motion, he took off his shirt. "What kind of birth control do you use?" he asked suddenly, his hands hesitating on the zipper of his jeans.

"I—um . . . I don't use anything," she whispered.

"What do you mean, you don't use anything?" He looked at her, hard, and the keenness left his eyes. "What do you mean?" he repeated.

"I mean I've never . . . I've never done it before."

"You're a virgin? Oh, don't tell me that. Jesus Christ, don't tell me that!" Abruptly, he began to pace about the room, muttering to himself. She lay very still, feeling terrible. What had she done wrong? She thought men liked to have girls who were virgins, liked to deflower them, take their cherry. She curled into a fetal position, knees beneath her chin so that her poor tiny breasts were hidden, and dimly watched him. In jeans, with his dark hair and his smooth-skinned brown chest, he could have been just a boy, any boy, even someone she knew from Allentown. And that made her angry. "You're a shit, you know that?" she said.

"What?"

"You heard me."

He came and sat beside her, and his eyes softened as he saw

how tragically frail and young and innocent she looked curled up in that fearful knot on the bed. "I'm sorry," he said. "It's just that I hadn't realized. I thought you were . . . I thought you knew what you were doing." He regarded her tenderly. He placed his hand on her thin, long, honey-colored flank, and began slowly to caress her. "All right," he said, and his voice was filled with emotion. "All right, we'll just take this slow and easy, okay? Please don't be afraid of me."

A burst of applause interrupted her reverie. The speaker had finished, and it was time for announcements and the break. Musette wrenched herself back to the present, staring at the broad shoulders of the woman in front of her. With a wave of revulsion, she realized that this was the wife of the man she was told never to fear, whom she had just been remembering so vividly. A drunk! Charlie's coat had slipped even farther off the chair, with a few inches of hem now lying in a puddle of coffee. People were getting up, wandering around the room, greeting friends. "Vivian!" screamed a woman across the aisle. "Vivian! Over here! I've got to tell you the funniest thing!" Musette leaned forward and in a soft voice said, "Excuse me." When Charlie didn't respond, she once again tapped her on the shoulder.

This time Charlie's heavy brows were knitted together in a frown of annoyance. "What is it?" she said, swinging around in her chair.

"Your coat," said Musette, pointing.

"What about it?"

"If you'd look, you'd see."

Charlie stared along Musette's slim, manicured finger. "Oh," she said. She reached down and carelessly pulled the bottom of the mink onto her lap, not bothering to wipe the wettened fur.

"My name's Musette," she said before she could lose Charlie's attention.

Charlie gave her a look that said, "I don't give a shit who you are," but Musette ignored it, smiling for all she was worth. She was determined to become acquainted with this woman, and she held out her hand so that Charlie was forced to shake it. "What kind of name's that?" said Charlie. "Sounds like a hairdresser."

"My agent thought it up years ago," said Musette. She pretended not to mind the tactless remark, but really she was furious that Charlie hadn't recognized her for the public personality that she was. "It derives from the Greek word for 'muse.'"

"I know what it derives from," said Charlie. "Don't you have a last name?"

"We don't use them in AA." She was about to add that in any case she never used a last name, she was just plain Musette. Instead, she said, "I think we've met before."

"Surely not," drawled Charlie, putting a cigarette between her lips, snapping open a small gold lighter, and exhaling a gust of smoke into Musette's face. The air around their seats smelled richly of the French perfumes they were both wearing, and, beneath that delicious scent, of the scotch on Charlie's breath. "What are you—some sort of actress?" she asked, eyeing Musette with vague interest.

"Something like that," said Musette, whose major achievements had really been as a model. "I was married to Miroslav Vlk—the Czech director, the one who does all those art films? I did a lot of work with him."

She waited for Charlie to respond, but the woman just stubbed out her cigarette and gave a ladylike yawn, raising a slim hand to her lips and turning around to face forward. The meeting was about to begin again. People were returning noisily to their seats, and at the front of the room the speaker had resumed his position at the podium. Feeling dismissed, Musette stared with venom at the long neck of the woman in front of her, wishing she could do something to hurt her, perhaps lean forward and whisper into one of those flat, elegant ears, "Hey, guess what? I've fucked your husband." But she restrained herself, twisting a diamond ring that suddenly felt too big and too flashy round and round her finger, telling herself she would get even, drowning out the speaker's voice with thoughts of what she would do next.

Half an hour later the meeting was over. Musette had decided to ask Charlie out to coffee, but the fat little man named Theo H. beat her to it. "Let's go to Le Cirque," he said, helping Charlie into her mink. "You could use some dinner."

"I don't think so," said Charlie.

"Well at least let me take you back to your mother's."

"I'm not staying at my mother's."

"You're not?" His voice sounded excited. "Where are you staying?"

"Rita Rutherford's."

"Good lord, why?"

Charlie gave a light laugh. "Wouldn't you like to know! Now if you'll excuse me." She pushed past him and started down the aisle toward the exit, her silk scarf, which was tied around the gold link strap of her Chanel handbag, dragging on the floor.

"Wait, you ought to take some of these," yelled Theo, running after her. He grabbed a handful of AA pamphlets from a table in the rear, caught up with her, and deftly slipped them into the pocket of her mink. "Come back tomorrow," Musette heard him say. "You should go to a meeting every day! It's important!"

Charlie raised her hand in an impatient wave, and the last Musette saw of her was her back in its dark impressive coat as she was carried along on the tide of people. The door opened and a blast of cold air entered the church hall. Musette was now next to Theo. She could see by the look on his face that he was considering following Charlie out onto the street, and she quickly reached over and tugged at his sleeve. "You know what she's going to do, don't you?" she said loudly.

"Hmmm—what?" He turned bulging eyes on her, blinking rapidly, as if he couldn't believe his luck when he saw how beautiful she was.

"I said, you know what she's going to do?"

"I know who you are!" he exclaimed, ignoring her question. "I remember you from years ago, the model—Musette." He clucked his tongue. "And you just had an *awful* time with your husband, didn't you? And then you went into Betty Ford, yes, I remember reading about that. How was it? I've never been to that place, and I've always been curious."

"It was all right," said Musette, who had hated every minute in the clinic. "A little too much regimentation for my taste. But listen, about Charlie Gallagher . . . she's going to go to a bar and drink."

He stared, fascinated, as Musette pulled on a pair of black kid gloves, smoothing the leather carefully over each long finger. "Really? How on earth do you know that?" he asked.

"I've seen her do it." She smiled at him, wetting her scarlet lips with her tongue. "Yesterday. After the lunchtime meeting on Seventy-fourth Street."

"Ah."

"Shouldn't we do something to help her?"

He shook his head. "Not at this point."

"Why not?" She was still smiling at him, her head cocked to the side, and she could sense that he was captivated by the small red velvet cap she had set at a rakish angle on her wild curls.

"Well," he said, nodding to several people he knew, obviously very happy that they should see him in the company of this beautiful woman, "in AA there's a saying: 'You can carry the message, but you can't carry the drunk.'"

"What's that mean?"

He pulled the name tag off the lapel of his jacket, and began to button his coat. "Come out to coffee with me, my dear, and I'll tell you."

heo took her to an espresso place two blocks away, on Ninety-first and Madison Avenue. Up front, by the cash register, was a glassed-in case filled with colorful little pastries. "You want to choose something before we sit down?" said Theo, nodding at the pastries.

"No thanks, I'm not hungry," said Musette, who had trained herself, during her long years as a model, to be totally blind to sweets.

"Well, I hope you don't mind if I indulge."

While he spent a few minutes studying the assortment of cakes, she settled herself in the last of a row of booths by the window. Other people from the meeting were there, she noticed, and the place was noisy, with lots of visiting back and forth from table to table. Theo was stopped five or six times before he got to where Musette was sitting. "Perhaps we should have gone someplace more private," he said.

"No, this is fine," said Musette, already looking forward to the espresso she had just ordered. She took a jeweled cigarette case from her purse and laid it on the table. "Want one?" she asked Theo, tapping a long red nail on the case.

"Ah no, my dear, I gave those up years ago."

"Really? I thought everyone in AA smoked."

"Mostly newcomers." He took off his coat, carefully folding it and placing it on the bench beside him. Then he ran his fingers through his thick yellowy white hair, glancing sideways at his reflection in the window to see how good he looked. "Give people a little time in the program, and they start shedding all their vices," he said with a laugh.

"Including pastry?" Musette asked, raising her brows as a waitress placed a large slice of angel food cake with coconut icing in front of Theo.

"Ah, but you mustn't look at me. I'm a good boy as far as cigarettes go, but otherwise, my dear, it's pure gluttony." He laughed and wiped his fork on his napkin. Then he bent his head over his cake, and began to eat with small rapid bites.

"Tell me about Charlie Gallagher," Musette said when he had devoured half the cake and was pausing for breath. She had a feeling other people were going to join them at their table, and she wanted to get as much out of him as she could before it was too late.

"Well, I don't hold out much hope for her marriage," said Theo, sighing happily. He took a small sip of espresso, wiped delicately at his lips, and started in on the cake again.

"Why not?" Musette asked, gripping her hands together beneath the table. She wished he'd hurry up and finish the damn cake.

"Because she's up here staying at Rita Rutherford's apartment, and he's down in Washington with the kids. Do you know Rita?"

He glanced at her, his mouth once again full of cake. Musette shook her head.

"She's a businesswoman, divorced, and she has an apartment two or three blocks from here. Right now she's away in Europe, which is what makes me wonder." He took another bite of cake.

"Wonder what?" said Musette.

"Why Charlie's staying at Rita's, and not at her mother's— Helene Vandermark has one of the most gorgeous apartments in all of New York." He winked at her, the lid going down slowly over his protuberant eye. "I should know, considering I spent a whole year redecorating the place."

"You think she's having an affair?" Musette asked pointedly, ignoring his attempt at puffing himself up.

"Well, there *have* been rumors." He wiped his mouth and smiled at her. At last he was finished with the cake. He slyly let his alligator belt out a notch and leaned forward, resting his elbows on the table. "I was at Helene's for Christmas—in fact, I was seated right next to Charlie, who was so drunk she knocked over her wineglass. A fine mess that was! She got drops the size of quarters all over my shirt, and now the thing is ruined. Anyway, I can tell you from personal observation that not a word passed between her and her husband, Neil. Either the two had had a colossal argument, or they simply don't care about each other anymore."

"Which do you think it was?"

"Probably the latter. A lot of eyebrows were raised a year ago when Charlie went off to Barbados on her own. Who knows what happened there? Neil, of course, needs to keep a very tight lid on things if he intends to run for president in 'ninety-six, but you can be pretty certain Charlie was doing more than just working on her suntan."

Musette took a cigarette from the jeweled case on the table, and waited as Theo reached into his jacket pocket for his lighter. "Is there any chance that he might divorce her?" she asked, slowly exhaling smoke as if she didn't care.

"Oh, none whatsoever. At least I don't believe so. Neil's a Catholic, remember, and they had a church wedding, which means getting a divorce would be awfully tough—not to mention ruinous to his career. On the other hand, trying to run a political campaign while your wife's having all sorts of adventures ain't such a good idea, either. Who knows? It's awfully interesting though, isn't it?"

An hour later, Musette lay curled up on the huge gunmetal-gray sectional in her living room, staring idly around her, and wondering if she should have Theo come and redecorate. The apartment, with its thick white wall-to-wall carpeting, zebra skin rugs, chrome lamps, and leather couches, was definitely a little bland. She needed a few antiques, and perhaps one or two of those old portraits of English dogs or horses to give it some class. Especially if she was to rekindle her romance with Neil.

Theo, gossiping about the possible demise of the Gallagher marriage, had stirred up all sorts of fantasies, and now she had a vivid picture of herself and Neil making passionate love on this very couch. Giggling softly, she placed a pale pink throw cushion behind her neck and let her thoughts wander.

She had never told anyone about her relationship with Neil, and that had been quite a credit to her since the girls in the office where she worked were always talking about him. How smart he was, how handsome and sexy—Mr. Neil Gallagher, who had been to Harvard Law School, and came from a rich Philadelphia family. He was thirty years old at the time, twelve years older than she was, and a desirable bachelor. His father worked for the State Department, and his mother, whose photo was on his bureau, didn't do anything, and looked like a cold bitch. They were devout Catholics, but Neil, in the eight months she knew him, never put his foot inside a church.

Her one error of judgment had been to think that he loved her as passionately as she loved him. And why not? When she arrived on his doorstep on Friday nights he seemed delighted to see her. "Oh Maggie," he would whisper, grabbing for her, pulling off her clothes as he maneuvered her down the hall to his bedroom. He would make love to her over and over again, insatiable, and he was always buying her gifts of perfume and sexy underwear (all of it genuine silk), always telling her how beautiful she was, how much joy she gave him. And yet, even in the very beginning, there were things she didn't dare examine too closely, things that made her wonder. His secrecy, for instance. It was of extreme importance that no one in either of their families know about the affair. "My parents just aren't ready for someone as hot as you," he would say. "And yours—well, your father would probably come after me with a shotgun if he knew what was going on."

Nor did he want her to meet any of his friends. When he spent weekends at people's houses in the country, she was never included, and she did not attend a single party with him or accompany him to any of the posh places where he might run into someone he knew. This began to bother her; it began to bother her a great deal. Somehow, in her mind, their relationship had always meant eventual marriage, and when Christmas, which marked their four-month anniversary, came and went with her being excluded from all the family festivities, she knew she must do something.

She waited a few more months. Their lives continued in the same way, with her traveling down to Philadelphia by train, falling into bed with him, listening with a quickened heartbeat as he told her how gorgeous she was, and how she made him happier than any woman he had ever known. Late in February, on the day she turned nineteen, she decided time was up. She secretly stopped taking the pill.

Two months later she missed her period.

She consulted a doctor to be sure, and then, with her heart in her mouth, told Neil.

"I've got some good news for you, honey. At least I think it's good news."

"Oh yeah. What's that?" He gave an amiable grunt, and rolled over, taking her more firmly in his arms. They had just made love, and were both feeling languorous and heavy and sated.

She let him hold her for a minute, and then sat up and lit a cigarette. "What it is, is this," she said, hugging her knees. "I went to the doctor the other day, and he told me I was going to have a baby."

Neil's hand, about to caress the silky flesh of her back, froze in midair. "That's impossible!" he exclaimed.

"It's what he said. I missed my period."

He stared at her, appalled. "But you were taking the pill! I don't understand."

"Apparently sometimes these things happen."

"Not when you're taking the pill, they don't."

He got out of bed, put on his pants and shirt, and went into the bathroom, where she heard him run water into the sink. When he came back, his face looked fresh and alert and extremely angry. "Let's go talk in the kitchen," he said. "I want some coffee." It was ten-thirty at night. She pulled on her panties and one of his shirts, which she neglected to button, and followed him into the kitchen. "You'd better tell me what happened," he said.

She shrugged, pushing her long blond hair out of her face. "I *told* you. Nothing happened."

"That's a lie. You must have stopped taking your pills. That's right, isn't it, Maggie?"

She looked at him out of sullen eyes. "Maybe I forgot to take one once." Instantly she regretted admitting anything.

"Forgot! Jesus! Well, what do you think you're going to do about it now, hunh? Just tell me that." The kettle whistled and he grabbed it, pouring water over his Nescafe, his movements quick and jerky. Maggie waited for him to come and sit with her, but he remained standing at the counter, a lean, disheveled, unhappy-looking man in faded jeans and a T-shirt that showed his ribs. She was beginning to feel alarmed. Especially when, in a corrosive voice, he said, "You did this on purpose, didn't you, Maggie? Oh, come on, it's such an old sad trick."

Her face turned scarlet. "I thought you loved me," she whispered.

"What's that got to do with anything?"

"What do you mean, what's that got to do with anything?"

"If you think we're getting married because of this, you're wrong. Dead wrong. Now listen, I know a doctor who—"

"I'm not having an abortion," she stated.

Neil looked at her sharply. She stared down at her thin beautiful hands holding the shirt together over her breasts. They were white at the knuckles. "Oh yeah? Well, what *are* you planning to do?"

She faced him bravely. "Stay with you. Marry. I want to have this baby."

"Well, you can't!" he snapped. "That's fantasy time."

"I thought you were Catholic."

"Oh Jesus, now you're going to pull that on me! Okay. All right." He ran a hand wearily over his face. "My family's Catholic, Maggie. Personally I don't give a shit about that stuff. Personally I think it's a bunch of crap. And you know what else is a bunch of crap? A silly little bitch like you trying to force me into marriage. So I want you to just get off the subject because it's not in the cards. Not now, not ever. Understand?"

Maggie's eyes were brimming. But when she spoke, her voice was fairly steady. "You said you loved me, you—"

"Sex love, physical love. Not the love of two people who are going to share a life together."

"But it was your lies that got me into this mess. All that crap about how happy I made you, how wonderful I was. I believed

43

all that bullshit, that's the point, and now..." She paused and wiped her nose on the sleeve of his shirt. "And now I don't see why it should be so goddamn easy for you. Mr. Harvard. Mr. Big Shot Lawyer. If you...if you aren't going to marry me, then you just goddamn well better pay me nicely. Know what I mean? A big check. Otherwise...otherwise there'll be trouble."

"Oh really? Look, I'm not the one who told you to quit taking those pills." He laughed bitterly, but she could see that he was worried. It gave her a glimmer of hope.

Neil slept on the couch that night, and Maggie, alone in his bed, sat up worrying and smoking cigarettes, even though they made her feel sick. The next morning they barely spoke to one another. She packed up her few things, and when she was ready she said, "Well?"

"Well what?"

"Don't we have some unfinished business?"

"Look, Maggie, I only have your word for it. I haven't even seen a doctor's report."

"You could call him," said Maggie. "Like right now. I've got his number."

"But it's Saturday."

"He works on Saturdays. He said if there were any problems—you know, morning sickness, stuff like that—to call."

Neil hesitated. Then, in a surly voice, he said, "All right, give me the number."

She stood, tapping her foot, shamed and embarrassed as he spoke to the doctor. When he was finished he disappeared into his bedroom, and came back moments later with an envelope. "You can look at this when you're gone," he said. "You'll see it's ample. In the meantime—well, I guess it had to end sooner or later. I'm just sorry it ended on this note."

And he held open the door.

Lying on her sofa in a luxurious Park Avenue apartment almost sixteen years later, Musette, who had once been a scared, defiant, pregnant teenager named Maggie, thought how very ironic it was that Neil's religion, about which he had professed to care so little, should keep him trapped in a loveless marriage. It's fate that Charlie and I should both be getting sober at the same time, she thought, sitting up and reaching for a cigarette. From the street, five stories below, came the wail of an ambulance. She left the couch and went to the window, staring sightlessly out into the dark canyon of Park Avenue. Those two, Charlie and Neil, owed her something, that was for sure. Because of a cheap, poorly performed abortion, she had been unable to have children, a condition that had ruined her life, ending more than one of her marriages, and turning her into a lonely and miserable woman. She took a deep, unhappy drag on her cigarette. As always, when she thought about her barrenness, she felt an overwhelming urge to put some chemical substance in her body, to get high.

Well, she wouldn't do it this time. She squashed her cigarette out in a jade ashtray that was really an antique. Instead, very soberly, she would stalk Charlie at AA meetings and become friends with her. And through Charlie, who looked used up and sour, she would get to Neil, making him love her again with her strong silky body, which was so much nicer than Charlie's, her soft sexy voice, her beautiful golden eyes. And then...She smiled fondly at her reflection in the dark window.

a A ruins your drinking," Theo had told Musette on the night they went out for coffee. "I'm willing to bet a rather large sum that we'll see Madame Gallagher in the rooms again." He was right, although for Charlie giving up alcohol was a terrible struggle. She would go on a binge for several days running, and then, not even understanding why, race to an AA meeting. "I despise AA," she told her friend Tanya. "The people are awful, and this business of having to say a prayer . . ." She shuddered as if the idea of mentioning the word *God* aloud in public were as disgusting to her as wearing a pair of Spandex stretch pants.

But she kept coming back. At one of the meetings she heard a speaker say, "I got sick and tired of being sick and tired," and that seemed to describe her own situation exactly. She couldn't stand the hangovers anymore. She couldn't stand not remembering what had happened the night before, or waking up with bruises on her body from stumbling into furniture or falling down when she was drunk. Above all, she couldn't stand not being allowed to see her children, although, in good conscience, she knew that Neil was right: it was dangerous for her to be alone with them, even for a weekend, as long as she was drinking. She wanted what the other people in the meetings had: clearheadedness and sobriety. Even Theo, whom she had always avoided because of his bitchy tongue, she considered, in the context of AA, a happy and fortunate man.

But as much as she craved sobriety—and it had come to that point—she could not seem to stop drinking. She would go through a whole day or two without a drink, and then an enormous thirst for liquor would overtake her, and she would have to run to a bar—breaking even her minor vow to Neil that she would drink only in private. And once she was in the bar she would get drunk, and there was no saying where that would take her. Luckily she did not, as Neil had feared, attract the attention of the press, but there were several mornings when she awoke with lumps and swellings on her body and no idea how she had gotten them. On one such morning her friend Tanya came over, took one look at her, and said, "You don't *have* to drink, you know."

This struck her as a novel idea, especially coming from Tanya, who years before, when they were schoolgirls, had been expelled from Ethel Walker for her habit of decanting bourbon into emptied-out bottles of shampoo or mouthwash, which she would then openly place on her dresser. Tanya was one of the worst drunks Charlie had ever known. She had married fairly young, at the age of twenty, and had never had children—her husband, Lyle, as she liked to say, being child enough. Together they had run a horse farm in Kentucky (there were rumors that her childlessness was the result of a nasty fall), had made and lost vast sums of money, had traveled and lived well and been excellent drinking partners. When Lyle died in a car crash in 1990—rumor had it he'd been driving drunk—Tanya retired to the farm and began to drink around the clock. That was the last Charlie heard of her until several weeks ago, when she ran into Tanya at a New Year's Eve party. "You!" Tanya had exclaimed, waving an arm in front of Charlie's face.

Charlie, drunk at the time, wasn't quite sure who was talking to her.

"It's me, your old friend," urged Tanya. "Don't you remember?"

"'Course I do," said Charlie, giving her a sloppy kiss. "It's just that there're so goddamn many people here."

"Unh-hunh," said Tanya. She looked at her evenly. "And you've had a lot of champagne. Look, my dear, I'm taking your bag, and I'm putting my card right in here in your coin purse where you'll easily find it. If you need me, call."

In the morning Charlie had stared at the card uncomprehendingly. She and Neil were staying at her mother's Fifth Avenue apartment, and there had been an unpleasant scene at the breakfast table about the noise Charlie had made coming home drunk the night before. "All that caterwauling," said Helene with a brisk shake of her white curls. "It's so common of you, Charlotte, to scream at your husband like that."

"You must have been dreaming, Mother," said Charlie, who had no recollection of fighting with Neil.

"That shriek I heard was no dream. Nor was the glass I heard shattering when you broke one of my favorite snifters. You really must change your ways, Charlotte. It's such a bad example for the children."

No one could make Charlie feel shame and rage like her mother, and she left the table knowing that it would be a long time before she stayed there again. But she also knew she needed time away from her family, and so she decided to spend a week or two in New York, using Rita Rutherford's empty apartment as a base. Staring down at Tanya's card, she thought, Oh good, I'll call her and we'll have such fun getting sloshed together. She pictured the two of them in a bar, talking about old times, and so it was a shock to learn of Tanya's involvement in AA.

"You could use it too," said Tanya bluntly. They were lunching in a restaurant in Soho, and Tanya had told Charlie all about how her brother had forced her to leave the Kentucky farm and go into a rehab before the booze killed her. "That stuff's poison," she said, pointing at Charlie's wineglass.

"Not for me it isn't," said Charlie, feeling red splotches of anger rise in her cheeks.

"Oh really? Well then, tell me why you're slurring after only two glasses of wine. Most people don't do that."

"The people I know do."

"Then you're in with the wrong crowd."

Two weeks later Charlie was at her first AA meeting. Now, a month after that, she and Tanya were sitting in her living room, drinking coffee. On Charlie's cheek was a blackening bruise, which she kept gently touching with her fingers.

"You have no idea how you got that, do you?" said Tanya, pointing at Charlie's cheek.

"None," said Charlie, not bothering to lie, as she would have with most people. "I was at a bar on Third Avenue, that's all I remember."

"You don't remember coming home?"

Charlie shook her head.

"For me that was always the worst part, not remembering, and then having to worry all the next day about whether I'd hit someone with my car, or done some other horrible thing." She studied Charlie, who was still in her bathrobe although she had showered and applied powder and rouge to her disfigured face. "You look as if you could use another cup of coffee," Tanya said after a moment. "I'll go make us some more."

While she was gone Charlie lit a cigarette with shaking fingers and stared dully into space, wondering if she would ever be able to stop drinking. A long piece of ash fell onto her robe, and absentmindedly she brushed it off, thinking how remarkable it was that she could start the day with a promise to herself that she would not go near alcohol, but that after several hours her brain would click off, and she would find herself in a bar or liquor store, almost as if her feet had a mind of their own. As she was thinking how hopeless it all seemed, she heard Tanya calling her to the kitchen.

"Coming," she said, getting to her feet.

The maid had just cleaned the kitchen and everything sparkled and glowed, hurting Charlie's bloodshot eyes. She sat down quickly, noting that Tanya had set the table with bright white napkins, a vase of yellow flowers, and a navy blue cloth that matched the tiled floor. It was a sunny day, and patches of golden light fell across the creamy counters. If she craned her neck—which was the last thing Charlie wanted to do right now—she could see the East River through Rita's small kitchen window.

"I thought we'd have our coffee in here," said Tanya, as if she, and not Charlie, were the hostess.

"That's fine," said Charlie. "I feel so lousy I don't really care where I am. As long as what's-her-name doesn't come in and start making a lot of noise."

"Marie-Josephe," said Tanya quietly. "You ought to know your maid's name." She poured their coffee and waited till Charlie had drunk half a cup. Then she said, "While I was looking around for coffee filters I found three bottles of scotch in the pantry."

Charlie's face reddened. "Really?" she said.

"You can't get sober, Charlie, if you keep booze in the house."

"I meant to throw them out. I guess I forgot," she said sullenly, twisting the cord of her robe around her finger.

"Oh come on! You can't fool me with that crap."

"Well, they're my safety net. It's not as if I'm going to drink them. I just need to know they're there. Otherwise I won't sleep at night."

"You'll sleep better at night if we pour them out. Consider it a symbolic act, or a rite of passage, whichever you prefer."

She stood up, pulling at the waist of her knee-length tweed skirt, and strode into the pantry, returning with the bottles hugged tightly to her breasts, the lapis beads she wore clinking against the glass. "I'd make you pour the stuff out yourself if that weren't a real AA no-no," she said, placing the bottles on the counter. One by one, with a closed look on her normally lively face, she began to empty them, and for a few minutes the kitchen smelled sickeningly of scotch. Watching her, Charlie noticed that the hem of her thick tweed skirt was held up in one place with a safety pin.

"Light me a ciggie, will you?" said Tanya when she had finished. She had washed her hands thoroughly, working up a thick lather of soap, and was drying them on a dish cloth.

"Sure," said Charlie. She lit two cigarettes, holding Tanya's out to her with shaking fingers. The sight and smell of those bottles being uncapped and emptied into the sink had horrified her, bringing back memories of other times—childhood punishments, a favorite doll her mother had tossed into the garbage because she had been naughty. How she had cried! Big wracking tears that caused her mother to send her to her room for what had seemed like days. After that incident, some thirty years ago, she had never played with dolls again.

"You know I meant what I said before," said Tanya. "You don't *have* to drink if you don't want to."

"I don't understand," said Charlie.

Tanya sighed. "It's kind of like not following an order that someone gives you. When you get an urge to drink, you don't give in to it. You call me, or you go to a meeting, or you have a glass of juice. There's a lot of sugar in juice, and that's what your body's really looking for. And...here's what's really important: *you do this a day at a time.* You're not going to drink today. You might drink tomorrow, but that's not your problem right now. It's today that counts." She took a final drag on her cigarette, and when she spoke again smoke gushed from her mouth. "One other thing," she said. "You ought to get yourself a sponsor. Know what that is?"

Charlie knew from the half a dozen meetings she had gone to that a sponsor was a person you chose from the rooms to help you with the steps and guide you through your sobriety. Everyone was supposed to have one, but she had decided that the rule—if that was what it was—didn't apply to her, since she hated the idea of anyone poking a nose into her business. "I don't particularly want a sponsor," she said to Tanya.

"Well you're not going to get sober without one."

"I've got *you.* Doesn't that count?"

"No," said Tanya. "Not unless we make it official."

Charlie traced a patch of sunlight with the toe of her slipper. "That sounds awfully serious. Like getting married or something. Let me think about it, okay? I mean I really love you, Tanya, but all this AA stuff is so new to me. I need time to adjust."

"Don't take too much time, honey, or you'll end up with your throat slit walking home from a bar one night."

Tanya's visit that bright mid-February morning signaled a change in Charlie. It was as if a nerve in her had gone dead, as if something that had ached had stopped hurting. She would go to a restaurant and watch someone at a nearby table sip a cocktail and think, I don't have to do that! It was all very bewildering. From minute to minute she expected to be hit by the desire to drink, and when that didn't happen, she wasn't quite sure what to do with herself. For the past fifteen years she had had a drink just about every day of her life, and for the last five of those years she had gone to bed in an alcoholic stupor. Sober, she was a stranger to herself.

Frightened of this new, unknown Charlie, she went to meetings every day. Up till now she had always gone hung over, or with liquor in her system, and it was interesting to watch what went on in the rooms without a haze of alcohol distorting her vision. One thing she noticed was that the people, for the most part, looked pretty normal. There was the black woman she had seen weeks ago, at the lunchtime meeting on Seventy-fourth Street, whom she now realized was Gwendolyn Thomas, the author. And she recognized a famous opera singer who had sung at a White House gathering she and Neil had attended, and an Italian *principessa* one often saw at parties, and—although out of embarrassment she did not acknowledge his presence—an old banking friend of her late father's. In this sort of company, she did not feel *too* out of place. But she couldn't bring herself to say anything in meetings, and she certainly couldn't bring herself to utter aloud the words, "My name is Charlie. I'm an alcoholic."

For a week or so she sat in the back, in the last row, always quickly leaving before it was time to join hands and say the Serenity Prayer. She would return to Rita's empty apartment, where she was accustomed to filling the evening hours with the consumption of alcohol, and think, Now what? Tanya's words, "You're not going to get sober without a sponsor," haunted her. She could see that it was true, she needed someone to explain what the hell was going on, but she didn't want that person to be Tanya. Much as she adored Tanya, there was something slovenly about her—that safety-pinned skirt!—that put her off.

Because she didn't know anyone in AA, getting a sponsor was difficult, rather like choosing a name from a hat. One was advised to stick with the same sex, but apart from that there were no rules or regulations. She was very confused until, at a large Saturday night meeting in a church on Madison Avenue, she spotted the woman whose story she had heard the first time, the one who had given up a child for adoption. Without thinking twice about it, she made a beeline for her.

"Is this seat free?" she asked.

The woman, who had been looking at some papers in her lap, glanced up at her and nodded.

"Good. I wanted to talk to you about something."

The woman was sporting the same sort of tight little minidress she had worn at the first meeting, and around her neck was a gauzy red-and-green scarf. Her ash-blond hair was held out of her face by a thin tortoiseshell headband. "Oh really?" she said. "What about?"

"I need a sponsor."

"Ah."

"I thought I'd ask you. You were the first person I ever heard speak."

"I see." She picked up her papers, bunched them together on her smart little black-stockinged knees, and slid them into a briefcase. "How long have you been sober?" she asked.

"Maybe a week."

"Maybe?"

"Well, I've been slipping and sliding around a lot."

The woman stared at Charlie out of eyes that were a pale, clear, intelligent blue. "The last time I spoke was over a month ago." She snapped her briefcase shut and set it down on the seat beside her. "What did you say your name was?"

"Charlie."

"Mine's Felicity. All right, I'll sponsor you. But I'm strict. I expect a phone call every day, even if it's just for two minutes. And I expect you to raise your hand at every meeting and identify yourself as an alcoholic. Starting now. Think you can do that?"

Charlie looked around the room, which suddenly seemed vast. Up in front, standing at the speaker's table, a man in jeans and a sports jacket was adjusting the mike. The meeting would begin in two minutes, and just about every seat was taken.

"I guess I'll have to," said Charlie, a large lump of fear forming in her throat.

A few minutes later, when the chairman asked for day counts, Charlie held up a trembling hand and, in a voice that nearly broke, said, "My name is Charlie, I'm ... an alcoholic, and I have approximately one week sober."

As people clapped for her, her heart beat so fast that she thought it would fly right out of her chest. But she felt wonderful, as giddy as she had at the age of thirteen, when she had secretly gone around sipping from all the guests' glasses at one of her parents' garden parties, and gotten drunk for the first time.

*D*on't you think I look good?"

"Yeah, you do. You look wonderful."

"It's all this clean living," said Musette, raising slender arms up in the air and twirling with a noisy swish of her ice-blue pleated silk skirt. She was with her agent, Harry Langhart, whom she had decided to visit since she felt so marvelous. Today was her thirty-fifth birthday, though with her long blond curls and her smooth honey-colored skin she could easily have passed for ten years younger.

"Well, it's really paid off, that's for sure," said Harry. He was a heavyset man in his early forties. When Musette had met him fifteen years before he had been thin and wiry, with love beads around his neck and a messy page-boy hairdo. Now he wore suits from Brooks Brothers and his graying hair was trimmed short at the ears and neck. In a striped tie, horn rims, and gleaming black wing tips, he could have been an investment banker instead of a talent agent who spent most of his time in L.A.

"The moment has come, don't you think, for me to get back to work," said Musette, stopping abruptly in front of his desk. She rarely visited him in either of his offices, but today, hearing he was in New York, she had burst in unannounced, and the secretary, a twenty-year-old gum-cracking girl who had never laid eyes on her before, had given her a hard time. "Sorry, but Mr. Langhart's got wall-to-wall appointments," she had said, and when Musette had brushed past her, she had yelled, "Hey, you can't go in there!" Harry, on the phone, had given her a big grin of welcome and mouthed the words; "I'll be off in a sec."

Now, pressing his fleshy fingertips together, he said, "I don't think so, Maggie."

"What?" Her wonderful catlike eyes narrowed in astonishment.

"You heard me, Maggie. It's not the right time yet."

He was the only person besides her mother and sisters to call her Maggie. This was because when he had met her she had been as young and raw as his current secretary, only instead of working in an office she had been waiting tables, a skinny, scared-looking, peroxided blonde who had come to New York with all her savings and an inferiority complex because her boyfriend had kicked her out and made her get an abortion. She had been staying in a hotel near Times Square, and he had taken her phone number, and within a few days moved her into the East Village apartment of a friend of his, and arranged for her to take dance classes. She never told him anything about her sad love affair, and if she had, he wouldn't have been interested. He saw only one thing in her, and that was the dollars her fabulous face and body would bring both of them once he had bought her the right clothes and taught her about hair and makeup.

"Why isn't it the right time? I'm in great shape, I'm off the pills and alcohol, and I haven't felt—or *looked*—this good in years."

"Yeah, true." He swiveled his chair around so he was facing her directly, his blue eyes sharp behind the horn rims. "Look, Maggie, I don't know how to tell you this except straight out. I've been sniffing around and . . . well, there isn't really anything out there for you."

She froze as if someone had just threatened her with a gun. "What's that supposed to mean?"

"Just what it sounds like. You're smart. You know what I'm

talking about. People don't want to work with someone who's gotten herself fucked up on pills and alcohol."

"But I'm off the pills!" she shouted, flinging her blond curls angrily out of her face and glaring at him.

"Yes, I know that," he said calmly. "But you've kind of screwed it up, Maggie. Especially with that last stunt you pulled, throwing all of Miroslav's clothes out the window. People just don't want to take a risk with you."

She stared at him, breathing fast. The final act of her dramatic marriage, taking scissors to her husband's wardrobe and flinging the whole mess out on the front lawn, had been the talk of Hollywood for months. "I don't see why not. I'm clean. I'm sober. I'm in AA. That stuff wouldn't happen again. It's all in the past. Anyway, people have short memories, Harry. I want you to find me work. Maybe something in TV. You know—a miniseries. Otherwise I'll go crazy."

He sighed. "Then I guess you're gonna go crazy, Maggie. No one's interested right now. Believe me, I've looked."

"Well, what am I supposed to do?" she whined. Her eyes blazed with fury, but she knew it wouldn't do to make a scene. Throwing tantrums never worked with Harry.

"Concentrate on your meetings. Maybe get involved with some sort of public-interest thing, like homelessness or the environment, that would help build up your credibility."

"I'm not sure that's me, Harry." She tapped her long red nails noisily on his desk. "I did get myself a sponsor, though."

"A what?"

"An AA sponsor. Someone who kind of guides you through your sobriety."

"Well, good," said Harry, rising from his chair to indicate that their meeting was over. "Use her. God knows you need all the help you can get."

Her new sponsor was Felicity Rettinger, the same thin young woman who sponsored Charlie. When Theo had poked her in the ribs at a meeting one night and said, "See that cute female in the tight dress over there? That's Charlie's sponsor," she hadn't wasted any time. Now, the day after her visit to Harry's office, Felicity phoned her.

"I'm giving a party," she said in her soft southern voice.

"Well, not really a party; that's misleading. I thought I'd invite you and Charlie, my other new sponsee, and one or two others to my house for dinner since you're all under ninety days. Interested?"

"Of course," said Musette. "I'd love to come."

"Good, then I'll give you my address."

With a smile of happiness, Musette took down the information. She had seen Charlie across the rooms once or twice in the past week, but this would be the first time she would have a chance to meet her socially. She knew deep down that it was probably a bad idea for her and Charlie to have the same sponsor, but she didn't care. If her scheme to meet and make friends with her old rival paid off, that was all that mattered.

Gwen Thomas had also been invited to the party. As she was getting dressed, her husband sat on the bed grading papers and secretly watching her. "You know what, honey?" he said suddenly. "I have to tell you I really kind of resent this."

"Resent what?"

"Your having dinner with these women. Driving all the way out to Brooklyn."

Gwen, who was trying to fasten the button of one of last year's skirts, glanced at him. "Felicity's my editor," she said. "I don't understand."

"This has nothing to do with Felicity or work. This is an AA thing, right?"

"Oh, Jesus, Walter. You treat me as if I'm about five years old." She began to struggle again with the waistband of her skirt. Since getting sober seventy-five days ago, she had put on a lot of weight. In fact, when she had gathered all her courage this morning and climbed onto the bathroom scale, the needle had hovered darkly at 156, which was sixteen pounds more than she was supposed to weigh.

"Well, we never spend time together anymore."

Gwen peeled off the skirt and tossed it onto the bed. She'd wear a pair of silky black evening pants with an elasticized waistband instead.

"And look at you getting all tarted up!"

"I'm wearing the only thing that fits," she said irritably. "Look, Walt, I need these women to stay sober. That's what

AA's all about. Talking to friends, talking to your sponsor. You wouldn't want me to start drinking again, would you?"

"Of course not," he snapped. "But I'd like to see you some-times, instead of the back of your head as you waltz out the door."

"You see me plenty. It's not as if we're newlyweds." She rubbed perfume into her wrists, narrowed one of her palms, and drew on her bangles. At least she could still get *them* on. "Anyway, I'll be home by ten-thirty or eleven, so we can snuggle up together and watch the news."

"Sounds like fun," Walter observed dryly. "Gwennie, you will promise to drive carefully, won't you? There're a lot of drunks out there on the road."

"Yeah, I know. I used to be one of them, remember?" She stood up and went to him, giving his beard a playful tweak before grabbing her keys and a pack of cigarettes from the dresser and stuffing them into her bag. "Have fun with those papers," she said as she sailed out the door.

Charlie had never been to Brooklyn before. In her mind only shop girls, drug dealers, and religious Jews lived in Brooklyn, so on the night of Felicity's dinner she borrowed her mother's driver, a swarthy little Colombian named Hector Ruiz, to get her there. "You'll be back for me at ten sharp," she said as Hector helped her from the car. She had no intention of being stuck in this strange place, although, as she stood on the pave-ment looking up at Felicity's house, she had to admit the neigh-borhood didn't look too bad. It was a little out-of-the-way perhaps, but the trees and quaint gas lamps and fancy iron grillwork were really quite charming. Felicity's house was cov-ered with ivy. Through tall parlor windows, Charlie could see rows and rows of books and the soft, plump, curving back of a sofa.

At the door she was greeted by Felicity's husband, Michael, a big smiling man with lots of curly black hair whom she had met at several AA meetings, and their four-year-old daughter, Bessie, who was dressed in an undershirt and droopy white panties. Michael took her coat and disappeared with it upstairs, and Bessie led her through the house to her mother. "You're the second person here," the little girl announced.

"Really?" said Charlie, glancing quickly at the toy-strewn parlor with its high ceilings and magnificent art deco fireplace. She would have liked to take a good look around, but the child tugged insistently at her hand, pulling her through partially closed, glassed-in double doors to the dining room at the back of the house. There, at a table set with a white damask cloth, tulips, and pretty silver, sat Gwendolyn Thomas, the writer. She was sipping Coca-Cola from a wineglass, and was dressed in a yellow tunic and wide black pants that resembled a maternity outfit. Since Felicity didn't seem to be anywhere in sight, Charlie extended her hand and introduced herself. "I'm Charlie Gallagher, and I know who you are—I adore your books."

"Thanks," said Gwen, as if she were accustomed to easy praise. "Why don't you sit down? Felicity's in the kitchen doing something tricky to a leg of lamb. She should be out in a minute."

"Oh. She doesn't have someone to help her?"

Gwen gave a snort of laughter. "You mean like a servant? No. Even if she had the money, she'd insist on doing everything herself." She considered Charlie, who looked like a prep-school girl in pearls, a dark green crew neck sweater, and a longish woolen skirt printed with tiny plum-colored flowers. "So you're one of Felicity's new pigeons."

"Pigeons?"

"AA slang for newcomer. An extension of which, by the way, is 'pigeon-fucking.' Beware."

"Not seriously?"

"Oh, yes. There're lots of guys waiting to leap on the innocent newcomer. Another term for it, here in New York anyway, is 'thirteenth-shtupping.'"

"Lord."

Simultaneously imagining this thirteenth step, the two women looked at one another and laughed. From the kitchen came the slightly nasal trill of Bessie's voice as she chattered to her mother. A warm doughy smell filled the room along with a sharp sweet scent of cherries. Charlie, who had been dreading this first social occasion without alcohol, suddenly felt light-headed and happy. "How long have you been sober?" she asked Gwen.

"Seventy-five days. You?"

"Fifteen. Each one of them filled with the most enormous terror and anxiety."

Gwen gave a husky laugh. "Don't worry. It gets better, I promise you that. The thing is to use AA like you used to use the booze. You know—addictively."

"Did I hear the word 'addictively'?" Felicity asked, coming into the room, her cheeks flushed from her work in the kitchen. She was wearing a blue-and-white striped canvas apron over a svelte pair of leggings, and her little daughter tagged behind her, carrying a big green bottle of ginger ale.

"Yeah. We were talking about getting high on sobriety," said Gwen, staring with mock distaste at Bessie's droopy panties. "Can't you get some clothes on that child?"

"Ha! You try," said Felicity, turning to Charlie with a warm smile of welcome. "You made it here. Good. Did you take a taxi?"

"No," said Charlie. "I borrowed my mother's driver."

"La-di-da . . . some of us have all the luck," said Gwen, smiling to show she meant no harm.

"I wouldn't talk what with all those hefty advances of yours," said Felicity. She continued to look at Charlie, who was biting nervously at one of her cuticles. "What can I get you to drink? The choices are juice, soda, Perrier, tea, or coffee."

Charlie gave a long sigh. "I guess coffee," she said.

"Right on!" Gwen laughed. "Good old caffeine'll do it every time."

Musette entered the room a few minutes later, accompanied by Bessie, who had raced to the front door as soon as she heard the sound of chimes. Felicity introduced the three women to one another and then returned to the kitchen, this time without Bessie, who couldn't keep her eyes off Musette. Clearly the child had never seen anyone so beautiful. She brushed up close to Musette, staring at her sparkling jewelry, her glorious curls, her high-heeled shoes, her red-painted lips. "Is that real?" she said, pointing to a diamond ring that flashed on Musette's wedding finger.

"Sure," said the actress. "Want to try it on?"

The child nodded ecstatically and everyone watched as the ring was slipped onto one of her tiny fingers. "A little big," said

Musette without the slightest trace of sarcasm in her voice. "Tell you what...you can wear my fur boa till bedtime. When is bedtime?" She removed her fluffy silver boa from the back of her chair and draped it around Bessie's shoulders.

"Right now," said Felicity, coming into the room with a glass of Perrier water for Musette. "Bessie, go find Daddy, honey. He's going to give you a bath and put you to bed tonight."

"Do I have to?"

"He'll read you a story."

"I don't care about a stupid story."

"You can take that boa with you if you're very good," said Musette.

Bessie turned wide eyes on the actress. "Okay," she said.

When the child was gone from the room, Musette pronounced her very cute.

"Yeah, she's cute when you can bribe her like that," Gwen muttered beneath her breath.

"Oh, I grew up with lots of younger sisters," said Musette. "I know how to handle them. You, I take it, don't have children?"

"Nope," said Gwen. "Not likely to have any, either."

"Why's that? If you don't mind my asking."

Gwen bit into a cracker. "I had what we black women call 'fireballs of the uterus.' Fibroids. Had to have a hysterectomy."

"Oh. Sorry. Well, I know what that's like. I don't seem too fertile either."

Gwen gave her an inquiring look.

Trying to keep her voice light, Musette said, "I had a bad abortion. That was back in the seventies when I was young and innocent and didn't know how to go about choosing doctors."

"Gee, rough," said Charlie.

"Yeah, well, it didn't help that the baby's father, who's actually known to some people in this room, hated being parted from his money. The piddly little bit he gave me was hardly enough to feed a cat." She smiled at Charlie, whose blue eyes, much brighter now that she was sober, were studying her with curiosity. "He said I was better than any woman he'd ever had in the sack, but the minute I needed him, it was fuck you, get out of here."

"Lord," said Charlie with a shudder, "he sounds awful. Who was he?"

"Forget it, my lips are sealed. All I'll say is that the abortion I had to have because of him accounts for the failure of my last marriage. Miroslav wanted a baby and I couldn't supply him with one, and voilà, here we are in kaputsky land."

"That's why you went after him with a knife?" asked Gwen, who had followed Musette's tormented Hollywood existence in the tabloids.

"It wasn't a knife, it was a pair of scissors. And I didn't go after *him*—I went after his clothes."

Charlie, who had been trying to follow this, said: "I don't understand. Please explain."

"Yes, please *do*," echoed Gwen.

"Well," sighed Musette, "it's complicated. I came home from lunch at Spago one day and discovered Miroslav in our pool house screwing this very young, very pretty actress who also happened to be a good friend of mine. So I ran up to our bedroom, took all his goddamn clothes out of the closet, cut them up with a pair of scissors, and scattered the pieces all over our beautiful Bel Air lawn. Ha! You should have seen people driving by in their Jags and Bentleys, craning their necks. The best was his mink coat. That was his pride and joy, although the only time he ever wore the goddamn thing was when he was in New York."

"Were you drunk when all this happened?" asked Charlie.

It occurred to Musette that Charlie had no recollection of having met her before, that on the night she had said Musette's name sounded like a hairdresser's she had already been half in the bag. She decided not to let this bother her. "Oh, yes. Very," she said.

Dinner was served with a minimum of fuss. "What about your husband? Isn't he joining us?" Musette asked Felicity.

"Not tonight. I wanted it to be just us ladies. He's upstairs working."

"Boy, are you lucky," said Gwen. "Walter would hover like one of those big noisy flies."

Felicity, smiling at the image, glanced around to see that they all had what they wanted, and then removed her apron and sat down. Everyone agreed that the food was delicious—which it was, lamb and tiny green peas and roasted potatoes and an arugula salad. For a few minutes they ate in silence. The dog came in to beg, and Felicity shooed him into the parlor and closed the sliding doors. From deep in the house came the boom of a grandfather clock, and instants later, from the street outside, the nagging screech of a police siren.

"Somehow one doesn't expect to hear that sound here," said Charlie.

"Why not? This is the city," said Gwen.

"It's so peaceful. In fact, I could quite easily see myself living here. Perhaps I should look around."

Musette glanced sharply at her.

"I need a bigger place," explained Charlie. "There's no room at Rita's for the children. Anyway, Rita's coming back soon."

"You mean you're leaving your husband?" Musette asked as casually as she could manage.

Charlie shrugged. "I don't know. Probably not. It's just that I can't go back to Washington. I wouldn't be able to stay sober there. Put me in that house with Neil and the children, and all the skeletons dancing around in the closet, and I'd be drunk in five minutes."

"Probably less," laughed Felicity. "In AA we call it 'staying away from places and things'—in other words, avoiding all the old haunts of the past. I'm glad you know about that instinctively. But as your sponsor, I should tell you that it's unwise to make drastic changes, such as buying a new house, in the first year."

"I could always rent," said Charlie.

"You could. But try to remember that getting sober is the biggest change in your life right now. Anything else—moving, or having a love affair, or getting a new job—could lead you straight back to a drink."

"We have to wait a year to have a love affair?" said Musette, tossing her blond curls and bunching her sultry lips into a comic pout.

"Well, it's suggested. And that's enough lecturing from me. Anyone want seconds?"

For dessert Felicity had baked a cherry tart, which she served with tiny cups of espresso. Musette, always careful of her figure, refused the tart, but had two cups of espresso. "Lord, I don't know where you get the willpower," said Gwen. "I can't seem to stop eating no matter what I do."

"Exercise helps," said Musette, studying Gwen's heavy chin and thick, pregnant-looking body. She was baffled by Felicity's relationship to this middle-aged black woman. "What do you do all day, anyway?"

"Well, right now I read a lot. And I go to the movies and visit friends."

"No, I mean for a living."

The room grew quiet.

"You mean you don't know?" said Charlie.

"Know what?"

"Gwen's a novelist," said Felicity. "Her books have been on the bestseller list. I'm her editor."

Musette's high-boned cheeks flushed a hot pretty pink. She gave a squeaky laugh of embarrassment and said, "Out in L.A. we don't have too much culture."

"Aw, that's not it," said Gwen, grinning at her. "'Fess up, girl. You were probably too zonked out on all those pills you took ever to read anything but the trades."

It was nearly midnight when the evening ended, and Gwen, feeling like a big wretched Cinderella, was suddenly nervous about what her husband would have to say. She was the first to leave, racing out the door without buttoning her coat, yelling, "Good-bye, see you all soon," over her shoulder. The other two waited for Felicity, who had gone upstairs to look for Musette's boa.

"Now I know where I met you!" exclaimed Charlie, looking down at a caky patch of fur on the hem of her mink. "It's been bothering me all night."

"Yeah, well, you'd already had a few. You asked me if I was some sort of actress."

Charlie laughed. "I never was much good on Hollywood lore, drunk or sober."

"Here we are," said Felicity, running lightly down the steps with the boa in her arms. "I'm afraid Bessie got some glue or something on it. I knew it wasn't a good idea to let her play with it like that."

"Don't worry," said Musette. "It's just something I wear for fun."

"It can go to the cleaners along with my mink," Charlie pointed out wryly. She had agreed to give Musette a lift, and the two women walked down the front steps talking about the best places to go to have fur cleaned in New York. Hector helped them into the car. "We'll be dropping my friend off at Park and Eightieth," said Charlie.

The car was a Peugeot station wagon that Charlie's mother used for shopping and for driving back and forth to the country, and there was no partition between the chauffeur and the backseat. Charlie immediately lit a cigarette. "Well, that was kind of fun," she said.

"Yeah, not too bad," agreed Musette.

"Somehow one expects an evening without alcohol to pass slowly, but I must say I totally forgot the time." She tapped ash into her palm. A moment later she opened the window and flung out her cigarette. "God, look at the view!"

They were crossing the Brooklyn Bridge, and the huge buildings and shimmering lights of lower Manhattan hung silhouetted before them like a glowing tapestry against the rosy nighttime sky.

"I'll have to come back here during the day," said Charlie.

Musette glanced at her curiously. "Your marriage must be in pretty bad shape if you're thinking of moving to Brooklyn. Were you serious about that?"

Charlie gave her a warning look and pointed without saying anything at Hector's back.

"Whoops, sorry," said Musette, mouthing the words.

Aloud, Charlie said, "It's just that I can't stay where I am for too much longer. And Brooklyn seems awfully charming."

"Well, you know what—I'll go house hunting with you. It happens to be my most favorite thing in the world."

"Are you serious?"

"Absolutely. My agent's putting me out to pasture for a few months while I get used to being sober, so I have nothing better to do."

"Well then, you've got yourself a deal. Give me your hand and let's shake on it."

Musette held out her hand, conscious of her long red nails and the diamond she wore on her middle finger, as Charlie, whose nails and fingers were unadorned, crushed her palm in her own with the firmness of a former hockey player. "We'll make a date soon," said Charlie.

At about the same time as Musette and Charlie were crossing the bridge, Gwen was unlocking the door to her apartment. When she was inside, she slipped off her shoes and tiptoed across the foyer. There were no lights on, and the place was very still, almost eerie. She would have liked to go into her study to smoke a cigarette, but she thought she'd better have a talk with Walter first. Probably he was fixing for a fight. She could actually feel him, the heaviness of his anger and resentment, in the silence of the apartment. The silence seemed to deepen as she walked down the hallway to their room, pushed open the door, and padded in on her bare feet. "Walter?" she said.

In the dark she could just make out his inert form on the bed, but he didn't answer. The quilt was pulled up to his ears. A digital clock stood on the bedside table, and Gwen could see that the time was 12:25. Somehow she knew that Walter's eyes were open, and that he too was staring at the clock.

"Look Walt, I'm sorry," she said. "The evening flew by, and..." No response. She gave up trying to explain and went to the bathroom to brush her teeth and undress. When she climbed into bed a few minutes later, Walter held himself stiffly away from her. Tentatively she reached out to touch his shoulders, but the clenched muscles were hard as rock, and she withdrew her hand as if she had been burned. For the rest of the night they lay as far apart from one another as they could, their bodies aching from the effort of not touching, their breathing fitful and disturbed. In the morning he got up early and left for work, not bringing her a cup of coffee as usual, not rousing her from her sleep. And she, with fiercely closed eyes and a rapidly beating heart, dug herself down deeper beneath the sheets and was relieved.

The Charlie who used to sleep well into the afternoon, keeping the curtains drawn so the light wouldn't bother her swollen eyes, was up at seven o'clock on the morning after Felicity's party. In the shower she hungrily planned what she would have for breakfast, remembering that only two weeks ago anything other than coffee and a glass of juice would have made her sick. Now her stomach groaned for food. Hurriedly she stepped out of the shower and reached for her robe, splashing her favorite Chanel No. 19 cologne liberally over her body. Running a brush through her thick chestnut hair, she thought how remarkable it was that she could wake with a clear head and remember everything that had happened the night before. No more hangovers! And none of the awful paranoia that had seemed, in her drinking days, to accompany her wherever she went—the sense that people were laughing at her because she said foolish things and her memory was unreliable and her breath, even in the middle of the day, smelled of stale liquor. Suddenly she had more energy than she had had since she was a girl. And she was happy! She liked this business of building her day around AA meetings, and the hell with everything else. "Put your life on hold for a while," Felicity had advised, and that was exactly what she was doing.

In the kitchen she wolfed down two slices of bran toast, half a cantaloupe, and a bowl of corn flakes with a banana. She was considering a third slice of toast when the phone rang. "Hello," she said, cradling the receiver on her shoulder and pouring herself a cup of coffee. It was her mother, back from a trip to Aruba, and she took the phone to the kitchen counter and sat down.

"Charlotte, I was terribly distressed to learn that you were in New York," Helene began.

Groaning inwardly, Charlie said, "Why's that, Mother?"

"Because you belong in Georgetown with Neil and the children! What's going on, Charlotte? Are you having an affair?"

This made Charlie laugh. "Of course not, Mother! Look, it's a long story. What's happened is I've gotten sober, I'm in AA. Isn't that wonderful?"

There was a long silence. At her mother's end Charlie could hear the yipping of one of Helene's little Yorkshire terriers. She had a vision of the dog squatting and peeing on her mother's Aubusson carpet, adding a pale streak of yellow to numerous other streaks. "Well, I'm glad you're not drinking, Charlotte. It's about time. But I hate to think of you going to those dreary meetings with all those dreary people."

"Oh, the people aren't dreary at all, believe me," said Charlie, thinking of Musette with her dyed blond curls, her sultry red-painted lips, and lively language.

"Well, it's not something you want to make public, you'd better be careful about that," said Helene.

"It's an anonymous program, Mother. That's the whole point."

Five minutes after she had hung up with Helene, she had a call from Neil. "When are you coming home, Charlie?" he asked, first thing.

"I don't know. Maybe in a few weeks."

"A few weeks!"

"I need to get used to being sober, Neil."

"But you can do that here in D.C. Jesus, don't you ever think of anyone but yourself?"

"I *have* to think of myself if I'm going to be any good to you or the children." She paused, remembering that Felicity had told her that AA was a selfish program, especially in the beginning when newcomers went through a period of becoming reacquainted with themselves after their long years of drinking. "Don't let anybody guilt-trip you," she had warned.

At his end Neil gave an impatient sigh. "That's a lot of crap," he said.

Charlie imagined him rubbing his hand along his cheeks, feeling for patches of stubble. "It's not a lot of crap, and while we're on the subject, I'd like to see the children. I want them to come up here this weekend."

"No way."

"I'm not drinking, Neil. That was our deal. It's been two weeks."

"I don't care. Why the hell should I trust you? I've seen you stop before."

Now it was her turn to sigh. "Because this time I'm in AA."

She heard a buzzing sound as he turned on his electric razor. "If you want to see the children, you come here!" he insisted. "*That's* the deal."

"In that case," she said angrily, "all deals are off!" She slammed down the phone.

His stubbornness and lack of understanding made her want to speak to someone from AA. Without bothering to look at the time, she went to her bedroom, rummaged in her purse for Musette's card, and picked up the phone. She would go look at houses today, she decided. With Neil being such a shit she wasn't sure she ever wanted to return to Washington.

"My, my—you're an early bird," said the actress, who was still in bed.

"Oh, did I wake you? Sorry. It seems to be a gorgeous day, and I thought we might go house hunting."

"Hmmm . . ." Musette stared at a thin yellow ray of sun that lay like a line of fire on her white satin quilt. It was only about eight-thirty and she had intended to have a lazy morning. "Let me get my book," she said, stalling for time.

While Musette was gone, Charlie tapped an impatient foot and thought how different the actress was from anyone she knew. That story about cutting up her husband's clothes! About how she had caught him screwing—was that the word she had used?—one of her best friends. And coming right out and saying some creep had made her have an abortion! Neil would kill her if she ever talked so openly about their marriage and the dark shadow that lay at its core. He'd positively take her apart. But there was something refreshing about Musette's honesty, and the lush sleazy glamour of her up-from-nowhere-to-Hollywood background. Charlie decided she would make an interesting friend.

"You know what," said Musette, coming back on the phone, "we should do this tomorrow. I mean, you have to make appointments with realtors first. Give them a chance to go through what they have."

"Oh, really? I hadn't thought of that."

"If you like, I'll set it up for you. But you'll have to tell me what you're looking for."

"Four bedrooms. A big garden. High ceilings. A tree-lined street." In her mind she was seeing her Georgetown house, only transplanted to Brooklyn. "Like Felicity's," she added. "Quaint and charming."

"All right. Let me make some calls and see what's out there. I'll get back to you in an hour or so."

Charlie hung up, smiling, glad to have Musette take care of these details. Now that she had thought of it, she was anxious to move. Rita's place was just too small, and she was sick of living with someone else's furniture. She wanted to be surrounded by her own things, paintings and furniture chosen by herself rather than by Neil or her mother or Theo Hammond. It struck her that she was tired of the English landscapes and horse portraits with which she had grown up. Maybe it was time that she pleased herself and hung the work of some weird, way-out painter on her walls. She could have a lot of fun wandering around the Soho galleries, going to art openings and exhibits, maybe even taking a course in painting or drawing at one of the art schools. She had majored in art history at Vassar, but had never had a chance to start a career. Now, perhaps, her chance had arrived. As she thought of this she gave a little pirouette and flung off her heavy terry-cloth robe, dancing naked around the room, feeling wonderfully free and alive for the first time in years.

* * *

The following morning Musette picked Charlie up in her little red Porsche, and they drove out to Brooklyn where they had an eleven o'clock appointment with a realtor. Since it was already a quarter to, Musette roared down the FDR Drive, only dimly aware of the choppy gray water of the East River to her left, and the brick walls and gardens of Sutton Place to her right. She had stayed up most of the previous night reading *Homegirl,* the first of Gwen's four novels, and her mind was filled with the heat and torpor and slow bitter language of the South. When Charlie asked her to please slow down a little, she said, "Sure thing," in a honeyed southern accent, and let up on the gas. But a few minutes later, as they drove past the UN and the hospitals and Peter Cooper Village, her foot had inched down and she was speeding again.

They saw four houses that morning, and not one of them was any good. A carelessly dressed woman named Mrs. Clark took them around, and Musette found herself growing more and more angry with Charlie, who seemed to find fault with everything. Instinctively she pitied Neil for having to live with such a woman. Stairs were too steep, gardens were too rocky and narrow, there was an odd smell, the rooms were damp, the kitchen was old, the street was noisy . . . each house had a problem, and it was a relief when Mrs. Clark finally showed them all she had on her list, and they could say good-bye to her and go for lunch. At Charlie's insistence, they walked along the Promenade first, among the classic brownstones and apartment buildings that overlooked New York Harbor and the mouth of the Hudson. "Oh, I love this place, don't you?" she cried.

Musette was amazed. After the many disappointments of the morning, she would have expected Charlie to say, "The hell with this, let's go back to Manhattan," but instead she planted herself on a bench and stared out over the water. It was a joyous sight. Boats slipped by, and the towers of Manhattan rose in a majestic formation just ahead of them, glass pinnacles of blue and gray and green that reflected the clouds. In the distance Musette could see the Statue of Liberty, and all about them was a scudding brightness in which birds flew, and small planes hovered like toys on strings. It was early March, a perfect day, the air fresh and clear, with just the slightest hint of warmth to it. Charlie wore a heavy, caped, olive-green trench coat, and she sighed, pulling the wide lapels tightly around her throat. "I could start life over here, couldn't you?" she said.

"I don't know," said Musette, who was having trouble lighting a cigarette in the wind. "It's a little far, don't you think?" Then she wanted to bite her tongue because, of course, the whole point was that Charlie and her children should live here, apart from Neil, in a snug out-of-the-way house in Brooklyn.

"Far? Not at all. Look, the city's right there. You can practically touch it."

They decided on a coffee shop for lunch. It was one-thirty, and they had only half an hour before they were to meet the next real estate agent, a Mr. Lyons, who had promised over the phone that he had some wonderful houses to show them. "Not like that last one, I hope," said Charlie. "She was a real dud. And she dressed the way her houses looked, poor dear."

"Why are you in such a hurry to move?" asked Musette, wanting to test Charlie, get her talking. "I thought you were all right where you are."

"It's a borrowed apartment."

"I know that."

"I'm used to living in a house. Anyway, Rita will be back in a few weeks, and I want to start getting ready to move out of there."

"What's your husband have to say about that?"

"Neil?" She laughed. "He doesn't know anything about it. When he finds out he'll be royally pissed off."

"He wants you back?"

"Does he ever!"

Musette, feeling distressed, watched as the waitress put their sandwiches on the table. Charlie waited until she had gone. "It has nothing to do with me, of course. Well, not entirely, anyway. His big worry is that if I'm not with him, all sorts of nasty rumors will start circulating in the press, and boom"—she slammed the flat of her hand on the table—"that'll be the end of his political career."

"Not necessarily," said Musette, taking a careful bite of her turkey on rye. "Look at Ted and Joan Kennedy."

Charlie's face paled slightly. "I'd rather not."

Musette glanced at her. "Too close for comfort, hunh?"

"Anyway, it's not as if I'm going to leave him. This is a temporary hiatus. I need to be on my own for a while."

"Good idea," said Musette, pushing her plate away and lighting a cigarette. "How'd you meet him, anyway?"

"Neil?"

She blew out a stream of smoke. "Yeah—Neil."

Charlie leaned back and lit her own cigarette. She had removed her coat, and the bright red crew neck sweater she wore underneath clashed slightly with her chestnut hair. "That's a long story," she said.

"We have time," said Musette.

"Well, let's see, it was nineteen seventy-five and I'd just graduated from Vassar. My parents had promised me a year abroad, and of course I was very excited about that. I was going to be a painter and I was young enough to be sure I had talent. I pictured myself going to art school and living in a tiny rooftop garret in Paris. But then, a week before I was to leave, I met Neil." She looked at Musette and smiled. "You know what a goose one is at that age. It was midsummer, and we were at my parents' country house in Pennsylvania. Someone, a cousin of mine, had brought Neil along as a guest for the weekend, and I fell madly in love. Suddenly the idea of going to Paris seemed tragic." She stubbed out her cigarette.

"What happened then? Did you go?"

"Sure I went. My parents insisted. They thought it was crazy for me to jump into anything, and they didn't know Neil's family. He's Catholic, you know. But then, after about two weeks in Paris, I started feeling sick in the morning and I realized I'd missed my period. I don't know why I'm telling you all this."

"Because we're both in AA," Musette said smoothly.

"Maybe. Anyway, I was a real ninny back then, and I phoned Neil in tears, and he flew over and took me to a doctor."

"He did?" Musette leaned forward, trying not to stare at Charlie, but staring anyway. She could feel her face go white and cold.

"Yeah. He was really good about it. My parents had a harder time, but they rallied and managed to pull together a beautiful wedding. My daughter, Petra, was born the following April."

"When did you say you met him?" asked Musette, feeling as if the breath had been knocked out of her.

"Late July of seventy-five."

"You didn't know him before then?"

"Of course not," said Charlie. "Why?"

"Oh, I don't know," said Musette, relieved that at least he hadn't been screwing them both at the same time. "It just sounds so quick."

"Well, it was," said Charlie, signaling the waitress for more coffee. Then she said, "Good lord, what's the time? Aren't we going to be late for Mr. Whosit?"

"Mr. Lyons," said Musette through clenched teeth. "And yes, we will be late, unless you take that coffee to go."

They saw another four houses that afternoon, but Musette, wounded to the quick, paid very little attention. It took every ounce of her dramatic skill not to lash out at the woman who was Neil's wife. What a bastard Neil was, running to the altar with his rich society love, kicking *her,* Musette, out into the cold. That check for five hundred bucks was supposed to keep her quiet and happy. Hah! She'd been the wrong girl, she knew that, but what, except for her money, was so right about Charlie? As they traipsed from house to house, Musette decided quite cold-bloodedly that she hated the woman: hated her stiffly voluminous olive-green trench coat, her habit of smoking cigarettes only halfway down, her flippancy, her abrupt manner, her slouchingly elegant bowlegged walk. Above all she hated her for being Neil's wife.

When they got to the fourth and last house on Mr. Lyons's list, Charlie grabbed Musette's hand. "Yes, this is it! This is it!" she exclaimed.

Musette reclaimed her hand and stuffed it deep into her jacket pocket. "How do you know? You haven't seen the inside."

"I just know. I love the location, and look at all that ivy growing up the front. Charming!"

The house was a warm red brick with white shutters and a white door. A magnolia tree whose buds were already thick and pink grew out front, and directly across the street was a small, red-painted church with a delicate pointed steeple. Mr. Lyons led them inside, and they saw that the house, which was still filled with its current owners' furniture, was much larger than it appeared from the street. From the entry hall a curving red-carpeted stairway led to two floors of bedrooms above, while the parlor floor had been opened out into a single, huge, loftlike space. The ceilings were high, the windows were tall, the floors were of a smooth polished tawny wood, and in the back was a fully planted garden whose light gave the room a green glow, a feeling of country. Charlie walked up and down, admiring the marvelous fireplaces, the exposed brick walls, the thick wooden beam in the kitchen from which hung pots and pans and strings of garlic. Then she turned to Mr. Lyons. "How much do they want for this?" Against Felicity's advice, she had decided to buy rather than rent.

"Eight hundred thousand."

"Really? That's a lot."

"Well, this *is* Brooklyn Heights. The house is spectacular, and as you can see, you wouldn't have to do anything to it."

"I'll pay seven and a quarter. No more. What do you think, Musette? Do you like it?"

Musette looked up from some framed photographs on the grand piano, squinting her eyes as if to bring the room into focus. "Yeah, it's terrific. If I were you I wouldn't hesitate. It's got everything you want. Space, charm, atmosphere. It's perfect." She gave Charlie a big sweet smile of encouragement, adding silently to herself, And it'll break up your marriage, bitch, which is just the way we want to go.

Gwen and Walter had begun to have continuous picky little fights. She wasn't home for dinner enough; her clothes were too tight and sexy to wear in public; she never seemed interested in the things he had to say anymore; why didn't she want to make love? In the week following Felicity's dinner they had one of their worst arguments. It started when she forgot to attend a poetry reading of his at Hunter College, going to an AA meeting instead. When they met up at home later that evening, he came very close to slapping her in his rage and jealousy. "I just don't understand!" he shouted. "I go to all your events. I hold your hand when you're nervous about giving a lecture, and I even accept an award for you when you're too goddamn drunk to go up and speak for yourself, and yet you can't come to one function of mine."

"That's not true! I usually go to your readings."

"This was an important one, Gwen."

"Look Walt, I'm sorry. What more can I say? I was wrong and I apologize."

They glared at each other. Walter, in an unaccustomed dark suit, looked more like a merchant than a poet, and Gwen suddenly felt sorry for him. "I don't want to fight," she said.

"Nor do I, nor do I. But I can't live like this anymore. Everything has to rotate around you and your schedule and your meetings while I'm some dumb little schmuck who doesn't seem to count anymore. I mean, I bring out a book of poetry and your attitude is, 'So what?' How's that supposed to make me feel?"

She could see he was getting all wound up again, and she backed up slightly, her hand rising to pat her hair into place and to pluck at her lower lip, which had begun to protrude obstinately. "My attitude is not 'So what?' Walter; I'm very proud of you, you must know that."

"Don't go patronizing me."

"I'm not patronizing you."

"Oh, yes you are, yes you are!" He loosened his tie, his black eyes staring harshly into hers. As he did this he moved closer to her, and there was something about the way his neck hunched forward out of his shoulders that made her think he was about to attack. "I've had just about enough of you!" he shouted.

"And I've had just about enough of you! Your jealousy and your insults and your paranoia. I'm getting out of here for a while, and you just goddamn well better calm down!"

She stormed out of the apartment without her coat and for the next twenty minutes strode along Twenty-third Street, feeling the chill March wind push itself up against her ribs. If a man in ripped clothing with a stocking cap on his head hadn't come up and said, "Hey lady, wanna fuck?" she would have gone on like that for hours, marching through the streets of Chelsea and Gramercy Park, the wind at her back; but instead she returned to the apartment where she and a quieter Walter apologized to one another and made tepid love. In the morning it seemed to her that everything was all right. "I'm going to a meeting at six o'clock," she said, wanting no more misunderstandings. "The one I always go to, my home group. I'll be back around . . . oh, seven-thirty or eight."

"Fine," said Walter, picking up his briefcase and giving her a quick scratchy kiss good-bye.

That night at the meeting, which was in a church in Gramercy Park, she ran into Theo Hammond and they decided to go out for coffee. They invited two others to join them, Tanya and a man named Keith who worked for a travel agency and had about a year's sobriety. As they were going down the church steps, Gwen put her arm through Theo's and said, "I count on you to cheer me up, my friend."

"Really? Why's that?"

"I haven't written a fucking thing in months."

"You mean since getting sober?"

"Before, after, what's the difference? I'm totally, monumentally, supremely blocked." She would have said more, but just then she spotted Walter standing across the street in front of a Korean vegetable stand, trying to look inconspicuous with the collar of his old army trench coat turned up around his bearded cheeks. She groaned and dropped Theo's arm.

"What's the matter?" said Theo, looking around.

"My husband," explained Gwen.

They both watched as Walter, a veteran jogger who was extremely light-footed and graceful, made a dash across Twenty-second Street and came toward them, his face unreadable in the patchy light. "What the hell are you doing here?" demanded Gwen.

"I thought I'd come and meet you. Anything wrong with that?" He sounded innocent enough, although his burning eyes could have scorched holes into Theo.

Gwen didn't answer, and Theo quickly said, "We were just going out for coffee. Why don't you join us?"

"Sure, I'd like that," said Walter, glancing at the others, particularly at Keith, who was tall and handsome, with a dark mustache and a tanned virile face.

They went to a Greek diner on Twenty-third and Lexington, squeezing themselves into a booth that had its own jukebox and a low-hanging imitation Tiffany lamp that hit Walter in the head as he was sitting down. After the waiter had taken their orders, Tanya, in a baby-blue cowl neck sweater that was tight over her large breasts, turned to Walter and said, "So . . . are you a writer too?"

"A poet."

"Gosh, I don't think I've read any poetry since college. Except maybe for that crap in *The New Yorker*. I used to love Keats, though. Keats and Swinburne and Tennyson, and of course, Eliot and Yeats and sometimes Wallace Stevens. And that other guy, too... oh yes, Hart Crane." She broke off and stared at Walter, twisting one of her thick ginger curls around a stubby, nail-bitten finger.

"I'm not quite in that league," said Walter, not wanting to admit that some of his finest poems had been published in *The New Yorker*.

"Oh, come on, Walter, don't be bashful," said Gwen. Turning to the others, she explained that Walter had just brought out a book of poetry.

"That's nice," said Keith, lighting cigarettes for himself and Gwen, who with a tinkle of bangles had held up two fingers to indicate she wanted one. "Well, what did everyone think of tonight's qualification?"

"Jesus, what a barn burner," said Gwen, taking a puff on her cigarette and coughing hoarsely. The man who had told his story at the meeting that night had spent fifteen years in jail for a murder he had no memory of committing.

"Imagine waking up and finding yourself under arrest for killing some guy you'd never even seen before," said Theo, who had been a high-bottom drunk, and loved hearing low-bottom stories about knife slashings, barroom brawls, and life on skid row.

"He must have really been blitzed," said Keith, shaking his head in admiration. "Jeez, the guy starts in Chicago on a Thursday afternoon, and the next thing he knows it's Saturday night and he's in a police station in Vegas."

Gwen coughed again, and Walter grabbed the cigarette from her hand and scratched it out in the ashtray. "You shouldn't be smoking, Gwennie," he complained.

"Hey man, if she needs to smoke, let her smoke," said Keith. "It's hard enough giving up the booze."

Gwen felt her face go hot. "That's all right," she said quickly, although what she really wanted to do was strangle Walter. She drained her coffee, put some money on the table, and stood up, slinging her tote bag over her shoulder. "Come on, Walter," she said, leaning down to give Theo a good-bye kiss, and waving at the others. "We've got all that stuff to do at home, remember?"

Out in the street Walter grabbed her and gave her a frantic hug. "I didn't mean to embarrass you, honey. I'm sorry."

"Forget it, okay?" said Gwen. His breath touched her ear in fierce little puffs, and over his shoulder she could see Theo staring at them through the coffee shop window, his face a pinkish yellow in the multicolored glow of the Tiffany lamp. Much as she loved her husband, she felt lonely standing with him on the sidewalk and wished she could be back in the coffee shop with the others. Hating to think of what that meant, she pulled out of his embrace. "Come on, let's go home," she said.

CHAPTER 9

Several days after her jaunt with Charlie to Brooklyn, Musette had lunch with Theo Hammond at his favorite restaurant, Le Cirque, on East Sixty-fifth Street. She was breathless when she arrived, her beautiful chiseled cheeks pink and rosy, her long blond hair blown every which way by the March wind. Under her fur coat, she was wearing leggings and an Irish fisherman's sweater, clothes that were a little too casual for Le Cirque with its elegant clientele, and she leaned over and gave Theo a sweet kiss on the cheek before sitting down.

"My, my, aren't we happy today," he said, looking at her with a raised brow.

"Not happy—healthy. I've been to the gym for a workout, *and* I've been working on my mind too." She giggled and pulled Gwen's novel *Hey Look at Me Mister* from her bag, holding it up for him to see.

"Ah yes. That's the one that won the Mendelsohn Award."

"Have you read it?"

"I've read all of them. Let's hope she keeps going—she's suffering from the most awful writer's block. Hasn't written a thing in months. Still, I think she's pretty amazing, especially considering the fact that she comes from a totally different world from the one she's describing."

"She grew up in Harlem, didn't she?"

"Yes, she did. But there's Harlem and there's Harlem."

"What's that supposed to mean?"

"Her parents were Jamaican," Theo said. "They worked like dogs so they could send darling Gwen to the best schools, et cetera, et cetera. I know that because she went to Calhoun with a niece of mine, and I was always hearing about this brilliant black girl in Jennie's class."

"But her books are so violent." Musette glanced at the fierce black face on the book's cover, and the calmer, but equally forceful portrait of Gwen on the back. *Hey Look at Me Mister* began with a brutal rape, and went on from there to describe the ordeals of a teenage girl growing up on the streets of Harlem. "I assumed that she had, you know, *been* there. She even talks kind of tough."

Theo smiled, showing horsey white teeth. "Sure she does. She's Gwendolyn Thomas, spokesperson for the nation's most impoverished class. But in reality, all her friends are white. So is her husband, Walter Rudin, a nice guy who writes the most tedious poetry I've ever read. And so is her way of life, with that apartment of hers in Chelsea, and the summer house up in the Berkshires. It's only her skin that's black."

Musette thought about the contradiction for a moment; then pointed a long red nail at *Hey Look at Me Mister* and said, "Who cares what she's like, or what she does. This book would make a dynamite film."

But Theo, whose ears were usually so finely tuned for every shift and nuance of the spoken word, wasn't listening. He had half turned in his seat and was looking at a woman with snow-white hair, carrying a Yorkshire terrier, who had just entered the restaurant. The maître d' was making a big fuss over her. "Look, there's Charlie's mother, Helene Vandermark," exclaimed Theo. "I thought she was still in Aruba. Goodness— now what could she be doing back so soon?"

"Perhaps she's worried about her daughter," murmured Musette. She watched as the elderly lady, who was with a younger man who carried her coat for her, walked swiftly across the restaurant. She had Charlie's tall build and the same snooty looks, and Musette could just imagine what it must have been like having her as a mother—a constant cool barrage of criticism. "Pull your socks up, my dear." "No, we hold the fork this way." "Your nails are dirty." Not that she would have minded some of that from her own mother, Lucille, who had been too drunk half the time to know, or *care,* what any of her children were doing.

"What did you say?" said Theo, swinging back in his seat, all ears again.

"I said maybe she's worried about Charlie. You know, I went out to Brooklyn with her the other day to look at a house."

"A house?"

"Yes. To buy."

"You're not serious!"

"I am. It's a beautiful house in Brooklyn Heights that costs a fortune, nearly a million dollars. She's planning to move in on her own, without Neil. In fact, probably at this very minute, she's with her lawyer going over financial arrangements."

Charlie Gallagher moving to New York—that was big news! By evening word got to Helene Vandermark, who was furious with her daughter for taking such a step without informing her first. "It's so embarrassing, Charlotte! Now everyone will assume that you and Neil are finished." There were several angry phone calls back and forth between mother and daughter until finally Charlie had enough and unplugged her phone. No one could say exactly where the rumor had started. In the morning, when Charlie reinstated the phone, the first person to call her was a very agitated Neil.

"What the hell is this I hear!" he exclaimed.

"What the hell is what?" said Charlie, knowing perfectly well what he was talking about.

"Your buying a house in Brooklyn. Charlie, what's going on?"

"Who told you?" said Charlie calmly.

"Peter Salzman. He heard it from Belle, who'd been out to dinner with Theo Hammond. Is it true?"

"Yes, it's true."

"Why didn't you tell me first? I can't believe this."

"It was kind of spur of the moment."

"Buying a million-dollar house in Brooklyn Heights is spur of the moment?"

"Not a million dollars. Only seven hundred and twenty-five. Anyway, the papers haven't been signed yet. And it *is* my money," she reminded him.

"But what does this mean about us? What am I supposed to say to the kids?"

Charlie sighed; that was her big worry, the children. She didn't want them to be caught up in a battle between herself and Neil, didn't want them hurt, didn't want them reading anything nasty in the papers. "I thought we could say that we've bought a big beautiful house with a garden so we don't have to stay at my mother's every time we're in the city."

"That doesn't make any sense. And it's not 'we.' It's you. And get this clear: as long as you go on acting like this, you won't have access to Petra or Colin."

"What?"

"You heard me. You'd better do some thinking, Charlie."

"But that's not fair! You have no right—"

"I have every right in the world," broke in Neil. "You deserted us to go on a drunken binge, remember? That won't look too pretty in a court of law. As I said, you'd better do some thinking, Charlie."

"And so had you! There's the whole Gil Hoffeld business. If that got into the papers . . ." She let the sentence hang. Her affair with Gil Hoffeld, which had had a disastrous ending for both of them, was something they never dared talk about.

"Ah, so now it's blackmail, is it?"

"It's not blackmail, Neil. I just want to see my children. And I want to learn about being sober. I have no idea who Charlie Gallagher is without the fumes of alcohol. Once I've done that, we can talk about the direction of our lives. For now, I need this time of peace and quiet."

"What about the press—what do I tell them?"

"I don't know. You're the politician. I'm sure you'll think of something."

That evening he phoned her once again to say he was coming to New York with the children; reporters had gotten hold of the story that Charlie was buying a house in Brooklyn, and he wanted, despite all appearances, to make it seem as if the marriage was still intact. "Charlie's just up in New York exploring different business possibilities," he said in a brief press conference. "I'm a great believer in women going back to the workplace or starting new careers, especially once their children are older."

They slept in separate bedrooms that weekend and the atmosphere was very tense, though the small group of reporters who had been hanging around Rita's building since the story broke got dozens of what looked like happy family pictures. A grinning Neil told one reporter that they had decided to purchase the Brooklyn house for the sake of the children, who needed more exposure to cultural events.

"He's such a goddamn liar," Charlie told Musette over the phone. With reporters dogging her every step, it was hard for her to get to meetings, and she spent a lot of time on the phone with AA friends.

"You don't regret buying the house, do you?"

"Never! It's just that because of the children I have to go along with whatever stupid thing he decides to tell the press. And I hate that. It makes me feel like such a phony."

But she refused to do the thing Neil most wanted, which was to go back with him. On Sunday afternoon, while the children were visiting their grandmother, they had a terrific argument, and he left Rita's in a fury, telling her it would be a long time before she saw the children again.

"Oh yeah?" she shouted after him as he went to the elevator. "What will your precious journalists think of that?"

"Nothing," he yelled back. "Not as long as you keep your big goddamn mouth closed."

They stared white-faced at one another for a moment, both of them thinking of her affair with Gil. Neil pressed the button for the elevator. "I'd better go before we say things we really regret," he said.

"Yes, you'd better," said Charlie, her heart sinking miserably and tears forming in her eyes as she realized that it might be weeks before she saw her beloved children again. But that was the way it would have to be—for the time being, anyway.

That same Sunday, Musette talked Gwen into coming along with her to the Atrium Club for a swim and a sauna. "Have a massage too, treat yourself," said Musette, staring at the writer's husky body in a way that made Gwen shrink with embarrassment. Now, after Musette had done fifty laps, they were stretched out side by side on the wooden sauna steps.

"No, this is fine," said Gwen, mopping at her face with a towel. "Mmmm, I just love this heat. So relaxing." She buried her head in her arms and felt about to go to sleep until she became aware of Musette, who could never sit still for long, regarding her heavy body. In the pool, wearing a purple swimsuit that was far too tight, she had hardly been able to keep up with Musette. After ten laps she had quit, and gone to lie on one of the lounge chairs.

"I hope you don't mind my saying this," Musette said, "but you ought to go on some kind of diet."

Gwen gave a loud groan. "I know."

"And you need to exercise. Get some of that flab off your body. I could help you."

Gwen rolled over. "Help me how?"

"With weights and stuff. It's not that bad once you get started. In fact, it's kind of fun."

Gwen opened one eye and squinted at her. "Could you get me to look as skinny as you?"

"It would take some work, but yeah, probably."

"How much work exactly?"

Musette dangled her long legs over the sauna step. She had allowed her towel to drop to her hips, exposing tight little pink-nippled breasts. "You'd have to come here four or five days a week."

"Is that what you do?"

"Yes. I have to. It's part of my job, like your sitting down to write every day."

Gwen's face clouded. It was her eighty-seventh day sober, and three days from now, when she hit day ninety, she intended to go back to her desk. "I'd have to think about it," she said.

"That's your problem," said Musette. "You think too much. You ought to just do it. A month or two on the machines and your ass'll be as tight as a steel spring."

"All right, all right, I'll do it."

"Good. And here's something else you should do. Something that'll loosen you up, get all your juices flowing again. You ought to let me make that book of yours, *Hey Look at Me Mister,* into a film."

"What?" Gwen struggled to a sitting position, suddenly a little cold in the dry heat.

"It'd make a great movie," said Musette.

"But you've never made a movie before."

"No, but with my knowledge of the industry, and my female point of view, I'd be great at it. I grew up poor, you know. I've lived with that kind of violence and horror."

"Maybe," said Gwen, unconsciously feeling along her wrist for the golden bangles she had left in Musette's locker. "But I've always refused to let my work go to Hollywood. I hate the idea of anybody fiddling with it." She grimaced and pulled her towel unhappily over the thick bulge of her stomach.

"You could write the script yourself," said Musette.

Gwen shook her head. "I've never written a script before. It's not something that happens one-two-three."

"And of course we'd arrange it so you had full control over what was going on."

They fell silent as the door opened and three middle-aged women entered the sauna. Musette stood up. "Think about it, Gwen. Now that you're a friend of Bill's there's a whole new world out there for you."

Despite the ill humor that Musette's suggestion had caused her, Gwen had to laugh. Bill Wilson was the founder of AA, and saying one was a friend of Bill's was a secret way of saying one was in the program. "I'll think about it, girl. But I can tell you right now what the answer's gonna be. It's gonna be no."

"You might think so, but I always get my way," said Musette in a voice so soft that Gwen wasn't sure she had heard right. She stared up at the model, who was now hooking her bikini top into place, a gentle smile on her lips; after a minute, her eyes met Gwen's, eyes that were an innocent, friendly, molten gold. "Here, let me give you a hand," she said, reaching out to help Gwen up from the hot sauna steps.

hree days later Gwen awoke with a feeling of dread. This was her ninetieth day without alcohol, an AA milestone since it took three months for a fairly healthy body to be restored to a fairly healthy predrinking state. After today she would no longer announce her day count in meetings. The applause would stop, which meant the holiday was over, and it was time to get back to work. With a heavy heart, she forced herself out of bed, threw on some clothes, and went to the kitchen to make breakfast for herself and Walter. He came in while she was reading the paper. "What're your plans for today?" he asked, pouring himself a cup of coffee.

"Believe it or not, I'm going to lock myself in my study for a few hours."

"Really?"

"Yes, and I'm terrified."

He brought his coffee to the table and sat down. "Maybe you should wait a little longer."

Gwen glanced at him. Sometimes she had the feeling that he wanted her to stay heavy and unproductive. When she had announced three days ago that she would be spending weekday afternoons at the gym with Musette, he had been very negative.

"What do you want to do that for?" he had said, reaching out and pinching the roll of fat at her waist. "I kind of like having something to hold on to."

She took a sip of her coffee. "No, I can't afford to wait," she said. "I'll go crazy if I wait any longer."

He had a morning class, and as soon as he left, she made a fresh pot of coffee and went to her study. It was nine o'clock. She rattled around for a while, adjusting the window blind to the right level, and rinsing out an ashtray. Then she switched on her computer. Her routine had always been to slip off her bangles, put her feet up on her desk, and smoke a cigarette as she reviewed the previous day's work. Today she decided she would look at the manuscript she had been having such trouble with three months before—no point in starting something new. She lit a cigarette and pressed some buttons on the keyboard. Chapter 1 of her fifth novel appeared on the screen. She took a giant swig of coffee, and began to read.

Within five minutes she knew she hated it. She exited from the file, and brought the second chapter up on the screen. That was no better. God, what had she been thinking when she wrote this crap! She had a look at the two remaining chapters, and decided the only sensible thing was to destroy the whole awful manuscript. That was accomplished in a few seconds—seventy pages of prose she had spent months agonizing over down the tubes. Then she sat with her chin in her hands, staring at the blank screen of her computer. It was ten o'clock.

An hour later she was still sitting there, tears rolling down her face. Her worst fear had come true—she was as dead inside as she had been when she was drinking, no words left in her, no whispered music, only an echoing silence, her muse as remote as an icy northern star. With a vicious jab of her thumb, she switched off the computer. What the hell was she supposed to do now? Live with this emptiness for the rest of her life? Or end it all by jumping off the nearest roof? As she was half-seriously considering the latter possibility, a phrase began to dance in her brain, the only decent one she had gotten all morning: *Don't drink and go to meetings.*

* * *

"Well, you know what they say in the program," said Margot Sibley, Gwen's sponsor. "It takes five years to get your brains back, and another five to learn how to use them."

"Oh, great. That's wonderful news. That really makes me happy," said Gwen. The two women were sitting in a coffee shop on Seventy-fourth Street and Second Avenue. After the morning's dismal failure, Gwen had gone to the noon meeting at Saint Hilda's, where she had run into Margot.

"Anyway, you did the right thing showing up at the meeting."

"Uh-hunh."

"Gwen, you're only three months sober. Give yourself a chance."

Gwen stared at her sponsor, who was sixty years old and had thin platinum blond hair, which she wore tied back in a ponytail with a velvet bow. She also wore designer clothes and always made a habit of bringing a big bag of knitting to meetings. Gwen had chosen her out of the crowd her first week sober for the simple reason that Margot, with her black-framed glasses and imperious, tight-skinned face, reminded Gwen of her ninth-grade English teacher at Calhoun. Luckily it had been a good choice. Margot, who came from the same sort of society background as Charlie Gallagher, and had never had to work for a living, was extremely kind and loving. Right now, however, Gwen felt like killing her. "I thought that once you had ninety days, you were ready to go back to real life," she complained.

"Whoever told you that? Most people are just a little less foggy, that's all."

"Well, what am I supposed to do? I can't not work. I'd only get crazy and suicidal all over again."

"I think," said Margot, removing her glasses and staring into Gwen's face with kindly blue eyes, "you should tell your story at a meeting. Now that you've got ninety days, you're eligible to do that."

"No way!" exclaimed Gwen.

"Why not? It would help you."

"I just couldn't, that's all."

"But Gwen, you've been on TV, and you've lectured all over the country. How could you be nervous about speaking at an AA meeting?"

Gwen gave her sponsor an exasperated look. "It's one thing to talk about work. That's easy. You just kind of push a button in your brain and out comes a lot of blah blah blah. But talking about life, real life, is something else. I refuse to do it."

Gwen had very concrete reasons for not wanting to talk about her life. As a girl growing up in Harlem, she had had to make choices, and to this day they were choices that caused her pain. Her parents had slaved to get her out of the neighborhood, away from the tough kids on the street. She was their only child, their miracle baby, and they wanted the best for her. She was sent to a predominantly white school on the Upper West Side, and there she began to dream that her mother, who cleaned houses, was a rich white lady whose skin didn't smell of Ajax, and that her father, a transit worker, was a smart white man in a three-piece suit instead of a subway car driver in a blue uniform that was shiny at the seat of the pants. Slowly she began to pretend she was white.

The local kids hated her. "Hey bitch, where you goin' with that stuck-up look on yo' ugly black face!" they would yell as she walked up the block in her knee-highs and loafers. She didn't care. She had her downtown friends, her white friends, and they were the only people, besides her parents, who counted. She hung out with them after school, slept at their houses, attended all of their parties and celebrations, had crushes on the same boys; and eventually, when she was eighteen, went off to one of their small, safe, expensive New England colleges.

By the end of her sophomore year she knew she was going to become an academic. Her chosen field was sociology, but as the years passed, she found herself growing more and more interested in black feminist studies. The Negro female in literature...this fascinated her. It was a way of studying herself, Gwendolyn Thomas, one step removed, so that any pain or anger she might feel on her own account appeared really to be someone else's flowing slowly into her from the pages of a book.

Once she had her Ph.D. she decided to try something new, accepting a teaching position at an all-black college in Mississippi. Almost immediately she knew it was a mistake. In a town where racial lines were strictly drawn, she felt like a stranger, an alien. She hated the heat, hated the white southerners, hated being confined on campus in what felt to her like a ghetto. It had been years since she had lived among her own people, and she was miserably unhappy. As a child she had suffered from asthma, and now the condition returned, and she went around in the humidity wheezing and coughing and feeling as if she would die.

Her contract at Tulsa College was for two years. She had a heavy teaching load, and she didn't know how she was going to make it. As early as November she wished she could quit. And then one day in the middle of the term, she was assigned a remedial student, a girl named Glady Johnson who worked as an aide at a nursing home outside the town. Glady could neither read nor write. Her English was terrible, and after a single session with her, Gwen was more depressed than ever.

In their second session, two days later, the girl said something that made Gwen want to cry. "You ain't happy, is you?"

They were in Gwen's office, a tiny room furnished with a battered old desk and two chairs. On the wall above the desk was a map of the United States, with a red thumbtack stuck in the state of Mississippi. Though it was November, it was warm and sticky outside, and a fan was blowing. "What makes you say that?" asked Gwen.

"'Cause I bin there."

"I'm homesick," said Gwen simply.

"Oh," said the girl. "Fo' New Yawk?"

"For New York."

"New Yawk's where all we down-South niggers fixin' to go. New Yawk, Chicago, Washington, D.C."

"Is that where you're fixing to go—one of those places?"

Glady shrugged. "I'm fixin' to learn to read. Won't know nothin' till then."

She was thin, bony, homely. Her skin was the color of an eggplant and had no sheen to it, but her eyes, Gwen thought, had a patience and intelligence that meant she was teachable. She was twenty years old. Her hands were calloused from hard work, and she kept her bushy hair short, clipped like a privet. Twice a week, late on Wednesday and Friday afternoons, she came to see Gwen in her office—sessions that were supposed to last only an hour, but that grew longer and longer as she told Gwen the story of her life.

She was born in Owen, Georgia, to a stern, tall, ugly woman named Leatrice Johnson who was a cook in the house of a wealthy white family. Glady had been unexpected, and from the first she was harshly treated by her mother. Since she was slow in talking, Leatrice assumed she was mildly retarded, and no one ever bothered to educate her. Instead she stayed with Leatrice in the kitchen of the big house, where she learned to kill and pluck chickens, plant herbs, make a fine pie crust, polish silver, and understand the moods of white folk. That last was very confusing to her as she was allowed to play with the son of the family, a boy named Teddy Caldwell who was a few months older than she was. For the first seven years of their lives, she and Teddy were best friends. Together they climbed trees, and swam in the creek, played dare, wrestled, and hid in the bushes, listening to his parents' idle chitchat from the veranda above. When they turned seven, the adults restricted their hours of playing together; slowly they grew apart until the time came when they hardly saw one another at all. Glady continued to help her mother in the kitchen, and Teddy was sent away to school. When he came home on vacations, an important young man now, he ignored her, and she grew accustomed to that.

The year they turned fourteen, Teddy began to shave. His voice had deepened, and in a coat and tie he looked several years older than he actually was. Glady had matured too, though she was not yet menstruating. One day, when she was on her hands and knees in the kitchen garden, he came by and said, "Glady, you're looking pretty."

No one had ever told her that before, and she beamed.

"I got an idea," he said. "Want to earn some money?"

She stood up, wiping her palms on her ragged skirt, and said, "Sure, how?"

"I'll show you," said Teddy, leading her across the lawn into the nearby woods to a grassy spot where he told her he'd give her a dollar if she let him touch her breasts.

Without a moment's hesitation, she agreed. Teddy had seen her naked dozens of times when they were children, and besides, her breasts hardly amounted to anything yet. So she pulled up her shirt and watched his mouth go loose and hungry as he plucked at one side and then the other. "Pay you another dollar if you let me kiss 'em," he said, breathing fast, and she agreed to this too, and it was the first of many such transactions. From then on, during his vacations, he'd take her to the grassy spot in the woods. Sometimes he'd bring along two or three friends, and they'd circle her, staring as she removed her shirt and bared her skinny chest, and even though her breasts were a disappointment—flat, with swollen blackberry-shaped nipples—each of the boys would grow excited and breathless and want to touch her.

By now she couldn't get out of the encounters. Teddy would say, "You don't come, I'll tell your mama what you've been up to . . ." So she would meet the boys in the woods, and it wasn't long before they began to push her down on the grass, making her lie there while they examined between her legs, squeezing and pinching and prodding until her flesh was raw. They didn't pay her anymore. One would hold her wrists, the other would spread her legs apart, and the third would mount her, and in this way she lost her virginity.

One day Leatrice followed her into the woods, and when she saw what was happening, she gave Glady a good beating. It was the girl's fault, she said, being provocative and full of devilment. Why else would boys like those surround her like bees to honey? Glady was bad, evil, and as punishment she would be sent to her uncle T. J. Walker who lived down in Louisiana.

Although Glady had heard a good deal about T. J. Walker, she had never met him before. The husband of Leatrice's late sister, Rose, he was a self-styled preacher whose congregation consisted of the poorest of the poor: a scraggly band of migrant workers who traveled from field to field all across the rural South. Reverend T. J. was their minister, the succorer of their souls, the wise, fierce, Bible-spouting man of God who took from them a small but precious percentage of their wages in return for noisily and rapturously connecting them up with Jesus and the world everlasting. Glady hated him on sight. He was small and rodentlike, with sharp black eyes, a wizened little face, and a smell of something old and musty. As soon as she stepped off the bus, he told her that her duties would include cooking, cleaning, marketing, doing laundry; and that if she didn't behave herself and perform her chores satisfactorily, he would take his belt—he pointed to a silver-buckled, snakelike strip of leather at his waist—and whip her black bottom till she saw stars.

What choice had she? She was fifteen, and she had no home, nowhere to go. She had never been out of Georgia, and the world was a scary place. Her mama didn't want her. At night she would lie on her thin little mattress on the floor and fight back tears. But she didn't have much time for crying...T. J. had meant what he said, and if he didn't like the way she pressed his shirt, or cooked his supper, or polished up his shoes, he would drag his belt from his waist and make her bend over so he could give her three or four good strokes. In front of the members of his church he would say what a good girl she was, but at home he was mean-mouthed and nasty, always cussing her out, threatening to beat her. They lived so for about a year and a half, and in that time, traveling in his Volkswagen bus, she saw six southern states, but to her each of them had the same gritty shiftless feeling—what was the difference between one shanty town and another? The same red dust. The same chickens pecking at the earth. The same barefoot children playing in the road. If she herself could have connected up with Jesus, she might have felt a little happier, but Jesus, both as word and symbol, made no sense to her. Why would a white man go let himself hang from a cross?

Toward the end of Glady's sixteenth year, T. J. decided there should be a change in their relationship. She was about as tall and as womanly as she was ever going to be, and people were talking; it didn't seem right that she and T. J. should live under the same roof without God's blessing...especially as they weren't blood related. T. J. had enjoyed the sight of Glady's tight black buttocks each time he whipped her, and now he told her that it was God's will that they marry. As if to prove his point, he began bothering her in the evenings, creeping into her bed, fondling her, pinching her skinny breasts, making her play with his penis. Put her mouth on it. That was horrible, but for a little man he was strong, and she couldn't fight him off. She tried hiding a meat cleaver under the pillow, but the idea of actually wounding his flesh sickened her almost as much as having to put her mouth on his penis, so she decided to do what he said until she had gathered together enough money to run away.

She did this as quickly as she could. Ten dollars from household money, twenty from the back of a radio where he hid church funds, another ten from out of his pants pocket, and another twenty that he gave her, as he did every Monday, to buy a week's worth of groceries. That was the Monday she left. She took with her the dress she was wearing, and a small cotton satchel containing a change of underwear, a hair brush and ribbon, a frayed picture of her mama, a sandwich, and a pair of tennis shoes. She accepted a lift into town from one of T. J.'s followers, and from there boarded a bus for Jackson, Mississippi, which happened to be the first bus out.

And so commenced a journey that took all of that day, and part of that night, and all that she would ever remember of it was the fear she felt as she stared out the window at the passing Texas landscape, convinced that T. J. was just behind them in his VW minibus. By the time they reached Jackson, her body was so bone-tired and hot and stiff that she could barely get her legs moving. She spent the rest of the night in the ladies' washroom, sharing a pack of Lifesavers with the attendant, who told her about an employment agency that might help her out.

Glady had never been bothered by the fact that she couldn't read. She could wash floors, make beds, and cook just fine, so when the lady at the employment agency asked if she could read, she shook her head and said she didn't see how it made any difference. "Well," said the lady, "the only job I got's one that requires reading."

"Oh," said Glady, thinking quick. Then she said, "Sure I can read. Been readin' all my life."

"All right," said the lady. "You look strong and sensible enough, so I'll take a chance on you." And she gave her directions to the house of a Mrs. Lydia Phelpps, who lived on the outskirts of the city.

Mrs. Phelpps was old—certainly over eighty, though it was hard to judge with white people. She lived in the same sort of house the Caldwells had lived in, large and white, with columns in the front, and a veranda all around it. Her only company was a cook and a manservant and a big, silky, gold-colored dog named Idaho. "Why Idaho?" asked Glady after she had gotten over being shy. "Ain't that the name of a state?"

"*Isn't,* not ain't," said Mrs. Phelpps. "And yes, it's the name of a state. He was born there."

The job with Mrs. Phelpps was easy, except for one thing: each night before dinner, while Mrs. Phelpps sipped a cocktail, Glady was expected to read to her. This was terrifying. The first book was *Great Expectations* by Charles Dickens, and Glady's hands were so sweaty that dark damp palm prints were left on the leather cover. Glady, of course, had no idea who Dickens was, but it reassured her to see that Mrs. Phelpps took one large swallow of her drink and then closed her eyes behind her glasses. "Let's see here," said Glady, opening to the first page. The lines of print seemed to move in a serious purposeful way, like dozens of columns of ants around three or four cracker crumbs. Her voice grew small. "Wonst upon a time," she said.

"Speak up!" said Mrs. Phelpps.

"Wonst upon a time, there was this...unh...boy named ...unh...Dick...who...unh...got himself in a mess of trouble..."

"Go on," said Mrs. Phelpps.

Glady did go on. Holding the book in her sweaty palms and occasionally turning the pages, she made up what turned out to be a lengthy saga about the adventures of one Dick Caldwell, his various friends and servants and relatives, and a bus trip he took through the South. During the trip Dick's money was stolen and he learned what it was like to be poor, taking up with a group of migrant workers. The story continued from night to night, and when, after several weeks, she had finished it, Mrs. Phelpps gave her another book, this one by a man named Lawrence. And so began a ritual that lasted for the next year: Glady would pretend to read, and Mrs. Phelpps, snoozing over her cocktail, would pretend to listen, and for some reason this nightly ritual drew the two of them together, each secretly enchanted by the wildness and foolishness of Glady's tales.

At the end of the year, Mrs. Phelpps had a little talk with Glady. She told her that she was seriously ill with heart trouble, and that she had arranged to have Glady provided for after her death.

"What you mean exackly?" said Glady.

Mrs. Phelpps smiled. "I'm going to die, Glady. I'm eighty-eight years old and I've been here long enough. I'm leaving you some money, which, it states in my will, is to be used specifically for your education."

"Ejication?"

"Yes—so that you can learn to read and write. God knows you've got enough imagination. I'd like to die knowing you can write some of those stories of yours down."

And that was what brought Glady to Tulsa College and to Gwen. Mrs. Phelpps died a few weeks after their conversation, leaving, as she had promised, a bequest for Glady's education. It wasn't a large bequest. Glady needed the job at the nursing home to support herself, and it took her a full year to work up the courage to inquire about courses at Tulsa. But she felt good knowing that someone had believed in her, and she was determined to honor the old lady's dying wish.

At least that's what she told Gwen, who would lean back in her leather swivel chair, put her feet up on a crate of books, and listen, enjoying the semidark, and her own fatigue, and the husky pitch of Glady's voice as she talked on and on about her childhood, and the meanness of T. J. Walker, and the wry humor of old Mrs. Phelpps, listen with her eyes closed, and her heart slowly beating, until the stories seemed to knit themselves right into the fabric of her soul. In their sessions together, Glady learned to read simply, and Gwen was given a strong taste of the backward South. It seemed like a fair exchange.

At Christmas Gwen flew to New York, and as soon as she got off the plane, she knew she'd never return to Tulsa. Angry letters were sent back and forth. Gwen got a doctor friend to vouch for her, saying she couldn't work because of her asthma, and after a few months the legal suit brought against her was dropped. If she felt guilty, she didn't show it. She spent the rest of that winter locked up in a library carrel at Columbia University, where she worked like a fiend, writing down everything she remembered of Glady's story. Every shift, every nuance, every detail, every turn of phrase—all that she had heard, adding and embroidering, using her own imagination, until out of these notes a new story emerged, and this story formed the basis of Gwen's first novel, *Homegirl*.

Once she had everything on paper, it took her only nine months to write the novel, and with it she won instant fame.

Overnight Gwendolyn Thomas, who had never had a black friend in her life (and who had just married the white poet, Walter Rudin), became *the* authority on what it meant to grow up poor and degraded in the rural South. She was invited to speak on TV talk shows, was interviewed by the press, was asked to dinners, benefits, functions. All of this would have been fine if she hadn't, with her privileged upbringing, felt like the biggest fraud there ever was. To protect herself, she adopted a blacker, more street-smart style, but she made it a rule never to talk about her personal life, and she granted as few interviews as possible. The name Glady Johnson was one that never crossed her lips. As time passed, she developed a whole new persona for herself, and she tried to forget that poor, loquacious Glady had ever existed anywhere outside of her brain.

But she never quite shook the feeling that she was a thief.

One morning in the middle of April, Musette opened the *New York Times* to the Sunday society pages and saw a photo of herself and Charlie Gallagher standing together at a big party at the Guggenheim Museum. Both of them wore evening dresses that showed their beautiful shoulders and long necks. "Actress and model Musette, recently moved to New York from the West Coast, deep in conversation with Charlie Gallagher, also recently moved to New York. What can these two be talking about?"

Musette studied the photo for a moment, and then put the paper down, smiling thoughtfully. She was still in bed, a breakfast tray beside her, and she lay back against a mountain of pillows and sipped her coffee. For the past few weeks she had been running all over the city looking at paintings and furniture with Charlie, but this was the first time their names had been linked in the press. She glanced at the photo again, remembering the long-ago Sunday when she had come across Charlie's nuptial announcement in the *Times,* the picture of that dark-haired radiant girl whom she had felt, with such bitterness, ought to have been she. She still felt bitterness, but now she was older and wiser and knew what to do with those kinds of feelings.

Pushing the tray aside, she climbed out of bed and went to her desk, taking a sheet of heavy cream stationery from the top drawer. Uncapping a gold Cartier pen, she wrote, in a small, girlish hand,

Dear Neil:

Thought you might be interested in the enclosed, if you haven't seen it already. Perhaps you aren't aware that Charlie and I have become good friends in the past few weeks. Of course I haven't said anything to her about our relationship, and it's clear you haven't either. I don't know whether or not you want to keep it that way. How about lunch sometime soon? It would be good to talk about old times.

She deliberated over whether she should sign it Maggie or Musette, and decided on the latter—that was who she was now. Half an hour later, wearing gym clothes beneath a camel hair coat, she slid the letter into a mailbox on Lexington Avenue. Ball in your court, mister, she thought, wondering how long it would take him to answer.

"You know you're doing too much, Charlie. You're going to wear yourself out if you're not careful."

Charlie looked up from her packing. Felicity, seated at the vanity table in Rita's bedroom, was watching her with concern in her eyes. She had her back to the mirror, and was wearing her usual tight little dress, with her shoes kicked off and her stockinged toes digging into the carpet. "But I'm always like this," said Charlie. "I like to keep busy."

"I'm worried, that's all. I mean, look at you: you're two months sober, and you've bought a house, and you seem to have left your husband—"

"Temporarily," interjected Charlie.

"—okay, temporarily, whatever. But having those journalists on your tail like a pack of hounds must make you nervous as hell."

Charlie laughed. "I can't say that I like it."

"And then running around the way you've been doing the past few weeks, going to all the auction houses and galleries."

"I need to do that," said Charlie. "It's good for me."

"And worrying about when you're going to see your children."

Charlie's face clouded. She didn't say anything, although it was agonizing to her that Neil had control over her visits with the children. He still wouldn't allow her to be alone with them, and so she had to make do with seeing them at her mother's Fifth Avenue apartment, which was always difficult, or driving down to Helene's Pennsylvania farm and meeting them there. It was still too early in her sobriety for her to dream of going to Washington and being together as a family. The weekend they had spent in New York, posing for the press, had shown her that.

"And now packing and leaving Rita's," continued Felicity. "I'm just afraid for you, that's all."

"But I get to a meeting every day," said Charlie. She began, carefully, to fold a silk blouse. "Sometimes two. And I have to leave Rita's. She's coming back this week, so I can't stay here."

"I know that," said Felicity. Charlie was moving into the Carlyle, where she would stay until she had closed on the Brooklyn house in the beginning of June. "I just wish you'd relax a little."

"Relaxing is the one thing that could lead me back to a drink," said Charlie with a grin. "Which reminds me—are you free Thursday night? There's an opening down in Soho I'd like to go to. South American painters."

Felicity shook her head. "You know what, Charlie? You're on the proverbial AA pink cloud."

"I am? What's that?"

"Being newly sober and in love with your sobriety. You're lucky. Not everyone experiences it."

"Oh. Well, that's good then." She dropped the folded blouse into her suitcase, looking pleased with herself. "So do you want to come with me to the opening or not?"

"I can't. That's my night to be with Bessie."

"All right. Then I'll ask Musette."

On Thursday morning Musette received a note in the mail from Neil Gallagher. *Dear Maggie*, it read. *Lunch would be fine. So would talking about old times. I'll be in New York the week*

after next, and will call to make arrangements. Until then ...
Neil.

Well, that's a start, thought Musette, noting with amusement that he had used her old familiar name. She wondered where he would take her for lunch. Probably somewhere hidden and out-of-the-way because of the press. All he needed was to be seen with a gorgeous blond actress while his marriage was rumored to be on the rocks.

She had agreed to go to the art opening with Charlie and now she could secretly revel in her contact with Neil. What a delicious high it was to know that she would soon see him. On Thursday night she wore a diamond choker and a clingy hot-pink dress that reached the middle of her slim thighs. Charlie, in pearls and a straight black sheath, looked much more sedate, and for a long moment Musette felt awash in envy of Charlie's easy elegance. Her hair was in a neat chignon while Musette's hung loose and wild around her shoulders. On the afternoon she met Neil perhaps she would go for that dressed-down look, tying her hair back and wearing only one piece of jewelry so that he would immediately see how classy she had become.

The gallery, a huge, echoing space that had once been a warehouse, was extremely noisy and crowded, and Musette felt it was the quintessential New York social arena, more fantastical to her right now than any Hollywood movie could be. Every other woman seemed to have on a ballgown and weird face paint, and the men wore florid, gangster-style shirts, dark suits, slicked-back hair, and earrings. For a while Charlie and Musette stayed together. Neither of them knew anyone, but it wasn't long before an admiring circle of men had gathered around Musette, who was—to her delight—recognized by a great many of the people there. Charlie, with a glass of ginger ale in her hand, wandered off by herself to look at the paintings. Even though there were none that sparked her interest, she was amazed at how inexpensive they were. When she was growing up, her parents had thought nothing of spending hundreds of thousands of dollars on a Constable or Turner, so for her a canvas priced at two or three thousand was a steal.

And then, in the back room of the gallery, she saw a row of portraits that made her heart beat quickly with excitement. There were eight of them, four men and four women, each bright-colored, large, and energetically painted. She examined each closely, peering at the artist's brushstrokes and then backing away, so she could study them from a distance. She did this several times. There was something about the portraits that made her feel as if she were walking through the streets of an exotic city at carnival time. As she was checking the price list, a man came and stood beside her.

"Like those, hunh?" he said.

She glanced at him, wondering if he was the artist. He was about forty, had gray spiked hair, and wore a black shirt and dark suit, no tie. His face was craggy, slightly rough-looking, and there were faint paint stains on his big hands. "I think they're very good," she said.

He smiled at her. "If you like Gauguin derivatives."

"Oh, I don't think these are like Gauguin at all. There's something very raw and angry about them."

The man laughed. "Yeah, they're raw, okay. That's because Rolando Cruz, the artist, doesn't know how to paint."

"Well, I don't agree," said Charlie, annoyed. Who was this guy to come up and give her a lesson in art appreciation? "He's got good technique, and some of the faces are marvelous. Look at that one there, the man smoking the cigar. So expressive."

The man gave another laugh. "If you call that expressive, you ain't seen nothin'. Anyway, the paintings only work as a group."

"That's right," said Charlie. "I agree with you there. And that's why I intend to buy them as a group. It would be unthinkable to do anything else."

She turned on her heel. Until that moment she had not known she would buy the portraits, and it gave her great pleasure to know the man was staring after her, mouth agape, as she pushed her way through a forest of people and walked across the gallery toward the front desk. How she hated know-it-all types like that. She saw Musette standing near the bar, talking to a man in a white suit, and rushed up to her. "Hey, guess what? I've just made up my mind to buy some paintings."

"Really?" said Musette, speaking loudly because of the noise in the room. "Which ones?"

"They're in the back. Come on, I'll show you. I want to know what you think."

Musette glanced apologetically at the man she had been

speaking to, and followed Charlie, who dragged her first to the front desk. "I want to buy the Cruz portraits," she said, taking her card from her bag. "Give this to your director, and tell him I'll be back in a few minutes." Without waiting for a reply, she took Musette's arm and guided her to the rear of the gallery. "Well, what do you think?" she said as they arrived at the portraits. She was glad to see that the gray-haired man had disappeared.

"They're good, I guess. You're really going to buy all of them?"

"Of course. They only work as a group."

"How much are they?"

"About sixteen thousand." She giggled. "That's not bad, considering what my parents used to spend on a single painting."

"Yeah, but your parents probably bought Cézannes and Picassos. Whoever heard of this guy Cruz?"

"No one," said Charlie. "Which is just the way I like it."

Musette was interested to see how elated Charlie became after writing out a check for the paintings. The two women stood together in the very center of the main room of the gallery, and Charlie, her face flushed, her eyes sparkling, couldn't stop babbling. At one point she nearly picked up a glass of white wine, mistaking it, in her excitement, for ginger ale. Musette watched her fingers flutter over the rim of the glass, and then quickly put a restraining hand on her wrist and stopped her. "Oh thanks," Charlie said giddily. "You know, I haven't been around this much alcohol since getting sober."

"Maybe we should leave," said Musette. They had been at the gallery for nearly two hours, and she had just about had enough of it.

"Why?" said Charlie. "This is terrific fun." She stared around her. "Lots of good-looking men here, don't you think?"

"If you like the mafioso look."

"Oh, come on. They aren't all like that." She craned her neck to see if she could spot the gray-haired man. "Anyway, most of them are gay."

"Oh, no they're not, honey," said Musette, who had spent a good part of the evening refusing to give out her phone number. In her clingy pink dress she was easily one of the sexiest women there. She considered Charlie, who looked a little reckless with her shining eyes and a lock of dark hair escaped from her chignon. She decided now was the time to ask the question she had been burning to ask for weeks. "Charlie," she said, "have you ever had a love affair?"

"What?" said Charlie, startled.

"I mean as a married woman. Have you ever been unfaithful to Neil?"

Charlie's face, glowing with excitement a moment ago, slowly turned a chalky white. Her voice became shrill. "Of course not. How could you ask such a thing?" She pursed her lips and gave Musette a hard look. "Don't ever ask me that again, understand? I won't accept it."

"All right, all right," said Musette. "I didn't know it was such a big deal." But instinctively she knew that Charlie, with her scared white face, was lying. Her eyes had grown veiled and distant. And look at the sudden droop to her shoulders, she thought. Musette was convinced that Charlie had not only had a hushed-up love affair, but that the man, whoever he was, was behind Charlie's precipitous move to New York.

When they left the gallery, Charlie refused dinner and went straight home to the Carlyle where she ordered a light meal from room service. But when she tried to eat her throat closed up, and she had to push the omelette away, practically untouched. Musette's casual question had opened the door to one of the darkest areas of her life—her love affair with Gil Hoffeld—and she knew she would spend the rest of the evening going over and over, in obsessive detail, the terrible thing that had happened at the end of the affair. Pouring herself a cup of coffee, and wishing desperately that it were scotch, she went and stood at the window. Instead of a deserted Madison Avenue, she saw Gil's face in the dark glass.

She had come back from her trip to Barbados a little over a year ago looking exhausted. At least that's what Neil had claimed, insisting that beneath her dark tan, her face was haggard. "What happened, darling?" he kept asking. "You're not yourself." As she couldn't very well tell him she'd had a wild love affair, she pretended, her first week home, that she'd eaten something that hadn't agreed with her, that she'd been ill during the sail around the islands. But he was too clever to fall for that. "If you were so goddamn sick, why didn't you tell me when we talked on the phone? Come on, Charlie. I want the truth."

Eventually he wore her down. She missed the sun on her shoulders. She missed Gil and the lines of coke he had laid out for her every few hours. She missed the movement of the boat, and the movement of his body thrusting itself into hers. In a flat voice she told Neil the whole story. "It was something I couldn't stop myself from doing," she concluded lamely.

For a few minutes he was very quiet. Then he said, "You're not going to see this guy again, are you, Charlie?"

She twirled a strand of chestnut hair around her finger. "I don't know. I might."

"I won't permit it, Charlie."

She looked at him. "How the hell are you going to stop me?"

He didn't answer. "If you do this, you're likely to destroy everything," he said finally.

She felt a perverse surge of excitement. "It's a chance I'll have to take," she said, knowing that as soon as the conversation was over, she would go upstairs and call Gil in Boston.

And so began the next phase of her love affair. Neil looked the other way. He moved out of their bedroom—she was grateful for that—but otherwise their life continued with the normal round of parties and social events. Once or twice a month she flew up to Boston to see Gil, but she never stayed overnight, and their times together were very discreet...a few hours of sex in his apartment in Beacon Hill. He was divorced, without children, so on his side, at least, the affair involved nothing more than telling his secretary he would be out for the afternoon.

In the summer the affair became more complicated. She spent two weeks with the children on her mother's farm in Pennsylvania, so she couldn't see him then. In August she and Neil had to make a trip together to the Soviet Union. And in the intervening weeks she was too busy visiting relatives to think of Gil. Though she didn't like to admit it, the excitement had begun to wear off. Gil had told her that he had some business worries, and she was leery of becoming involved in that part of his life. Sex was all she wanted from him, and the tense, chain-smoking man who insisted on talking about his money problems was frankly a turnoff.

Still, she had a crude kind of feeling for him. When he asked her to spend a weekend with him at his house on Cape Cod, she agreed. She had just returned from her trip to the Soviet Union, and needed badly to get away from Neil, who at that point was trying to control her drinking. As it was after Labor Day, there was very little chance of her running into anyone she knew.

She flew up to Boston on a Friday, and that same night they drove to Barnstable in the dark, where they had a lovely, relaxing time. His house was small, a tiny white cottage with roses growing up the front. Behind it, at the end of a green clipped lawn, was a dock where a boat was moored, and they spent most of Saturday sailing up and down the bay, remembering old times. Although Gil still had business worries, he seemed in much better spirits, and they agreed to come back one more time before the winter set in.

They chose the first weekend in October. Once again Charlie flew up to Boston, but unfortunately it was raining, and the drive to the cape was long and unpleasant. Gil, brooding over problems with the SEC, was in a difficult, sullen mood, and he kept his eyes fixed on the road and barely spoke to her. That night, climbing into his soft bed, she expected kisses and caresses, but for the first time since she had known him he was unable to make love. "Sorry, I just can't," he said, and she turned her head to the side so he wouldn't see her angry disappointment. With Gil there was sex, just sex, and without it, without the architecture of touches, it was as if they were strangers. She lay on her stomach and heard the wind in the trees outside, and wished she had stayed in Georgetown.

The next morning was gray and cold. Gil had not stayed in bed the night before (she found him asleep on the living room couch), and she decided there was no point in waking him. She had some coffee and went out for a walk. On the narrow strip of beach she kicked stones around for a while. Then she found a rock to sit on and stared out over the misty water and watched the gulls. When she had enough of that she went back to the house, feeling more and more depressed. The house felt damp and chilly, and Gil was still asleep. And so the morning went. She had a bath, and tried to read a mystery, and at about noon Gil woke up. "Jesus, do I feel shitty," he said.

"Oh?"

"Yeah, I must have really tied one on."

"You want some coffee?"

"Coffee would be good. Also a beer. No, not a beer—a slug of brandy. Would you mind, honey? Bottle's over there somewhere on the sideboard."

His speech was thick and vague. Charlie brought him a glass of brandy and had one herself, and then, while he was in the shower, made some sandwiches and coffee. The sun came out, and that was a good sign; and when Gil emerged from the bath, she saw that he had shaved, and that his eyes looked brighter. He was wearing jeans and a thick white fisherman's sweater. "I'm not sure how hungry I am," he said.

But he ate quite a bit, and between them—as he talked dejectedly about his failing business—they consumed nearly a gallon of wine, and by the time Charlie rose from the table, she saw to her amazement that it was three o'clock. Gil wanted to go sailing.

"Do you really think we should?" said Charlie. "Isn't it pretty late for that?"

"It's only the middle of the afternoon," said Gil. "Come on. I've got to get outside."

Charlie didn't particularly want to go outside. She had that sensation she always had when she was a little drunk: her tongue felt thick and fuzzy, and her brain had tunneled down to a point where it could only focus on one thing at a time. She was unsure of her body. Somehow she pulled on a jacket, and then she clung to Gil as they left the house and walked across the lawn to the dock. It had grown quite windy. Loose strands of hair kept flying into her face, and she saw that there were whitecaps on the water. Surely this wasn't a good idea. She tried to say as much to Gil, but already he was busy with the boat, and he shouted at her to help him with the sheets. She did that, and once she was in motion, with the heaving boat beneath her feet, and the flap of the sails, the ringing of metal on wood in her ears, she decided that this would be fine, this would be an adventure. The sun threw wide swaths of gold over the choppy water, the thousands of waves, and behind it the sky was a tough blue, and she had to squint to see anything. Hunkered down in the cockpit, Gil was trying to light a cigarette, and she noted that his hair was the same gold as the water. She clambered over to him. "Here honey, have some of this, it'll do you good," he said, and she realized that what he held in his hand wasn't a regular cigarette, but a thickly rolled joint. She had only a little, not liking its effect on her, and he took four or five deep pulls on it, and then stubbed it out, wrapped it in cellophane, and stuck it in his shirt pocket.

Later she would say she remembered almost nothing of that journey: she had had too much to drink and the little bit of marijuana had paralyzed her brain so totally that the world—that crazy wild sea, the golden sunshine, the small scampering boat—was, for a period of time, lost to her. They crisscrossed the bay, she knew that; they got drenched with water, and Gil kept yelling "Coming about! Coming about!" and laughing wildly as the boat tilted nearly onto its side. She must have lowered her head to avoid the boom like someone in a dream, doing it over and over again automatically, and like someone in a dream she must have watched Gil's large hands on the rudder, and felt quite safe. But all this was speculation. All she really knew was that at some point in time Gil made an error of judgment, stood up when he shouldn't have, and got knocked in the head by the boom. She didn't see it, but she heard it: a *thwack* as definite and horrible as gunfire, and when she looked up he was already falling. The boat veered so that it seemed to be hanging perpendicular to the water, the sail bedding itself down flat over the racing waves, and she reached for him, trying desperately to grab whatever part of his body she could get, but in that moment he was gone.

He went in headfirst, and when he did not come up gasping for air she knew that he was unconscious; but already she was moving, acting, racing to pull down the sails, start the engine. Her brain was very clear now. She began to look for him, shading her eyes against the sun, steering the boat this way and that, zigzagging across the water, calling his name, calling, calling, but she knew that it was hopeless. She remembered how his hair matched the golden water—any sunlit wave could be he, his head—and she knew that she should give up, go for help, but she kept on looking anyway. She was wet, she was frozen, the wind was an enemy punching her face, hurling itself at her, but none of this mattered; nothing mattered except finding him.

How often she sent the boat back and forth across that same rough patch of water she did not know. In the end her hands were simply too numb to work the rudder, and she had to go in.

The first person she called was Neil. She used a pencil to dial because her fingers were useless, and when she heard his voice she started crying.

"Honey! Honey what is it?"

Brokenly she told him.

"Okay," he said. "Okay, I don't know if I've got this right, but I want you to stay where you are. Do you hear me? I want you to stay exactly where you are, and not do anything, *any-thing*, until you hear from me. Understand? Now give me the number there."

She gave him the number, and a few minutes later he called her back. "Now listen," he said. "We're in luck. The Salzmans are there this weekend, and they're on their way over to get you. Charlie? Do you understand? The Salzmans are coming over right now."

"But what about the police?" she stammered. "Shouldn't we—"

"No, no, Peter will take care of all that. Just stay where you are, and if the phone rings again, don't pick it up!"

She did as she was told. Shaking in her wet clothes, she sat and waited for the Salzmans, not daring to turn around, look out the window, catch sight of the rough, empty, incriminating sea. When the phone rang at one point, she jumped and reached out her hand and then quickly stopped herself, her heart pounding so loudly in her chest that it seemed like an actual sound in the room. Hours seemed to pass, and then she heard tires on the gravel driveway, and the slamming of a door. Peter Salzman came in. He was an old friend of Neil's from boarding school, and she thought she had never been so glad to see anybody. "Okay, okay, tell me what happened," he said, and as she told him they went outside to the dock, and Peter stared anxiously over the water.

"Did anybody see you?" he asked. "Were there any other boats?"

"I don't know. I don't think so." Her body was shaking so hard it was difficult for her to get the words out.

"We've got to call the Coast Guard," said Peter. "Oh thank God, here's Belle." His wife must have come in a different car. She raced across the lawn, a large harried-looking woman in a bulky pink sweater, and Peter gave her quick instructions. "Take Charlie inside," he said, "and get a blanket on her. Then I want you to comb that house and get her stuff—*all* her stuff!—and put it in her suitcase, and get the hell out of here. Did anyone know you were here?" he demanded of Charlie. "Did you go anywhere in public?"

She shook her head.

"No? Okay. Well then, Belle's going to take you home to our place, and when you've had a bath and feel a little better, she's going to drive you down to New York, and you'll fly back to Washington from there. All right?" He put his arm around Charlie, and led her quickly up the lawn. When they were inside the house, he said, "What I'm going to tell the police is this: that I had lunch with Gil today, and then we went for a sail, and then, because of all the booze in him, he somehow lost control of the boat for a minute and had an accident. Could have happened to anyone, really, but the point is, the important thing is, that *you* weren't there with him. You were—"

"Doesn't matter where she was, darling!" said Belle, throwing a blanket over Charlie. "Just help me find her things so we can get the hell out of here!"

Charlie was never in any way implicated in Gil's death. The body washed ashore two days after the accident, and in the autopsy two things were determined: that the deceased had sustained a heavy blow to the base of his skull, and that there was an extremely high content of alcohol in his system. This dovetailed with Peter's story. "I begged him not to go out sailing," he told the police. "But there was no arguing with a man like Gil, especially when he'd been drinking." The newspapers reported that Gil had been severely depressed because of business reversals. No mention was made of a woman, and Peter Salzman's role in the affair was described as that of a "concerned friend." Thus it was unnecessary to cook up a story about Charlie's whereabouts that weekend. No one ever seemed particularly curious, and if, on her return to Washington, she appeared shaky and broken, if her eyes were heavy with tears, and her moods were dark and fretful, it was attributed, as always, to an excess of alcohol. In time the whole unfortunate affair blew over. Neil's good name was as clean as it had ever been, and Peter Salzman, who owed him several favors, was able to feel that he had repaid a debt to an old and dear friend. As for Charlie, she would have liked to run to the ends of the earth to get away from the nightmare memory of Gil falling off that boat. But a temporary move to Manhattan, and then the purchase of a house in Brooklyn, was the best she could do.

And the best I can do right now, she thought, is wallow in a nice hot tub. She turned away from the dark glass of the window, so badly shaken from reliving Gil's death that what she really wanted was a drink. A few sips of scotch would soften her up, blur her memory so that the fatal episode would disappear behind a wall of fog and she wouldn't have to think of it. No one would know the difference unless she told them. She could call room service as easily as snapping her fingers.

With three long strides she was at the phone. "Yes," said a voice, "what would you like?" She opened her mouth to order a double scotch, but her throat closed against the words, and instead of scotch she heard herself ask for orange juice. It was one of the strangest moments of her life, discovering she was physically incapable of ordering alcohol, the nectar that had sustained her for so many years—that had killed her lover, and come close, on many occasions, to killing her. Replacing the receiver, she took a deep breath and thought with pleasure that the filmy pink cloud on which she had drifted for the past few weeks was now as solid beneath her feet as the gritty pavement of Manhattan.

$\mathcal{M}$usette, very keyed up waiting to hear from Neil, went to the gym more often than usual. Swimming relaxed her, made her feel sensual, and as she knifed through the water she would think of Neil, imagining what it would be like to see him again, to feel his hands on her body. In her mind he was always the Neil of the past, young and athletic with thick dark hair, devilish blue eyes, and an appetite for lovemaking that wouldn't stop. As she swam with strong steady strokes from one end of the pool to the other, she pictured the two of them in bed together, heard his voice whispering promises into her ear. By the time she was out and wrapped in a towel, she was the next Mrs. Gallagher, and Charlie was a has-been living on her own with two adolescents and a houseful of ugly paintings in Brooklyn.

As she had promised, she took Gwen to the club with her several afternoons a week, and though exercise was an ordeal for the writer, the hard work was beginning to pay off: Gwen looked better in a swimsuit than she had a few weeks ago. She also put herself in charge of Gwen's diet. "See," she said one afternoon, when they were lunching on salads in the club's dining room. "Thanks to me you've lost at least eight or nine pounds. You ought to let me manage your work life, too."

Gwen raised her eyebrows, but didn't say anything.

"Seriously, Gwen. You'd write a terrific film script, I know you would."

"It's just not something I ever wanted to do," said the writer.

"Why not?"

Gwen shrugged. "Doesn't have the same breadth as a novel."

"But you've never tried. Anyway, it might free you up. Help you get rid of that writer's block."

"Oh," laughed Gwen, "I'd do anything short of taking a drink to get rid of that. But I don't think writing films is the answer."

Absentmindedly, she removed one of her golden bangles and spun it around on the tablecloth. Musette watched for a moment, and then said, "One thing I've been wanting to ask you is how you came to write *Homegirl*. It's so different from your other novels."

The question hung in the air for a few seconds. Gwen returned the bangle to her wrist, took a sip of water, and said nervously: "It's not something I like to talk about."

"Gwen, this is me, your AA buddy, remember?"

"All right, okay. It's just that it was so long ago, and I'm kind of sensitive on the subject. I mean I feel guilty. I guess I can say that to you since we're both in the program." Sighing, she took another sip of water. "Thirteen years ago I spent a term teaching at a black college in the south, and I had a remedial student named Glady Johnson. She was really in bad shape, couldn't read or write, and she chose me as a...a confidante. Twice a week she'd come to me with all her problems. I'll never forget those big trusting black eyes. Anyway, by Christmas, when I went home to New York, I had her whole story and I started writing it down in little notebooks. I never asked her permission, just went ahead and did it."

"*Homegirl* was based on her?"

Gwen nodded. "The thing is, I didn't go back to the college. I never saw her again. I guess on some level I thought, Shit, the girl can't read anyway, so what's the difference? But in all these years I've never felt right about it."

Gwen made it so easy for Musette to get what she wanted from her. "If you made *Homegirl* into a movie, you'd get rid of some of that guilt," she said, watching the writer out of impassive golden eyes.

Gwen reached for a piece of bread, and changed her mind. "I'm afraid I'm not following you on that one."

"The problem is you never acknowledged Glady. How could you have since she was illiterate? Now, if you made *Homegirl* into a movie, there's a chance she'd go see it, identify with the main character, and think, Wow, there's someone in this world who wanted to tell my story. For her it would be a blessing, like winning the lottery, only on a psychic level. See what I mean?"

"I guess." Gwen gave a snort of laughter. "Thank you, Doctor."

"Will you think about it?"

"I don't know. Maybe."

Just when she was sure she would never hear from him, Musette had a phone call from Neil. "Hi," he said. "This is weird, isn't it?"

His voice, cutting through sixteen long years, sounded deep and strong. She shivered and let out a silent breath. "Yes."

"Are you free for lunch Wednesday?"

"I think I am. Let me check." She flipped through the pages of her desk calendar, fingers trembling as she sought the first Wednesday in May. "I'm free," she said softly.

"Good, then how about sandwiches in the park? We could meet at that little café at the pond on Seventy-sixth Street."

"All right," she said. "But what if it rains?"

"If it rains, I'll come to your place."

Wanting to be alone with him, she prayed for rain. But Wednesday dawned bright and hot with sunshine. Cursing, she climbed out of bed and went to her vast mirrored closet. What the hell would she wear? She remembered the first time she had had lunch with Neil all those years ago, the low-cut pink rayon dress she had worn, the ugly high-heeled shoes, the white plastic handbag, and those sad false pearls from Woolworths. She must have seemed so pathetic to him! Well, this time she would floor him with her beauty and elegance and sophistication. She reached through the masses of clothes she had flung on her bed, snatching up a black linen sleeveless dress. Yes, that with a pair of low-heeled black patent leather sandals, a thick ivory bangle, and classic golden earrings from Tiffanys. Keep it simple, she thought. She'd wear her hair loose to catch the sunshine in her beautiful golden curls, and carry a wide-brimmed straw hat with a black grosgrain ribbon. This time she would be the woman Neil wanted—a chic but sexual denizen of his privileged world.

The morning passed quickly. She was too nervous to eat breakfast, and she found herself pacing up and down her bedroom, wishing she could have a drink. When she had moved back to New York, she had instructed her maid, Carmen, to get rid of everything in the living room bar, so that was out—there wasn't a drop of liquor in the house. But she couldn't bear being this agitated, and half an hour before leaving the apartment, she decided to take a Valium. She had purposely stashed some away in a bathroom cabinet in case of emergencies, and this first meeting with Neil certainly qualified as an emergency. Besides, Valium had never seemed like a harmful drug to her. When she had been in the Betty Ford Center last fall, they had talked of the addictiveness of Valium—but in her case it never did much more than bring her down, even her out, soften the edges of everything around her. In AA the use of any kind of mood changer was taboo, but what the hell: no one would smell the tranquilizer on her breath, it wouldn't make her drunk, and she'd be able to face Neil with a calmness and serenity that was far better than the craziness she was really feeling.

Musette walked as slowly and nervously as a bride down the wide, sun-dappled path to the boat pond. The hat she carried in her slender palms reminded her of a bouquet of flowers and she felt virginal and young, loving the soft spring air on her skin and the way the light of this beautiful golden day danced and rippled over everything it touched—the gleaming waters of the pond with its tiny sailboats, the children scampering in the playground, the distant meadow with its yellow crop of daisies. As she walked she glanced from side to side, looking for Neil, and when she saw him she had to stop short and take a deep breath. He was sitting beneath the trees on the last bench before the path opened to the pond; he had taken off his jacket and was wearing a white shirt that contrasted sharply with his dark hair; his eyes were hidden behind a pair of sunglasses. On the opposite bench an elderly man was sharing a bag lunch with a flock of pigeons, and Neil seemed totally immersed in the sight.

After a moment, she continued down the path, glad that she had the advantage of seeing him first. When she got closer she saw that his hair was gray at the temples—she loved that! And that his face, his thickened jawline, had a gritty maturity that had been missing years ago. But his body looked sleek and young, and in his white shirt and loosened red tie he was one of the handsomest men she had ever seen.

Now she was next to him. She took a last deep breath and reached out to touch his shoulder. "Neil?" she said tentatively.

"Maggie!" he said, springing to his feet. It was clear that he didn't know whether to kiss her or shake hands. She decided to take charge, leaning forward and quickly brushing her lips against his cheek. Oh, the remembered smell of him—English soap, tangy after-shave, and the dry woodsiness of his hair. She felt her body grow weak.

"Well, it's good to see you," he said.

"Yes," she murmured.

"Are you hungry? Shall we get something to eat?"

"I'd just like to sit down for a minute."

"Of course." He gestured to his bench. "Let's sit here."

Aware of his eyes on her long legs, she decided that her surest strategy for the moment was to play prim and proper, hard to get. Crossing her legs at the knee, she smoothed the material of her dress down over her thighs and placed her wide-brimmed straw hat demurely on her lap. "Gosh, I haven't been to this place in ages," she said, wishing he would remove his sunglasses so she could see directly into his eyes.

"Neither have I. Charlie and I used to come here sometimes with the children, but of course that was a long time ago."

The mention of Charlie—and so casually!—caused a spurt of anger to run through her. She fought it down, saying, "It's scary how quickly time passes. Do you remember the first time we had lunch together?"

He laughed uneasily. "How could I forget?"

"I was wearing those ridiculous clothes and I was so frightened I thought I would die."

"I remember being a terrible host," he said almost as if he were apologizing.

She glanced at him. "Why don't you take off your sunglasses," she said. "I have no idea what you look like."

"All right. But you may not like what you see." He removed the glasses, putting them in one of the pockets of his suit jacket.

"Why shouldn't I like what I see?" she murmured, cocking her head to the side as she studied him. Without the glasses, his eyes were blue and soft, with smudgelike circles beneath them, and a network of tiny worry lines fanning out from the corners.

"Because I ain't young and handsome anymore," he said with a laugh.

"I think you're very handsome," said Musette, pleased that he had wanted to hide his circled eyes from her. Was it Charlie's leaving that had chiseled those little lines of worry and fatigue into his skin? Her fingers ached to smooth them away. "You look as if you could use some sleep, though," she added.

"Yeah, well..." He stared openly at her. "You're very changed," he said after a moment.

"Really—how?"

"Oh, I don't mean in a bad way. It's just that you've become so... sophisticated."

She laughed. "You mean as opposed to the trashy blonde you kicked out of your apartment 'cause she had something in her belly?"

"Let's not fight. That was years ago. I behaved badly, and I've always regretted it."

"Uh-hunh." She looked at him closely. "Tell me something, Neil. If I'd had money back then, would you have married me?"

He shifted uneasily on the bench, his soft blue eyes clouding over. "I can't answer that, Maggie. I wish I could say money had nothing to do with it, but I'd be a liar if I did. In those days, it was always my career that came first, my plans for the future."

"And now?"

He shrugged. "I don't know about now."

"You married Charlie after knocking her up one soft starry night under the rosebushes."

"Jesus. She told you about that?"

"Sure. Didn't I say we'd become good friends?"

"Yeah, but..." Their eyes met. For an unbearably long moment they stared at one another, and then he reached for her hand. "Let's leave Charlie out of this," he said in a low voice. "I don't want her to know anything about us, past or present. Agreed?"

"Agreed," she murmured, feeling tiny shocks of electricity run through her body at the touch of his hand.

"One other thing, Maggie. You have to believe this. Writing that check that day was one of the hardest things I've ever done."

"Because you were stingy," she said flatly.

"No," he said. "Because, despite what you did, I really had strong feelings for you. And," he laughed, "for whatever it's worth, I was crazy about you in the sack." He let go of her hand, and stood up. "Well, shall we go and get something to eat?"

They ordered café au lait and slabs of Brie on buttery golden croissants from a concession stand that called itself a café, and went and sat down at one of the white wrought-iron tables on the terrace overlooking the boat pond. Since it was very crowded and they had to share a table, they couldn't talk about anything important. Neil told her he was glad her career had gone so well over the years, and that he had been sorry to read about her divorce from Miroslav.

"Were you really sorry?" said Musette, licking a crumb from her lip and narrowing her golden eyes at him.

"Well, that's a *façon de parler*. I don't like to think of you as unhappy."

"I don't like to think of you as unhappy, either," she said.

Neil glanced nervously at the other people at the table—two very proper-looking British nannies and their young charges. "Let's take a walk around the pond," he said.

The wide pathway was filled with lunchtime strollers happy to have an hour in the sun away from their offices. Neil and Musette stayed close together, their arms brushing occasionally as they walked. She was very conscious of the swing of her hips and the firmness of her body beneath the slim black sheath she wore. Neil walked with his tan suit jacket slung over his shoulder, whistling to himself. It was a while before either of them spoke. Finally, in a voice that she hoped sounded casual, she asked, "What are you going to do now that Charlie's gone?"

"Hope that she comes back," he answered without hesitation.

They were midway around the pond. She was aware of a tall black man on roller skates swooping past her, of violin music from a street musician who had set his hat out a few feet from where they were. "Do you still love her?" she asked, forcing the words through stiff lips.

He slowed to a halt and turned to face the boat pond. Two little sailboats, one red and one blue, zipped back and forth across the water, their excited owners jumping up and down at the side of the pond. Musette held her breath waiting for him to answer the question.

"Of course I love her," he said. "She's my wife."

Musette gave a flat, hard laugh. "Oh, come on, Neil. That doesn't necessarily mean anything."

"Well, to me it does."

"Oh, really? Well, then tell me something, Neil. Is she as good in the sack as I was?"

He had turned to face her again, and she could see a shadow enter his eyes. "I'd rather not answer that," he said.

"Well, you just have," she said and, staring into his eyes, she smiled at him. "Come on, let's walk some more."

She went ahead of him this time so that he could appreciate the firm round shape of her bottom beneath the dress, and the softly suggestive back-and-forth motion of her hips. After a moment he lengthened his stride so he was beside her. He had put his sunglasses back on, and now he took her arm, just above the elbow, and gave it a little squeeze. "Between you and me things will always be . . . complicated," he said in a gruff voice.

"That's because we're attracted to each other," Musette said, smiling at him with her even white teeth. "Nothing can change that."

Ignoring the remark, he let go of her arm and slipped on his jacket. "How do you know Charlie—through AA?"

Musette nodded.

"I thought so. I read about your going into the Betty Ford

Center. I was always nervous about sending Charlie to a place like that because of the publicity."

"No one gets sober until they want to," said Musette. "Anyway, Charlie would have hated it there. Too many rules and too much group therapy."

"But it worked for you."

"I don't mind spilling my guts out." Musette laughed. "Wearing my heart on my sleeve. You ought to know that."

They had veered off onto the winding path that led up to Fifth Avenue. Beneath the trees it was shadowy and cool, and Musette felt her spirits drop as she sensed Neil getting ready to leave her. Walking along, he tightened the knot of his tie and pushed back his sleeve, glancing at his watch. "I've got a meeting in Washington at six o'clock, so I'm really going to have to make tracks," he said apologetically.

"Oh, too bad," said Musette. "Well, we should do this again."

"Yes, we should," Neil said, keeping his voice neutral. "I'll call you, all right?"

"All right."

They were just about to exit from the park, and impulsively she pushed her body against his and gave him a little hug. It was important, she decided, that he should fly back to his lonely Washington bed with the fragrance of her perfume in his nostrils, and the feel of her body, with its soft subtle curves, firmly planted in his mind. She didn't kiss him, but she nuzzled her cheek against his, and then, before he had a chance to get nervous about anyone seeing them, she quickly loosened her arms and backed off. "Ta, ta," she said, waving her hat in his direction, the ribbons fluttering in the light breeze. "See you soon." And she was gone, melted back into the crowd, before he could even form the word *good-bye*.

That night, too keyed-up to sleep, Musette took another Valium. What the hell, she thought as she pried off the plastic cap and popped a five-milligram pill into her mouth. One more can't hurt me. Drifting down into a deep well of sleep, she saw Neil— his grizzled hair, his taut, athletic body, the lines etched into the corners of his eyes...and drowsily wondered when she would see him again. Should she wait for his call, or send him a note on thick, scented paper? Should she perhaps fly down to

Washington and pay him a surprise visit? As she was picturing herself sitting on his desk, legs swinging seductively back and forth, the phone rang, its shrill ring startling her out of her dreamy state.

"Hello-who-is-it?" she exclaimed, grabbing up the phone, certain this was an emergency.

"It's Gwen. Jesus, what's the matter with you? Your voice sounds funny."

"Oh, *Gwen*." Relieved, she sank back on the pillows. "I was asleep, that's all."

"Whoops—sorry. I figured you'd still be up. It's only eleven o'clock. Want me to call back in the morning?"

"No, that's all right," Musette yawned. "What's up? You're not canceling tomorrow are you?" The two women had a date to meet at the gym.

"No fear, much as I'd like to. I still have all that flab to lose. This is about something else."

"Well, what?"

"Now listen, girl, I don't want you to say told you so, but I started playing around with *Homegirl* to see how it would be as a movie, and I've written a few scenes. I'm having a great time."

Musette sat up, completely alert now. "Gwen, that's wonderful! That's the best news. When can I see them?"

Gwen chuckled. "When I'm good and ready. Right now I'm learning how to format the goddamn thing. It's a whole other language."

"Yes, I know. Gwen, I'm really glad you're doing this. I'm sure you won't regret it for a minute."

They hung up a few minutes later and Musette, sighing happily, switched out the light and lay back on her satiny pillows, resolutely closing her eyes. But it was no use. Her heart kept skipping beats, and her eyes kept opening and staring into the darkness. She felt her stomach tighten with excitement, and knew that if she didn't do something she'd jump out of her skin. First the anxiety of meeting Neil and now this good news of Gwen's—it was too much for her.

Without turning the light back on, she got out of bed and went to the bathroom, where she opened the medicine cabinet. Five more milligrams of Valium were all she needed—kid's stuff to a person who used to get so strung out on coke she couldn't see straight. With fumbling hands she removed the pill from the vial and swallowed it down with a few sips of Perrier. In twenty minutes the pill would take effect, and she'd feel that wonderful calm and serenity again. Sleep would come to her as easily as a child running to its mother; she had only to lie back and open her arms, and in the meantime she could daydream of Neil, the handsomeness of his face as he turned to her in the park today, the soft blue eyes in which she still read love and desire. Oh yes, he wanted her—she knew that, even if he didn't; the problem was now simply one of strategy. Yawning softly, she left the bathroom. In the morning, when her mind was fresh and clear, she'd work out a plan; for now all she wanted to do was imagine Neil's hands on her body and float away.

---

wo weeks passed, and there was no word from Neil. Musette's plan had been to wait and see if he contacted her; if he didn't, she would send him a note saying she needed some legal advice on a private matter—a matter that would, of course, be breathlessly woven into a very elaborate game of seduction.

But as it turned out, she didn't have to get into that sort of game at all. One morning as she was lingering in bed, she read in the *New York Times* that Neil Gallagher, congressman from Pennsylvania, would be speaking at a lunch organized by the National Organization of Women at the Marriott Hotel at twelve-thirty that afternoon. Immediately a new and wonderful plan formed in her mind, and with a giggle she jumped out of bed and raced to the bathroom to get ready.

An hour and a half later she was at the Marriott. She wore a tight and very chic red silk suit that was cut low enough in front to reveal the shallow cleavage between her breasts. Around her long throat was a stunning three-stranded pearl choker that had been a gift to her from Miroslav on their first wedding anniversary—it was the only jewelry she wore aside from her rings, and she happened to know it had cost him a small fortune. Pausing only once to ask for directions, she walked quickly and purposefully down a corridor toward the banquet halls, her hair a loose golden cloud around her shoulders. She knew she would stand out in this very vociferous political group of women, but she didn't care—in fact, she counted on that.

Today almost more than any day she could remember, she appreciated the tedious acting classes her agent had insisted she take through the years. At a desk set up outside the banquet hall in which Neil would be speaking, a crowd of drab-looking women stood on line. Musette took her place at the end, aware of receiving curious—and in some cases, hostile—glances. The others all wore simple dark clothing and comfortable shoes, and here she was in a chic but vampy suit and three-inch heels. It made her want to throw back her head and laugh. The line moved quickly and when her turn came she said to the woman checking names off the list, "I'm Musette."

"Musette who?"

"Just Musette."

The woman at the desk studied her sourly. "Don't you have a last name?"

"I've had several last names and I don't use any of them."

"Well, there's no Musette here." She checked her list and shook her head. "I don't see your name or anything like it."

Musette squared her elegantly broad shoulders. In her black suede high heels she was a willowy five feet eleven, and she loomed threateningly over the woman, looking every bit like the glamorous actress she was. "There must be a mistake," she said in a voice that was showily calm. "My secretary reserved a place for me at this luncheon over a month ago. Either let me see the list, or call the program coordinator. I'm tired of standing here arguing."

"I'm not arguing," said the woman, sucking in thin cheeks. "I'm just doing my job. What organization did you say you were with?"

"I didn't," growled Musette.

"Well, if you'll just wait a minute."

She left, coming back moments later with another woman who looked more official in heels and a mannish suit. "I'm Nina

Teitelbaum," the second woman said unnecessarily, since her name had been inked onto a label across her breast pocket. "What seems to be the problem?"

Musette explained that she was an actress interested in becoming affiliated with NOW. "I find it pretty disturbing that you've managed to lose my reservation," she said.

"Please accept my apologies," said Nina, smiling gummily at her. "I know you've been inconvenienced, and what I'm going to do is put you at a table right at the front. If you'll just come with me."

And so it was that Musette, looking like a big lush rose in a field of dandelions, was seated at the table right beneath the speakers. On one side of her was a woman wearing a crew cut and big hoop earrings who did something connected with teen pregnancies, and on the other was a woman in a T-shirt dress and owlish horn rims who told Musette she was a professor of public health at Columbia. "And what's your connection?" she asked.

"I'm an actress," said Musette, choosing her words carefully, "who once had a bad abortion. I'm not sure how public I'm going to go on that, so don't quote me." But already she was thinking it would be fun to be the Jane Fonda of the pro-choice movement.

Neil came in and found his place on the dais, and she could tell he saw her almost instantly. His face tightened and reddened as if something had gotten caught in his throat, but then, after a moment, he regained his composure and acknowledged her with a small nod of the head.

She waved back. She was sitting almost directly beneath him, and she was glad now she had worn the low-cut suit and that her hair, with its masses of golden ringlets, shone like a beacon. She raised a glass of ice water to her lips, and watched him involuntarily follow the movement of her hand, and in that moment she knew that she had him.

The lunch itself passed in a blur. When Neil spoke she hung on his words, leaning forward slightly so that he could see the swell of her breasts, licking her lips every once in a while as if she were nervous for him. It amused her no end that he tried, in his politician's way, to include the whole audience in his sweeping gaze, but that his eyes kept coming back to her. He wore a gray suit and robin's-egg-blue shirt, and Musette thought he looked terrific with the silvery patches at his temples glinting and catching the light, and his shapely hands lifting from the podium every time he wanted to make a point. In an hour, she thought, those hands will undress me. Already she could feel them kneading her breasts and moving down over her stomach to the golden fluff between her legs, and as she imagined how it would feel to have him thrust his fingers inside her, her lips parted and her eyes met his in an open, frank, sexual stare.

At that point he faltered. He looked helplessly down at her, his cheeks flaming, and gave a little cough to cover up his agitation.

Very coolly she looked back up at him, and winked.

A smile crossed his lips. "You women," he said, "have always been known for your chutzpah, and I'm glad to see that nothing has changed."

After the lunch, Musette stood in the knot of women that had gathered around Neil. Everyone seemed to have a lot to say, and impatiently she pushed ahead, placing herself next to Neil and saying in a low voice, "Mr. Congressman, I'll be in the bar next to the Broadway exit in twenty minutes. See you then." Without waiting for a response, she swung away, leaving the room in the company of Nina Teitelbaum, who wanted to know if they could expect to see her at a big rally at the end of May. "I don't know," said Musette. "Here's my card. Why don't you call my secretary and set it up with her."

In the bar she sat at a small corner table, ignoring the stares of several businessmen who tried aggressively to catch her eye, and doing her best to pretend to herself she wasn't nervous. Her watch said two-thirty, and then two-forty-five, and then two-fifty, and then three o'clock, and she was on her second diet Coke, and seriously thinking of giving up, when Neil walked through the door. "I don't know whether to get mad at you, or laugh," he said, sliding in beside her on the banquette.

"Laugh," said Musette. "It's much more pleasant. Anyway, I made it fun, didn't I?"

"Well, you made it *interesting*."

"Good, and I can make it much more interesting. How are things down in Washington?"

He laughed nervously. "Fine."

"A little lonely, aren't they?" She moved closer to him on the banquette, her thigh very subtly brushing against his.

"Maggie, I want to tell you right now that I've never been unfaithful to Charlie, and I don't intend to start now."

"Really?" she said, noticing that he kept his leg where it was. Intensifying the pressure of her thigh against his, she said, "Well, you must be pretty horny then. Charlie tells me the two of you haven't had sex in over a year."

"Not because I haven't wanted to!" he said angrily. "What else did she say?" He removed his leg and shifted position so that he was facing her squarely.

"Nothing much. Oh, don't go getting all pissed. Women *do* talk, you know." She took a small gold compact out of her purse and studied her face, bunching her lips together in a pout and smoothing away a smudge of lipstick with her little finger.

"Did she ever say anything about why she left Washington?"

"No. Only that you two needed some time away from each other." She studied him over the rim of her compact. "What happened, Neil? Was there another man?"

"Of course not," he said firmly. "She's a drunk, that's what happened. Booze infiltrated our marriage and drowned everything good out of it."

"I thought you said you loved her."

"I do love her. Or I love the girl she used to be." He ran his hands over his face. "Let's talk about something else."

She applied a shiny coat of bright red gloss to her lips, closed the compact with a little snap, and returned it to her purse. "All right. What would you like to talk about?"

"What you're doing at a NOW luncheon. Those women are hardly your speed."

"Hmmmm," said Musette, shifting restlessly and curling one of her legs sideways on the banquette so that her skirt rode up to the top of her thigh. "As you know, the subject of abortion concerns me a great deal. I'm very interested in making sure that women have the right to do whatever they want with their bodies—that the choice of continuing, or *discontinuing*, a pregnancy is theirs, and theirs alone." She glanced sharply at him, and decided this was not the time to tell him about her own sad experience—an experience she would always blame on him.

"Well, that's admirable," said Neil, his eyes resting on the silky flesh of her thighs.

She shifted once again so that the skirt rose a little higher and her underpants were visible. "Yes, isn't it?" she agreed, watching his eyes travel up to the lacy patch of silk between her legs. She allowed him to stare hungrily for a moment, before closing her legs and sliding them back down to the floor. Placing her hand on his knee she said, "Well, you know what? It's getting awfully hot and steamy here in this bar. As it happens, I have the key to room sixteen-seventy and I think I'll go up there and cool out for a while. You're welcome to join me if you like." She felt the warmth of his knee creep into her fingers, and gave the hardened flesh a little squeeze. Locking her eyes onto his, she removed the card key from her bag with her free hand and wiggled it at him. "See you," she said, rising from the table.

From there it was touch and go. She was almost certain he would follow her, but she knew he wouldn't risk taking the same elevator, and as she stepped into the glassed-in cage that would carry her to the sixteenth floor she glanced around the lobby to see if she could spot Neil. No sign of him, and her heart sank as the doors closed and the little cage lifted with a slight jolt and began its dizzying ascent up the lobby wall. Holding her breath, she leaned over and looked down; beneath her, the swarms of people had turned into toylike figures, and one of those figures was Neil. She felt sick with anxiety. If he decided against joining her, she wasn't sure what she should do next. Call him and tell him what a chicken he was?

She was the only person to get off the elevator at the sixteenth floor. Her heels sinking into the carpet, she made her way to room 1670 and fitted the key in the lock, glancing up and down the corridor as the door swung open. No one. Entering the room, she felt lonelier than she had ever felt in her life. In her current mood, the luxurious room seemed drab and lifeless—a large space with a king-sized bed, soft lighting, a desk and chairs, a window with a gauzy white curtain overlooking an airshaft. How dreary! Kicking off her shoes, she sat down on the bed and opened her purse, withdrawing the small gold box that contained her Valium. She was about to pop a pill in her mouth when there was a soft rap on the door.

Her heart began to thud. Jesus, was she imagining this? No, there it was again. She sprang to her feet, thrusting the pills back into her purse, and ran to the door. Before opening it, she moistened her lips and fluffed her hair up with her fingers. "Who is it?" she said in a low voice.

"Who do you think?"

She opened the door and Neil came in. His first words were, "God, I hope I don't regret this."

"You won't," she said tightly.

Without really looking at her, he moved into the interior of the room, putting his briefcase down on a chair. "Well," he said.

She was standing just behind him and their eyes met in the mirror. "Well what?"

A smile flitted over his lips. "Well, let me kiss you."

He turned around then and took her in his arms. "Oh, Jesus," he muttered as she fitted her body against his. He began hungrily to kiss her. She let him have her warm mouth and then arched her head back as his lips began to move along her throat. He unclasped her pearls, flinging them to the floor, and moved his hands into the jacket of her suit, stroking her creamy shoulders and feeling for the hook of the bra she had worn to push up her small breasts. When he had her bra off, he squeezed her nipples hard between his fingers, just as she had so often dreamed of his doing, and she heard herself give a little moan of pleasure.

"Like that, hunh?" he whispered.

She nodded mutely.

"Well, here's something you'll like even better." He pushed her skirt up and lifted her so that she had to wrap her legs around his waist, and for a few minutes he held her that way, stroking her buttocks and kissing her on the mouth, the throat, the shoulders. Then, still in that position, he carried her to the bed and gently lay her down, peeling off her tights and panties and pushing her skirt up around her waist so that the flat slope of her stomach and the mossy golden vee of curls beneath it were fully exposed.

"God, I've missed this," he said.

"So have I," she murmured, looking up at him.

He unbuckled his belt, and in a neat movement was out of

his pants. She reached for him and they began to writhe together on the bed; it wasn't until the very last minute that he handed her a condom that he must have bought while she was waiting so nervously in the hotel room. "Here, why don't you help me with this," he said, pulling her hand along the length of him.

She did as he wanted, too excited to speak. Then she kissed him and pulled him on top of her, guiding his erection between her legs, moaning and weaving her hips as he thrust himself inside her with a knifelike motion. Oh yes, this was it! He belonged to her now! He was hers and not Charlie's! She found herself clawing his back as they moved together in perfect harmony, each pushing the other closer and closer to the edge, until finally she couldn't stand it anymore and her body shuddered in a series of intense spasms. "Neil!" she screamed. "Oh, Neil!"

The first time they made love they were in such a hurry that they didn't bother to take off any more clothing than they had to. The second time they relaxed and enjoyed themselves, and by early evening they had made love three times and they were both exhausted. "Jesus, what time is it?" Neil asked in a hoarse, sated voice.

Musette sat up and felt for her watch. "Six," she said.

"Is it? I'm really sorry, Maggie, but I'm going to have to get going. I'm supposed to meet some people for dinner in half an hour."

"Can't you call and cancel?" said Musette, watching as he stood up and crossed the room to the bathroom.

"No," he called out, turning on the shower. "It's a political thing."

While he was in the shower she remembered, as she had off and on all day, that she was supposed to meet with Gwen at six-thirty to go over some of the scenes she had written for *Homegirl*. The two women had planned to work together for an hour before going to a meeting in Greenwich Village where Charlie, who had just celebrated ninety days, was to tell her AA story for the first time. Well, that was pretty ironic, thought Musette, standing up and gathering various articles of clothing and jewelry from the floor.

While Neil dressed, she went into the bathroom to fix her hair and makeup. Wanting to keep the smell of him on her body as long as possible, she had decided against taking a shower.

"I think you should leave first," Neil called to her from the bedroom.

"All right."

"And I insist on paying for the room."

Narrowing her eyes, she reached back and fumbled with the clasp of her pearls. "Too late. It's already on my card."

"Next time, then."

He came into the bathroom and watched as she ran a brush through her tangled hair. She could sense that he was in a big hurry now, and it made her nervous. "When is next time?" she asked, her eyes seeking out his in the mirror.

"I don't know. I want to think a little, Maggie. This is a big step we've taken."

She slipped the brush into her purse. "I see," she said, turning to face him. "Well, while you're thinking, think of this." Moving like a cat, she put her arms around him and held him very close, kissing him with a moist, newly lipsticked, open mouth, and thrusting her deft little pink tongue between his lips. "You're the best, Neil," she whispered, before disengaging herself. "So don't go disappointing me, okay?" She threw him a loving look, picked up her purse, and sauntered gracefully out of the room, her tall heels moving soundlessly over the carpet as she opened the door and closed it behind her with a little click.

*I*t was seven-fifteen when Musette arrived at Gwen's apartment. She was breathless and disheveled and her cheeks were flushed. Gwen took one look at her and knew she had been up to something. "Jesus, girl, where've you been?" she said, eyeing Musette's slinky, tight-fitting suit and beautiful pearl choker.

"Oh, I was at a fashion show at the Marriott, and then I had appointments all afternoon. I never had time to go home and change."

"Well, you look great, so I wouldn't worry about it," said Gwen, noting the dreamy expression in Musette's eyes. She was sure the actress had been with a man. With her messy hair and swollen lips, she had the appearance of someone who had just gotten out of bed after hours of lovemaking. "Come on, let's go to my study. The meeting starts at eight, so that gives us hardly any time."

She led Musette into her austere little workroom and installed her on the love seat. "I want you to make yourself very comfortable," she said, nervous because Musette would be the first person to read her attempts as a scriptwriter. "What can I get you to drink?"

"Diet Coke would be fine."

"Okay, I'll bring it in a minute. In the meantime, here are the first five scenes." She handed Musette a wad of manuscript, conscious of the actress's eyes drifting over the bare walls of her study, the gray metal filing cabinets and neat rows of books. At nearly seven-thirty, rays of late afternoon sun filtered in through the bamboo blind that covered her only window, and tiny white dust motes danced in the air. Reluctantly she left the room, returning a few minutes later with a glass of diet Coke and a bowl of cashew nuts. "How is it so far?" she asked.

The actress looked up at her, a strangely drugged expression in her glittering eyes. "Fine. But I can't concentrate with you hovering over me, so get lost, will you?"

"Okay, okay, I'm out of here," Gwen laughed. She went to her small galley-style kitchen where she rummaged around the fridge, looking for a decent piece of cheese she could serve with crackers. Not that they would have time to eat; she just needed something to do. While she was slicing a hunk of cheddar, she heard Walter's key in the lock. "That you, honey?" she called out automatically.

"Sure it's me. Were you expecting someone else?" He came into the kitchen, and gave her a hug from behind, kissing her neck and running his hands over her breasts. "What's for dinner?" he murmured. "I'm famished."

"Oh, honey, don't you remember? I told you this morning. Musette's come over to read a few scenes for me, and then we're going down to the Village to hear Charlie qualify."

His face fell. He let go of her silently, and went to the bedroom to change his clothes. When he returned he was wearing blue jeans and a Yale T-shirt. His thick black hair was rumpled, as if he had angrily run his hands through it a number of times. Ignoring Gwen, he opened a cupboard and took out a can of tuna.

"You could go out," said Gwen.

"Yeah? Where to?"

"The Empire Diner."

"I'm sick of the fucking Empire Diner."

"Well, I could make you an omelette."

Musette appeared in the doorway just then, her face glowing with excitement as she held out the pages of manuscript. "Gwen, this is marvelous!" she exclaimed. "Keep going. You're doing just great." Sensing the tension in the room, she stopped, her eyes falling on Walter, whom she had not met before. "I'm Musette," she said, extending her hand. From the look of surprise on her face, it was clear that she had forgotten Gwen was married to a white man.

"Oh, I'm sorry, I should have introduced you," said Gwen.

"Walter Rudin," he said curtly. Gwen watched him study the actress, aware of his eyes flitting over her tall, slender body, her ripe little breasts, her tousled hair. She saw the blood creep into his cheeks when Musette, with a wriggle of her shoulders and a look that said he was the only man on earth, told him how nice it was to meet him. She wanted to laugh out loud a moment later when he turned to her and said, "You know what, honey? Suppose I come with you to the meeting. We could go out for dinner afterward, which would solve everyone's problem."

Since it was an open meeting, which meant nonalcoholics were welcome, she couldn't very well say no.

At seven-thirty that evening, Charlie walked into a large and almost empty church basement in Greenwich Village. The room had the look of most AA meeting rooms: coffee brewing on a scarred table that had probably been donated by a church member, rows and rows of metal auditorium chairs, two large white charts on which were written the Twelve Steps and the Twelve Traditions on the wall behind the speaker's table, and on a ledge at the side of the room, stacks of AA literature. There was a certain dreariness to the place that Charlie, used to church basements, no longer noticed. She was going to qualify here tonight. It was her ninetieth day sober, and she had allowed Felicity to pester her into telling her story.

Not wanting to bare her soul in front of people she or her family knew, she had signed up to speak at a meeting in the Village. She had asked only a few friends to come and hear her: Musette, Gwen, Tanya, and, of course, Felicity. But none of them were here yet, and as she looked around the room she felt lonely and frightened. She had arrived early—too early—on purpose. Feeling a little foolish, she went into the kitchen to see if she could find the person in charge. Under blinking fluorescent lights, two women and a man chatted amiably as they stood at a long wooden table, opening cartons of milk and packages of cookies and cups. All three of them wore black. The man's hair was cut so short that one could see the ashen color of his skull, and the women both had wild perms and wore as many hoops and studs as they could along the outer edges of their ears. Charlie, in a white linen skirt, a pale green crepe de chine blouse, pearls, and a beautifully cut off-white Armani jacket, felt distinctly out of place. "Excuse me," she said in her loud voice. "I'm tonight's speaker. I'm not sure what I'm supposed to do."

The man looked up. "Welcome," he said, holding out his hand. "I'm Paul S."

"Charlie G.," said Charlie, holding out hers.

He introduced the two women, and then said, "Why don't you grab yourself a cup of coffee, and take a seat in the front row. I'll let you know when it's time to go to the speaker's table."

Feeling even more lonely, Charlie did as he suggested. The room was beginning to fill up. She looked around for her friends, but there wasn't a soul she knew, just a sea of people dressed in black; both sexes in inky jeans and T-shirts, the women with that wild permed hair, and the men scalped like little boys about to go off to summer camp. She fingered her own hair, which was clipped back with two large gold barrettes, and thought that despite the drab uniformity of their clothes, everyone here looked arty and interesting, while she, in her expensive skirt and jacket, looked like what she was: a rich, untalented society matron.

Reaching into her tote bag, she removed the May edition of *HG,* and began to fan her cheeks. It was hot! At ten to eight, the room was nearly three-quarters full. Where was Musette? She needed her badly. It was so odd sitting here, an alien creature, a pale white dove in a flock of crows. She felt a hand on her back, and jumped.

"Nervous?" said Felicity, putting her briefcase down on the chair beside Charlie's. Though she must have come straight from the office, she was wearing the same slim black pants and long, loose T-shirt as almost every other woman in the room. Charlie felt more apart than ever.

"God yes."

Felicity smiled encouragingly. "Don't worry. It'll all seem okay once you're up there talking."

"I'm afraid of going blank."

"You won't. I promise. The words will pour out, and you'll feel the most wonderful sense of release."

Charlie doubted that very much. Felicity knew only the bare bones of her story. She had no idea how much horror it contained, how much had to be kept hidden, secret. She knew nothing about Gil.

"I always look at it this way," said Felicity. "When you qualify, you're not up there to entertain people, but to help them stay sober, and as long as you do that for one person in the room—perhaps the newest, the one who was planning to go out after the meeting and get drunk—then you've done your job. Understand? It's really an act of great kindness."

Despairingly, Charlie said, "I'll try to keep that in mind." Her lips felt stiff, and she bit down on them, wishing she'd never agreed to do this. All around her she heard coughs and scraping sounds and hello-how-are-yous as people came in and claimed chairs and settled themselves. For the first time in months, she had that odd tunnel vision she used to have when she was drunk. Steeped in alcohol, her brain hadn't been able to deal with objects more than a few feet away from her, so that she was always tripping over things and misjudging what other people said because their faces were blurry. Now the room simply wouldn't hold still. When someone off to the side waved at her, she squinted and waved back, but she had no idea who it was.

Felicity tugged at her sleeve. "You'd better go up there. The chairman's motioning to you."

Charlie saw Paul S., the man from the kitchen, at the speaker's table. He had told her earlier that he would make announcements and ask for day counts before introducing her. "Where are Gwen and Musette?" whispered Charlie, getting up from her chair.

"I don't know. Don't worry. They'll be here any minute."

"Will you walk with me?"

"Yes, of course. I'll walk with you, and I'll hold your things, and I'll even get you another cup of coffee, loaded with sugar, just the way you like it."

Feeling extremely self-conscious, Charlie sat down at the speaker's table beside Paul S., who grinned at her and said, "Hey man, relax. No one's gonna shoot you." She hid her trembling hands in her lap, and tried desperately to remember the things she had planned to say. She was aware of someone, a man whose voice sounded familiar, reading the preamble.

"Alcoholics Anonymous is a fellowship of men and women who share their experience, strength, and hope with each other that they may solve their common problem and help others to recover from alcoholism. The only requirement for membership is a desire to stop drinking..."

Glancing up, she saw that he had gray hair, but she was too distracted at the moment to think of who he was or where she might have seen him before. Her heart thundering in her chest, she heard Paul say, "And with us tonight is Charlie G. from the Fifth Avenue Group." She opened her mouth, nervously wetting her lips, and was surprised when her voice didn't come out in a croak.

"My name is Charlie," she said. "I'm an alcoholic." And she began, just as Felicity had counseled her to do, at the beginning—when she got drunk, at the age of thirteen, at one of her parents' parties, and her mother's butler had to carry her upstairs and put her to bed. After that, the words seemed to pour out.

Charlie was nearly halfway through her qualification when Gwen, Musette, and Walter arrived at the church. They couldn't get three seats together in the front, and so they sat in the back, craning their necks to see Charlie. Her voice was surprisingly loud and clear, but in her pale, well-cut clothes she looked incongruous in the dreary room. Gwen, distracted by her husband's presence, tried to force herself to listen. Charlie was talking about her ambition to become a painter, and how that goal had been thwarted when she stumbled into marriage at a young age and had children. "Once I had the babies, the drinking really took off."

Gwen's mind wandered. She was intensely aware of Walter sitting beside her. What had made him want to come along tonight? Clearly he had been attracted to Musette in some way— was that it? Or was it his usual fear of losing her if she went to too many meetings alone? He was always so certain she was having an affair with another recovering alcoholic.

"Having to run two houses, entertain, cope with my children, and help my husband with his career was too much for me. I started drinking earlier and earlier in the day. Pretty soon I was hiding bottles all over the house, and I was becoming forgetful. I'd make a date with someone, and not show up because I was drunk when I made it. It was awful."

Walter leaned over and whispered, "Well, at least you didn't do that."

Gwen ignored the remark. She hated it when he came with her to meetings. He always found a way to start trouble. She glanced at Musette, who was sitting on the other side of him, listening to Charlie's story with parted lips. She didn't seem to be having any trouble concentrating. "My marriage began to fall apart," said Charlie. "I resented my husband for trying to control my drinking. As the years passed he became the enemy, and my one big desire was to get away from him. So at Christmas I moved up here to New York where I could go on a real spree. But things never turn out quite the way we plan, and within a week I ran into an old friend who twelve-stepped me into this program. I can't say I came in here willingly. It took a few more weeks of slipping and sliding."

She looked out over the audience, her face suddenly full of anguish. "The thing I regret most about my alcoholism is the way I treated my children. I wasn't there for them when they were growing up—not in the normal sense. At night I'd get sloppy drunk, and then I'd be overaffectionate, wanting to kiss them and embrace them when they couldn't stand the boozy smell of me. They must have thought I was crazy, slurring my words and lurching all over the place. And then in the day, I'd be so hung over and irritable that I didn't want them anywhere near me. 'Just leave me alone, leave me alone!' I used to shout at them all the time. And now...now, going through this business of getting sober, I've had to temporarily give up access to them, and I'm not sure if, or when, I'll ever live with them again. And that's been hell..."

Charlie was almost finished. What Gwen dreaded most was the end of the meeting, when people stood up and joined hands to say the Serenity Prayer. Walter always got so nasty about that, muttering, "Jesus, is this hokey!" under his breath, and refusing to hold anyone's hand but hers. And then he would stomp out like a jealous lover, dragging her with him, not letting her stay to talk to people.

"What I want to do now," Charlie was saying, "is find the girl I used to be, the one who loved painting and art and adventure, and put her back in my life. If I could have her and my children I'd be a truly happy woman. And I know that the only way I can get those things is by coming to meetings and listening to all of you."

There was a sharp burst of applause. Gwen glanced at her watch. Eight-thirty. Another half hour till the end of the meeting.

Up in front, feeling drained and shaky, Charlie lit a cigarette. It had been easier than she thought. She had managed to skip over all the business about Gil Hoffeld, and jump right to her move to New York. And it had been so good to talk about her children—the guilt she had suffered because of being drunk around them, and now the pain of missing them. While the secretary made some more announcements, she glanced around the big, smoke-filled room. Felicity, just in front of her, mouthed the words, "You were great." Charlie smiled in acknowledgment, and let her eyes wander farther back, to the last row, where, with a bearded man sitting between them, she saw Musette and Gwen. She hadn't realized they were here while she was talking, although Musette, in a bright red dress, was like a flashing neon sign in the tide of black surrounding her.

When the secretary's break was over, people raised their hands to share from the floor. Charlie picked on an arty-looking woman in the middle of the room, who spoke very emotionally about a fight she had had with her daughter. When the woman finished, Charlie made no comment, but chose someone off to the side who went on at length about the ordeal of looking for a job. Charlie forced an expression of sympathy onto her face. She was having trouble concentrating. Had it been a mistake to mention her failing marriage? Neil would kill her if word ever leaked out. And she had more or less admitted that her move to New York was permanent. Suddenly, confronted by a sea of faces and white waving arms, she felt exposed and vulnerable. Any of these people could go out and talk. Give her story to the press. But they wouldn't do that, she thought, choosing a girl with a tattooed wrist in the front row. They couldn't. It was an anonymous program...

There were still a good number of people who wanted to speak when the chairman raised his hand from the back of the room to give her the time's-up signal. "Well, I guess that's it," she said, standing. In a way this was the moment that called for the greatest poise, as she had to step forward and join hands with people in the first row, and start the room off in the Serenity Prayer. "God," she said uncertainly, and to her the word sounded tinny and false.

Grant me the serenity, responded the rest of the room,
To accept the things I cannot change,
Courage to change the things I can,
And wisdom to know the difference.

As she stood there, mouthing the prayer, her hands gripped strongly on either side, she felt such a warm rush of happiness course through her that she wished she could freeze this moment in time forever.

Afterward she was surrounded by people. Tanya, who was heavily perfumed, and who just wanted to give her a quick kiss before rushing off to a party. The girl with the tattooed wrist, who wanted to tell her what an inspiration she had been; she too was struggling to become an artist. A man with white flowing hair who looked as if he were a writer or poet, and who gave her a big hug, and said, "Marvelous sobriety, my dear. Keep it up." Charlie said she would try. Her mouth hurt from smiling so much. She saw Felicity and Musette waiting at the outer edge of the crowd, and wished she could get to them. And then suddenly there was only one person left to talk to, a man who looked vaguely familiar as he walked toward her, pushing a hand through his thick gray hair. In a flash she remembered. Of course. It was the man from the opening she and Musette had gone to in Soho, the one who had been so negative about the Cruz portraits.

"We meet again," he said, smiling. She noticed that he had

a chipped front tooth. He was wearing the same dark clothes he had had on that night at the gallery.

"Yes," she said. "What a coincidence."

"Ah, but in the program we learn there are no coincidences." He glanced at Felicity and Musette, who were standing off to the side. "I see your friends are waiting, so I don't want to keep you. I just wanted to say it was a pleasure hearing you, and to wish you lots of luck."

"Thanks," said Charlie.

He hesitated. "I know we didn't exactly agree about those portraits, but if you're serious about studying art, I'm a good teacher."

"Oh?" said Charlie, surprised.

He grinned so that the little lines at the corners of his eyes deepened. "Well, what's AA for, if not a little networking? Anyway, here's my number, and if you're interested, just give a call." He handed her a small white card, waved his arm in a salute, and walked away.

Charlie stared after him, and then glanced at the card. DENNIS MACLEISH, it said. It listed an address in Brooklyn.

*C*oming out of the church, Musette felt a warm sooty wind push the thin material of her dress against her body, and was reminded of how rumpled she must appear to the others. As if reading her thoughts, Charlie said, "Where've you been all day, Musette? I kept calling you and getting your machine."

"I went to a fashion show at the Marriott. That's why I'm dressed this way."

Charlie glanced curiously at her. "I would have gone with you if you'd told me," she said. "Which designer?"

"Just a bunch of kids from FIT. No one interesting."

"Oh," said Charlie. "Well, where shall we go to eat? I'm starving."

"How about the Coffee Shop on Union Square?" suggested Felicity. "That's always fun."

"Good idea," agreed Musette. "We can get a cab on Sixth Avenue."

As they walked along, three in a row, doing their best to avoid the Village crazies who seemed to be out en masse that night, women with shaved heads and painted skulls, men dressed like weird Biblical characters, Charlie said, "What happened to Gwen? I thought she was coming to dinner with us."

Musette sighed. "It's that husband of hers. There's something really wrong there. She wanted to at least stay and congratulate you, but he kept nagging at her about how hungry he was." She made her voice whiny. "'Come on Gwen, let's get out of here, I'm starved, nah nah nah nah.' I don't give that marriage very long."

"Doesn't sound good," agreed Charlie.

Holding out her arm to signal a cab, Felicity said, "That happens a lot when people get sober."

"What does?" asked Musette.

"The person who's recovering becomes so much stronger than he or she used to be that the whole dynamic of the marriage shifts."

"And then what?" Charlie asked as a cab screeched to a halt.

Felicity opened the door, gesturing to the other two women to climb in ahead of her. When she was inside she said, "And then either the marriage breaks down, or they go to a shrink and start all over again."

Musette, seated in the middle, glanced sideways at Charlie. I'll bet she's wondering which it'll be for her, she thought: reconciliation with Neil, or divorce. With her thigh pressed against Charlie's in its crisp white skirt, she was suddenly intensely aware of the fact that she hadn't showered after making love with Neil three hours earlier, and that she must still reek of sex. She wondered if Charlie noticed, or was on some unconscious level suspicious.

The Coffee Shop was a fifties-style diner, decorated in a funky Afro-Brazilian style, that was dimly lit and noisy and filled with some of the most trendy-looking people in New York. As soon as they walked in the door, a tall, impeccably dressed black woman rushed over and threw her arms around Musette. "Hey baby, it's great to see you!" she said in an extremely deep voice. "Come on, don't tell anyone, and I'll sneak you to a table." She led them to a booth in the back, and as they sat down, Musette murmured to the others, "She's in drag. Isn't that totally amazing? If it weren't for her voice, you'd never know she was a man." Another beautiful black woman brought menus; when they had ordered, Charlie fished around in her jacket pocket and said, "Has anyone ever heard of Dennis MacLeish?" She held up the card he had given her.

"Is he the man you were speaking to just before we left the meeting?" asked Felicity.

Charlie nodded. "It seems he's a painter, and he has this idea that I should study with him."

"That's kind of nervy, isn't it?" said Musette.

"You think so?" said Charlie.

"Well, don't you? Listening to someone's drinking story, and trying to take advantage of them?" Musette could feel her competitive instincts rise straight to the surface.

"Anyway, you don't want to start painting now, do you?" said Felicity. "Surely, you've got enough going on?"

"Well no, not now," agreed Charlie. "But maybe once I move into the house."

"I wouldn't use him as a teacher," said Musette. "He looked pretty seedy to me." She thought of Neil in his beautifully cut clothes, and the man she had seen talking to Charlie, a man in white sneakers and a dark rumpled suit, and thought how lucky she was to be back with her old lover. Everyone else was pale and dull in comparison.

In the excitement of closing on the Brooklyn house, Charlie forgot all about Dennis MacLeish. She moved in on an extremely hot day early in June, and a week later Neil flew up from Washington to meet with her. They hadn't seen each other in several months, and she wasn't prepared for his reaction to the change in her looks.

"Jesus, Charlie. You could be a different person," he said as she showed him around the house. She was wearing a long slim skirt that had a slit up the back, showing her beautiful legs, and a jade green halter top. Her hair was pulled up in a high, girlish ponytail with several strands escaping around her neck.

"How do you mean?" she asked, her cheeks going pink as she felt him stare at her.

"I don't know. Your hair's thicker. And you seem more . . . alive somehow."

She had to smile to herself as he said that. She knew what he saw: now that she had stopped drinking, her skin glowed with health, her eyes shone, and the bitter lines of unhappiness at the corners of her mouth had virtually disappeared.

"You look ten years younger," he added.

"It's because I'm sober," she said.

"You've really done it, haven't you? Gotten off the bottle."

"Yes, I have. It's taken a long time, but I have."

She took him on a tour of the house, which was filled with boxes and packing crates, and then sat him down on a stiff Victorian sofa in the living room. "I'll get us something to drink," she said. "Is iced tea okay?"

"Fine with me."

When she returned, he had removed his jacket and was looking around. The room was vast and had, as yet, almost no furniture in it. Boxed canvases leaned against the bare walls, the windows were uncurtained, and the wide-planked wooden floors had no coverings on them. Because of the tall ceilings, their voices seemed to echo as they spoke. "I'm sorry I can't offer you anything stronger," she said, handing him his iced tea.

"That's all right, I understand." He placed the glass on the floor at his feet, and cleared his throat. "We really should make some plans," he said.

She was quiet, unsure of what to say.

"It's been almost six months since you left home, Charlie."

"So?"

"Originally it was just going to be two weeks. Then you had to stay up here to get sober. Now you've bought this house. What next?"

She reached down for her drink, uncomfortably aware that he could see the dark line of her cleavage beneath her halter top. "Suppose I told you I don't want to come back?" she said.

His face went pale. "What do you mean?"

"What do you think I mean? This marriage has played itself out. That's fairly obvious. It's time we ended it."

Neil gave a bitter laugh. "It doesn't seem as if it's played itself out to me."

"I'd like a divorce," she said, surprised that she had even been able to form the word on her lips.

"You know that's out of the question," he said quickly.

"Oh, come on, Neil!" Angrily she pulled the elastic band out of her heavy hair, pushed the hair up higher off her neck, and twisted the band around it again. "Eventually you'll have to give me one."

He didn't say anything. He seemed to be fascinated by the sight of her large breasts straining against the taut material of her halter top as she raised her hands to her hair. She had a sudden memory of how he used to watch her as she nursed Colin and Petra when they were babies, the softest look of love on his face. Sometimes he would press his lips to the flat, dark nipples and insist on tasting the milk, which he told her was thin and very sweet.

"Neil?"

"Do we have to talk about this now, honey?"

"Yes, we do."

He raised his eyes to hers and she saw a desperate look of sadness in them. "I'm not ready to talk about divorce, Charlie. I'm just not. Let's focus on the children instead. You can have them for the summer, which is what you want, isn't it? I'm not blind—I can see how much you've changed now that you're sober, and I want Colin and Petra to see that, too. It'll be the best thing that ever happened to them."

Charlie felt her spirits soar with happiness. What did she really care about a divorce, as long as she had her children? In her jubilant mood she almost felt like kissing Neil, and he must have sensed that because, as they stood in the doorway just before he left, he grabbed hold of her and began to rub his body against hers. "I want you so much, Charlie," he whispered into her hair. "Can't we just forget about the past few months, and go upstairs and make love?"

"It's not just the past few months," she said, drawing away from him, shocked that he could talk to her this way after the hour they had spent discussing divorce. "It's our whole marriage, and my alcoholism, and your career, and the thing that happened with Gil, and . . . *everything*."

He stared at her, almost as if he didn't comprehend. "I don't know what to do to make things better," he said sadly.

"There's nothing you can do. Just give time time." She smiled at him. "That's an AA saying—you'll have to forgive me; I seem to be full of them. Now get the hell out of here. I have this whole house to unpack."

* * *

Later that night Charlie took a break from her unpacking, made herself a tall glass of iced tea, and called Musette to tell her about the meeting she had had with Neil. "I couldn't believe it," she said, smiling into the phone. "There I was telling him I wanted a divorce, and there he was, staring at my boobs and asking me to go to bed with him!"

"He wanted to sleep with you?" said Musette, her voice hollow with disbelief.

"Yeah, he did. It made me feel—I don't know—kind of tender and sad for him."

"If I were you it would make me feel like puking. He's just manipulating you, don't you see that? He wants to flatter you to get you to quit talking about divorce."

"Maybe," said Charlie. "Frankly, I don't really care as long as I can have my children back."

"Yes," murmured Musette. "That's wonderful."

"Is anything the matter, Musette?"

"I don't feel too well. I think I ate something that didn't agree with me. I'll talk to you tomorrow, okay?"

After hanging up, Musette sat in her living room staring into space, so shaken she could hardly move. So Neil was still interested in Charlie. That made her feel sick with grief, especially after the good time she had given him in bed these past few weeks. Fighting off waves of nausea, she forced herself out of her chair and began to pace the thickly carpeted floor. What a shit he was! After their wild afternoon at the Marriott, he had come up to New York twice to see her. She had bought sexy Victorian underwear, had worked out harder than ever at the gym, had gone to a tanning salon, had even—she paused, staring with indifference at a Ming vase—had Theo Hammond buy some exquisite objets d'art on her behalf. And for what? For nothing. The bastard still wanted his wife.

She felt her heart grow rock-heavy in her chest, and knew that if she didn't do something immediately she would fall apart. Her hands itched to pick up the Ming vase and hurl it to the floor, and she had to force herself to back away, turn around, and race to her bathroom, sobbing as she ran along the hall. In the bathroom she opened the medicine cabinet, reaching blindly for the bottle of Valium and thrusting two pills into her mouth.

After that, breathing quickly, she stared at herself in the mirror. "He's yours," she said firmly. "All yours."

She stayed that way, her hands pressed against the sink, until the Valium began slowly to take effect. Then she went and lay down on her bed. Everything would be all right, she decided, if she could get Neil to take her out in public, instead of only meeting her here in the privacy of her apartment. She wanted the whole world to see them together, their names linked in gossip columns, their pictures all over the press. Once that happened, Charlie would become a relic of the past, and she, Musette, would never have to worry about losing Neil again.

A week after Neil's visit, the children came to stay with Charlie in Brooklyn. After six months on her own, this wasn't easy. She was used to her own tempo, to moving through the day with a care only for herself and her own wishes. A lunch date with Musette, Felicity, or Gwen. An AA meeting. An hour or two wandering around Soho, looking at galleries. In the few weeks she had lived there, she had filled her house with classical music, with the smells of flowers, with a feeling of peacefulness and quiet. But once the children arrived, all this was finished; she was delighted to have them with her, but felt rusty, even inept, as a mother. Her children had changed drastically in the last months; to Charlie they felt like strangers, understandably resentful of a mother who had been a drunk, and then had abandoned them to get sober. Fifteen-year-old Petra slept late and when Charlie tried to rouse her, she was greeted with an angry "Oh, come on, Mom! It's my vacation!" Nine-year-old Colin, on the other hand, followed her around the house from the moment she was out of bed, whining that he had nothing to do. The house was filled with the most awful music, with the heavy smell of Petra's perfume, with the sound of the children arguing, which they did constantly. By the time they had been there half a week, the upstairs bath had flooded, and Petra had made friends with the girl next door and was never home. Colin, still lonely, had discovered the local video store and the thrills of skateboarding. Charlie found herself worrying about them constantly.

She decided to take them to an AA meeting. When she had first gotten sober she had explained to them about her alcoholism. "It's an illness," she had said. "Like diabetes, or a heart condition. Only there's no test for it. One doesn't *know* one's an alcoholic until after lots of heartache and trouble."

"What do you mean?" said Colin. They were at her mother's farm in Pennsylvania, had just come in from a walk in one of the pastures, cast off their muddy boots, and lit a fire in Helene's low-ceilinged, rustic living room. Colin was lying on the floor with one of his grandmother's puppies.

"I mean that the only thing that lets you know you're an alcoholic is that you can't stop drinking. You crave alcohol, although your body is allergic to it and it makes you very sick. It's kind of paradoxical. In my case, the liquor affected my speech—remember how slurry I sounded? And my memory. I would have what are called blackouts, periods when I seemed aware and conscious, but I really had no idea what I was doing. Kind of like sleepwalking."

"I don't remember that, Mom," said Petra.

"No, because I just seemed like a weepy drunken woman. But I'll bet you remember how angry and irritable I was the rest of the time. Remember how I screamed at you once when you wanted me to help you with a Halloween costume?" She had locked nine-year-old Petra out of her room because her head ached so badly, she didn't want to have to deal with her.

Petra nodded.

"Well, what you didn't know, and what I didn't know, was that when I was angry like that I was withdrawing from alcohol. On the one hand my body was worn out from processing the stuff, and on the other it needed more to feel normal and happy. Most people call it a hangover."

"Oh," said Petra, glancing at her nails, which she had just painted a hot bright pink.

"If you're so sick, Mom," said Colin, looking up from his puppy, "how can you get better?"

"The cure is simply not to drink," Charlie said. "And to go to lots of AA meetings."

As soon as the children came to New York, she took them to an anniversary meeting. This was something Felicity advised. "Your children are old enough," she said. "There's no reason why they shouldn't see for themselves what AA is all about." In her short time in AA, Charlie had been to quite a number of anniversary meetings, and she found them cheerful and festive. Cake was served, lights were dimmed down, candles were blown out, and everybody clapped like mad. The celebrant (or celebrants; often there were several) sat in the front, blushing and smiling and accepting gifts of flowers and cards. And the speakers were usually positive and upbeat in what they had to say.

Before going, Charlie warned Petra and Colin not to stare at anyone, not to repeat anything they heard, and not to be too surprised if there were occasional outbursts of anger, tears, or emotion. "Just keep your mouths closed, and listen," she said. "If you have questions, I'll answer them later."

This particular meeting was in a church in Brooklyn Heights. Charlie shepherded her children to seats near the windows, and noted with relief that among the many people who filled the church hall, there appeared to be only one crazy: a man in soiled clothes, who stood in the back, muttering to himself and eating cookies.

Nor was she the only one who had brought children. A trio of little girls, and a boy who was about Colin's age, sat in the front row, and Charlie realized they must be related to the celebrants. Four people sat at the table facing the room. Two— a man and a woman—were celebrating; the others had been chosen by them as speakers. Of these, the first was a man who smiled at the room and said, "What you see here is an extremely grateful recovering alcoholic." For a few minutes he talked about the female celebrant, Susan, who had just completed her first year of sobriety. Colin, bored, started fidgeting in his seat. "Mom," he whispered, "when are we going to have the cake?"

At the very beginning of the meeting the lights had been lowered and a cake had been wheeled in. There had been singing and clapping, and together the celebrants had blown out the candles. Colin, impressed, had been disappointed when the cake had been taken back to the kitchen to be sliced into pieces. Now he whispered, "Do you think there'll be enough for everyone?"

"Yes," whispered Charlie.

"But when will it be served?"

"At the break," whispered Charlie. "Now *shh!*"

On the other side of her, Petra had grown interested in the speaker. He was a thin, wiry, balding man in his early forties, and once he stopped talking about Susan, his voice became loud and angry. Apparently he had gone right down to the bottom in his drinking years. "Booze'll kill you!" he shouted. "Turn you into a raving lunatic." He leaned forward in his chair. "One morning you wake up and what do you see? Not your wife lying next to you—oh no, she's run off long ago, and who can blame her? So . . . what do you see?" He paused, smiling sourly. "You see a lot of fucking little mice and insects scurrying up and down the walls, that's what you see."

Colin gasped. "What's he talking about, Mom?"

"I'll tell you later," whispered Charlie.

"But how come he saw mice?"

"Later!" hissed Charlie.

"Anyway," continued the man. In a tie and jacket, he looked as if he had just come from Wall Street. "There's no one there to tell you those little mice aren't real. So what do you do? Reach for the bottle, of course. A big swig'll take care of everything. Only trouble is . . . you drank up everything you had the night before. All the booze is gone, and now you're really in trouble."

Why, wondered Charlie, had Susan chosen someone quite so grim for an anniversary meeting? But when he got to the end of his story she understood why. The man was an inspiration, a glowing tribute to the wonders of AA. "After I was sober a year," he said, "my wife and children came back to me. A lot of marriages break up when people quit drinking, but in my case . . . well, I guess I was lucky. Now it's four years later, and this guy you see here has just taken every bit of courage he's got and started his own law practice. That's right. And for a man who not *too* long ago did time on the Bowery, that's just plain fucking miraculous!"

The applause was thunderous. Colin whispered, "*Now* are we going to have cake, Mom?"

"Yes, I think so," said Charlie.

"Can you make sure I get a piece with a flower on it?"

To Charlie's relief, he seemed to have forgotten all about the speaker's hallucinatory visions of mice and insects.

Two mornings later, Neil phoned her. "I'm flying up to New York today. I'd like to take the children out to dinner."

"It would be nice if you phoned in advance," said Charlie. "We may have had plans."

"Do you have plans?"

"No."

"All right then. I'll see you around six."

When Neil, usually so punctual, arrived a little disheveled-looking at six-thirty, Charlie was busy with a pair of pruning shears in the garden, and Petra was upstairs taking a shower. Colin excitedly gave his father a grand tour of the house, and then took him to the garden where they had hung a hammock between a fence post and a big flowering mimosa. "Want to lie here and have a drink, Dad?" he asked. "I could bring you some lemonade."

"That would be nice, but I think I'll pass," said Neil. He glanced at Charlie, who was bent gracefully over a rosebush, a large wicker basket at her feet. "There are some things your mother and I need to talk about," he said pointedly.

Colin took the hint and went to his room, where he had a stack of new comic books.

"He's pretty diplomatic," said Neil.

"Yes," said Charlie, tossing a freshly cut rose into the basket. "He's wonderful. Don't you want something to drink? Actually the lemonade isn't bad. We have this new housekeeper, Gloria, who squeezes it fresh."

"Maybe later," said Neil. "Right now I'd just like to stay out here and talk." While Charlie continued to poke at her rosebush, cutting the larger, riper blooms, he sat down on a small stone bench and watched her. At this hour the garden, with its beds of tall colorful flowers, smelled sweetly of the wisteria growing on the back fence.

"I'm pretty pissed off at you," said Neil after a minute.

"Oh? What for?" Charlie dropped her shears, and reached into the pocket of her skirt for her cigarettes.

"You took the children to an AA meeting. I think that's an absolutely asinine thing to do."

"Is it?" said Charlie, coloring. "Why?"

"Oh, for God's sake! That's not a place for children. Colin told me he heard a man talk about mice and insects running up and down the walls. He was scared, and why wouldn't he be—

he's only nine years old. I can't believe you subjected him to that!"

Charlie suppressed her fury. The man with the d.t.'s might have repaired his marriage, but could she save hers even if she wanted to? Neil seemed as hard and uncomprehending as ever. "Did he tell you about the cake and candles?" she asked.

"What?"

"The cake and candles. It was an anniversary meeting. There was a woman there celebrating her first year sober, and *she* had *her* children with her. Younger than Colin, I might add, and none of them seemed scared. Neither, for that matter, did Colin. He gobbled up his cake, and wanted to know if he could come to more meetings with me."

"Well, he can't!" snapped Neil. "If you want the children to stay with you, he can't."

"And Petra?"

"Not Petra either. The last thing our kids need is to be hanging out with a bunch of ex-drunks."

"I'm an ex-drunk, Neil. Remember?" She put her cigarette between her lips, picked up the basket of roses and pruning shears, and placed them both on a table that was covered with small pots filled with herbs. Taking the cigarette from her lips, she said, "You seem to think AA is some sort of seedy place filled only with Bowery bums. Well, it's not. It's very inspirational, and a lot of the people there are just like us. I shouldn't tell you this, but Theo Hammond is in AA. So are a great many highly regarded and well-known people." She crushed her cigarette out in a terra cotta saucer, and studied him thoughtfully. Neil looked a little stunned, perhaps more by her tone than her words. "You know, you ought to go to a meeting or two yourself to see what it's all about."

He didn't answer, and a moment later Petra came waltzing out into the garden in a filmy yellow sundress Charlie had bought for her in a Soho boutique. "Hi, Dad," she said, throwing back her shoulders and attempting to walk like a model. "Like my new dress?"

Charlie, staring at her and thinking how pretty she was, fought down the tiniest wave of resentment. It was just like Petra to come along and steal a scene before the final, clarifying word had been spoken.

That same evening, while Neil and his children were eating in a Chinese restaurant in Brooklyn Heights, Gwen was in her bedroom changing her clothes to go to a meeting. She had been working on her film script all day, going over and over a scene that was giving her trouble, and felt extremely tired and irritable. As she stepped out of her shorts and turned sideways to study herself in the mirror, Walter came in. "You're looking good," he said.

"Thanks." She had lost fifteen pounds, and her body, from all the stretch exercises and aerobics, was very firm.

"Though I kind of prefer you with a little excess flesh." He came over and put his arms around her, rubbing his hands over her belly. "Know what I mean?"

She smiled and gave him a little push. "I've got to get ready," she said.

"Oh? Are you going to a meeting?"

"Yes, and afterwards I'm having coffee with Musette. I've got some scenes I want to go over with her."

His hands tightened on her shoulders. He turned her around so that they were facing each other, and kissed her on the mouth, slowly and rhythmically grinding his pelvis into hers. "You really turn me on," he murmured. "Especially when I see you naked like this."

"Thanks," she said wearily, trying once again to push him away.

"Why don't we get into bed for a little while?"

"Oh Walt, I can't right now. Come on, leave me alone. I'm in a hurry."

She could feel his erection pressing into her and tried to pull away, knowing suddenly she couldn't bear for him to touch her when she had already said no. Sensing that, he gripped her harder, his fingers becoming painful on her flesh. They began to struggle. He had never forced her to have sex before, and she wondered if she shouldn't just give in and get it over with. In her current exhausted state that would be easier than fighting him off. Arching her head back, she saw that his face was white with determination, the dark eyes filled with intense anger and resentment as much as with desire. "You're always in a hurry these days!" he spat out, reaching down and yanking at her panties.

She became so angry that she forgot how tired she was. "Don't you dare, Walter!" she exclaimed.

"Dare what? You're my wife. Or have you forgotten?"

Instinctively she raised her knee to his crotch, but he was too quick for her. He pushed her roughly onto the bed, slapping her hard across the cheek to shock her into lying still. "I can't believe you're doing this!" she yelled, her eyes smarting from the force of the blow. Realizing that nothing was going to stop him, she let her body grow limp and heavy, offering no resistance as he mounted her, just gritting her teeth and praying he would hurry up and get it over with.

When he had finished, he began almost immediately to beg her to forgive him. "I didn't mean it, Gwennie," he said over and over again. "I love you—you know that, don't you?" Without answering, she got slowly off the bed and went to the closet, trying to control her sobs as she yanked a dress from a hanger. Hurrying into the bathroom, she locked the door behind her. After what he had done, she couldn't stand the sight of him. Even hearing his voice made her skin crawl. Pulling the dress over her head, she made a firm decision: she would sleep somewhere else tonight, and she wouldn't return to the apartment unless she had a friend with her for protection. It didn't take a lot of soul-searching to know she never wanted to be alone with this man again.

When Neil brought the children home from dinner, he hung around for a few minutes, talking to Charlie in her front hallway. "I'm sorry if I was harsh before. It doesn't really do either of us any good to argue."

"No, it doesn't," she agreed.

"In fact, I think we should find some way of having a friendlier relationship."

Oh no, not this again, Charlie thought, worried that he would make a pass at her. "I think we're friendly enough for the moment," she said.

"I mean the kind of friendly where we do things together as a family. Maybe take the children on a trip out West at the end of the summer."

"I don't know if I'm ready for that," she said, opening the door and slipping quickly back into the shadows so he wouldn't be able to take her in his arms as he had the last time. "You shouldn't have any trouble finding a cab," she said. Behind her the phone began to ring, but she stayed where she was, knowing Petra would answer it.

"Well, speak to you soon," he said. In a well-cut summer suit he looked trim and youthful, and Charlie felt an unexpected twinge of desire for his clean sexiness, the male authority he seemed to carry so easily.

"Hey Mom," yelled Petra, "Musette's on the phone. She says it's urgent."

"Okay, coming," Charlie called back. "I've really got to go," she said to Neil. In the dim hallway light she saw that his face suddenly wore an anxious expression, and she was reminded of a puppy being put into the street on a cold day. He was alone, after all; Charlie at least had her children, but right now all Neil had was politics—no one in the world really wanted or needed him. Feeling sorry for him, she leaned over and gave him a light peck on the cheek. "Now get out of here," she said, pushing him toward the door.

On the phone, Musette told Charlie there was trouble between Gwen and her husband.

"What sort of trouble?" said Charlie, trying to recall Gwen's husband, whom she had met only once. A man with a dark beard, curly hair, and an air of resentment, the kind of man who consistently sent food back in restaurants.

"They had a fight. There was some physical violence."

"Good lord. Did he hurt her?"

"She's pretty badly shaken up. We need to figure a few things out, and I thought it would be a good idea if we came over and talked to you."

"Of course. Do that. Come right away."

While she was waiting, she made coffee, sent Colin up to bed, and gave Petra permission to sleep next door at her friend Shelley's house. Twenty minutes later the two women were on her doorstep. Gwen looked frail and unsure of herself. She was wearing a mauve dress that gave her skin a yellowish cast, and in the lamplight Charlie saw that a heavy bruise was forming under her left eye. "Jesus!" she exclaimed. "What happened?"

"To put it in a nutshell, he socked me good," said Gwen with a thin attempt at laughter. She sat down heavily on the sofa and leaned her head back as if she was very tired. The bruise beneath her eye had an oily tinge to it, blues and blacks and violets emerging, like the rainbow sheen on a gas spill. Charlie considered her and said, "I'll get the coffee."

Within moments she was back with a tray, which she set on a beautiful black-laquered Korean chest that served as a coffee table. Gwen still sat with her head back and her eyes closed. Over by the piano, Musette was running her fingers softly over the keys. Impatiently, Charlie said, "All right, ladies. How do you want your coffee?"

Gwen took hers black. She stirred at it listlessly and told Charlie about what had happened with Walter. Musette moved over to the mantel, where she smoked a cigarette and peered at framed photographs of Charlie and Neil and the children. When Gwen got to the point in her story where Walter physically assaulted her, she said, "He was like a total stranger. It was as if I didn't exist as a person, a woman, and he was going to do what he was going to do no matter what. I didn't know he had built up so much resentment against me, that's the scary thing. I never want to be near him again."

"Of course not," said Charlie. "What happened then?"

Gwen laughed bitterly. "He got himself all nice and zipped up and began apologizing."

"And what did you do?"

"I was pretty weak. But then the adrenaline started pumping through me, and I managed to pull on this dress, throw some things into a bag, and get the hell out of there."

"He didn't try to stop you?" asked Charlie.

"No. He was in the bedroom crying big crocodile tears when I left."

"Jesus. He needs a shrink," said Musette.

"He already has one," said Gwen. "That's what's so weird." She looked at the other two women, and suddenly her face grew immensely sad, her eyes taking on a new solemnity, as if she had just seen a vision of the richest human gravity and potential. "You know," she said slowly, "in the past, if something like this had happened to me, I would have gone out and gotten drunk. That's exactly what I would have done. Called down to the liquor store for a whole fucking case of scotch, and proceeded to go through those bottles till every last one of them was empty. But now . . . Jesus, I just want to keep my mind clear and deal with this. Know what I mean?"

The other two nodded, although Charlie, remembering the dramatic increase in her consumption of liquor after Gil's death, wondered if she would have been so virtuous. "What are you going to do now?" she asked. "You can't go back to the apartment."

"Well," said Gwen, "I was wondering if I could stay with you for a while, till I get things sorted out. I can't go to my mother's, and Musette's expecting house guests."

"Sure," said Charlie. "But I warn you, it gets noisy around here with the children."

"Children," breathed Gwen, "are just what I need after an experience like this. I think I could use some of their magic and innocence."

As much as she admired Gwen, Charlie was ambivalent about her presence in the house. She had plenty of space, but she herself was just getting used to living in Brooklyn. She wasn't sure she liked the way her children acted around Gwen. Because Gwen was famous and carried herself with quiet authority, Petra seemed more deferential to her than to her own mother, and Charlie overheard her boasting that they had a famous writer living with them. She had to scold Colin several times for sneaking into Gwen's room and playing with her computer. The boy was confused by Gwen's blackness, by her sadness, by the tough language she sometimes used, by her not always private tears. The day their grandmother's driver drove to Gwen's apartment and returned with a carload of luggage, books, electronic equipment, and a little gray cat named Miss Fish, the children sat nervously watching as all these things were brought into the house and carried down to the basement. There they would remain until Gwen was ready to make a permanent move. When the last load had arrived, Charlie, suppressing her fury, confronted Gwen. "I didn't know there would be so *much!*" she said, still trying to sound like a hostess.

"*This?*" Gwen laughed. "It's nothing. I only took the essentials."

"But I don't see why *you* had to be the one to leave. Doesn't he have a place upstate? Couldn't he have gone there?"

Gwen shook her head so fiercely that her hair trembled. "I will never stay in that apartment again," she declared. "Never." Her eyes met Charlie's and she gave her a warm smile of friendship. "I don't know if I'll ever be able to tell you how much I appreciate this. It's so important for me now to be with friends, especially friends from AA."

On the other hand, since Charlie and the children would be away most of the summer, it wasn't altogether a bad thing to have someone living in the house. And Charlie liked Gwen. She was savvy, ironic, and comforting, and they spent several evenings talking late into the night—about Walter, about Neil, about how Musette's dramatic style amused them. Charlie came close to telling Gwen about Gil; to stop herself, she developed a habit of quickly turning personal conversation back to Gwen. For example, it amazed Charlie that Gwen could work with such concentration when her life had just fallen apart.

"But it's not as if it's me who's doing the work," said Gwen.

"What in the world are you talking about?" said Charlie.

They were stretched out on lawn chairs after dinner on Charlie's back deck. It was an evening of low-lying, heavy clouds, unmoving air, black, drooping June leaves. On the table between them burned a citronella candle, and in its flickering light Charlie could vaguely make out the details of Gwen's face: her wry smile, the shine of her eyes.

"I hear the words in my head," explained Gwen. "I'm not conscious of formulating them, or putting them together in sentences, or anything else. I just hear them, and then write them down."

Charlie slapped at a mosquito. "So you really do believe in all that business about communing with a muse? I thought it was just some sort of joke."

"It's no joke to me. Not when it comes to my work."

"And what about AA?"

"You mean the concept of a higher power?"

Charlie nodded.

"Well," said Gwen, "in AA there's a saying that the bottle's bigger than you are, so there has to be something bigger than the bottle. You can call it anything you like—God, or a force of nature, or—"

"I can't cope with that God stuff."

"Oh, I don't mean God in the ordinary sense. Look, Charlie, there was a time, not long ago, when alcohol had more power over you than anything else in your life. It had more power over you than the love of your children—think of that."

Charlie was silent.

"Well," continued Gwen, "now the alcohol is gone from your life—at least we hope it is—and in its place is something much bigger, much more magnificent."

"Oh really," said Charlie. "And what is that?"

Gwen leaned toward her, her eyes looking moist and saucer-like in the candlelight. "AA. All the people clapping in the rooms. Their stories, and the energy created by their stories. The incredible spirit they emit as they come together and help one another defy the compulsion to drink."

"It's the first time I've heard it put that way," Charlie said wonderingly, her voice sounding soft and thoughtful in the dark.

"Well, to me that's the core of AA. You don't have to believe in God—just in the healing power of two or more recovering alcoholics talking about booze."

Above them a light went on, and a window opened. The heavy June stillness was suddenly broken by a loud blast of rock music.

"Good God," said Charlie. "There's Petra. I'd better go up and tell her to turn down the music." She rose from her chair, but before leaving she said, "Thanks, Gwen."

"For what?"

"For showing me what people mean when they talk about God."

$\mathfrak{M}$usette sat naked at her vanity table, her slim body a honey gold from the summer sun, her sinewy back arched as she ran a silver-backed brush through her hair.

"I love watching you do that," said Neil, who was lying on the bed.

"Oh? Well, then I'll do another hundred strokes," Musette giggled. She leaned forward so that the heavy mane of hair fell over her beautiful face, and her spine and small dimpled rump were entirely exposed; she brushed her hair that way for a moment before once again leaning back, curving her neck luxuriantly so that her hair flowed down past her shoulders.

"Everything you do makes me happy," Neil said in a hoarse voice.

Her eyes were closed as she steadily drew the brush through her hair, but she heard him get up off the bed and walk toward her. When she sensed him standing just behind her, she opened her eyes a fraction; he was watching her closely in the mirror, very aroused. He took her head between his hands and pressed it back against his belly, running his fingers along her throat. "Oh Neil," she moaned, dropping the brush to the floor.

"Neil what?" he whispered. "Is there something you'd like me to do to you?"

"Whatever you want," she whispered back. "Whatever makes you happy."

He cupped his hands over her small breasts, pinching at her nipples and running his nails in small circular movements over her sternum. Then, slowly, he pulled her up and guided her in front of him to the bed. She wanted him so badly that she stumbled almost as if she were drunk. Her mouth was open, slack with desire, and without saying anything he pushed her down on her stomach and entered her from behind, moving slowly and rhythmically until her body responded in a series of tight spasms. It thrilled her that she could not see his face, that she was completely in his power, almost a slave to him, as he thrust himself more and more deeply into her. At last he pushed her over the edge, and she couldn't control her screaming or the thrashing of her hips as she was caught in a long, pulsating orgasm. From a long way off she heard him shout her name— "Maggie! Maggie!"—as he reached his own wild climax; then, for a few moments, crushed beneath the weight of him, she felt as rich and complete as she had in the early days of her addiction to cocaine.

Afterward she lay curled up in his arms. It was nine o'clock in the evening. An hour before they had had a light dinner of sandwiches and fruit, and now both of them felt peaceful and happy. "You're not going home tonight, are you?" she asked, reaching up to stroke the hollow of his neck, which always made him quiver, and then running her hand along the day's bristly growth of beard on his chin. She adored the feel of his stubble against her fingers.

"I'm afraid I have to."

"Oh. I thought since Charlie has the children..." She let the rest of the sentence hang. Talking about Charlie made him uncomfortable, and she knew she had to be careful.

"I don't think it's a great idea for me to stay here," he said, taking her hand and pressing it to his lips.

"Why not?" she asked softly.

He grinned at her. "Because it might become a habit."

"Nothing wrong with that." She sat up, her golden eyes studying his face closely. "Neil...?"

"Uh-hunh?"

"What's going to happen to your marriage? It's only fair for me to know."

"Yeah, I suppose it is," he said, sighing. "The answer is, I don't know. Charlie wants a divorce, but I'm not prepared to give her one. She also wants to keep the children, which is fair—they're better off with her right now. Beyond that, I'm unwilling to make any decisions."

Neil's statement put her at a distance, almost as if she were a reporter at one of his press conferences. There was a firmness in his voice that told her she'd better not ask any more questions. She saw him glance at the bedside clock, and quickly slid down on the sheets, planting a soft kiss on his lips, and running her long red nails against the muscular flesh of his thighs. She knew that she could ensure with her body what she could not demand otherwise: that he stay the night.

Early in July Charlie moved to her mother's farm in Pennsylvania. There had been a change in her life: Neil had agreed to let her have the children on a full-time basis, provided, over the next year, there be no discussion whatsoever about divorce. "I mean none," he said when he presented her with this option.

"All right," Charlie agreed. Felicity had persuaded her that she was too newly sober to consider divorce, that she should try to change as little in her life as possible. She would see a lot of Neil now; it was his wish to visit the children every other weekend, although he had promised he would never violate her independence by asking to spend the night.

She traveled up to the city every other week, leaving the children in Pennsylvania with their grandmother. Gwen was still at the house in Brooklyn. Charlie herself might have to wait a year before taking legal steps to dissolve her marriage, but Gwen had already filed for a divorce. She was in fine high humor. Her screenplay was coming along nicely, and she had found an apartment on the Upper West Side that she was thinking of buying. She took Charlie to see the apartment one night, and afterward they went out for dinner.

"So—did you like it?" asked Gwen.

"The apartment? Yes, I think it's perfect."

"But you wouldn't live there yourself, would you?"

The apartment was on 104th Street between West End Avenue and Broadway. It had a tiny little roof garden, and was very bright and cheerful, but in Charlie's opinion it was too noisy; and she didn't like the neighborhood, which was full of derelicts and junkies. Avoiding Gwen's eyes, she said, "Well, you're talking to a girl who grew up on..." And then she stopped. They were in a Mexican restaurant on 100th and Broadway, a place where she would never have dreamed she would see anyone she knew. But sitting across the room, with her back to them, was Tanya Hendricks, and in Tanya's hand was a glass of beer. "Jesus," whispered Charlie. "You won't believe who's here, or what she's drinking."

Gwen turned around, stared for a moment, and turned back. "Who's that she's with?" she asked in a disturbed voice.

Opposite Tanya sat a big, dark, rough-looking man whose unbuttoned shirt revealed a tanned chest and a thick black tangle of hair.

"I don't know," said Charlie, suddenly feeling ill. "That *is* beer she's drinking, isn't it?"

"Yes, look—the waiter's bringing another bottle."

"Oh lord, what do we do?"

"Nothing," said Gwen. "We carry on with our dinner, and we make as little fuss as possible."

For the rest of the meal the two women did their best to avoid looking at Tanya. It wasn't easy. Charlie's eyes were continuously drawn to the hand lifting the beer stein, the curly head thrown back in laughter. It seemed to her that Tanya's husky voice was singled out from all the other voices, and that it was thick and sloppy; that her companion, leaning over the table, took the kind of liberties men only took with drunken women; that her body sat a little too stiffly in its chair. But these things could have been her imagination. When Tanya rose to leave, her gait seemed steady, and her cheeks were flushed with happiness. She passed through the door without seeing them.

In the morning Charlie called her to make a date.

"Oh, Charlie, is that you?" said Tanya in a sleepy voice. "I haven't spoken to you in ages. It's been too long, hasn't it?"

"Yes, it has," agreed Charlie. "In fact that's why I'm calling. I wanted to invite you over for dinner this evening."

"This evening? Let me think a minute... All right. Yes, that would be good. I've never been to your house, have I?"

"No," said Charlie with an uneasy laugh. "Now listen, are you ready for the address? You'll take a cab, of course."

Their date was for seven o'clock. Charlie had her housekeeper prepare curried chicken breasts and a green salad and strawberries with fresh whipped cream, but Tanya never showed up. After an hour, Charlie phoned Tanya's apartment. The line was busy. She tried again fifteen minutes later—still busy. Half an hour later she checked again, and the operator told her there was trouble on the line. Frightened, Charlie decided to go to Tanya's in person.

By now it was after nine o'clock. She left a note for Gwen, who had gone to a meeting, and rushed into the street, looking for a cab. Tanya lived on East Sixty-eighth Street, in an apartment she had inherited from an aunt. Normally it would have taken twenty minutes to get there, but tonight, in sweltering weather, every car in the city seemed to have overheated. When the taxi finally pulled up in front of Tanya's building, Charlie threw twenty dollars at the driver, telling him to keep the change, and rushed into the lobby. After the heat of the city, the air inside was shockingly cold. A doorman behind a large console asked her whom she wished to see.

"Mrs. Hendricks in Nine G."

"Mrs. Hendricks? Just a minute."

He punched some buttons on the switchboard. In the cool air Charlie shivered, suddenly aware that her silk blouse was damp beneath the arms.

"Doesn't seem to be an answer," said the doorman.

"You mean she's not there? She must be."

"I haven't seen her all evening."

"How long have you been here?"

"I came on at four."

Charlie glared at him. "Look, I know she's upstairs. I've been trying her for hours, and I think there may be a problem."

He scratched at his head beneath his visored cap. "I don't know what I can do about it, ma'am."

"You can call the super."

This took some negotiation. When the super finally arrived,

he looked annoyed, as if someone had just woken him from a nap. He kept blinking at Charlie, and he muttered angry Spanish sentences beneath his breath. "You want me to take you to Nine G?" he said. "All right, I take you." They rode the elevator in silence. When they reached the ninth floor, he strode ahead of her and rang Tanya's bell a full twenty seconds before using his key.

Inside the lights were on, and from the far end of the apartment came the sound of a TV. Charlie called, "Tanya? Tanya!" but got no answer.

"She's probably at the back," said the super. They moved down the hall, and everything seemed as it always was in Tanya's messy household: a jumble of mail on the hall table, shoes kicked off on the floor, a pile of clothes from the cleaners on a chair, still in their protective plastic. This gave Charlie a feeling of hope. But at Tanya's bedroom door her heart faltered. Through it she could hear the smooth, murmurous sound of the TV, and above that something else—a woman talking and singing to herself in a thin, high-pitched voice.

"See—she's there," said the super.

"We'd better go in," said Charlie, opening the door without bothering to knock.

The room was in terrible disorder, with a trail of spilled powder on the carpet, an overturned vase, a whole drawerful of clothes on the floor, photographs everywhere. In dismay Charlie stared at the mess, and then at Tanya, who lay on the bed, among half a dozen colorful throw pillows, holding a glass of whiskey to her chest. She wore a green silk kimono whose sash had come untied, and beneath it Charlie could see her big pink breasts and the white mound of her stomach.

The super made a disgusted sound in his throat. "I could have told you she'd be like this," he said. He shook his head, backing from the room, muttering to himself in Spanish. "It's the same story for weeks now." Charlie heard him slam the front door behind him and turned her attention back to Tanya, who was eyeing her suspiciously. "Oh, Tanya," she breathed. "What happened?"

"What do you mean . . . what happened?" said Tanya, but very slowly, wrapping her tongue with great care around each word. "I'm sick . . . that's all. How'd you get in here?" She sat up and fumblingly put her glass on the night table, sliding a lamp in front of it to hide it, as if Charlie hadn't yet seen it was scotch. Then, supporting herself on the pillows, she heaved herself off the bed. Her kimono was still open; it was long on her, and as she walked toward Charlie, its soiled green hem dragged along the floor.

"The super let me in," said Charlie.

"Really? Well, that's rotten. That stinks. I should report him to the board."

"Tanya, don't you remember you were supposed to have dinner with me? You were supposed to come to my house?"

"Sure, sure," Tanya enunciated carefully. A crafty look entered her face. "But I got sick. The doctor gave me cold medicine, and said the most important thing for me to do was sleep." With one hand she closed her kimono over her breasts, and with the other she grabbed Charlie's arm and began to propel her from the room. "And that's why I want you to leave. Right now!"

Her grip, for someone so drunk, was surprisingly strong.

Charlie pushed her off. "No," she said. "You need help."

"I don't need help. Not your kind of help. I need to sleep. That's what the doctor said. Now get the fuck out of here!"

"But Tanya, this is insane!"

They were in the hall, and there they did a little tug-of-war. Charlie very firmly removed Tanya's hand from her arm and started into the kitchen with the intention of making coffee.

"I didn't say you could go in there," slurred Tanya, getting behind Charlie and giving her a hard shove.

"Hey, quit that!" yelled Charlie, whirling around. She had to give up. There was a look of hatred and defiance in Tanya's eyes that she couldn't bear, and the smell of liquor rising from her friend's skin was revolting. Taking thin, shallow breaths, she allowed herself to be led to the front door, knowing that the instant she was out of the apartment she would burst into angry tears. She didn't want to think that if Tanya had gotten drunk, the same thing could happen to her. And so, with real hostility, she pulled her arm from Tanya's, saying, "Your medicine stinks. If I were you I'd change doctors." She didn't wait for Tanya to answer. Already her eyes were swimming with tears, and she ran from that apartment as if it was filled with sickness.

From a pay phone in the street she called Felicity, and in a choked voice said, "Something awful's happened. I've got to come see you right away."

"What is it?" said Felicity, alarmed.

"Tanya. I found her drunk."

"Oh, Christ! Where are you? Never mind—just jump in a taxi."

Felicity was waiting for her at the door, and she gave her the sort of hug someone would give a person who'd just witnessed a terrible disaster. "I'm sorry," she said. "Let's go in and have some tea. Michael's upstairs asleep."

At eleven-thirty at night, Felicity's house, even in summer, gave out cozy, creaking sounds. In the dining room a big grandfather clock ticked somnolently, and from the mantel came the honeyish smell of freesias. The two women sat down, and Charlie was conscious of the whirring of a fan, and of moths beating against the tall screened windows. Until walking through Felicity's door, she had felt driven by a breathless panic, but now a feeling of calm began to wash over her. Felicity gave her a cup of tea and said, "Drink this. It's warm and it'll soothe you."

After Charlie had taken a few sips, she said, "All right. Now tell me what happened."

Charlie described the whole chain of events, and when she had finished, Felicity exclaimed, "But how awful for you! Why didn't you call me? I would have gone with you."

"I don't know," said Charlie. "I guess I didn't think of it. I was so afraid she'd had an accident."

With a patient sigh, Felicity rose and wandered over to the other end of the table, where she absentmindedly pushed at a pile of books and papers. "Do you know who her sponsor is?" she asked after a minute.

"No. She may have told me, but I've forgotten."

"Pity . . . Well, there's nothing much we can do about it then."

"What do you mean nothing?" said Charlie, astonished. "Aren't we supposed to try to help her? Isn't that the whole point?"

"No," said Felicity. And then, firmly, she repeated herself: "No."

"But—"

"Look, Charlie, Tanya knows exactly where to go when she's ready to stop drinking. She's not ready, that's the point, and right now the only person you can help is yourself. I hope you understand that. Because you *can't* help Tanya. Only she can do that, and if you go up there and start making coffee and throwing out bottles, the chance of your being pulled down with her is very great."

"All right, *I* can't, but couldn't you? You've been sober for years."

"Not me either," said Felicity. "I don't know her, and I wouldn't dream of putting myself into a situation like that. It's just too dangerous." She sat down and looked thoughtfully at Charlie. "The best you can do is call someone from her family. Otherwise, my advice to you is stay out of it."

In a low, unhappy voice, Charlie said, "What I want to know is why? Why'd she do it? Jesus, she's the one who got *me* sober." That Tanya could slip—Tanya, who had been so relentlessly firm with her—terrified her more than anything else.

"Because she stopped going to meetings," said Felicity. "Oh, that may not be the actual reason. Anything could have triggered it. But when people slip like that, it's because they've lost contact with AA. They think, 'Oh, I can have just one drink.' They think, 'Maybe I'm not really an alcoholic after all.' They delude themselves, and then pretty soon they're on that horrible merry-go-round all over again." She smiled at Charlie. "The point is, to an alcoholic taking a drink is as natural as drawing breath, and the only way to keep from drinking is to go to meetings. You understand? You'll be safe as long as you go to meetings."

"You're sure?" said Charlie.

"Yes, of course I'm sure."

But Charlie was worried. In the sleepy Pennsylvania town where she was spending the summer there was only one meeting a week, and days would pass with her in dangerous proximity to her mother's liquor cabinet. She would play tennis and afterward she would think, An ice cold beer would be terrific right now. At dinner she would watch her mother's guests drink wine, and feel that old, almost lusting thirst at the back of her throat. And at bedtime there was the empty space on her night table where she used to keep a brandy bottle and snifter. Sometimes, in the weeks that followed, as she was drifting off to sleep in that lonely Pennsylvania farmhouse, she felt as if the ghost of that bottle were calling to her, and then she would force herself to remember Tanya's slow, angry, drunken voice, and her messy pink breasts beneath the open kimono. "No, it won't happen to me," she would whisper to herself. "I won't let it."

And the next day, no matter what was planned, or who was there, or what was expected of her, she would get in her car and drive up to the city to go to a meeting.

*J*n the middle of August Musette decided to spend two
weeks with her agent, Harry Langhart, who had a house
on Cape Cod. It seemed to her that everything in her life
was at a standstill. Neil, who was still treating her as his
secret mistress, had taken his children on a trip to San Francisco
and would be gone till the end of the month. She had begged
him to let her fly there separately, staying in the same hotel and
meeting him clandestinely in the middle of the night, but he had
refused. Charlie had impulsively flown off to join some friends
on a yacht off the coast of Sardinia. And Gwen, busy with the
move into her new apartment, had put off writing the last few
scenes of her screenplay until she was more settled.

She needed to be with Harry to discuss production plans for
Homegirl. When she had first told him about the project, he
had been dumbfounded. "Jesus, how'd you do that? Gwen
Thomas has always refused to let anyone get near her work."

"Let's just say I have the right touch," Musette said with a
complacent smile.

"Well, I hope you're up to this, Maggie. It's a tremendous
undertaking, and you're going to have to attract a lot of money.
And if you screw it up . . ."

"Yes?"

He looked at her bleakly. "You can kiss your career good-bye forever."

"It seems to me you said I had more or less done that already."

They spent hours talking about casting and film crews and how Musette should go about setting up a production company. She had brought the first part of the screenplay with her, and Harry, reading it, whistled and said, "God, this is really hot!"

She also talked to him a little about her private life. Musette had never done well with friendships, particularly friendships with women, and of all the people she knew, Harry was the closest to being a confidant. She felt safe and at home in his rambling house with its French provincial furniture, colorful scatter rugs, primitive paintings, and large baskets of fruit and dried flowers. He loved to cook; in a corner of his kitchen he had placed a rattan couch so that guests could sit and chat with him while he worked at the stove. One afternoon, as he was making a bouillabaisse, Musette told him about her love affair with Neil. Harry whistled over that just as he had over Gwen's film script. "Playing with fire, aren't you? I mean, the man's going to run for president."

"Yeah, but that doesn't mean I shouldn't go to bed with him."

Harry looked up from chopping onions. He was wearing khaki cutoffs and a white Izod T-shirt, and his blue eyes were smarting from the onions. "What about his wife?" he asked. "You don't think he's going to leave her for you?"

Musette shrugged. "I don't want to go into details, but Neil and I have a long history. Anyway, the marriage stinks."

"I know that."

She peered at him. "How? From reading the papers?"

He picked up his knife and began chopping again. "I never believe anything I read in the papers. I know it because one Sunday morning, a little over a year ago, I saw Charlie Gallagher coming out of our local deli with a man named Gil Hoffeld, and it was clear there was something going on between them."

"That was up here?" Musette's heart skipped a beat.

He nodded.

"The guy has a place here, or what?" It was urgent that she know it all.

"Used to. He died in a sailing accident last October."

She leaned forward on the couch. "Wait a minute. Let me get this straight. How do you know Charlie wasn't just a casual weekend guest?"

"I watched them go from the deli to their car. I knew who Charlie was, and it seemed odd that she should be with someone like Gil, who was kind of crude. After he put the groceries in the trunk, he grabbed hold of her in a way that, believe me, had nothing to do with casual."

"And you're sure the woman was Charlie?"

Harry hated having his memory challenged. "Of course I'm sure. I remember she pushed him away as if she was embarrassed."

Musette had a sudden recollection of Charlie's white angry face at the art gallery months ago when she had denied ever having had a love affair. Suppressing a tight smile, she said, "Tell me about the sailing accident. What happened?"

"I don't really know. I was in L.A. when I heard about it, and I never followed up on the story. All I know is he'd been drinking heavily and somehow managed to fall overboard." He swept the finely diced onions onto a plate, rinsed his hands, and wiped them on a dishcloth. "Aren't you glad you stopped drinking?" he asked grimly.

Determined to learn more about Charlie's affair with the drowned man, Musette made a dinner date with her as soon as she returned to the city in early September. They met in an Italian restaurant in the East Seventies, and both made a production of kissing one another on the cheek. "God, you look great!" said Charlie, admiring her friend's sun-streaked hair and tanned skin.

"So do you," said Musette, thinking to herself that the Charlie who sat across the table from her now really was different from the tense, uptight woman she had met half a year ago. That woman had been angry and judgmental. This one was far softer, with a ready smile on her lips and an open and eager spirit. She had had her hair cut in Paris, and the chestnut waves fell prettily to the nape of her neck. Her makeup was different, too: the eyebrows had been thinned, and the splash of freckles across her upturned nose now seemed girlishly becoming. She wore a bright red lipstick, and her clothes were chic and youthful. Long turquoise earrings grazed her shoulders.

"Like my new style?" said Charlie, aware of being studied.

"Yeah. What happened?"

Charlie shrugged. "Can't run around Soho looking like a dowdy old matron. By the way, you should come over and see some of my latest acquisitions. I swear my house looks more like an art gallery than a home."

"Do your children mind that?"

Charlie gave a low chuckle. "What do they care? They're so busy with their new school that I could move out all the furniture and they wouldn't notice."

They ordered a bottle of San Pellegrino, and a big plate of antipasto. For the second course each decided to sin and have lasagna. Over coffee Musette said, "You know, there's something I wanted to ask you."

"Ask," said Charlie, waving away smoke from her freshly lit cigarette.

"Have you ever heard of a guy named Gil Hoffeld?"

Charlie's skin turned deathly white. The freckles stood out against it like little flakes of soot. She drew in her breath sharply and said, "No. Why?"

"Just wondered. My agent said he once saw you with him up on the cape."

"Well, your agent must need glasses. I haven't been on the cape in years."

"It seems this Gil Hoffeld died in a boating accident."

"Did he? I'm sorry to hear that. But since I never met the guy, it really has nothing to do with me." Her voice was loud now, the angry voice of the old Charlie. People at the adjoining tables stared as she stabbed out her cigarette and reached into her purse for her compact. "Call the waiter, will you? It's late and I want to go home."

"All right," Musette said quietly.

In the morning Musette asked her secretary, a woman named Patsy Shroeder who came to the apartment twice a week, to find out everything she could about the death of Gil Hoffeld.

"Who's he?" asked Patsy.

"An acquaintance. I'm a little suspicious of the way he died, that's all. You should be able to get information from the Boston papers. Also the Cape Cod weeklies."

"Will do," said Patsy cheerfully.

Then she tried, without success, to reach Gwen. "This is the Thomas residence," said the recorded message on Gwen's machine. "Leave a message at the sound of the tone, and I'll get back to you."

"I'm sick of leaving messages," growled Musette. "Have you died or something? What the hell's going on?" She slammed down the phone. She had been calling Gwen every other day since her return from the cape.

An hour later the phone rang. "What's going on is this, baby," Gwen crooned in her husky voice. "I've moved into a new apartment. I'm trying to get ready to teach a course up at Columbia. And I'm doing my best to avoid Walter, who has a habit of calling me up late at night to tell me what a bitch I am."

"Sorry," said Musette. "Well, here's some good news. A lot of people are interested in backing the film. How's it going?"

"Five more scenes and I'm done."

"Great! Want me to read anything?"

"Not yet. I'll call you in about two weeks. Oh, and we should get our agents talking. Want to start setting that up, baby?"

Over and over again during the summer and early fall, Gwen gave herself little pep talks about how strong and brave she was. That bastard did an awful thing to you, she would say, staring at her thin face in the mirror. No cause for misery or regret, baby. You've just got to pick up the pieces of your life and carry on.

And yet, when she stepped back from it, she saw that her life was a ragged, dark dream she didn't understand. She kept herself busy—that helped—but sometimes, as she was unpacking, or putting books on shelves, or getting dressed to go out for a meal, she wondered who the person was inside this whirl of activity. And then she would want to stop everything and lie down on her bed, be very still. Eventually she began to do just that, and she became strangely aggressive about guarding her time and privacy, breaking dates with friends, ignoring the phone when it rang, disregarding her answering machine. She left letters unopened, didn't return messages, and saw only a handful of people: her sponsor, her lawyer, her agent, some colleagues at Columbia. Walter was continually calling her up or ringing her doorbell, wanting to get together and discuss what had happened, and she knew that some of her new reclusiveness was a reaction against him.

But she continued writing. And she went to meetings—not her usual ones in the Village or on the Upper East Side, but new ones where no one would know her. One evening she ventured into a meeting not far from where she lived, and she was shocked to see that all the people there were black. Not the well-heeled, dignified, God-fearing blacks who had been her mother's churchgoing friends when she was growing up, but street blacks: poor, nasty-looking, lower class.

The meeting was already in full swing, and Gwen wondered if she should stay. In a beautiful Missoni dress, with a soft leather bag hanging over her shoulder, she didn't feel safe. The people looked like muggers and thieves. The speaker was in his late teens or early twenties—it was hard to tell because he wore pitch-black sunglasses, and she couldn't see his eyes. His hair was in a brutal flat top, his voice was jivey, soft, seductive, and on his feet he wore enormous white Nikes with the laces untied. He sat, almost sullenly, with his legs stretched out before him, and Gwen had trouble catching what he said. But that was all right—she was leaving.

Thank God she had chosen an aisle seat. Quietly, stooping a little—half expecting whispers of "Look, ain't that Gwen Thomas, the writer?"—she stood and, in her French designer sandals, tiptoed to the door. She was sweating. Beneath her silk dress, her sides were wet, and she could feel beads of perspiration on her forehead. She couldn't wait to get out of here and into the cool breeze of the street, among the throngs of people moving up and down Broadway. But at the door a hand reached out, and a voice said softly, "Hey baby, you ain't leavin' yet..."

It was a woman of about fifty. She was tall and stern-faced, with a big sweep of iron-gray hair that sat stiffly on her forehead. Dangling from her ears were two enormous gold-plated dollar sign earrings. She had large breasts and very dark skin, and Gwen instantly knew better than to disappoint her. "No, I—"

"'Cause you ain't heard nothin' yet, so you stick right here by me."

It was true—Gwen hadn't heard anything yet. Whispering that her name was Audrey, the woman put a cup of coffee in Gwen's hand and nudged her into a chair. Gwen felt like a prisoner. She looked around her. Rows and rows of smiling black faces. There must have been sixty or seventy people there, and every one of them looked as joyous as if the Lord himself had come down from his throne to speak to each of them directly. And all because of the surly young man in the sunglasses and white sneakers. He would say, "There was a time I used to break into people's houses, smash up everything of no use to me, but I don't do that no more because I got this here fellowship."

And everyone in the room would clap, and shout: "We hear you, man! Amen! Amen!"

He would say, "I've been in prison, but now that I've got these Twelve Steps to guide me, I can rest assured I won't never go there no more!"

And there would be cries of "Hallelujah!"

He would say, "The Third Step tells us to turn our lives and our will over to the care of the God of our understanding, and I know if I do that every day—*every day!*—my life is gonna be just fine..."

Whistles and cheers.

Crazily, Gwen found herself cheering along with everyone else. She couldn't help it. She understood only half the references the speaker made, but the waves of energy and excitement that pulsated through the room caught hold of her, too, and she felt a joy rising in her chest that sent shivers to her hands and feet. With her bag clutched to her side, she clapped and cheered and joined hands with her neighbors as they all said the Lord's Prayer. It was the most sonorous rendition of the prayer she had ever heard, and when it was over people embraced one another hard, some of them with tears in their eyes. Gwen allowed herself briefly to be held to the breast of the woman named Audrey, who patted her back and said, "Listen to me, baby, I'm gonna give you my phone number, and if ever you need me, you just call, hear?"

Shortly afterward Gwen began an AA Fourth Step, the step most dreaded by recovering alcoholics since it involved a "searching and fearless moral inventory" of one's life. She didn't know what prompted her to do this. One night, without giving much thought to it, she sat down at her kitchen table with a yellow pad and wrote, "I was born in New York City forty-four years ago. My parents, who came from Jamaica, were very poor, and they had to struggle hard to give me the things they thought any bright young American child should have. Even a child who was black..."

That first night, in her small, dense scrawl, she covered ten pages. The next evening she sat down again, and the result was another ten pages. Within a week she had written forty pages, and within three weeks she had covered most of her life. Whew, she thought when she was finished, I really had a lot of stuff to unload. As far as she knew, most people only wrote a handful of pages listing their strengths and weaknesses.

She locked the pages away in her filing cabinet. She felt as if she had learned something vitally important, but she wasn't sure yet what it was, or how it could be of use to her. The expanse of her life—her childhood, her parents' trials, her writing, and her marriage to Walter—now stretched behind her, all in place, like a rough and curving road, and she could actually bear to look back at it. The next step was to share what she had written with her sponsor, but she was still in her reclusive phase and didn't feel up to it. Her best energy had to go into finishing the remaining scenes of her screenplay. Other than that, all she wanted to do was sit in the cozy white-and-yellow kitchen of her new apartment, drinking innumerable cups of tea and stroking her little cat, Miss Fish.

And dreaming...not of anything specific, but vague amorphous dreams. The screenplay was almost finished, and she wasn't sure what she would do next. A new novel? Short stories? It frightened her to be so uncertain, and the most frustrating part of it was that she felt bits and pieces of an idea, fragments of a story pressing against her brain. She would take long walks, hoping the story would knit itself together, but all she saw were floating, disparate images of her family. Her father leaving the house carrying a lunch pail. Her mother wearing men's shoes to work because they were more comfortable. Herself as a little girl hurrying through the streets, tensing her shoulders against the vicious remarks of local children.

Sometimes, during her walks, she would stop in at what she thought of as "that black meeting." She had returned there several times because... But she couldn't think why exactly. Only that, after the years of being Gwendolyn Thomas, best-selling author, it was a relief to put aside her persona, and become just a black person whom no one particularly noticed among other black people. One night, after the speaker had stepped forward, holding out his hands, and said: *"Whose Father?"* and the room had responded with a deep, happy: *"Our Father!"* moving on then into the Lord's Prayer, a man came up to her and said, "Hey babe, how's it goin'?"

The prayer was over, people had finished hugging and embracing, and were now putting away chairs, emptying ashtrays, looking for their jackets. Gwen stared at the man. She had never seen him before, or if she had, hadn't noticed him. He was about her age, perhaps a little older, wearing blue jeans and a black sweatshirt; his hair, instead of being in a stylish flat top, was rounded and woolly. His skin, which had a reddish mahogany tinge to it, was as shiny and lustrous as a piece of well-oiled wood, and his eyes were flat and black, the whites slightly inflamed as if he had been drinking. Gwen sniffed at the air, but there was no telltale odor of liquor. "I don't believe I know you," she said.

"No, but *I* know *you,*" said the man, holding his fingertips delicately to his chest, and then flipping his hand over and gesturing at her with a yellowy-pink palm. "I know you."

"Oh," said Gwen, her heart sinking. She dug her hands down into the pockets of her jeans, feeling for her keys. She had no wish to talk to this man. Across the room, through a haze of cigarette smoke, she saw Audrey with her big iron-gray sweep of hair, and began to move toward her.

"Wait," said the man. "I ain't done talking."

"Yeah?" said Gwen. "Well, you don't seem to have much to say."

"I got this to say," said the man. "I read your books."

Gwen's heart sank even further. If this man had read her books, there was nothing to stop him from telling everyone at the meeting who she was. She turned and faced him unsmilingly. "Look," she said, "this is an anonymous program. I want to be private here. Understand?"

Once again he held his hands out to her, yellowy palms up. "Hey baby, don't fret. Everyone feels the same way you do. How long you been coming round?"

He was standing quite close to her, and now she could smell his after-shave, which was strong and sweet, and the coffee and cigarettes, heavy on his breath. "I don't see that that's any concern of yours," she said.

He laughed. "My, my, ain't we little Miss Snob," he said, and his eyes, which had been a flat mud black, sharpened and seemed to cut through her. "And that's something because, you know, I gotta tell you, I really like your books."

"Well good, I'm glad," said Gwen. "But that still doesn't give you the right to know anything personal about me."

People were milling around them. "Hey John!" someone yelled, and the man turned and yelled back, "Hey bro'—what's happenin?" to a flat-topped, swaggering youth in a leather jacket. Then he turned back to Gwen. "Oh come on, lady. This is AA. Sooner or later we all get to know personal things about each other."

"Yeah? And what's your personal thing?" she snapped, immediately regretting it. She wanted to get away from him, not stand here listening to his life story.

"My personal thing," he said, "is that I once spent three years in prison." Her eyes must have widened slightly, because he laughed and said, "Never kept company with scary low-life dudes like us before, have you?"

"I've kept company with all sorts of people. Now if you'll excuse me ..." She pushed past him and walked quickly to the door that led upstairs to the street. She wouldn't come back here again so soon, she decided. She would miss Audrey, who gave her a warm hello every time she entered the church basement, but she didn't want to be bothered by some creep like that John whatever-his-name-was. Wasn't worth the effort. At the top of the stairs she zipped her jacket and glanced behind her. There he was in the stairwell. She heard his low laughter and his ghostly voice saying, "Sure I'll excuse you, baby. You give me a good reason and I'll excuse you all you need." Annoyed, Gwen opened the door and hurried out into the cool October night.

One golden Sunday in early October Musette was pushed into a mood of angry despair when Neil called and canceled their date for that evening. "You can't do this to me," she complained. Stripped of makeup, wearing Reeboks and a plain gray sweatsuit, she had been on her way out to the gym when the phone rang. Now she unhooked her fanny pack and abruptly sat down in a paisley-covered armchair next to the hallway phone.

"Maggie, I'm really sorry. It won't happen again."

Ha, she thought. It was not the first date he had canceled in recent weeks, and she was beginning to get good and tired of it. "Why can't you meet me?" she asked, her voice thin with annoyance.

"The usual reason—too much work, not enough time."

"But I thought you were coming up here anyway to spend the afternoon with your kids."

"I am. Which cuts hours out of the day. Look Maggie, you're going to have to be understanding about this. I can't disappoint my children. With you it's different—you're an adult and you know what my life's like. But Colin and Petra have been put through hell this past year, and I refuse to let them down."

"So have I," she wanted to scream at him. Instead, she tried to push him into making a date for the following week.

"I just don't know what my schedule's like yet. I'll call you from the office tomorrow, okay?"

They said good-bye and hung up, but after a moment she grabbed the phone again and dialed Charlie's number. Screw the bastard. She'd show him. "Hi honey," she said sweetly when Charlie answered. "Got any plans? I have this tremendous urge to come to Brooklyn."

"My only plans are to sit around and enjoy the peace and silence. Neil should be here around lunchtime to pick up the kids, and he won't be bringing them back till around five."

"Good. I could use some peace and silence myself. Why don't I join you?"

To her surprise, Charlie sounded delighted. "It *would* be nice to talk to a grown woman. You know the way."

Pulling her sweatshirt over her head, Musette hurried to her bedroom, showered, put on a light makeup, and rummaged through her closets, agonizing—as she always did when she knew she would see Neil—over the decision of what to wear. Finally she chose easy, comfortable, sexy clothing: soft rust-brown ankle boots, black jersey leggings, an oversized fawn-colored sweater that blended beautifully with the gold of her skin. Before leaving the apartment she took a Valium. She was up to fifteen milligrams a day, which she knew was taboo in AA circles (unless in a medical emergency, taking a mood changer of any sort was considered a slip), but she couldn't help herself. Without the calming effect of a tranquilizer, she felt as if her skin was too tight for her body, as if she might explode.

Charlie, in a pair of faded jeans, flung open the door, happy to see her. "Hi darling," she said. "I'm glad you've come. I want to show you my latest." She seemed to have forgotten the awkward moment of a few weeks ago when Musette had brought up the subject of Gil Hoffeld. Tossing her chestnut hair out of her face, she led Musette into the huge living room. Her nails, Musette noticed, were painted the same scarlet as her mouth.

"Well, this place has certainly changed," said Musette, looking around. Charlie had bought ten or twelve paintings since moving in. On one wall were the eight Cruz portraits. On another was an enormous canvas whose subject was hard to determine, although the colors, mosaic splashes of reds, oranges, purples, and yellows, were very bright and hard. Above the two fireplaces were matching canvases: skeletons dancing in a green sunlit field, and thin, gaunt nudes cavorting in the same field in the black of night. The paintings were carefully placed, and Musette felt as if she were in an art gallery. There was very little furniture, just a black Steinway at one end of the room, and a seating area of two sofas, an armchair, and a Korean chest at the other. Near the kitchen was a rolltop desk where Charlie did paperwork. The tall windows were draped with some sort of filmy fabric that let in a good deal of light.

"Like it?" said Charlie.

"The room? Yes, it's very impressive."

"No. I mean my new Dick Norris painting." Seeing that Musette was confused, she pointed at the orange-and-red abstract. "Wait till you see it at night. It practically glows."

"I'll bet," said Musette dryly. She sat down on one of the sofas and Charlie brought her coffee. It was three-thirty. For the next hour they gossiped idly. Charlie was intending to take a painting class, possibly with the man who had given her his card the night she qualified in the Village.

"You mean that seedy-looking guy with the gray hair?" said Musette.

Charlie nodded, her scarlet lips turning up at the corners in a girlish, conspiratorial smile.

"Well, why not?" said Musette, sensing that Charlie might want more than to be taught painting. That meant she and Neil were probably not growing closer; that was certainly fine. "He looked as if he knew his stuff."

At about four-thirty, Musette began to grow nervous. The numbing effect of the Valium was wearing off, and she considered going into the bathroom to take another. "I hear Gwen's script is almost finished," said Charlie. "Have you guys signed contracts yet?" This new topic of conversation was very intricate, and by the time they had finished it, there was the sound of a key in the door, and then a girl's voice calling, "Mom?"

"In here," yelled Charlie.

Musette, frightened, moistened her lips with her tongue. The door banged, and there were noisy footsteps. A young girl came into the room. She was wearing a long black skirt and a denim jacket, and behind her was a boy of about ten carrying a baseball glove. "Mother," said the girl in a kind of wail, "I want to go to Shelley's to do homework. Is that okay?" Behind these two was Neil. He was halfway into the room before he saw Musette. When he did, he froze, a look of shock stiffening his face. A moment passed before he became the politician again.

"Neil, this is Musette," said Charlie. "You may know who she is. She's been in several films."

"You mean you're an actress?" said the girl, turning to stare at Musette.

"Yes, I am," said Musette, though lately she felt like an impostor when she answered that question. In fact, even when she was acting she felt like an impostor.

"Gosh, that's fabulous," said the girl, sitting down beside Musette. "What films have you been in?"

Musette told her, keeping a wary eye on Neil, who had barely acknowledged her presence. He was across the room, talking a little too loudly to Charlie about child-care arrangements. When she saw him grab his Burberry trench coat from the back of a chair, she quickly stood up and said, "Look, I've got to be going myself. Perhaps I could give you a lift back into town? My car's just outside."

"Oh, that's a good idea," said Charlie, leaning over and giving Neil a kiss on the cheek. "Children, say good-bye to your father."

"What the hell kind of stunt was that?" said Neil when they were in the car.

"Was what?" responded Musette with mock innocence. "Charlie and I are good friends. She invited me over to see what I thought of you."

"I don't believe that."

"It's true."

"Well, I wish you'd stay away from her."

Musette's hands tightened on the wheel. "If I stayed away from her, she'd really get suspicious. Anyway, I don't see why you're keeping me such a deep dark secret. It's not as if Charlie doesn't do what she damn pleases."

"What's that supposed to mean?" Neil squirmed beneath his seat belt. He clearly didn't like to be the passenger in a car driven by a woman, especially if that woman was Musette.

Pressing her booted foot down hard on the accelerator, Musette said, "Who's to say there aren't guys in her life?"

"Hey, don't drive so fast. What do you mean, guys?" Neil's voice had in it the edge men's voices always had when they sensed competition.

"Boyfriends. Lovers." She glanced at Neil, who looked terribly upset. A surge of jealousy shot through her. "I'm just guessing," she said quickly. "She never actually mentioned anything."

"Well, maybe you should keep your guesses to yourself."

They had stopped at a light. "You know, you can be a real shit when you want," Musette said coldly.

There was a silence. The light changed, and she pressed her foot down hard again so that the little car shot forward. Neil gripped his seat belt. "Sorry," he said. "Look, supposing we go back to your place? We need to be alone together, that's obvious, and I'll put off my other plans till tomorrow."

"Fine with me," said Musette, swerving quickly and jamming on the brakes to avoid a cab.

In bed he was as passionate as ever. "I love these tits of yours. Did I ever tell you that?"

"Lots of times," she laughed.

"Well, I'm telling you again. And I love putting my face right here, between your legs."

She groaned. "Oh, that's good," she murmured. "That's good."

"Now put your mouth on me," he said, hoarsely. Happily she complied, and it was his turn to groan as her lips closed over him. When he could bear it no longer, he pulled her head away and thrust himself inside her, coming almost immediately. "Oh baby!" he yelled. "You're the best thing that ever happened to me!"

"Did you really mean that?" she asked moments later when they were lying exhausted on the sheets.

"That you're the best thing that ever happened to me?" Neil

moved his arms from above his head and crossed them over his chest. "Yes."

"Well then, Neil, don't you think it's time we went public? I can't stand this sneaking around anymore. It reminds me of years ago when you made me feel like your little whore."

He raised himself on an elbow. "I made you feel like that?"

"In the end, yes."

"Well, I won't do it again, Maggie. I promise. But at the same time, please try to understand. The press'll jump on us like a pack of wolves if they find out what's going on. Would you want that? Would that be good for *your* career?" He lowered himself, taking her head between his hands, stroking her hair. "It takes time to work things out, lots of time. So don't push too hard, okay? There are several people's lives at stake here." He kissed her gently on the lips. "Okay?" he said again.

"Okay," she murmured, although she didn't think it was okay at all. She knew how lonely her bed would feel when Neil got up to leave it. She knew how miserable she always felt when he walked out the door. She didn't see why she alone should be the one to suffer, taking forbidden drugs to keep calm, sitting around waiting for the phone to ring, secretly building her hopes and dreams around this man. What she had to do was find some way to bind him to her. Otherwise she'd go crazy.

The next afternoon Charlie phoned Dennis MacLeish, the gray-haired artist she had now several times bumped into at AA meetings in Brooklyn Heights. He answered on the fifth ring. "Dennis?" she said.

"Yeah? Who's this?"

"Charlie Gallagher. You know me from AA." She gave a nervous cough. "I'm the one who bought those Cruz portraits you hate so much."

"Sure, I remember. You were leaving your husband. Is that still happening?"

"Is that...? Well—yes."

She heard the click of a cigarette lighter.

"And you wanted to learn to paint. That's obviously why you're calling me."

She lit her own cigarette. "Yes."

"Had any experience?"

"I beg your pardon?"

"With painting. Have you had any classes?"

"While I was at Vassar. But that's ancient history."

"Doesn't do to date oneself, sweetheart. All right, here's what I suggest. I teach a basic painting course at the School of Visual

Arts Wednesday nights. You could come to that. Do you have supplies?"

"No—not yet."

"Go to Pearl Paints on Canal Street, and they'll give you everything you need. Be sure and bring charcoal and a large sketch pad. Oh, and wear old clothes, Vassar. We get pretty messy in this class."

She hung up, thinking she didn't like his tone. But what the hell, she'd try one or two classes. If he was a bad teacher, she'd go somewhere else.

On Wednesday night, wearing jeans, sneakers, and an old blue work shirt, she appeared at his class at the School of Visual Arts with a box of paints. Under one arm she carried a sketch pad, under the other a large canvas. She saw he was busy with a student, so she stood in the doorway, looking around.

The room was enormous and quite depressing. Tubes of fluorescent lighting gave off a cold merciless glare. At one end of the room was a row of sinks, at the other a flock of derelict easels and several stacks of folding chairs. In the middle, on a raised platform, stood a couch. Charlie realized they would be painting from life, and tried to locate the model. Ten or fifteen men and women talked companionably to one another as they set up their easels and laid out their paints, but the model was nowhere to be seen. Dennis MacLeish had finished with his student, and now he came forward, clapping his hands. "All right, class. *All right!* Let's come to order."

The gentle hum of conversation stopped. Dennis MacLeish moved to the center of the room and stood by the couch. He was wearing an olive-drab army jacket over a black T-shirt and khaki pants. On his feet were muddy, paint-spattered work boots that had bright red laces. His gray spiky hair was tousled, and on his long, thin, rather battered-looking face was a stern expression. "We're going to work *very* hard tonight, aren't we?" he said. "Otherwise we're wasting everyone's time, and poor Ruth might as well not have come out in all this rain."

By Ruth he meant the model, who appeared just then in a dingy blue candlewick bathrobe. She was a woman of about thirty-five, with curly bleached blond hair that showed dark at the roots, and a ruddy, uneven complexion. When she took off her robe, Charlie saw that her stomach was fat and doughy. Without a word from Dennis, she lay down on the couch.

Nonchalantly, with the tip of his heavy work boot, Dennis flicked on a small heater that stood beside the couch. "Now I want every one of you to look closely at Ruth," he said. "Study her—the way the thigh extends from the hip socket, the hand joins the wrist, the neck rises from the collarbone. Squint your eyes and back up and notice her as a form. Then sit down, and for the next five minutes I want you to keep your eyes on your pads, and draw from memory."

The class groaned good-naturedly. For the first time Dennis's face relaxed into a smile. "Come on, cowards, just do it, and then we'll get on to the good stuff." He turned toward Ruth, indicating to her that he wanted her to shift one of her hands. Then he swung around so that he was looking directly at Charlie and said, "Well, Vassar, what's it going to be? Are you gonna stand in the doorway all night, or are you maybe planning to come in and join us?"

Charlie blushed violently. For a moment she considered leaving, but then in a soft voice Dennis said, "Just put all that stuff down and take a seat." He pointed at a chair beside a woman whose white hair was held out of her face with a leather thong. "All you need is your sketch pad and a stick of charcoal and you're in business."

Unfortunately her charcoal was buried in her shiny new box of paints. She kneeled where she was and began fumbling with the clasps.

"Well, you're not going to get anywhere like that," Dennis said with a laugh, pushing his way through the easels and coming toward her. He handed her a piece of charcoal, and helped her to her feet. "Okay now," he said. "We're already three minutes into this exercise, which doesn't give you much time. Go ahead and draw like a son of a bitch."

Her drawings were terrible. Big blobby figures whose limbs were all out of proportion and who bore no resemblance whatsoever to the model. "That's okay," said Dennis, looking over her shoulder. "At least you're drawing big. You've just got to get the kinks out of your hand." This little bit of praise offered some comfort. She would work very hard, she decided. Dedicate herself to getting the human form just right. As she looked some more at Ruth she began to think of how her own very different body worked. It was good to be in touch with the physical this way.

After that first exercise the model took a break. The woman beside Charlie smiled encouragingly. "He's a wonderful teacher," she said. "Just put yourself in his hands, and you won't believe how quickly you'll develop."

"Oh really?" said Charlie. She had noticed that the woman drew with almost photographic precision. "How long have you been studying with him?"

"Six months. He's taught me a lot about color."

Charlie wanted to ask more, but once again Dennis clapped his hands and called the class to order. "All right, now that we've warmed up, let's really get to work. We've got an hour and a half. I want to see those canvases covered—not an inch of white space, understand?"

Everyone stood and went to their easels. Charlie was about to go to the back of the room for an easel, when Dennis stopped her. "Not you, Vassar," he said.

"What?"

"You need to spend the time drawing."

"I do?" She looked at his face, which was neither friendly nor unfriendly. The brown eyes were shrewd, and the skin along his sallow cheeks was rough and pitted. "I came here to paint," she said.

"Yes, I know. Everyone did. But you don't have the experience yet. It's a matter of hand-eye coordination. Practice. You should carry a small sketch pad with you everywhere you go."

"But this is a painting class," she said obstinately.

"Yes, Vassar, yes—we all know that. But before you can paint you've got to be able to draw. Now sit down and get a move on. I want the whole form—big swooping exaggerated lines. I'm going to time you. Two minutes per sketch."

By the end of the evening she was exhausted. Her hands were black and sooty with charcoal dust, and her lower lip felt sore from where she had bitten down on it in her effort of concentration. As far as she was concerned, it was a wasted evening.

Her last drawing looked just as primitive as her first, even though Dennis had assured her that there was a looseness and confidence that had not been there in the beginning.

Dennis, she thought wearily as she packed her things, was a hard taskmaster. For a full hour and a half he had had her do two- and five-minute sketches, and now her vision was blurry and her body was filled with a tense, wired energy. The image of Ruth lingered in her brain. And she could still hear his voice, with its cowboyish twangy drawl, calling "Time's up, Vassar!" every few minutes.

She left the room without saying good-bye to anyone. The others were at the sinks, washing brushes, and Dennis was smoking a cigarette with Ruth, who had changed into street clothes. For the next ten minutes she searched for her locker—it turned out to be on another floor—and then was annoyed because it wasn't large enough to accommodate all her things. She'd have to take her sketch pad with her. Cursing softly, she banged the door closed and headed for the elevator, which was crowded with students when it finally came. She wedged herself in among them, pulling her sketch pad close to her, and gave a little jump of surprise when she heard Dennis's drawl in her ear. "Hey, Vassar, how come you left in such a hurry?"

"I really wish you wouldn't call me that," she muttered, grateful they were almost at the ground floor.

"Oh—and what should I call you?" he said as the doors opened.

"My name is Charlie. Why don't you try that?"

"All right. Though Vassar comes naturally to the tongue. But Charlie it shall be." He fell into step with her, walking across the lobby. Outside it was raining heavily, and she paused to button her slicker and pull her umbrella from her bag. "Where're you going, Charlie?" he said.

"Home."

"Where's home?"

"Brooklyn."

"Oh yeah, that's right. Well, maybe you could give me a lift. That's if you have a car. I live in Brooklyn, too."

"Yes, I know," she said. He looked puzzled, and she added, "It was on your card. Sure, I'll give you a lift."

Her car was parked a block away. He grabbed her sketch

pad, sticking it up beneath his poncho, and she opened her umbrella, and they made a run for it. By the time they were in the car, their faces were as wet as if they had stepped from the shower.

"Whew—cats and dogs," said Dennis. He took off his poncho, and flung it, along with her sketch pad, onto the backseat.

Charlie switched on the engine. "Where are you from?" she asked.

"Wyoming. You?"

"Right here. New York."

"Ah. Thought so." With a large white handkerchief he rubbed at his face and hair. Then he leaned back against the leather headrest, closing his eyes as if he wanted to sleep.

"How long have you been here?" asked Charlie, inching the car carefully into the bumper-to-bumper traffic on Twenty-third Street. Because of the rain, people were driving badly. She had the ventilator going full force, but still the windows of her old Volvo were so fogged up it was hard to see.

"Oh lord, nearly twenty years. That dates me some, doesn't it?" he said, grinning.

"Some. Did you come here to go to art school?"

"Yeah, Pratt. Then I started teaching and I had a couple of exhibits, made some money, and lost it all drinking. That's my story pretty much in a nutshell."

"How long have you been sober?" she asked. They were on the FDR Drive, and every car that passed flung enormous wings of water on them. Ahead lay the bridges with their twinkling faerie necklaces of light.

"A year," he said. "A long haul, but it's okay now."

They didn't talk again until they had crossed the bridge, and Charlie had to ask where he lived. He laughed. "Right here under the bridge, Vassar. Whoops, sorry—that just seemed to pop out. I guess you'll have to think of it as an endearment. Anyway, you can practically see my building from here." He gave directions, sending Charlie through a confusing tangle of one-way streets. They were in a dark, spooky, industrial area where not a single building seemed to be inhabited. Finally, after bumping over what felt like an unpaved street, he told her to stop.

"You live here?" she asked incredulously. In the dark she

could make out steep loading docks and wide doors of corrugated steel.

"Sure. Why? Too slummy for you?"

"No. It just seems so empty."

"Oh, it's not empty, believe me." He pointed at a dark, hulking building. "Whole thing's been converted into lofts. There are ten or twelve of us living there. Painters, sculptors, even a woman who does weaving."

Charlie peered through the steamy car window. At the end of the street she could see the lights of Manhattan. So the river was just there. "I'd like to see your work sometime," she said.

He was struggling into his poncho. "Is that a pass?" His voice beneath the wet rubbery material sounded distant and hollow. When his head came through, the hair stood up in feathery clumps, and she had a sudden urge to smooth it down for him. "If you're really serious about it, you could go up to the Whitney," he said. "I've got paintings there in the permanent collection."

"Oh really?" said Charlie. "Good. I'll certainly do that."

"Yes, do that," he said, mimicking her. "In the meantime, Vassar, keep on drawing." He reached over, and with a rustle of his poncho, gave her a playful little punch in the arm. Then he opened the car door and jumped out. "Thanks for the ride," he said, and she watched as he ran up some steps and disappeared into a gloomy doorway.

What a creepy place, she thought, her headlamps cutting across piles of garbage and rubble as she drove away. She imagined it stank here on summer days, and in the winter it was cold and oppressive. And yet the idea of all those artists holing up in a dank building in the middle of nowhere was intriguing. And so was the idea of Dennis MacLeish with his red shoelaces and his stand-up hair and his blunt Wild West manners. Tomorrow she'd go up to the Whitney and find out about him. Then, if she liked what she saw, she'd invite herself up to his loft and see if he had any canvases worth buying. And maybe, just maybe, he could be more than her teacher.

*G*wen's mother, Sarah Thomas, was a small woman given to bouts of complaining and sulkiness. At seventy years old, she was still very delicate and pretty. Her teeth were white and beautifully even (Gwen was married and had written her first novel before she realized they were false). Her skin was the color of nutmeg, a pale fine brown, and her almond-shaped eyes were a deep gray that looked startlingly dark in the small, creased face. Though she had strong hair that grew in nicely, she insisted on wearing a wig because it was easier—now that she was elderly—a gray wig that seemed as natural on her as her teeth. Gwen had dinner with her once a month and was always surprised at how well her mother looked. Old Mrs. Thomas lived by herself in the apartment Gwen had grown up in. She had been a widow for nearly a decade.

Their dinners together were never easy. Mrs. Thomas had disapproved of Gwen's marrying a white man, and during the years of her marriage Gwen always visited her mother alone. Nor had Mrs. Thomas been particularly pleased with Gwen's success as a writer. With friends she would brag about her daughter, but when it was just the two of them she had little to say. And this made her resentful. She would argue with Gwen about the infrequency of her visits and the meager interest Gwen took in her poor, lonely mother. Of course, she felt threatened by Gwen's fine educated English. She couldn't read Gwen's books—they were too difficult for her—and she couldn't enter Gwen's world: that was light-years away. And so the easiest and most gratifying thing for her to do was to whine and pick at Gwen, hoping she could shame her daughter back into being a complaisant schoolgirl.

To some extent this worked. In Sarah's company Gwen became tongue-tied and anxious. The grown woman vanished and in her place was a clumsy twelve-year-old always sure to say or do the wrong thing. One cool fall evening Gwen arrived for dinner half an hour late, and this brought a frown of disapproval to her mother's pretty face. "Where you been at, girl?" she said, taking Gwen's coat.

"I had to go to a meeting." She had not told Sarah about AA, having always kept her drinking a secret from her family. She knew her mother assumed any meeting she went to would be with an agent or editor, but in fact she had gone to the AA meeting in Harlem; the uninhibited energy of the place kept drawing her back. She hadn't seen John, the man who had known she was Gwen Thomas, which was just as well, though in some secret part of herself Gwen was ready to give him another piece of her mind.

"You went dressed like that?"

Gwen looked down at her clothes. She hadn't had time to go home and change, and she was wearing a sweater and slacks and a pair of brown leather cowboy boots. "Yes—why? What's the matter with the way I'm dressed?"

"You might have put on a skirt. And your hair! Lord Jesus, why don't you ever get it fixed right? You used to wear it so nice." It was a real source of anguish to Mrs. Thomas that Gwen had let her hair go natural. She herself, in a silver wig and a checkered housedress, looked neat and ladylike, and she felt Gwen should look the same. With her usual disappointment weighing her shoulders, she led the way into the kitchen.

"What are you cooking, Ma? It smells good." Gwen wanted no contention tonight.

"Same as I always cook. Chicken."

"You don't always cook chicken, Ma."

"Most of the time I do. You know, girl, you're looking awfully thin." With a grunt, Mrs. Thomas bent to open the oven. "What's the matter with you? Still grievin' over that no-count husband?"

"Never!" said Gwen with a nervous laugh. "I was the one who left him, remember?"

"I only remember what you tole me, and that was that he started acting rough. Ain't that right, Gwen?"

"I don't want to talk about it, Ma. It's in the past."

"Hmmm. Well, you know what I thought of him in the first place." Mrs. Thomas put a dish of parsleyed potatoes on the table. She was a good cook, and it was true, the kitchen smelled delicious, but in her mother's company Gwen's appetite always dried up like a streambed in August. Alongside the potatoes, the old lady put hot buttered corn muffins, and a platter of vegetables, and finally the chicken itself, browned to perfection. Gwen knew better than to try to help her. Nothing irritated Mrs. Thomas more than someone poking around her kitchen, getting in the way.

"What you need is a real man in your life, not some poet. That'd fatten you up," said Mrs. Thomas, removing her apron and sitting down. "You too solitary. Always were."

Gwen stared at her mother in amazement. Mrs. Thomas rarely made references to sex. The life of the soul was what interested her. She lived for two things: the church, and her apartment, which she kept neat and tidy. Picking up a highly polished silver fork, Gwen said, "I don't have time for men right now. Hey, guess what, Ma? I've been asked to speak at a dinner at the Waldorf."

"Oh yeah?" said Mrs. Thomas, helping herself to chicken. "What kind of dinner's that?"

"A very fancy one. It's to raise money for Tulsa College. I think Jesse Jackson may be there."

"Well, ain't that something," said Mrs. Thomas, putting a piece of crispy skin in her mouth. "When's this?"

"Early November. I could get you a ticket if you like."

"Oh no, girl, I don't think so. I got a lot goin' on myself." She took a long drink of milk, and when she was finished her lips were circled with white. She dabbed at them with her napkin. "In fact you and me have to talk, because I made a major decision."

"Oh really? What's that?"

"What it is, is this," said Mrs. Thomas, staring hard at her daughter. "I've decided I've had enough of this place. The dirt and filth and crazy people. The winters that take the warmth from your bones. I'm moving back to Jamaica."

Gwen put down her fork. "You can't mean it!"

"Why not? It's where I was born. I still got the house in Saint Elizabeth. And I'd like to live out my days alongside my sisters."

But what about me? Gwen wanted to cry out. Instead she said, "How will you manage it all?"

"Manage what?"

"The packing and—"

"Ain't no hardship in packing. Friends from church'll help."

"But Ma, you love this apartment. It's your home."

It was also *her* home. In the living room, with its ugly plum-colored velveteen chairs and sofa, was the piano she had practiced on as a girl. The store-bought "Chinese carpet" was the same she had lain on Friday and Saturday nights when she was allowed to watch TV. Even the smell of the room was the same: furniture polish, Windex, floral spray, heat rising from the radiator.

"Doesn't feel like home these days," said Mrs. Thomas, hugging her arms to herself as if the freezing winter weather were already upon her. "I'm going back to where there's beauty to feast the eye on, and you don't have to worry who's behind you in the street."

"And where there are hurricanes to blow your house to bits," said Gwen bitterly. "Come on, Ma. You've been away from there so long you'll never readjust. And what about all your friends? And Dr. Mitchum from your church? How's he going to get through a service without you sitting there, singing like an angel?"

"He'll do fine without me," said Mrs. Thomas. "No one gonna roll over and die because I'm leaving." She made a tight mouth and glanced at her daughter. "Least of all you."

In the taxi going home, Gwen felt an acute pain in her stomach, and wondered how she would manage without her mother up there in Harlem in the small, redolent apartment where she was supposed to remain always. It didn't matter that she kept contact to a minimum, or that the thought of old plaintive Sarah sometimes made her want to tear her hair out. Her mother was her mother, and without her New York would be an empty place, a desert where she, Gwen, would suddenly be prey to all sorts of disasters. Where would she put all her memories?

Leaning back against the seat of the cab, she had the strangest vision of putting them in a metal urn just as the ashes of her father had been put. She closed her eyes against this terrible thought. And then, with her eyes closed, she burst out laughing.

The cabdriver glanced at her over his shoulder. "You got a problem, lady?"

Gwen laughed even harder.

"I don't need no crazies in my cab."

"It's just that I had an idea," gasped Gwen. "A realization, an epiphany."

The driver was white with an Italian name. He stared at her in the mirror and said, "Oh yeah? What kinda idea?"

But she was laughing again. She had to struggle for breath before she could answer him. "I'm going to write a book," she said finally. "About my parents, my family."

"Oh, a book," said the driver. "I bin tryin' to do that for years. Lotsa luck."

It was so obvious. Why hadn't she thought of it before? A novel that would begin in Saint Elizabeth, where her mother had been born. That would trace her family's history both in Jamaica and in New York. Use all the relatives. Her father's crazy sister, Hildie, who kept a market stall and smoked cigars and was said to be a witch. Her mother's mother, Celia, who couldn't read or write, but who kept bearing children because "that was why the Lord had put her here." Her grandfather Bill, who had two wives at the same time and pretended to be mute so he wouldn't have to talk to either of them. Her handsome uncle Peter whose fingers just loved to pluck out chords on a guitar, and whose rock-hard body was never so comfortable as when in bed with a rich white lady. Her cousin Francine who was light-skinned enough to pass, and who had run off to Paris and married a banker. Herself...oh yes, of course, herself...the lonely, solemn child who had, because of her parents' ambition for her, climbed up out of their world and become a kind of misfit. What freedom there would be in writing about all of that!

Upstairs in her apartment, she made herself a strong pot of tea, and for the next two hours paced up and down the kitchen, stopping occasionally to light a cigarette or to jot down a few ideas. This was what she was after, this intense hunger and excitement. Her mind was as fertile and green as the sugar fields of Jamaica, and the knot of sadness in her stomach had been dissolved into adrenaline. But by about two in the morning her energy began to flag. Her little cat lay asleep on top of a pile of magazines and unopened letters on the kitchen table, and tiredly Gwen sat down and stroked her, admiring the brownness of her fingers against the gray fur. Then, because she was not yet tired enough to get ready for bed, and no longer awake enough to continue working, she began idly to sort through her mail. One letter was postmarked August 30, and was from the planning committee for the Tulsa dinner. She opened it and read:

Dear Ms. Thomas:
Once again, we are so pleased that you have agreed to honor us by speaking on November 1 at the Waldorf. It will be a great occasion! Besides yourself, there will be six other speakers: the actress, Bethany Hunt, whom you probably know was a graduate of Tulsa College, Charlayne Hunter-Gault of PBS television, Faye Wattleton of Planned Parenthood, Mayor Tom Bradley of Los Angeles, Ambrose Smiley, and J. Hopeton Sinclair, editor of the *West Indian Voice*. Each of you should feel free to speak for approximately ten minutes, and to choose a subject related to your experience as a black professional in your field. The order of speakers will be . . .

Gwen stopped reading. J. Hopeton Sinclair? Hadn't he given her a bad review two years ago when she won the Mendelsohn Award? Yes, she remembered distinctly. She had received glowing praise from everyone; long articles had been written about the beauty of her prose, the acuteness of her vision, the extraordinary aliveness of her characters. "Gwen Thomas is more deserving of this honor than any writer I can think of," wrote the *Times*. But J. Hopeton Sinclair, whom no one had ever heard of, had disagreed. Alone among the reviewers, he had declared that, "While Ms. Thomas's prose is fluid enough, the thoughts and emotions she attributes to her characters too often do not have the necessary and inimitable ring of truth one would wish for in such an important piece of fiction. Perhaps this has to do with the fact that Ms. Thomas, educated in the finest white schools, has had to depend almost entirely on observation rather than actual experience. In tackling a subject such as hers—the alienated black of the inner-city slum—one needs to have been there, to have groveled in the mud of poverty, violence, drug addiction, prostitution, in order not to sound counterfeit. Ms. Thomas comes close, but her own voice, that of a black woman with white sensibilities, is intrusive to the knowing reader..."

She remembered being furious, and throwing the review away in the garbage. J. Hopeton Sinclair was no one important. But on some deep level his words had played on all her insecurities, had perhaps even been the beginning of the block that had crippled her as a writer. And now she was to appear with him! Angrily Gwen reread the letter, her lips moving as she scanned the page. There was no question of her getting out of the engagement. She would just have to ignore the man, say what she had to say, and hope for the best. It would be her first public appearance without liquor in her system.

usette felt as if she was operating on two fronts. There was all the excitement of producing *Homegirl,* an excitement that kept her in a whirl of activity from morning till night, and there was her relationship with Neil, which had begun to make her feel unhappy and degraded. What she had hoped for in the relationship was not only passion, but mutual support and love—the freedom to travel together, to go out to restaurants and the theater, to wake up beside each other in the morning, to plan a life together. She would even have liked cooking for Neil and sending his shirts out to the laundry. Instead they continued to meet secretly in her apartment, and their love was hot and hidden and dirty—an affair based entirely on eroticism rather than on true affection and regard. As she had years ago, she was beginning to feel like Neil's cheap plaything, especially as she only saw him at his convenience, usually once or twice a month.

But in the area of *Homegirl* she glowed. Once contracts were signed, Musette's office became very busy; she increased her staff, and her original secretary, Patsy Shroeder, began to come in every day. With all the letters and mailings and phone calls

Patsy had to do, she didn't have much time to gather information about Gil Hoffeld's death, and six weeks had passed before she handed Musette a folder of clippings. Musette went through these in half an hour, and then sat abstractedly at the Biedermeier desk in her bedroom, thinking about what she had read.

Almost all the clippings said the same thing—that Hoffeld, a Boston commodities broker who had a summer cottage on Rosewood Lane, Barnstable, had fallen from his boat late on the afternoon of Saturday, October 6, and drowned after receiving a contusion to the head; that he had been in the company of his neighbor, Peter R. Salzman, whose permanent residence was 900 Fifth Avenue, New York; that the two men had had a lot to drink; that Hoffeld was an extremely competent sailor; that his body had washed ashore two days after the accident. There were several quotes from Salzman, who was described as the president and CEO of Salzman & Bresslau Pharmaceuticals, a small New Jersey–based firm. "Gil was pretty depressed because of some business difficulties he was encountering. He invited me over for lunch to discuss a few things, and I guess we drank more wine than was good for either of us. Anyway, he said a sail would cheer him up. I tried to talk him out of it because the weather was bad, but there was no arguing with Gil when he'd been drinking. He was determined to get on that boat. And it all happened so fast . . . Gil stood up when he shouldn't have, got caught in the head by the boom, and there was this tremendous crack as he went overboard. It was awful, and the worst thing was I couldn't do a thing to help him . . ."

Musette read this particular quote several times, and then reached for the phone and dialed Harry Langhart's office in Los Angeles. "Hi, it's me," she said. "Quick idea. What do you know about Peter Salzman? He must live near you on the cape."

"I know more about his wife, Belle. She's real involved with the opera and ballet. Why?"

"I thought they might be good people to approach for *Homegirl.*"

"Well, they're rolling in money, I know that. Belle contributes regularly to all sorts of things. She's even had a bunch of Broadway flops."

"Think you could introduce me?"

"Sure, why not? Let me work on it, and I'll get back to you."

He called her the next evening.

"Maggie?"

"Yes?"

"Listen, I know you hate opera, but I've been invited to a gala event at the Met next week. Wanna be my date?"

"Not really. Those things bore me stiff."

"Even if you were sitting in Belle and Peter Salzman's box?"

Musette giggled. "No—then I'd be *very* interested."

"Good. Well then, get out your ball gown, baby. We're gonna do some dancing."

On the evening of the Met gala, Musette, nice and evened out on Valium, wore a black satin-and-velvet Scaasi gown that fit like a glove. Her honey-colored hair was pulled severely back into a French twist. She wore nothing around her throat, but in her ears glimmered diamonds, and on one wrist was a simple gold mesh bracelet. She looked, as Harry told her when he arrived in a limousine at seven-thirty, stunningly beautiful. "Like a million dollars," he said.

"Jesus, I better," said Musette, pulling her black mink cape around her shoulders. "I want to raise at least that much from them." Then she sighed. "I just wish we could skip the opera part and show up for the dinner."

"Come on, you'll love it—it's *Il Trovatore,* lots of gush and bravado."

"I don't give a shit what it is. All those fat women prancing around the stage always look stupid to me."

At Lincoln Center Harry took her arm and walked her slowly across the broad, white-paved plaza toward the blazing lights of the opera house. It was a cool night; beneath the fur cape her skin felt uncomfortably naked and exposed. All around them couples moved in the same direction. There was the click of heels on stone, the excited ringing out of voices, and now and then the rustle of silk, and a soft trail of perfume, as a woman in an evening gown swung past.

She and Harry didn't talk until they were inside the Met. "I've always loved this," said Harry, indicating the glittering spray of chandeliers, the winding arc of red-carpeted stairs, the tall windows, and incredible golden light. He looked at the architecture and design, while Musette looked at the people, wondering who, among the many women in long dresses and furs, was Belle Salzman, and who, among the men in evening jackets, was her husband, Peter. All her intelligence, she knew, must be focused on these two tonight, and as she ascended the stairs, lifting her dress in one hand so she wouldn't trip, she tried to empty her mind of everything else.

But she was conscious, as always, of hundreds of eyes upon her; of the occasional voice whispering, "Isn't that Musette—the actress?"; of men watching greedily. When they reached the Grand Tier level, and Harry gave her cape to the *vestiaire,* her flesh was ready for all that admiration. Glancing in a mirror she saw that her neck and shoulders were as golden as the golden light, and her eyes, sparkling brilliantly, had turned a dark amber. An usher led them to the Salzmans' box.

And there she had a shock. In the box to the left of the Salzmans was Neil Gallagher.

She saw him immediately. He was seated beside a woman who wore a tiara in her brown hair, and he was smiling and rubbing his hand along his jaw, listening to something the woman was saying. When he felt Musette's eyes on him, he looked up and the smile disappeared. It was as if someone had given him a blow. For a moment his face went blank, and then, just as quickly, his expression sharpened and the smile returned—a small private smile that was accompanied by a swift ducking of the head.

Musette, confused, ducked her own head in response. Harry was just introducing her to the Salzmans, and she shook hands, mumbling something about what a pleasure it was to be here, and blindly slipped into her seat. The lights began to dim. In a whisper, Belle Salzman introduced her to the other couple in the box, a Mr. and Mrs. Ignato Reye. Then she waved at Neil's box, and said, "And that's Carter Levy, and his wife, Mary Louise, and behind them, Neil Gallagher and Claire Armstrong, and behind *them,* Joey and Priss Herman. But you'll meet them all properly later."

"Oh," said Musette, surprised. "You mean we're all one party?"

"Yes, of course," said Belle. "I always take two boxes at functions like this. I'd take three or four if Peter would let me."

The opera could have involved genuine bloodshed and Musette would not have noticed. All she was aware of was Neil's tuxedoed body so close to her and yet so far away. But instead of doing what she wanted, which was to wrap herself around him, she spent the first intermission with Belle. "I'd like to know everything you're up to," said the large woman, accepting a glass of champagne from her husband, and then waving him off. She looked like a small, elegant whale in an Oscar de la Renta ball gown that did nothing but emphasize the thickness of her flesh with yards of rich maroon satin. Yet her hands, moving as she talked, had a certain dainty allure, and her wide mouth was intelligent. She had wavy copper-colored hair that gave her whole being a liveliness and made one forget how heavy she was. She must have been in her mid-forties. "Why don't we sit here," she said, indicating an out-of-the-way banquette. "No one will bother us, and we'll be able to have a good long natter."

That was one thing Musette immediately learned about Belle: she used British expressions that sounded forced and uncomfortable on her heavy New York tongue. "Of course I've seen every one of your films," she said. "I've always been a fan of Miroslav's, but you were the one who really lit up the screen."

"That's awfully kind," said Musette. "Miroslav and I *were* good together—in terms of work, I mean—while it lasted, but now..." She drew her beautiful shoulders up in a shrug.

"What *will* you do now? I thought it such a pity about the divorce."

Musette laughed throatily. "Oh, it wasn't a pity, believe me. That marriage had really come to an end." A short distance away several people stood chatting and laughing, and involuntarily Musette glanced at them, looking for Neil, who had left his box as soon as the lights came on, and who she sensed was avoiding her. With an effort, she returned her gaze to Belle. "What I'm going to do now is make a movie."

"You mean *star* in a movie?"

"No, I mean *make* a movie. Be the producer."

"Really? What a smashing idea."

"Yes, I think so."

"Which movie?"

Musette smiled at her. "You know the writer Gwen Thomas?"

"Of course. I adore her."

"Well, I've taken an option on one of her books—*Homegirl.*

Gwen's written the screenplay herself. She's done a fabulous job."

"And now I suppose you're looking for money?"

"Well—yes."

"Don't be surprised," said Belle with a laugh. "My style is to get right to the point. How much do you think the film will run you?"

Musette took a sip of ginger ale. "Not much, as these things go. We haven't worked out the total budget yet, but I'd say about twelve million. The film'll be made in Georgia, which is a right-to-work state, so that should keep expenses down."

"Interesting," said Belle. "Very interesting. And who is 'we'?"

"My production manager—he used to work with Miroslav—and myself. We're just putting the package together now."

"So you don't have any backers yet?"

"Oh yes, we have quite a few." In the past few weeks Musette had been very busy raising funds. "At the moment we're concentrating on finding the right director. We want someone very special and sensitive for a film like this."

"How right you are," said Belle. She was silent for a moment, drumming dainty pink nails on her champagne glass. Then she said, "Well, you know what? I'd like to read the script. Do you think I could do that?"

"Of course," said Musette. "What a terrific idea."

"Oh, I'd say it was your idea as much as mine," said Belle. "Let's keep this between us, shall we? If I like the script, I'll have a word with Peter. Otherwise you'll have it back in a few days."

Watching for Neil, Musette said, "I'm sure you'll like it; virtually everyone who's seen it has made a quick grab for their checkbook."

Though there were two more intermissions, Musette didn't actually talk to Neil until after the final curtain. While the others lingered in the box, she and Harry went out for a cigarette. On the promenade ushers were shepherding those people who would not be staying for the gala dinner toward the elevators and stairs. A dance floor had been set up by the balcony railing, and in a few moments tables would be wheeled out and the whole place would turn into a dazzling restaurant. Harry lit her cigarette and she took a deep puff and said, "Well, I'm glad that's over with. Now comes the fun part."

Squinting through the smoke of her cigarette, she saw Neil coming toward them with the woman in the tiara, Claire Armstrong.

"Who *is* that woman?" she said under her breath.

"His cousin," murmured Harry. "She's always at events like this. Big committee woman, but stingy as hell, so don't go looking to her for money. She makes a good companion for Neil to escort, because the press knows she's not a romance."

Neil, splendid in an evening jacket, gave them his crooked Irish grin and said, "Well, that was long and tedious, wasn't it?"

"Abominable," agreed Harry.

"I don't know," said Claire Armstrong, who wore a gray cocktail-length taffeta dress that showed her thin bowlegs. "I thought the soprano was rather good." She pronounced "rather" in the British way, and Musette took an instant dislike to her.

"Belle didn't tell us you'd be here," said Neil, turning to Musette, his voice casual. "How do you know the Salzmans?"

"Through Harry," said Musette, with a sweet smile. "He has a house near theirs on the cape."

"Is that so?" said Neil, a small line sharpening at the side of his mouth.

Just then a group of photographers descended on them. Musette gave Harry her cigarette to put out for her and drew a tiny gold compact from her evening bag. She knew her face looked lovely, but she touched up her lipstick and ran her fingers lightly over her chignoned hair before turning to the cameras. There was the whir of flash guns that she was so used to, and then the photographer from *Vogue* said, "That was great! Perfect! Now how about one of you and the congressman?"

But Neil, who had conveniently just spotted an acquaintance, grinned and said, "Another time, fellas," as he disappeared into the crowd. Musette was photographed with the dowdy Claire Armstrong instead.

At dinner Neil and Musette were seated at different tables. Musette found herself next to Peter Salzman, a big, open-faced, gregarious man who had a sweet smile and eyes that were warm and humorous behind thick glasses. At the beginning of the meal he said, "I told Belle I wouldn't talk to her for a week if she didn't seat you and me together."

Musette laughed. "Well, I guess she likes talking to you."

"She likes talking, period," Peter said, removing his glasses and staring closely into Musette's face. "Did you enjoy the opera?"

"You want the truth?"

"Of course."

A waiter appeared with a bottle of white wine and Musette quickly put her hand over her glass. "I didn't listen to a word of it."

"Ah, well, at least you're honest." He chewed for a moment on the stem of his glasses. Then he pointed at her wineglass. "How come you're not drinking?"

"Let's just say liquor and I don't get along too well."

"Oh, I know all about that. I have this odd little problem with alcohol myself. If I drink during the day I get sick as a dog."

"Really?" said Musette. "But that doesn't stop you, does it?"

He polished his glasses on the sleeve of his dinner jacket, and returned them to his nose. "Sure it does. I don't touch the stuff till cocktail time. Then I can drink as much as I want and nothing happens, except that I get a little drunk."

"But during the day . . . ?"

"During the day the stuff might as well have poison in it."

"So you *never* drink during the day?"

He looked at her a little oddly. "The last time I had a drink during the day was fourteen years ago when my daughter was born. I was so sick from a glass of champagne I thought my head would explode. I had to lie in a dark room for hours with the walls spinning."

She started to ask him about his afternoon of drinking with Gil Hoffeld, but thought better of it. She needed to be on good terms with this man. He must have been lying to the reporters, she decided. But why should he have done that? And wouldn't the police have expected to find liquor on his breath, since, according to his story, he and Gil had had more wine than was good for them?

Puzzled, she studied Peter as he spoke to the woman on his other side. He was no liar, she could sense that. Eccentric perhaps, but otherwise a witty, fun-loving, highly intelligent man. "How do you know Neil Gallagher?" she asked when he had turned back to her.

"Oh God, Neil and I go way back. In fact, I probably wouldn't be who I am today if it weren't for him."

"That's intriguing," Musette said, thinking that perhaps *she* wouldn't be who she was, were it not for Neil. "What do you mean?"

He drummed his fingers on the table, looking bashful. "Well, I'll tell you . . . Neil and I were at school together, Andover, but we might as well have been on different planets. He was one of those boys who came from the right family, a great student and athlete, and I was Jewish, which wasn't exactly the thing to be. I was also what my daughter would call a complete and total nerd. Coke-bottle glasses, more interested in books than sports, that sort of thing. My first year there Neil was the only person who would be friends with me. Looking back, I see that as extremely brave and heroic."

"And you've been friends ever since?"

"Ever since. He was the best man at my wedding, and vice versa, our daughters are the same age, our wives . . ." He trailed off as if there were some problem there.

"Your wives?" prompted Musette.

He looked at her. "You and Charlie know each other, don't you?"

"Just in the past year," Musette said carefully. It was AA protocol not to indicate how you knew a fellow recovering alcoholic.

"Well then, you can appreciate that she and Belle are totally different types."

Musette laughed in agreement.

"Anyway," continued Peter, "Neil and I share a passion for science, which is probably what's held us together over the years."

"I didn't know that," said Musette. "I thought his main interest was politics."

"Oh no. As an undergraduate at Yale, Neil was a brilliant biologist. I never understood why he chose to go into law, and neither did anyone else. But listen, enough of this. Care to dance?"

"You never told me you were a brilliant biologist," said Musette later in the evening when Neil cut in on her on the dance floor. She delighted in the touch of his hand on her waist because it reminded her of other, more intimate touches, and because it was so public.

He held her at a distance, staring into her face. "You've been talking to Peter, I see. Don't take everything he says seriously."

"Why?"

"He can get pretty gassy."

"Is it true he has a violent reaction to liquor if he drinks during the day?"

Neil laughed. "Yeah, that's true. Jesus, I've never seen anyone puke like he did at the Yale-Harvard game after one or two beers." He laughed again, and then drew her a little closer. "I wish we were alone together," he whispered.

"Really? Then why did you run off like a frightened rabbit when those journalists wanted to photograph us?" She leaned back so she could see the expression on his face.

"Oh, come on, Maggie, let's not go into all that stuff again. You know it's not wise for us to be seen together."

With a trill of laughter, she pressed up against him, rubbing her body suggestively against his hips and stomach, hoping the world would notice. "We're together now, aren't we? For everyone to see."

"Not for long, Maggie, if you pull this shit."

"Okay. I'll be a good girl." She pulled away a little and smiled at him mischievously. "Want to come to my place tonight? That is, after you take your cousin home."

"Uh-unh. I can't. I'm staying at the Salzmans'. Peter and I have some stuff to go over."

"What sort of stuff?"

"Just stuff."

The dance number ended, and reluctantly they dropped their hands and began to clap. "Oh God, Cousin Claire's beckoning. I'd better go back to the table," said Neil as the band started up again a moment later.

"Screw her," said Musette.

"Can't. It would be incest. Besides, I'd rather screw you."

He and Claire left shortly after that. Musette, who was once again on the dance floor, missed saying good-bye to either of them. "Apparently the cousin didn't feel so well," said Harry when she returned to the table.

"Oh," said Musette, fanning herself with her hand. Ignato Reye, her partner of a few moments ago, was a tireless dancer, and she could feel little trickles of perspiration along her ribs. "Well, you know what?" She took a sip of water. "I wouldn't mind leaving myself. It's been a long day and I'm exhausted."

"Fine by me," said Harry. "We achieved what we came here for."

"Let's hope we did," said Musette.

"Oh, I wouldn't worry. It's a brilliant script. Belle's gonna love it."

In the limousine she could hardly keep her eyes open. But upstairs, in her apartment, she was suddenly wide awake. It was one in the morning, and she moved through the rooms, changing her clothes, putting her things away, rummaging through the refrigerator for something to eat. She couldn't stop thinking of the connection between Peter Salzman and Neil. If they were such very old, very good friends, she decided, there was a possibility they would stick out their necks for each other. Judging from what Peter had said, he owed Neil a few favors. So . . . But she couldn't yet figure out what those favors might be. All she knew was that things didn't add up: Peter couldn't have been truthful about drinking with Gil the afternoon of the accident, and Charlie, whose face had gone chalky white at the mention of Gil's death, had been lying when she denied knowing him.

But what did all that mean? She was in her bathroom now, removing her makeup, and she looked at herself in the mirror and gave a little shrug. Her own face, glistening with cold cream, was ghostly pale in the pink bathroom light. She reached up and touched her fingers to the corners of her eyes, pressing against the tiny invisible wrinkles that lay beneath the cream. She had no idea what it meant, but she knew in her bones she would do everything in her power to find out.

ennis MacLeish had two paintings at the Whitney, and Charlie fell in love with them both. They were large, savage—one a wild tangle of black lines that were furiously drawn over so many layers of color that the whole thing appeared to be a dense dark cloud; the other a chalk-white house in a deserted landscape with a naked woman standing in front of it. The stylistic difference between the two were immense; she noted there were five years between them.

Wanting to see more of his work, and anxious to talk before her next class, she called him immediately. "Dennis," she said, "I've just seen your paintings. I'm very impressed."

"Hey—that's good, Vassar."

"I'd like to see more. Which gallery are you with?"

"Well, I was with Edith Pike on Wooster Street. But that was a while ago. We kind of parted company."

"Oh. Well, do you have anything at your loft? Canvases you're working on?"

There was a silence. Then he said, "Nothing current."

"Well, can I see what isn't current?"

"If you like. Be prepared for a mess, though."

"I've gotten good at handling messes," Charlie said. As soon as she hung up she phoned Edith Pike, whom she knew somewhat from her travels through Soho. "This is Charlie Gallagher," she said. "I understand you used to represent Dennis MacLeish. I really admire his work and I'd like to find out what I can about him."

"Well, for one thing he's a drunk," said a tough, cigarettey voice.

Charlie didn't know how to respond to that.

"He's brilliant, though," Edith continued, a little wistful under the toughness. "If it weren't for the booze he'd be a household name. It's something that always made me want to weep, a talented guy like that drinking himself—literally—into oblivion."

"But I've heard he's gotten sober," said Charlie.

"Have you? Well, that would be a big boon for the art world. I'd love to see what he's doing—that is, if he can stay off the bottle long enough."

"He was that bad, hunh?"

"Oh, he was terrible. Always making promises he couldn't keep. Getting into trouble." She laughed throatily. "One time he didn't show up for his own opening. The guests were there, the food was there, the press was there—everyone but Dennis. Turns out he was on a plane to Mexico. He'd been drinking all day, and kind of forgot about the rest of his life. That's the way he was. But look, there are lots of other wonderful painters. You should come over to the gallery one day, and wander around."

Dennis's loft was on the sixth floor of an old warehouse. Charlie visited him two afternoons later, riding up in a big freight elevator that moved so slowly it seemed to be standing still. Dennis greeted her nonchalantly, a cigarette hanging from his lip. "Hope you're not scared of dogs, Vassar," he said, indicating the sleek black Doberman who had followed him to the door.

"Not really," said Charlie, trying not to move as the dog mistrustfully sniffed at her.

"Don't worry. She's harmless, aren't you, Fortune?" said Dennis, giving the dog a loving shove. He led Charlie into the main part of the loft. The dog, Fortune, followed, her nails clicking on the wooden floor. Every so often she thrust her nose into Charlie's ribs, but Charlie was too busy looking around to take the time to be uncomfortable. Dennis hadn't been kidding when he said the place was a mess. The windows were filthy—long sheets of glass so soot-blackened that the light that shone through was a thin dismal gray.

"How can you paint here?" she asked. "The light's terrible."

"I told you, Vassar. It's been a while since I've worked."

"Why? You're so talented."

He grinned at her, a little defiant. "We can get into that later."

The loft was a large, raw, crudely furnished space, with a primitive kitchen, a lumpy couch, some chairs, and a TV at one end, and an easel and work table at the other. A short flight of steps led to a sleeping loft above. Books, papers, and clothing lay scattered all around. The place was almost a parody of what an artist's loft should be, and Charlie wondered if Dennis was a little self-consciously proud of the debris.

She wandered over to the empty easel. "So where are your paintings?" she asked. No art at all hung on any of the walls.

"I've sold most of my work," said Dennis, coming up behind her. "Sit down over there, and I'll show you what I've got."

Charlie sat down on the lumpy couch. Dennis disappeared into what she assumed was a storage room, reappearing several minutes later with a large canvas. He lifted this onto the easel, and wheeled the whole thing over to her.

"Jesus," said Charlie. She pushed her glossy chestnut hair out of her face and leaned forward.

"Like it?" said Dennis.

"It's great." She stared at the painting. "I've never seen anything quite like it before."

The painting was as savage and angry as the two she had seen at the Whitney: a disembodied head whose outlines were eaten away by the soft, opulent colors surrounding it. The face had a waxy pallor, eyes, nose, mouth harshly drawn to create a stony expression at variance with the warm reds and oranges in which the head floated. It took Charlie a full minute to realize that the face was Dennis's.

"Goodness, it's you," she said, feeling suddenly chilled.

"Me when I was drinking."

"God, what a great idea." Charlie looked at the painting even more closely. She felt as if she'd lived the life that it showed—as if, when she was drinking, she too had been this stony and numb, her sense of self melting messily into the world. She thought of Tanya Hendricks, drunk again, and shivered. "When did you paint it?"

"A year and a half ago. It's the last thing I did."

"You don't have anything else?" Charlie's eyes raked the empty shell of a loft.

"As I told you before, it's all been sold. I'm just hanging on to this because it's a constant reminder of what the booze did to me."

"So you wouldn't sell it?"

"Hell no."

"Would you paint something on commission?"

He stared at her out of amused brown eyes. "I'm not sure I could work that way. Besides, I haven't been in the mood to paint. I'm just getting used to being sober." He had been leaning against the easel, and now he straightened his lanky body and began to pace up and down the rug, hands pushed deeply into the pockets of his khaki trousers.

"But what do you do all day?" asked Charlie, appalled that someone so talented should let himself go to waste.

"Go to meetings. Teach that one class. Read. Walk around and look at things." He stopped pacing and stared at her. "Why?"

"Edith Pike says it would be a big boon for the art world if you started to work again."

"Does she now?" said Dennis, looking even more amused. He came and sat down on the couch beside Charlie. "And are you the person who's going to get me going again?"

Her face colored. "Well, I..." She had a vision of herself delivering a carload of canvases to the Pike Gallery, negotiating prices, hiring a PR person, relieving Dennis of all the small, draining tasks of life so that he'd be free to spend every minute of the day painting.

He smiled charmingly at her, and she wondered what it would be like to kiss him, to touch that leathery, pitted, masculine skin. Her flush deepened, and she raised her hands to her cheeks as if to stop it. He was watching her closely. After a minute, he reached over and gently pulled her hands from her face. "You didn't answer my question," he said.

"About whether I'd be the one to get you going? Well, I wouldn't mind."

"Ah, Vassar, that warms my heart. Truly it does."

They stared at each other, and then, wordlessly, moved closer together on the couch. He put his arms around her. She caught the faint, but not disagreeable, scent of his body as he began to kiss her, working his tongue deeply into her mouth. Automatically her tongue wriggled against his, and her hands went up and caressed the back of his head and neck.

For a long time he kissed her. Charlie could feel her body reacting, warming to him, hungry for more. It had been so long since she had kissed a man this way. "Supposing we get these off," he murmured, tugging at her sweater and the waist of her pants. He slipped his hand under her clothes, inching it up and around to undo her bra, while he went on kissing her, harder, more urgently now. And then her bra was unfastened, and she was pushing him away and struggling to sit up, staring weakly around, and wondering if she could really make love, here, on this dreadful couch. Dennis's face was flushed, ardent, thick with need. His lips already had the redness of hours of sex. "What's the matter, Vassar?" he asked softly, and just the sound of his voice, the feel of his eyes on her large breasts, which had slipped from the cups of her bra and were swinging free beneath her sweater, caused a tightening, a series of hot little spasms deep inside her.

"Isn't there someplace else we could go?" She was conscious suddenly of the dog lying near them, open-eyed, on the floor.

"You mean you want a bona fide bed?" Dennis laughed. "I can oblige. Let's go upstairs."

Folding her arms over her chest, she followed him across the loft to the wooden steps that led to the balcony. At the bottom of the steps was a small gate, which he closed so the dog couldn't follow and make a nuisance of herself. Even so, once they were upstairs, Charlie could hear the agitated click of Fortune's nails on the floor. "She'll settle down in a minute," Dennis promised. "She's jealous." The balcony consisted of a single large windowless area set up as a bedroom, with a queen-sized mattress on a box spring, a chest of drawers, several woven peasant rugs, and a straw basket containing books and magazines. Beside the bed was a dome-shaped lamp of white frosted glass, which Dennis immediately switched on. "We do want light, don't we?" he asked, and Charlie realized he was as nervous as she was. She sat down on the bed. "I haven't done this in a while," she said.

"Oh?" He opened his mouth in a grin that showed his chipped front tooth.

"No, really, and there are things I should ask such as do you, uh—"

"I may be a drunk but I'm clean, Vassar. I never did drugs. Anyway we'll play it safe." He went to the chest of drawers and produced a condom, which he held up victoriously. "See," he said. "Nothing to worry about."

Charlie thought, to the contrary, there was everything to worry about, starting with the fact that she didn't really know this man. It was three in the afternoon, her children would soon be coming home from school, and here she was about to go to bed with a stranger, a painter whose work was eerie and violent, and whose life was messy and unstrung. But she didn't care! Her mouth filled with saliva, so anxious was she to taste him, to be in his arms; and as he reached over and slowly pulled the sweater up over her head, she could feel the points of her breasts harden. "Beautiful!" he said, as if he were surveying a painting or landscape, when her large breasts were free at last. Charlie smiled at him, wriggled out of her pants and underwear, and lay down, panting, on the bed, wanting him to feast on her. The sheets smelled as if they could use a washing, and the last idle thought she had before Dennis's clothes were finally off and he was leaning over her, sucking at her nipples and pushing his stiff penis into her thigh, was that next time they would make love at her house, among her things, in her own clean, sweetly scented, spacious bed. Either that, or she would have to send her cleaning girl, Lucia, over here to fumigate the place, which she didn't really think would be appropriate. But by then Dennis had lowered his head to the wetness between her legs, had clamped his mouth over the soft flesh. She heard herself give a little scream of pleasure, and forgot everything.

---

*P*hone call," said Patsy Shroeder, sticking her head around Musette's bedroom door. "It's a Mrs. Belle Salzman. Shall I say you're here?"

Musette, who had just come from her bath, knotted her white terry cloth robe. "Yes, I'm here. But ask her to wait a minute, will you?" She poured herself a cup of coffee from the silver pot the maid had left on her desk, and lit a cigarette. She hadn't expected Belle to respond quite so soon. Less than a week had passed since the gala supper, and she was afraid it was bad news. "Hello, Belle," she said, picking up the phone. "How wonderful to hear from you! I can't thank you enough for the other evening."

"Yes, it was nice, wasn't it? I love putting together parties like that." She chuckled. "Though I must say, between Priss Herman's morning sickness and Claire getting one of her awful migraines, there was kind of a hospital feel to it."

"Oh, I hadn't known that Priss was enceinte." Musette liked to use French words whenever she could. "I thought she and Joe were just back from their honeymoon."

"Yes, isn't that a kick?" Belle chuckled again. "Hard to imagine little Joey Herman getting anyone in that condition. But look, I didn't call to gossip. I just wanted you to know that I read the script and I simply love it. I'd planned to save it for next weekend, but once I started I couldn't put it down. Now, the next thing is for me to talk to Peter. He's off on a trip to Oslo tomorrow, and we haven't had time for a chat yet."

"Does that mean you're interested in backing it?"

"Well darling, of course I'm interested. But I have to hash the whole thing through with Peter before coming up with actual figures. And of course we'll want to know who's directing, et cetera, et cetera. You said the other evening you were just putting together a package?"

"Yes," said Musette. "We are."

"Good. Well, when Peter gets back next week and I've had a chance to talk to him, we'll set something up. All right?"

"All right. Yes, that would be wonderful."

They said good-bye. Musette lit another cigarette, and stared at her wavery reflection in the coffeepot. She had to decide whether or not to inform Gwen of this latest development. According to their agreement, Gwen, as associate producer, had the right to make certain artistic decisions, as well as to approve (or disapprove) of casting. But in fact, when Gwen had relinquished the script a month ago, she seemed to have entirely lost interest in the project. Clearly she was a writer, not a manager—words were all that were important to her. And this was fine with Musette, who had worried all along that Gwen would push for a black director to the exclusion of all white candidates who might also be qualified. She crushed out her cigarette and stood up. Belle's phone call had come at the right time. Tomorrow she was scheduled to fly out to the West Coast to talk to Miroslav, who, despite their differences, she hoped would be interested in directing the film. No one, she had decided, could handle *Homegirl* as well as her ex-husband. Teaming up with him once again would draw a lot of publicity—and consequently a lot of money. Unless Gwen came to her with questions, she would continue to keep her as uninformed as possible.

On the evening of November first, Gwen put on a black velvet suit, an African necklace of warm beaten gold, a pair of tall black suede heels, and her many bangles. This was the night she was to appear at the Tulsa dinner at the Waldorf, and she was terrified. Talking to her sponsor, Margot Sibley, she had boiled the terror down to two things: her fear of speaking publicly about anything to do with her career, and her nervousness about encountering J. Hopeton Sinclair, newspaper editor and critic. "You'll do just fine," Margot had promised. "Knowing what frightens you is half the battle."

But Gwen wasn't convinced. It was the first time she would be speaking to a large audience without liquor in her system, and she was afraid of panicking and reaching for a drink. "Just do the Third Step," counseled Margot. "Turn your life and your will over to your higher power. That's more or less what you do every day when you sit down to work, isn't it?"

But it was one thing to surrender deeply to the creative force that seemed to guide her when she was in the privacy of her study, and another to let go like that at a dinner in a luxurious hotel. "I'll try," she had said to Margot, promising to call her at the end of the evening.

Now she studied herself in the mirror. Her hair, which had just been cut, was as soft and fuzzy as a lamb's. She put small gold hoops in her ears, sprayed on some Miss Dior, and backed up to see the effect. She wasn't pretty in the conventional sense, but she was a strong, handsome-looking woman. Her cheekbones stuck out, wide and flat, and she liked the fullness and darkness of her lips, the round shape of her nostrils, and the hard intelligence that beamed from her eyes. She had her father's height and dark skin, and her mother's high-boned Indian cheeks and almond eyes, all in all not a bad combination. For that moment, staring into the silver gleam of mirror, she was pleased with herself; then she saw the note cards she would be using at tonight's dinner scattered on the bed, and the queasiness rose once again in her stomach. Margot had said to do the Third Step. If she were to talk to Audrey at what she had dubbed the Black Meeting, the large woman would undoubtedly say: "Baby, when you confused, just repeat the Serenity Prayer to yourself. And if you ain't got the time for all them words, say it the short way: *Fuck it.*" Well, all right, thought Gwen, stuffing the note cards into her bag, and pulling on her heavy black overcoat. Fuck it, that's all. Just plain fuck it.

*　*　*

She entered the Waldorf with those two words running like a mantra through her head, and miraculously they made her feel a little better. The Tulsa dinner was being held in the Grand Ballroom, which was on the third floor. Gwen left her coat at the second-floor coat check and took the elevator up. Before the dinner was a cocktail reception in the East Foyer, and as she picked up her name tag at the table in the outer hall, she was glad she had had the sense to arrive late.

A pall of smoke hung over the East Foyer, and there were the sounds of laughter, conversation, clinking glasses. Gwen waved at a few people she knew. Maybe this wouldn't be so bad after all. In the center of the room, a crowd had gathered around the actress, Bethany Hunt, and Gwen craned her neck to get a better view. The woman was beautiful, but in a sleek, overrefined way that didn't interest Gwen, and she turned and headed for the bar.

Although she would have loved a scotch on the rocks, she ordered a ginger ale, and began to circulate through the crowd. It wasn't long before she, in her own right, was surrounded by people wanting to say hello to the famous novelist. Smiling, she shook hands and made intelligent small talk until finally the doors to the ballroom were thrust open, and the crowd moved forward in a slow, steady crush. Gwen found herself being carried along on a tide of people, most of them black and distinguished-looking: educators, politicians, members of the clergy, businessmen, artists, writers, entertainers. Once she was inside the vast room, she pulled away from the crowd and went up to the dais to find her seat.

There were eight speakers, four on one side of the podium, four on the other. Gwen took a quick look at the name cards. On her side were Ambrose Smiley, president of Tulsa College, the actress Bethany Hunt, and Bernard Shaw of CNN, the evening's master of ceremonies. On the other side were Faye Wattleton of Planned Parenthood, Charlayne Hunter-Gault of PBS, Tom Bradley, mayor of Los Angeles, and J. Hopeton Sinclair of the *West Indian Voice*. Gwen, pleased that Sinclair wasn't seated anywhere near her, didn't see him when she looked over at the other side. Her own seat was at the end of the dais, farthest away from the podium. Ambrose Smiley was to her left, and as he pulled her chair out for her, he said, "Good to see you again, Gwen."

Gwen didn't remember ever having seen much of him when she was at Tulsa all those years ago. He was a tall, rangy-looking, quite handsome man with ebony skin and graying hair. Gwen judged his age to be about sixty. She smiled at him, and said, "Yes, it's nice to see you, too."

Bethany Hunt, on his other side, put a cigarette to her lips, and Ambrose quickly turned to light it for her. "I know I shouldn't smoke in public. Bad for the image and all that," laughed the actress, waving smoke away with a thin beautiful hand. "But I really don't care. That is, unless you mind?" She glanced questioningly at Ambrose, who said he didn't mind at all. Gwen lit her own cigarette, and stared out over the enormous golden room, narrowing her eyes so that everything was blurry. She hated the actress's voice, which was thin and simpering, with the slightest hint of a Boston accent. How had the woman managed to star in so many roles with a voice like that? Ambrose broke in on her thoughts. "Do you two ladies know each other?" he asked, as Bernard Shaw stood up and began to present the speakers.

"No, I don't believe we do," lilted Bethany.

Don't believe, thought Gwen. Jesus, how false.

"Oh, well then, let me introduce you," said Ambrose. "Gwen, this is Bethany Hunt, whom I'm sure you've seen dozens of times—in fact, it's hard to turn on the TV without seeing her. And Bethany, this is Gwendolyn Thomas, one of our most distinguished authors."

The women reached across him to shake hands. Bethany gave Gwen a superb smile, but her dark eyes were placid, and her face, which was light-skinned with a wash of golden freckles across the narrow (and surely doctored) bridge of her nose, wore a bored expression. Gwen took an instant dislike to her. She was about thirty, though she could have been younger, and she had the sort of hair that Gwen in her schoolgirl days would happily have killed for: long and thick and abundantly curly. She wore a glimmering white-sequined gown that showed off the beauty of her café au lait skin.

Bernard Shaw introduced Bethany first since she was the evening's honoree. One of America's finest actresses. A graduate of Tulsa College. Known for her deep commitment to saving wildlife and the planet. Gwen let his words drift over her head, barely listening as she concentrated on the audience, the hundreds of dark, softly lit, upturned faces. A salad of goat's cheese and Boston lettuce had been served as an appetizer, and people were eating in respectful silence as Bernard Shaw spoke. There must have been fifty tables, each with a gleaming white cloth, flowers, and candles, and the effect, in the sparkly light of the enormous glass chandelier, was dreamy and ethereal. Gwen, who wasn't terribly hungry, forced herself to take a bite of salad. Bernard Shaw had moved on now to the other speakers: Ambrose and herself, and then Faye Wattleton and the others to his left. Putting down her fork, Gwen felt for the note cards inside her bag, fingering them for reassurance. What was she going to say to all these people? The speech she had prepared had fled her mind, and she was left with a dull, static, seashell roar. This had happened to her before, but each time there had been a glass of wine just at her fingertips, and she'd been okay. Except the last time. The time at Thornton College a year and a half ago, when she'd gotten drunk on whiskey in the ladies' room, and then had staggered across the stage to the podium and hurled abuse at the audience. Automatically, with a tinkle of golden bangles, her hand reached across the white-clothed table for her water glass.

"And last but not least, we have Mr. John Hopeton Sinclair of the *West Indian Voice,* a leading black weekly here in New York."

Gwen leaned forward, wanting a good look at Sinclair. At the same time, she raised her glass to her lips and took a small swallow. The editor looked familiar. Somewhere she had seen that bony, cynical face before. And then, as she remembered where, she gasped and spat out the liquid in her mouth. The goddamn stuff was wine! Wine, whose dry, slightly sour taste coated her tongue and caused, just that one mouthful of it, a familiar whirring in her blood. Beside her Ambrose murmured, "Are you all right, dear?"

"Yes," Gwen said thickly.

But she wasn't all right at all, and she hastily put down the glass and wiped at her lips, so confused she wanted to cry. She should have known better than to blindly drink from a glass without looking at its contents first. She picked up her water glass, the right one this time, and rinsed her mouth gratefully. At least she hadn't gone on and drunk the whole goddamned thing. When her mouth tasted fresher, she lit a cigarette and glanced again at Sinclair. She was almost positive he was who she thought he was—the man she had seen at the Black Meeting a few weeks ago. That harsh-spoken and seemingly uneducated man, the one who had told her, not without a certain undertone of menace, that he had read her books, and who had tried to shock her by telling her he had been to prison. *What for?* He hadn't said, and she hadn't asked.

Now she studied Sinclair carefully. He had the same burnished skin, the same woolly hair, the same sharp-eyed, thin, humorless face as that other man. Of course he was wearing a tuxedo, which gave him a far more prosperous appearance than a pair of jeans and a sweatshirt. But she was sure it was the same man.

She stared at him thoughtfully, squinting against the smoke of her cigarette, and suddenly he looked up and gave her a big, gap-toothed, ironic grin. When she didn't smile back, he raised his water glass and saluted her.

The first speaker was Bethany Hunt, who stood easily at the podium, radiant in her sparkling white gown, her thick hair falling over her shoulders. She gave what Gwen thought was a rather mechanical speech about the important influence Tulsa College had had on her life, but the audience loved her, and when she stepped down, there was a solid round of applause. "Not bad for a kid who partied all the time," whispered Ambrose.

"How'd she make it through?" Gwen whispered back.

Ambrose gave a snort of laughter. "Don't be naive. She flunked out of Vassar and then kind of drifted around until we took her. Her father owns a chain of shoe stores up in New England, and with the hefty donation he gave us, we were able to build a new gym."

"I see," said Gwen. She felt a little uncomfortable sitting next to Ambrose because of her own poor performance at Tulsa College. Nothing had ever been said, and she wondered if she should take this opportunity to do an AA Ninth Step, to make an amend. According to Margot and to everyone else she knew in AA, one didn't have to attempt that step until one had been sober for a while, but this might be the only chance she would ever have with Ambrose. She looked over at Sinclair, wondering what he would advise. The editor was puffing at a cigarette, staring down at his plate and looking bored. Just the sight of him made her blood boil, and she shifted her attention back to Ambrose. "You know," she said, "I've always felt bad because I didn't exactly give Tulsa my best shot."

"Water under the bridge," said Ambrose. "You were a different person then."

"You remember how I was?"

"Sure." He laughed. "It would be seventy degrees and a balmy day, and you'd be walking around huddled up in a shawl. You were kind of hard to miss."

"But as a teacher?"

"Don't remember anything about you as a teacher. But if you were unhappy there, you were right to leave. Anyway, I think you'd agree that your experience at Tulsa turned out to be a rich one for you and for everyone who's read your work. Isn't that so?"

"Yes," Gwen said, feeling immeasurably lighter than she had a few moments ago. She thought of Glady with sudden affection, not her usual stab of guilt. "Without that year at Tulsa I'd never have written *Homegirl*. In fact, I'm not sure I'd ever have written anything at all."

Gwen fretted through the rest of the speeches. She twisted her napkin in her lap. She left her dessert—raspberry sherbet in a silver cup—untouched, so that it melted to a gooey syrup. She drank three cups of black coffee, and she kept mentally repeating the short form of the Serenity Prayer—Fuck it, fuck it. Ambrose must have thought she was crazy, but he was very sweet to sit next to, and at one point he patted her hand and said, "You know, it's an honor to go last."

"Some honor," Gwen said. "I might die first."

"Don't drink any more coffee and you'll be fine. Anyway, the more nervous you are, the better you speak. That's my theory."

If his theory was true, John Sinclair, who walked to the podium with his hands in his pockets, was incredibly nervous. He was the only speaker Gwen listened to with total attention, partly because she was curious about what he had to say, and partly because he was so dramatic, so full of surprises. He was a small man, smaller than she remembered, and his face was crafty and fierce as he stood scowling at the audience. Several moments passed before he opened his mouth to speak. And when he did, he gave that amazing gap-toothed grin, and said, "My. *My, my, my.* We all sure heard a bunch of high falutin stuff tonight. Birth control for them teenage girls out there. Yeah, that's a good idea. That's important. Making *our* institutions of learning as influential, as *classy* as Harvard or Yale." He rolled his eyes heavenward as if only God could facilitate such a thing, and there was a nervous titter of laughter from the audience. "Gettin' some of those boys of ours . . . you know the ones, them homeboys who'd just as soon knife you for a few dollars as go out and do an honest day's work . . . getting *them* interested maybe in politics or social welfare. Well, that's a good idea too. But the question none of us fortunate niggers here at the top of the heap seems to want to address is: *How we gonna do it?*"

Shocked at his use of the word "nigger," Gwen glanced at the audience. The people nearest her were staring up at Sinclair, mesmerized.

"The way we gonna do it," he was saying, "is by being honest. Taking a good, hard, *shrewd* look at where we—the black part of this nation—are; figuring out, *honestly,* how we got here; and deciding what we're gonna do about it. And the first thing we gotta realize is that self-pity, concentrating on the past instead of looking forward, ain't gonna get us nowhere. Neither is the welfare check coming in the mail. And neither is the negative self-image that is a curse upon us, that is our biggest problem because it leads to violence, hopelessness, despair, and drugs. We are a wonderful people, a beautiful people. It's time for us to join hands with everyone else, the whole rainbow, and do what we can, not only for ourselves, but for the rest of this great nation. Believe me, it is only through rising above prejudice and fear and hatred, that we will find our way. Now, let's talk about honesty."

Honesty, for John Hopeton Sinclair, was a painful and merciless process of stripping away all the dreams and illusions, and presenting facts as they were. "We don't want to be lulled by pretenses, sweet talk, false ideas," he said. "We gotta know exactly what is what."

The only way to know what was what, he declared, was through a strong black press. Newspapers, radio, TV—the black points of view had to make themselves felt throughout the media with a forcefulness that would act as a real agent of change within the black psyche. That was his message, and it was a strong one. Gwen, who wanted badly to dislike him, was filled with a jittery kind of awe. He had a down-home, unhurried way of speaking that put the audience right in the palm of his hand. But he could turn around: without seeming to change gears, in an acid voice, he could say something so shocking and revelatory that a gasp would go through the room. And everyone loved that! The street English, the big evil grin, the fist brought down for emphasis on the podium—the audience couldn't have enough. His last words were, "Our point of view is valid, our language is colorful, we are a strong good people...isn't it time that we put down the needle, the drug, the gun, and found other, more productive ways to make ourselves heard in this society?"

Gwen wondered how she could top him. When Sinclair was finished, he looked over at her and gave a little nod, as if to say, "Your turn, baby." Then he stepped down.

Bernard Shaw strode over to the mike, holding up his hands as the audience continued to clap. "Now folks...now we're going to hear from the lady we've all been waiting for, and whose books have given us such pleasure and excitement: Gwendolyn Thomas!"

"Good luck," said Ambrose. Gwen threw him a grateful look, and walked, stiff-backed, to the podium. Fuck it, she was thinking. Fuck it, fuck it. She held her note cards tightly in her hand, but she knew damn well she wasn't going to use them. The lights shining on her were hot, as hot as suns, and she took a moment to push back her sleeves, and clear her throat. Then she said, "Well, Mr. Sinclair has just spoken convincingly of honesty, and so I'm going to tell you something about how I got here. You know, I never intended to be a writer—uh-unh, I intended to be a sociologist. I was going to sit in my comfortable university office, and read about the various patternings of human society, particularly our own black society. That was what I was going to do. But then two things happened: I became interested in black poets and writers, and I went to teach for a year at Tulsa College."

She paused for breath, and stared out at the audience. Then she laughed. "Now I've got to tell you, I was the most sheltered black girl you've ever met. I grew up in Harlem, but I was like a hothouse rose out there among the wildflowers, and so the last thing I wanted was to spend my life in any kind of ghetto. I mean I could talk big about helping my own people, but I didn't really know anything about them. I knew Lord and Taylor's, that was what I knew. I knew Bonwit's and Bloomingdale's, and the arty movie theaters on Third Avenue. And I knew, as I grew older, the peace and quiet of libraries, the joys of intellectual growth. Living in a white man's world, that was what I knew. So that when I went off to Tulsa College, it was ... well, I've gotta tell you folks, it was something of a shock. I wasn't happy. I wasn't happy at all."

She hadn't planned any of this. The words just seemed to fly out of her mouth. And she felt relaxed. She felt marvelous, almost as intoxicated as if she'd had a few drinks. She stood, her strong brown arms resting lightly on the podium, and without worrying about how any of it sounded, she told them about the dog days at Tulsa College; about meeting Glady Johnson, who couldn't read or write, but could tell a mean story; about how she had run home to New York. "That was the year I wrote *Homegirl*. And it was like fate playing a trick on me, because all I wanted to do, or *thought* I wanted to do when I got back to this civilized city of New York, was go to the movies, traipse through department stores, look up all my old friends. But instead I found myself in a library carrel writing down a bunch of stories. Not *my* stories, understand, but Glady's. And somehow those stories turned into a book."

She stared out at the blur of faces. She had been talking for about ten minutes, and she knew it was time to wind down. "Well, I want to tell you tonight that sometimes I feel a little funny writing other people's stories. And that's my point because, you see, I am not the lost black woman you meet in *Homegirl* or *Hey Look at Me Mister* or any of my books. I'm a different kind of black woman, the kind who gets lost moving from one class into another, one world into another."

She smiled, squaring her shoulders so that her necklace flashed. "I'll bet there are a lot of you here tonight who've had to deal with that problem. I mean, come on, this is the Waldorf Ass-toria, and you've each had to pay four or five hundred dollars to get in here. Let's be honest: our mammies and pappies never knew about money like that. No way. Most of them had to struggle to buy food and clothing for their poor children, and the idea of a banquet like this"—she shook her head—"well, if they were to walk into this room tonight, they'd think they'd died and gone to heaven. Which brings me back to where I started: sociology. We are a very odd segment of the black population. We've made it. We've climbed to the top. But the top is an extremely confusing and dangerous place for a black person to be, and if we're to keep our balance, if we're to function as writers and educators and politicians and journalists, then we must be very sure of who we are and where we're going. Without shame, without delusions of grandeur, but pridefully, and with a sense of humor, we must put one foot in front of the other, raise our eyes to the prize, and keep walking."

There was a burst of applause. "Here, here!" several people shouted. Gwen nodded her head in thanks, and walked quickly to her seat. She was sweating. Her upper lip and forehead were damp with perspiration, and she could feel wetness beneath her velvet suit jacket. As she sat down, Ambrose congratulated her. "You were wonderful," he said. "The best." His eyes were shining, and she saw that he meant it.

"I'm just glad it's over," she said. She put her note cards back in her bag, hoping she hadn't made a goddamn fool of herself. Inside her bag she found some Kleenex, and she wiped her face and the palms of her hands, and then took a sip of water. She didn't want to look at John Sinclair, but her eyes moved toward him as if he were a magnet. The outline of him. The small strong body. The woolly head, which had a shiny copper-colored bald spot at the crown. He was talking to someone, his back to her, and she decided that in a few minutes, when she had her breath back and Bernard Shaw had finished his closing remarks, she'd go over to him and ask why he hadn't told her who he was at the meeting. He must have known then that they would both be speaking at the Waldorf, so his reticence seemed odd and childish.

But before she had a chance to move from her chair, she was once again surrounded by people. Well-wishers. Admirers. Old friends. Journalists. Youthful writers hoping for advice. Bernard Shaw had wrapped up the evening with a joke, and now they all surged toward her from the tables on the floor of the ballroom. She was high. She was excited. She felt Glady with her here, and the feeling was good. She took her time and said a few words to everyone, and forty-five minutes passed before she was free to go and speak to John Sinclair. But by then his seat was empty and he was gone.

harlie waited till the maid's day off to invite Dennis to her house. She had promised herself she would not sleep with him again at his loft, where it was so dirty, but it was a promise she had been unable to keep. At home there were always people around, and so, mad to see him, she had driven to his loft at odd hours, and lain with him on unclean sheets, listening to the whimpering of the dog downstairs.

But today—bliss!—she had her house to herself.

She had asked him to come for lunch, which she figured would give them plenty of time. He arrived punctually at a quarter to twelve, carrying roses wrapped in white paper that he must have bought at a Korean vegetable stand. "Here, these are for you," he said, thrusting them at her.

The idea of a man as tough as Dennis MacLeish doing something as sentimental as buying roses both moved and embarrassed her, and she gave him a quick kiss and went to the kitchen to put them in water.

"Hey, this is some place you've got here," she heard him say with a whistle. He was in the living room, looking around.

"Yes, I know," she said. "I was very lucky to find it."

"Must've cost a fortune."

She didn't answer. She put the roses in a crockery vase, and went to join him in the living room, suddenly conscious of how she must appear to an artist who didn't have much money. Cashmere sweater, Cartier watch, pearl drop earrings, hair a mass of shining waves. All simple, plain, unpretentious as hell, but put it together and you had the dressed-down, careless look of the very rich. Walking toward him, she thrust her jaw out slightly, and pushed her hands down in the pockets of her tan trousers. She hadn't felt this way at his loft. There she had been an art student, an inferior being, a visitor from the outside world, but here everything about her spelled privilege.

He was at the far end of the room and he didn't look up as she approached. His eyes were fixed on her most recent acquisition, a huge colorful canvas by a young American painter, Gary Green, that was tilted against the wall as she hadn't yet had time to hang it. On his face was a hard look of envy that he made no attempt to hide. "This guy's vastly overrated," he said when she was beside him. "How much did you pay for it? Ten-twelve thousand?"

"Something like that," said Charlie, although she had paid considerably more.

"Boy, they sure know how to soak people like you. I mean look at this painting! The brushstrokes are amateurish, the colors are insipid, the composition's an outright bore, and yet he gets away with it. Makes me goddamn furious."

"You could be doing just as well if you wanted," said Charlie through tightened lips. She was stung by his last remark, the notion that she was not as discerning as she knew herself to be. "It's just a matter of work."

"Oh yeah, work work work. The famous W word. Well, let me tell you, it's not just a matter of work. It's a matter of being in the right place at the right time, having a clever manager, being packaged the right way so that people will like you and want to eat you up like candy. That's what it is. Talent—the pure blood, sweat, and tears of the thing—is really the least of it."

"But before you can be *packaged*"—Charlie spat the word out as if it had a bad taste—"you have to have work, canvases, something to sell."

He smiled at her sourly. "There you go with the W word again. All right, Vassar, I'll work if that'll please your gilt-edged soul. I'll produce paintings that'll blow your socks off, and trot them right over to Edith Pike, and make sure the spotlight gets shined on me. In the meantime, do you think we could eat? You promised lunch and I'm starving."

After cheese omelettes, fruit, and coffee, they went up to her bedroom. It was one o'clock. The children wouldn't be home till around four, so they still had plenty of time. Charlie had already put in her diaphragm—one thing less to deal with, though she insisted Dennis wear a condom—and now she sat down on her bed and watched Dennis admire her pretty room. She had intended to furnish it simply, but had found herself haunting the antiques stores on Atlantic Avenue, where she had picked up all sorts of bric-a-brac. Blue striped wallpaper complimented the blue of the Chinese rug and the velvet of the Victorian settee; bead necklaces were draped over the mirror of her marvelous old oak dresser; and the brass bed had been bought at a country auction. The effect of the room was one of coziness and clutter. But Dennis seemed to like it. After a minute he sat down beside her, untying his work boots and stowing them beneath the bed. "Want a cigarette?" she asked. The times they had made love before they had gotten right to it, hungrily, ardently, but now there was a certain strain between them.

"All right," said Dennis. He pointed to a book on her bedside table, the *Big Book,* which was the closest thing AA had to a bible. "Are you really reading that? I thought you hated that stuff."

"I'm reading it the way I read Proust," said Charlie. She lit his cigarette for him, and stretched out on the bed. "I used to fall asleep with *Swann's Way* on my pillow when I was in college. I had this idea that the only way to absorb it was if it was right there next to my brain while I was asleep and dreaming, and that seems to be the way it is with the *Big Book* too. As long as it's there, like some kind of icon, I won't get into trouble."

"Oh, yes you will," said Dennis, sliding his hand under her sweater. The cigarette was still in his lips, and his eyes, bothered by the smoke, were half-closed, which gave him a look of cunning.

"Not that kind of trouble," murmured Charlie. "I meant drinking trouble."

"Well, if you stick with me, Vassar, you won't have to worry about drinking trouble." And he started to undress her.

They made love twice, first quickly, almost violently, as if their bodies were looking for an immediate, explosive release, and then slowly and voluptuously. Dennis was not the passionate, innovative lover Gil Hoffeld had been, but when he touched her, it was with a bluntness and hunger that made her want to wrap her legs around him and moan. She knew she was infatuated with him. In the past week he had constantly been on her mind, vivid pictures of his face, his naked body, his rough, chapped, painter's hands. She had stopped going to his class because it was impossible to sit there, pretending she was nothing to him but a student.

After their second lovemaking she fell asleep. When she awoke, Dennis was gone from the bed. She sat up, rubbing at her eyes, and stared in the direction of the bathroom, where she assumed he was. But the door to that room stood ajar, and she could just discern a faint patch of dusky light from the window. No one was in there. "Dennis?" she called. "Dennis, where are you?" Around her the large, silent house felt suddenly gloomy, and she shivered. "Dennis?" she called again, wondering if he could have left while she was asleep. Disturbed, she swung her legs over the side of the bed, and went to the closet for her bathrobe.

Suddenly he was behind her. "Here I am, sweetheart," he said. His feet were silent on the rug.

She jumped, startled. "Jesus, where were you?"

"Exploring. I wanted to see the rest of your house."

"Why didn't you wake me up?" She didn't like it that he had looked around her house without her.

"Didn't want to disturb you." He moved forward to take her in his arms, pushing the bathrobe open, kissing her tenderly. "You looked so sweet and peaceful lying there under the quilt."

She pushed him away. "What time is it? Jesus, the children'll be here any minute." The gilt clock on the mantel said twenty to four. She ran to the bathroom and turned on the shower. She smelled of sex. There were sticky patches on her stomach and between her thighs, and somehow, even if her skin was hidden, she couldn't bear to face the children like that. Especially Petra, who seemed, these days, always to be watching her critically. The last thing she wanted to do was introduce her to Dennis.

She stepped out of the shower and toweled herself briskly, rubbing at her hair, spraying herself lightly with eau de cologne. "Dennis," she called, "are you dressed?"

"Not yet," he said, coming into the bathroom. "I need a shower."

"Well, take one at home. I don't want the children finding a strange man in my bathroom."

He grinned at her. "Why not? Be a nice little eye-opener into the character of their sexy mother." But he left the bathroom without showering, and quickly put on his clothes. Charlie threw herself into the pants and sweater she had had on before, and drew the quilt up over the bed. She glanced around the room, picked up the ashtray, turned off the bedside lamp, opened the curtains, and said, "Come on, let's get out of here."

But when they were downstairs, going into the living room, she heard the key in the door. "Damn!" she exclaimed. Dennis didn't have his jacket on yet, and their lunch dishes were still on the table, hard evidence.

"What the hell are you so worried about?" he asked. "I promise I'll be a good boy."

"They've never seen me with another man before."

Seconds later Petra was in the hall, dropping her backpack with a thud and calling, "Mom? You home?"

"In here, darling."

"Colin's over at Richie's. I hope that's okay. What's for dinner?" She came into the living room, her cheeks ruddy from the cold November afternoon, her brown hair strewn over her shoulders, her shirt tighter, for a schoolgirl of fifteen, than Charlie would have liked. When she saw Dennis, she stopped short. "I didn't know anyone was here," she said.

"Petra, this is my art teacher, Dennis MacLeish. He was nice enough to come over and have a look at our new Gary Green painting."

"Oh," said Petra. She came farther into the room and shook hands, accustomed to being polite from her days in Washington. "Mom's wild about that painting, but my brother and I don't quite see the point."

"Neither do I," Dennis said dryly.

Charlie watched Petra study him, trying to see him as her daughter did. He was wearing khaki pants and a frayed blue shirt, his hair was tousled, his fingers were yellow from nicotine, and his work boots looked as if he'd been stomping through mud and dirt for years. On the back of a chair lay his old cracked brown leather bomber jacket. She watched as Petra's eyes drifted to that, and then back to Charlie herself, who was standing at the fireplace, smoking. "What did you say was for dinner?" she asked.

"I didn't," said Charlie. "But we could go out and have Chinese if you like."

"Okay," said Petra. She looked beyond her mother to the dirty plates and glasses on the dining room table. "Well, I guess I'd better go upstairs and study," she said. "It was nice meeting you."

"Likewise," said Dennis.

She strode from the room, a tall pretty girl in tight jeans that accentuated her rounded bottom and the narrowness of her hips. It shocked Charlie that the school permitted students to dress like that. She and Petra had had several screaming matches on the subject of clothing, but when she saw it was a losing battle, she had given up. She just didn't have the energy for continual arguments with her children. Now she let out a long breath and said, "Well, I guess you'd better go."

Dennis reached for his jacket and put it on. At the door he tried to kiss her, but Charlie, conscious of her daughter, averted her head. "Not now," she whispered, annoyed that he could be so thoughtless. But once he was out the door, she started yearning for him again. Aching for him.

Two nights later she stood in that same doorway with her husband, Neil. It was Colin's tenth birthday, and they were going out to dinner as a family. "How are you?" said Neil, pulling her to him and giving her a quick kiss. She kissed him back, and said, "Fine," although this was untrue. She had just had a terrible argument with Petra over plans for the evening.

She took his coat and they went into the living room. "Where are the kids?" he asked.

"Colin's upstairs in his room, busy with a new computer game I bought him, and Petra's where else? On the phone. They'll be down in a minute."

Neil chuckled. "I'll bet the last thing she wanted to do was waste a Saturday night on her little brother's birthday."

"How right you are," said Charlie. She gave him a seltzer water with lime, and didn't bother to apologize for the fact that she kept no liquor in the house. Neil was used to it by now; in the past few weeks he had begun to go to an Al-Anon meeting in Georgetown, and knew as much about AA and the Twelve Steps as Charlie did. She appreciated that—it was an effort for him, she knew—but at the same time she vaguely resented his entry into this part of her world. He took a sip of his drink, and put the glass down. "She doesn't have a boyfriend, does she?"

"Petra? Of course not."

"Well, you never know. She's so—developed."

"Only physically. Inside she's still a big baby."

"I don't know," said Neil. "I get the feeling she's changing pretty fast."

"Jesus, remember what it was like being fifteen?"

Neil laughed. "I remember being terrified of girls. I remember being very excited about sports, and going skeet shooting with my father—"

"Who you hardly ever saw," interrupted Charlie.

"Who I hardly ever saw. And I remember this one guy always passing around sex magazines in our dorm. He was a real loud-mouth and I hated him. But boy, I envied him for having the nerve to walk into a store and buy those magazines."

"But did you *look* at the magazines?"

Neil grinned at her. "Sure I did. Secretly. They were the stuff of great fantasies, all those shaved, big-titted ladies, and I'd hole myself up in the bathroom with them like everyone else. But I didn't connect them with any of the real girls I knew till I was ...oh, about sixteen."

"And then there was no stopping you," giggled Charlie.

"That's right," said Neil, picking up his drink. "Once I got brave enough to actually test the waters. Which, let me tell you, in the early sixties, for a well-behaved young man such as myself, were not as warm as they are now."

"What wasn't as warm?" said Petra, coming into the room. She leaned down and gave her father a kiss. She was wearing a mustard yellow kimono top over a tight black miniskirt, and her shiny brown hair was loose over her shoulders. Over the kimono she wore a fringed shawl she had borrowed from her mother. Neil pretended to ignore the sloppily seductive look of her outfit. "Oh," he said, "your mother and I were talking about the travails of being a young man in the sixties."

Petra sat down in a chair across from him, drawing her legs up beneath her and starting in on a handful of pistachios. "What'd you get Colin for his birthday?" she asked, prying open a shell with a mauve-painted fingernail.

"Stuff for his computer," said Neil. "Tapes, a watch—"

"A new skateboard," said Charlie.

"Yes, a new skateboard. And tickets to an ice hockey game."

"Oh, he'll love that," said Petra, opening another shell and licking her fingers. Charlie watched her guardedly. You'd never know, she thought, that a little over an hour ago we were practically at each other's throats. The rage she had felt toward her daughter had been unlike anything she had ever experienced as a mother before. Petra, who had been out most of the day, had come into her room while she was dressing, and flopped onto the bed. "What time do you think we'll be back from dinner, Ma?" she had asked.

"I don't know. I suppose around nine-thirty or ten. Why?"

"Because a bunch of us are going out later."

"*Are* going out? What are you talking about?"

Petra pretended to examine one of her nails. "Eliza and Heather and Kate and I. We're either going to Nell's or the Limelight. Probably Nell's because Heather knows someone there."

"Somehow this conversation isn't making sense to me," said Charlie. She stopped buttoning her blouse, and stared at her daughter. "Perhaps you could elaborate a little. You know you're not allowed to run off into the night just as you please."

"This isn't running off, Mother. There are a whole bunch of us."

"That doesn't make it any better. You're fifteen, Petra. That's too young to go to nightclubs."

"Oh, *Mother!* This is the twentieth century, remember? Everyone goes to clubs now. It's not like when you were my age."

"Sometime in prehistory, you mean. Look, I don't care what century this is. You're not going."

Petra, sprawled on the bed, stared at Charlie out of eyes that gave nothing away.

"You're not going," Charlie repeated, "and that's final."

"Then I'll be the only one stuck at home," said Petra in a quavering voice. "No one else's mother is as strict as you."

"I don't believe that."

"Well, it's true. Eliza's mother's letting her go. So is Heather's and so is Kate's and so is Anna's. Even Shelley who always has to be home by midnight. We'd all be taking a cab."

"Uh-hunh," said Charlie. She sat down at her dressing table to brush her hair. "Tell me," she asked casually, "what happens at these clubs?" In the mirror she could see Petra sprawled on the bed, her body stiffer-looking now, tensed and knotted up like a kid about to have a tantrum. Her face was sullen, the lips turned down. Jesus, she hates me, thought Charlie.

Petra mumbled, "We just dance."

"What?"

"We just dance," repeated Petra. "What do you think we do? Sneak out in the alley and have sex? Shoot dope up our arm? That was in your time, but it's not in ours—"

"Now wait a minute, that's not—"

"You probably think people bring in beer and marijuana, but that's not true, that's what your generation did. Ours is a lot more savvy, and we wouldn't dream of getting ourselves all messed up like that." She sat up on the bed, and began to talk loudly, staring furiously at Charlie, who had turned around, brush in hand. "I mean, I got to see you drunk all the time, I saw what that was like and do you think I'd make the same mistake? Do you really think so? Well, I wouldn't. And anyway, if *your* parents hadn't been so uptight, maybe you wouldn't have gotten into all that trouble with booze."

"Petra, you're getting out of line."

"No I'm not! No I'm not! No one else's mother is as controlling as you are."

"Oh, we're back to that," said Charlie, stung. "Look, I just can't believe that any of those girls' parents would let them stay out till all hours at a club."

"Call them and see."

It was a dare, and Charlie knew it. She also knew that Petra expected her to back down, but this time she wouldn't. She had let her have her way with clothes, makeup, hairstyles, and had pushed her curfew back later and later till now she was allowed, on Saturdays, to stay out until one in the morning. And that was as far as she was willing to go. Staring at Petra, she picked up the phone and dialed her neighbor's number. "Diana," she said in a tense voice, "this is Charlie Gallagher. How are you? Look, the reason I'm calling is that Petra tells me Shelley and a whole bunch of other kids are going to a club tonight."

Petra sat hunched on the bed, her face greenish white beneath the glossy mop of hair.

At the other end of the phone Diana said, "It seems they are. Anyway, that's what Shelley told me. She said that you were letting Petra go, and I figured if you were letting her go, then it was probably all right."

"Well, this is the first time I'm hearing about it," said Charlie, "and it's not all right, and I can tell you right now that Petra's not going."

They spoke a moment longer, agreeing to check with one another in the future when their children made plans. Charlie hung up and looked at Petra. "I think you have some explaining to do."

"I don't have any explaining to do," Petra said nastily. She was close to tears, and she had to take a big gulp before she could speak again. "I could have lied, you know that? I could have said I was sleeping at someone's house, and we'd have gone to a club anyway, but I didn't, I was honest, and now you've messed everything up and they'll all hate me."

Watching her, Charlie felt such a confusing rush of emotions, she didn't know what to do. She wanted to defend herself, she wanted to strike out at her daughter, she wanted to weep at the loss of her little girl. Who was this sullen, awful stranger? Above all, she wanted to hold Petra, protect her from the hot, driving urges that were part of being fifteen. But she did none of those things. She sat there, all choked up, as Petra jumped off the bed and ran from the room screaming, "But you don't care about that! You don't care about me, or Colin, or anything else! All you care about are those stupid, ugly paintings and your AA meetings!"

And now she was sitting in a chair, eating pistachios, talking happily with her father. Charlie had made no attempt to smooth things over after their fight. Let her stew, she had thought; when she's calmer, we'll talk. What saddened her most was that she wasn't able to discuss any of this with Neil. She was afraid that if she did, he would accuse her of having lost control of their daughter, and would once again demand to take the children away. She felt like a single parent.

Unhappily, she rose from the sofa. "I'm going up to get Colin. Probably he doesn't realize you're here."

"No, that's all right," said Neil, pulling at her wrist so that she had to sit down again. "He'll come when he's ready. I wanted to talk to you about Thanksgiving."

Charlie groaned.

"Well, it's only a few weeks away. You don't really want to give it here in Brooklyn, do you?"

"Why not? It'd be fun. And I could invite some interesting people, like Gwen and Musette."

"Yeah," said Petra, girlish again, bouncing in her chair. "We could build a big fire in the fireplace. It'd be great. And Shelley could come over."

And Eliza and Heather and Kate, thought Charlie, picturing an endless stream of adolescent girls. Maybe it wouldn't be such a good idea to give it in her new home after all. And for personal reasons she wanted to get Thanksgiving over with as quickly as possible, and not get stuck with a lot of guests. Neil would be taking the children to Pennsylvania after the meal, which meant she would be able to have several nights alone with Dennis.

"If you give it here, your mother will be terribly insulted," said Neil. "You know she likes to have Thanksgiving at her place. I don't think she's changed the guest list or table setting in years, so let's not rock the boat. There've been enough changes already."

"You're probably right," agreed Charlie. "Oh look, here's the birthday boy." Her face lit up as Colin entered the room.

Neil hastily stood and held out his arms to greet his son. "Ready to celebrate the end of your first decade, old man?"

Thanksgiving was the last thing on Musette's mind. Business matters kept her out on the West Coast longer than she had anticipated. She was on the verge of signing a contract with Miroslav, who had been very picky about all the details, but agreed to fly back to New York for a day to meet with the Salzmans. Already she had raised a good deal of money, but she was counting on the Salzmans for the final amount.

An Irish maid in a frilled white cap showed her into the living room. There, on a shabby chintz-covered sofa, sat Belle, husky-looking in gray flannel trousers and a pastel-blue sweater and pearls. Beside her, its head on one of her chubby knees, lay a big yellow Labrador who stared adoringly at his mistress. "Ah, Musette darling, have a seat. Eileen will get you something to drink. What will you have? Tea? Coffee? A soft drink?" Tactfully, she left out the offer of anything alcoholic; she must have heard from Peter that Musette didn't drink.

"Coffee would be fine," said Musette.

"Good. Make that two coffees, Eileen. And see that we're not disturbed, please." When the maid left, Belle said, "My staff thinks nothing of calling me to the phone every five minutes."

"Yes, I know how difficult that is," said Musette. "Will Peter be joining us?"

"Well, he said he would *try* to make it. We'll give him a few minutes, shall we?" She pushed back her sleeve, glancing at a tiny jeweled watch. "It's only just a little after three."

Musette glanced around, wishing she would push the dog off the sofa. The rest of the room was handsomely done with a great deal of antique furniture, the usual de rigueur oriental carpets, fancy floral arrangements, family portraits interspersed with quaint eighteenth-century paintings of cows and horses. She wondered if Theo Hammond had had a hand in decorating the place. "How long have you lived here?" she asked.

"Oh gosh, ages. We have a house in New Jersey, but we only use that for the occasional weekend now."

"And a house on the cape."

"Yes, a house on the cape. But that's strictly for summers. I really think of this as my home."

Eileen came in with a silver tea tray, and the dog sat up, alert to the presence of food. "Cisco, if you're going to be a pain in the ass you'll have to leave," said Belle. She looked despairingly at the maid, who said, "I'll take him for you, ma'am."

"Thanks, Eileen. With him here, Mrs. Vlk and I will get nothing done."

With the expertise of one who had to do this several times a day, the maid grabbed the dog's thick collar and dragged him from the room before he could snatch any cookies off the tray. "That's a relief," said Belle, wiping a few yellow hairs from her lap. "How do you take your coffee? Milk? Sugar?"

"Black, please," said Musette.

"Ah, yes, as I should be doing, but I can't stand it that way." She added cream and sweetener to her own coffee, helped herself to some cookies, and leaned back on the sofa. "So . . . you were just out in Los Angeles. How did things go?"

"Very well. In fact, something *really* exciting has happened, which is that Miroslav has agreed to direct."

"No!" exclaimed Belle, putting her cup down in the saucer with a clink. "Why, that's marvelous. So you two must be getting along pretty well."

"In a working sense, yes."

"No chance of your getting back together as a couple?"

Musette thought of Miroslav, who had told her at their last meeting that he was planning to marry again. "Absolutely none," she said.

"Well, I'm sorry about that, but I'm glad to hear he's directing *Homegirl*. I suppose that means things are moving along pretty swiftly."

"They are," said Musette, sipping at her coffee. "Though we still have an awful lot to do. The fun things—you know, all the preproduction stuff like casting and scouting locations—won't happen till early next year."

"And when would you actually start shooting?"

"Late in the spring. Miroslav won't be free till then, and in terms of weather that's the right time of year for us."

"Hot as hell I imagine," said Belle.

"Yes, awful, but that's the atmosphere of the story."

Belle looked as if she was about to say something, but the maid came in just then, and in a hushed voice announced that Mr. Salzman was on the phone. "Oh damn," said Belle. "That means he won't be able to make it." She rose heavily from the sofa and left the room. When she came back she said, "Peter sends his apologies. His company's just been awarded an important government grant, which is wonderful, and we're all very pleased, but it means a lot of work with lawyers and budget people and... well, it needn't concern us. He said to go on without him, and promises to be here next time." She sat down, crossing one plump leg over the other, and reached for a cookie. "What I'd like to know is how you've managed the financial end of it. I suppose you've formed a limited partnership and sold shares?"

"Yes," said Musette, "and we've been incredibly lucky, although considering the script that's not surprising. I have the prospectus here, and I'll leave it with you so Peter can have a look at it." She removed a glossy booklet from her briefcase and placed it on the coffee table. "So far we've raised nearly two-thirds of the budget, and I'm negotiating with a distributor who's interested in putting up the final quarter."

"Which would leave?"

"About a million."

"Peter and I were talking in the four-hundred-thousand-dollar range." When she spoke about money, Belle's voice became solidly and flatly the voice of a Brooklyn-bred New Yorker.

"That would be wonderful," said Musette.

"Although," said Belle, "we might go a little higher. To tell you the truth, I don't see this as a regular investment. I see it as something that could really influence people. You know— change the way they look at blacks. That's important to me."

"I know what you mean," said Musette. "That's part of what sold me on making this film." A bald-faced lie, but after months of raising money, she knew that the do-good factor was what made the film so appealing to private investors. That and Gwen Thomas's prominence on the bestseller list.

"Who do you think will play the lead—the girl, Winnie?"

"Miroslav spoke about Bethany Hunt. He's worked with her

in the past, and he thinks she's tops. Of course she won't come cheap, but I tend to agree with him; I think she'd be excellent, and she's someone people really like to watch."

"You mean a box office draw?"

"Yes, exactly."

"Have you approached her yet?"

Musette took a cigarette from a silver box on the coffee table and lit it with her own gold lighter. She inhaled and blew out a cloud of smoke, smiling warmly at Belle. "No, we haven't. But I don't think it's an offer any black actress in her right mind could refuse, do you?"

"What does Gwen Thomas think?" asked Belle, not answering the question.

"Oh, she adores Bethany."

Gwen was so involved with her new novel, *Voyage to a Cold Land,* that she dropped any pretense of being interested in the film. She spent almost every waking moment at the library, researching Jamaican folklore and history, and when she wasn't at the library, she was with her mother up in Harlem, trying to learn as much about their family as she could. "What you asking all these questions for?" the old lady would grumble.

"Just curious. I have no idea who half the members of my family are, and since you're planning to desert me here in New York I'd like to know something about them."

"Honey, I ain't deserting you. You're free to visit me in Jamaica any time you like."

When Felicity questioned her about the book, Gwen was equally evasive. "It's going to be an epic about a Jamaican family emigrating to the States," was all she would say. "When I've got something down on paper, I'll show you." So far she had written dozens of character sketches, but that was all.

She had also, once again, started going regularly to the Black Meeting. When Audrey, who always stood by the door, saw her, she grabbed her and said, "Hey girl, where you been at? I haven't seen you in weeks."

"Oh," Gwen said uneasily, "I've been kind of busy. You know how it is."

"No, I don't know," said Audrey. "I ain't never too busy for a meeting, and if you know what's good for you, you shouldn't be either. You got somethin' to tell me? You in trouble?" Her dark eyes sought Gwen's. Though nothing formal had been said, and the two women had never even gone out to coffee together, Audrey treated Gwen as if she were a sponsee.

"No, I'm not in trouble," said Gwen. "I've just had an awful lot of work to do, that's all." She laughed. "And I *have* been going to meetings. Just not this one."

"Why's that?" said the older woman.

Gwen shrugged. She didn't want to admit that she'd been off and on avoiding John Hopeton Sinclair, whom she'd thought was a scary street person. All that had changed. Since hearing Sinclair's impressive speech on black identity at the Waldorf, she was looking forward to talking to him—explaining and challenging his ideas, maybe discussing her book. The idea of actually conversing with him scared her and excited her, and she knew why: she was ready for a smart, attractive black man.

"This is the meeting you belong at," said Audrey. "You got any other home group?"

"No."

"Well then, it ain't safe for you to stay away so long." She put an arm around Gwen, drawing her close. "Now listen, baby," she said, low-voiced. "I know who you are and I know you wrote all those books, but what I gotta say is this: one drunk's just like the next, no matter how much success he or she got in this life. You follow me, baby? We all the same beneath this skin of ours: bums headed for the gutter unless we stay clean, and go to meetings, and talk to each other. Talk, baby, talk. We stay quiet and secretive, and the disease of alcoholism's gonna come creeping up on us like a serpent on its belly. And once that serpent starts hissing in our ears, it's all over. So what I suggest is you do more than just wander in here every so often, taking a seat way in the back where ain't no one ever gonna notice you. What I suggest is you hang around and do some service. You followin' me, baby?"

Gwen nodded.

"Ever done service in the fellowship before?"

Gwen withdrew from the warm pressure of her arm. "Now don't go getting mad at me, but I haven't had time. My life's kind of fallen apart since I got sober."

Audrey made a clucking sound with her lips. "Why would I get mad at you, baby? What happened—your marriage go bad?" She stared at Gwen's ringless left hand, and Gwen wondered if she knew she'd been married to a white man. "That's what happened to me my first year. My husband ran out on me, leaving me with five kids."

"Good lord, how'd you manage?" Gwen was relieved to get the focus off herself.

"Went to meetings. Prayed. Eventually found me another man." She chuckled, her large breasts heaving. "At least this one's sober, but sometimes I feel like a woman's best off keepin' her own company. Know what I mean?"

"*Too* well!" Gwen said, so loudly that several people turned and looked their way.

The two women smiled at one another. "You and me's gotta talk, girl," said Audrey. "In the meantime, as I was saying, we need someone to come in early and make coffee Monday and Thursday nights. Think you could do that, baby?"

So she became coffee maker for the Harlem Twelve Step group, as the meeting was officially called. It wasn't a job that displeased her, though in the beginning she was sure she wasn't very good at it. She would wear jeans, sneakers, her oldest coat, and go to the church while the meeting room in the basement was still empty, lug the huge coffee urn from the closet, fill it with water, lay tin ashtrays on the table, set out plates of cookies, a carton of milk, tea bags, cups, sugar; and somehow the mindlessness of all this activity soothed her. Other people would slowly drift in, and some of them would chat with her, calling her by her first name, and giving her warm, gentle hugs. If they knew she was Gwen Thomas, the writer, they didn't make a big deal of it. They wanted to know how her day had gone, and to talk about politics, jobs, boyfriends, sex, money, the mechanics of staying sober. Within a very short time it struck her as odd that she had ever thought of this as a meeting where underclass blacks predominated, that she had been nervous about coming here. The indistinguishable blur of faces sorted themselves out into faces she knew: the stolid churchgoing faces of her mother's generation, the students, the career girls, the hustlers, the welfare mothers, the shop keepers, the street people, the occasional lawyer or teacher—everyone seemed to be represented. Even whites, for white speakers were booked in from other meetings, and would come in groups of five or six, acting as if there was nothing strange or uncomfortable about being lone fish in a sea of blacks. After all, this was AA. As Audrey said, "Don't matter what the color of our skin is; we're all just a bunch of drunks trying to stay sober."

One night, as she was lugging the big coffee urn out of the closet, Sinclair walked into the room. There were other people there, so she didn't notice him at first. He took a seat in the front, removed his jacket, and lit a cigarette. When Gwen saw him, he was sitting by himself, one leg crossed over the other, arms dangling, head back as he blew smoke rings toward the ceiling. His bald spot glittered like a polished piece of amber.

She watched him for a moment, thinking that for such a small man he certainly had a commanding presence. Somehow, even though the dozen or so people in the room were all standing by the coffee urn, the center of gravity seemed to have shifted over to where he sat. And yet no one went near him. The others waited for the coffee to be ready, and discussed holiday plans. It was a few days before Thanksgiving, and there was an excitement, a feeling of festivity in the air. People watched for friends coming in the door, calling out loud hellos and running over to embrace one another as the room slowly filled up. Gwen allowed herself to be hugged and kissed, but once she saw that the coffee was percolating, she grabbed her cigarettes and coat, took a long, long breath, and went over to Sinclair. "Hello," she said, sitting down next to him.

"Hello," he said sourly. He barely looked at her.

"I've got a few things to say to you."

He reached for a cigarette. "Ain't no one stopping you," he said. She noticed he had brought in his own container of coffee, and a Drake's coffee cake, still wrapped in cellophane.

"First," she said, "I want to know why you didn't tell me who you were that time you came up and talked to me. You knew we were both scheduled to speak at the Tulsa thing."

"Yeah," he said. "So what."

"That was pretty rude."

"Lady, *you* were pretty rude. You thought I was some kind of scum off the street, and you gave me the big brush-off."

This was true, and for a moment she was silent. Then she said, "If you'd told me who you were straight off, it might have been different."

"What would have been different? Ain't no changin' the fact that you think some folks in this world ain't good enough for you."

"Oh, so that's it," she said. She watched as he removed the lid from his coffee and took a slow sip. "You really have a lot of preconceived ideas about people, don't you?"

He didn't say anything, just sipped at his coffee.

"I suppose that's why you wrote those awful things about me a few years back."

"Maybe." He picked his burning cigarette up from the ashtray, dragged on it, and put it out. He wasn't going to look at her.

"Well, let me tell you this," she said. "I've been reading your paper every week. I didn't use to, but since hearing you at the Waldorf I decided to make it my business. It's a good paper. I'm sure you know that, but I wanted to say how impressed I am with the kind of stories you're putting together." It was true. She had always thought the *West Indian Voice* was a cheap, thin advertising rag, but in reality it was filled with interesting and lively pieces drawn from the cultural, as well as the political, scene. "I'd like to contribute to it," she said. "I'd be really honored if you'd let me write a series on . . . well, I have several ideas. Race relations between West Indian and American-born blacks. Child prostitution. What happens to the youngest of our children when they're cast out onto the streets. I could even give you short stories—fiction that hasn't been published before."

She stopped short and stared at him. He was smiling thinly, and for the first time since she had initiated the conversation he was willing to meet her eyes. But the look he gave her was ill-willed and amused and disgusted all rolled into one, and the words that accompanied the look were just as nasty. "Lady, hell's gonna freeze over before I ever publish one word you write," he said.

She got up quickly. The meeting was just beginning, and she didn't want to spend one more minute next to Sinclair. Through a scrim of tears, she saw Audrey beckon to her, and forced herself to cross the room and drop into the seat beside her. The chairman had just called on people to give their day counts, and beneath the staccato bursts of applause Audrey murmured, "What's the matter, baby? You look like someone just took a sock at you."

Gwen's throat was too constricted to say anything. Audrey studied her closely, and then took her hand between rosy brown palms and told her to breathe slow and deep. "When you're ready, you tell me," she said.

"There's nothing to say," Gwen whispered after a moment. She certainly wasn't going to report the conversation with Sinclair.

"Uh-hunh," muttered Audrey, her dark eyes grim with knowledge. "Cain't fool me, baby. John S. over there certainly knows how to make people feel like shit when he wants."

"Why does he do that?" whispered Gwen.

Audrey released her hand, picked up her coffee and gave it to Gwen. "'Cause he had a lot of misery in his life. Now shhh, baby, let's you and me quiet down and listen to the speaker. That's what we here for, ain't it? That's where all our healing's gonna come from."

On the Tuesday before Thanksgiving, at eleven-thirty at night, Dennis phoned Charlie, asking if he could stop by to see her.

"Is it important?" she asked, surprised that he should want to come over at this late hour. She had just put a Beethoven sonata into her sound system, and was lying back on her living room sofa, enjoying the clean, spare feel of the room, and the dying flames of the fire she had lit earlier. Although the children were upstairs in their rooms, she was nervous about having him there. As far as she knew, Petra might still be awake.

"Yeah. Kind of."

"Okay. But we'll have to be very quiet. I don't want my kids waking up."

When she opened the door, he was standing there, stamping his mud-caked boots and rubbing his hands to get some warmth into them. "Don't you have any gloves?" she asked, leaning close and kissing him.

"Too poor," laughed Dennis. He was wearing his old bomber jacket and a pair of thin-looking jeans. His ears and cheeks were red from the cold.

As they went into the living room, she asked, "You didn't walk here, did you?"

"Not directly," said Dennis. "I was at a meeting, and then a bunch of us went out for coffee, and then I saw a pay phone and decided to call you."

"I thought you said it was important," said Charlie, sitting down beside him on the sofa.

"It is." He looked hungrily at her. Then he encircled her waist with his strong hands and drew her to him. Within minutes she was under him and her bra was off. "Oh honey," he whispered, "touch me. Reach down and touch me." She did, tentatively, fumbling with his belt buckle, and sliding her hand into his pants. He was fully erect, but she drew back, aware of the vulnerability of their bodies there on the sofa, of the large and suddenly unfriendly room, of the possibility that one of the children might creep down and see them. "No!" she whispered. "I can't; I just can't."

He groaned and sat up, running his hands through his hair. "Honey, I don't know when we're gonna get another chance. I'm going away for the weekend."

"You are?" Charlie said bleakly, sitting up beside him. "I thought we'd have the whole time together. My kids are going to Pennsylvania with their father right after Thanksgiving lunch. I'll be here on my own." She drew her knees to her chest and wrapped her arms tightly around them, feeling forlorn, the picture of despair.

"Well, I thought we'd be together too," said Dennis, "but a friend of mine from Pratt called this morning to ask if I'd come and visit him upstate, and I said yes. Frankly, I could use the change of scenery. It's beautiful up there, mountains and everything, and...well, shit, Charlie, you're the one who's always after me to work work work, and I figured this might get me started again." He reached over and touched her cheek. "Understand?" he asked softly.

"Don't patronize me, I hate that," she muttered. Then, abruptly, she uncurled her body and stood up.

"Where are you going?" he asked, watching her in the dim firelight.

"To check on the children. If we're going to have sex, I want to make sure they're asleep." She picked up her sweater, draping it over her breasts as she left the room. A few minutes later she was back. "Okay, come on," she said. "Leave your shoes in the hall, and don't say anything, not one word, till we're in my room with the door closed."

Usually a sound sleeper, Petra woke with a frantically beating heart, and lay very still in her bed, trying to reassemble the fragile wisps of her dream. No use; the wisps faded, and she was left with the uneasy sense that something was wrong and she didn't know how to fix it. Rolling onto her side, she glanced at the phosphorescent numerals of her clock. It was one in the morning, and she decided to have a cigarette—in this house, even though her mother was a heavy smoker, always a complicated business. She had to put a towel at the door to hide the smell, she had to burn incense, she had to sit, with a blanket wrapped around herself, at the open window, ready to throw the butt away if she heard Colin or her mother or one of the maids anywhere near her room. Of course, at this late hour, with everyone asleep, she had much more freedom—a big plus for waking up in the middle of the night.

Yawning, she switched on her bedside lamp, swung her feet to the floor, and padded slowly across the room. She and her mother had a deal. As long as she kept her room fairly neat, she did not have to suffer the disgrace of having her drawers and closets inspected. And this was good because in the past few months she had accumulated an awful lot of things that were not for her mother's eyes. Cigarettes, for instance. And worse than cigarettes, condoms. And vaginal foam, which her friend Heather, who was not a virgin, had assured her was an excellent form of birth control. These last two items, which were hidden in an old tote bag beneath a pile of shoes, she had not, as yet, had a chance to use. But she was getting close, very close, every day imagining the unknown boy who would take her virginity, and she figured she might as well be prepared.

She put on her down jacket, removed a pack of Marlboros from the pocket, and went and opened the window. It was cold as shit outside. The first inhalation of smoke hurt her lungs, but then, as usual, she began to enjoy herself. When she had smoked cigarette number one right down to the filter, she tossed it over the ledge. She was now completely awake, and she decided to have a few tokes on the joint she had bought earlier in the day. That would make her good and drowsy, and she might even remember her dream. Using a bobby pin to get the end part of the joint to her lips, she sucked and held her breath, sucked and held her breath. And then sat awhile, smiling out over the deserted street, wishing she could play some music or call some people on the phone. She didn't know how much time passed before she realized she was cold. And hungry. Starving.

Before she left her room to go to the kitchen, she lit some incense. No one would be up now, but she couldn't take the chance of the telltale odor of marijuana seeping through the house. Then, light as a cloud, she closed her door and floated downstairs. She loved to be alone in the dark like this. Secret and quiet, with the loud ticking of the hallway clock coming at her like a heartbeat, and the stairs beneath her feet creaking like old bones. When she reached the second floor, she could smell her mother's perfume—the flowers that went into making that scent, lilacs and gardenias. She paused and sniffed deeply at the air. She was filled with love. She would have liked to tiptoe into her mother's room and crawl into her bed, as she used to when she was a little girl, before her mother was sick so much of the time. A yellow strip of light shone beneath Charlie's door. Her mother was awake, probably reading or having a last quiet cigarette, and there was no reason Petra shouldn't tap on the door and go in for the nourishment of a good-night hug. She raised her hand to knock...and then she heard laughter—soft, sexy, flirtatious laughter.

She backed away from the door. Although it was almost unrecognizable, the laughter was her mother's, and it was accompanied by another sound, another laugh, deep and guttural, the hoarse shuddering laugh of a man. Petra froze. She felt the hairs stiffen on the back of her neck. She felt the blood stop in her veins, felt her mouth silently open in a cry of "Oh no!" Her throat rose as if she would vomit. She stood there for she didn't know how long, and when finally her brain gave her the order to move, she felt as if a whole lifetime had passed. Slowly, so slowly, her teeth locked against that furious remonstrating scream, she inched her way down the stairs. Her one idea was to get away, get outside, to run as fast as she could, as far as her legs would take her, on and on until she was winded, until she collapsed in the street and the police had to come for her, sirens shredding the night.

When she was downstairs she realized she was coatless and barefoot. Her teeth were chattering, her cheeks were wet with tears, and her stomach had that sick loose feeling that meant she had better get to a bathroom. The hallway light was on, and for a moment she stood there indecisively, staring at herself in the mirror, a ghostly figure in an old faded nightie of her mother's, a girl poised for flight, tall and hopeless-looking. It was a moment she would never forget. She knew she had to go back upstairs, past her mother's bedroom door and that mocking, sexy laughter. But she didn't want to; she wanted to stand here forever, silent and desperate, in a night that wouldn't end, wouldn't reveal its secrets to anyone but her. Shivering with cold, she hugged her arms around herself, took several shallow nervous breaths, and started for the stairs. But something—she would never know what—made her stop, and, glancing behind her, she saw beneath the hallway table, hidden away as if they were shameful, a pair of heavy muddied work boots with bright red laces.

So now she knew who the man was.

Two days later, it was Thanksgiving. Neil, who had spent the previous night at the Salzmans', came by at noon to pick the family up. Petra watched him kiss her mother hello, a loose easy kiss on the mouth, nothing lingering or sexy about it. After he had kissed her, he held her at arm's length and told her how good she looked.

And her mother did look good. Today she had given up her usual arty clothes, and was wearing a short, close-fitting dark dress, and a flowing black-and-emerald paisley jacket. Her legs, in low heels, were magnificent. When she walked she swung her hips, and her curls fell prettily into her face so that she had to push them back with an elegant flick of the hand. Her nails and mouth were painted a smooth crimson. "Oh sweetheart," she said after Neil had kissed her. "You've got lipstick on your mouth. Here, let me wipe it off."

Sweetheart! thought Petra. How could she call him that after the other night? She watched with hatred as Charlie took a handkerchief and dabbed at Neil's lips. Such a wifely gesture.

Her way of looking at him and straightening his tie was wifely too, as was the concern in her voice when she said, "How was the drive up from Georgetown yesterday? Any problems?"

At lunch in her grandmother's stiffly formal, oak-paneled dining room, her parents were seated next to each other. This was different from other years, and Petra wondered what her grandmother was up to. From the sour look on the old lady's face, nothing that would bring on happiness or sunshine. The usual cast of characters was there: Petra's uncle and aunt, her two pain-in-the-ass cousins, an old maid niece of Helene's, that fussy decorator, Theo whatever-his-name-was, and an ancient man who walked with a cane and was somehow related to Petra's late grandfather, Cyrus Vandermark. But Petra, focusing on her parents alone, paid scant attention to any of these people. Even her cousin Julian, a year younger and a definite loser, failed to get her going when he whispered: "D'jou give it away yet?" He grinned evilly at her, and she gave him a haughty stare and said, "Wouldn't you like to know, asshole." But she didn't talk to him for the rest of the meal.

Theo Hammond, on her other side, kept her busy with questions about school, and about whether or not she liked living in Brooklyn. She strained to hear what her parents were saying. They seemed to be having a jolly old time, giggling and whispering to each other, and at several points Petra heard that new sexy laugh of her mother's rise and float above the table. "Well *they're* certainly happy, aren't they?" said Theo.

Petra's mouth tasted as if it were filled with ashes, and she didn't say anything.

"I remember how they were last Christmas—they barely had a decent word for one another. But now"—he glanced slyly at Petra—"it looks as though they've made up. I suppose you'll soon be moving back to Georgetown?"

"Dunno," said Petra, wishing the stupid old fart would shut up.

"It's not as if you're too young to talk about these things," remarked Theo. "Quite the opposite. You strike me as a particularly astute young lady."

Petra took a big gulp of Coca-Cola. Across the table and a little ways down, her mother removed a cigarette from a silver dish and waited with smiling eyes for Neil to light it. Their

hands touched—Petra felt that touch in the pit of her stomach—
and then Charlie leaned her head back, and blew out a long
stream of smoke.

"Well?" said Theo.

"I'd rather not talk, if you don't mind," Petra said rudely. A
river of tears was flowing inside her. Along its banks, women
in black veils and dresses screamed and beat their breasts. The
world had turned dark, had turned the color of ashes and smoke,
and through that darkness she watched her parents with mounting sadness and anger. It was sick, it was disgusting, it was
horrible the way her mother led her father on. He had done
nothing to deserve this, and she was a bitch who acted higher
and mightier than anyone else, while all along she was screwing
her art teacher. Well, Petra wouldn't put up with it. Her heart
would break, she'd get ulcers, she'd have to go off and see some
awful shrink if something didn't happen to set her mother
straight. To set them all straight. She glanced fiercely up and
down the table. Everyone was eating happily. Beside her, Julian
forced a burp. Theo Hammond, who had gone through two
large slices of pumpkin pie with remarkable speed, removed a
pill from a small gold box and swallowed it down with coffee.
"Aren't you going to finish that scrumptious dessert?" he asked.

Petra looked at her untouched plate. She didn't remember the
butler having put it there. "I'm not hungry," she said.

"I hope you won't turn anorectic on us."

"No fear," said Petra, although secretly she found the idea
appealing. If she starved herself, if she wasted away to nothing,
if she landed in a hospital with tubes up her arm, wouldn't her
parents have to pull themselves together then!

After lunch she and Colin drove down to their old house in
Swarthmore with their father, stopping once on the highway
for Colin to go to the bathroom and for Neil to get some coffee.
Colin, always hungry, insisted on buying hot chocolate and a
box of doughnuts, and when he offered some to Petra she refused, even though they were the powdered sugar kind that she
especially liked. She refused to eat the sandwiches their father
made for them that evening, claiming that she had stuffed herself
with too much turkey at lunch, and at breakfast the following
morning, all she would have was a glass of juice. Neil, reading
the paper, glanced at her curiously, but didn't say anything. He

didn't say anything at lunch either, when all she had was one bite of a grilled cheese sandwich and half an apple. Nor at dinner when she pushed the food around her plate. By then she was feeling light-headed, euphoric—a little like the way she felt when she got high on grass—and so the next morning, even though her stomach burned with hunger, she decided to continue the experiment. "Jesus, what's the matter with you?" said Colin, wiping syrup from his mouth and reaching for a glass of milk. "You sick or something?"

"Just not hungry," said Petra, pleased with this new ability of hers to control her body.

"Well, I don't see how you can stand it," said Colin.

At lunch her father asked if she was all right, and she smiled at him and said, "Yes Dad, perfectly all right." She had had a small bowl of cottage cheese, and even that seemed like too much to her. She spent the afternoon with a friend, and then in the evening the family went out to dinner at one of her favorite restaurants. And still she wouldn't eat. Colin had ribs, and her father had a steak, and they both had baked potatoes heaped with sour cream, side orders of salad, and apple pie for dessert, and she sat there, feeling like a saint, her mouth filled with saliva, and all she had was a little bit of fish. Something she never ordinarily ordered.

When they got home, her father said he wanted to have a talk with her. Alone. In the study. Colin, who had rented *Friday the Thirteenth*, his favorite movie, was sprawled on the living room floor, and Petra wished she could sink down beside him, oblivious to the problems of the adult world. Instead she followed her father with leaden feet. When they were in the study, Neil gestured at a chair and sat down at his desk, staring at her pensively. "All right, young lady," he said after a minute. "Suppose you tell me what this is all about."

"What what's about?" said Petra, stalling.

He went straight to the point. "Your loss of appetite. One or two meals, okay. But I've watched you, and a mouse wouldn't be able to survive on what you've had in the past two days."

"I just haven't been hungry, that's all."

"Are you sick?"

"No."

"Do you have your period?"

Petra blushed. "No."

"Then what is it? Look, I'm prepared to sit here all night if I have to." His blue eyes were cool and patient. He coughed softly, and began to tap the eraser end of a pencil on the desk. "Is it something with a boy?" he asked. "Love problems?"

Petra's voice broke as she said, "No, no—it isn't that." She looked down at her lap, ashamed. This was so awful.

"Then what is it?" he repeated.

Without looking at him, she said, "I can't tell you."

She heard the rhythmic *tap tap tap* of the eraser on the desk. "Yes, you can," he said softly. "You can tell me anything. You know that."

"Not this," said Petra.

The tapping of the eraser stopped. "Why not this?" he asked.

"Because," said Petra, fighting tears. "Because I can't, that's all." She continued to stare blindly at her lap, chewing hard at her lower lip, shoulders shaking. What she wouldn't give to be outside with her brother! There was silence in the study, and then a small scraping sound as Neil stood up and came around the desk. Kneeling, he gently put his hand under her chin, lifting her head so she had to look at him. The expression on his face was earnest and tender, and Petra, crying openly now, threw herself forward so her own face was hidden in his neck.

They stayed that way for a while, huddled together, Neil holding her tightly, stroking her loose brown hair, rocking her to and fro, as if she were a very young child. Then, with an edge of firmness in his voice, he said: "Okay baby, I want you to tell me what's going on."

"Mom's got a boyfriend," Petra whispered into his neck.

"What?"

"I said Mom's got a boyfriend," repeated Petra, wishing suddenly that her mother were there and could talk for herself.

Charlie didn't know what time it was when the phone rang, but she answered on the first ring, and her voice was wide awake and anxious.

"It's me," said Neil.

"Oh," said Charlie, disappointed. "Is anything wrong?"

"You bet something's wrong."

262

"Well, what is it? Come on, don't play games with me. It's too late at night."

"I don't give a shit what time it is," said Neil. "You know, you've got Petra so upset she's more or less stopped eating."

"What are you talking about?" said Charlie, her voice hardening.

"Think about it a minute, and see if you can't figure it out yourself."

She was silent for a moment. Then she said, "I don't have to take this, Neil."

"Oh, don't you? Well, all right then, I'll tell you. Petra heard you the other night. When you were having such a good time with your boyfriend or lover or whatever he is. Apparently she woke up hungry in the middle of the night, and went down to the kitchen to get something to eat, and on the way she heard ... well, you can imagine what she heard. And now we've got a pretty distressed teenager on our hands."

"Oh God," said Charlie in a stricken voice. "But why didn't she come to me and talk about it? Why didn't she come to *me?*"

"I don't know. She probably wouldn't have talked to either of us if I hadn't dragged it out of her. Why'd you do it, Charlie? I mean how can you be so stupid as to have some guy—some creep you don't even know—in the house?"

"What do you mean, creep?" Charlie had to stop to light a cigarette. When she spoke again a moment later, she was so angry and upset she could barely get her words out. "How can you suggest such a thing?"

"Petra told me he was your art teacher. Jesus, Charlie! How long've you known him, a month?"

"What difference does it make how long I've known him?" She paused for breath. "He's a fine person and I happen to be involved with him. I can see who I want, Neil. You and I aren't living together anymore, which means we're both—and I stress *both*—free agents."

Neil gave a harsh laugh. "We're not even legally separated," he said.

"Yeah, well. But for all intents and purposes we are."

"Not in the eyes of the law. Now listen to me. I've been pretty damn tolerant letting you move to New York and flit around doing exactly as you please, but I will not be tolerant regarding our children and the kinds of things you expose them to. Which means I will not put up with your openly dating anyone or having lovers in the house. You know how quickly the press gets hold of that sort of stuff. If you persist, Colin and Petra will come and live with me."

Charlie fought back tears as she stabbed out her cigarette. "Try to get them," she said in a thick voice. "I'd fight you in court."

"Yes, but don't expect to win. Not with your history of alcoholism."

He always had an answer, she thought bitterly, reaching for another cigarette. "Don't *you* expect to win," she said, coughing as she exhaled smoke. She waited a moment before going on. "You realize, of course, that I could ruin your career. All I have to do is talk about what happened on the cape."

Neil let out a long, unhappy sigh. "I guess both of us could get pretty ugly." He was silent for a moment, and Charlie imagined the look of anguish on his face. She wondered what room he was in and felt a sudden stab of nostalgia for her cozy Swarthmore house. "The main point here," he continued, sounding a little like the public man he was, "is to protect the children. And you're not doing that if you expose them to your sex life, or have boyfriends over to dinner, or anything like that."

"You mean you want us to continue this farce of being a happy couple," said Charlie angrily.

"For the children's sake, yes. At least until our situation is resolved."

"Neil, I know you very well, and what you're saying is you want me to go on playing the role of meek little wifey wifey until you've had your shot at the White House. Well, I won't do it. I can't anymore. It's just not me—you've got the wrong woman for that."

"I don't seem to have any woman at all," said Neil in a voice filled with irony.

It was Charlie's turn to sigh. "We could go on like this all night," she said.

"Yes, we could."

"All right, listen," Charlie said. "I'll be discreet, but that's all I'll be, and not for very long. I know you said a year, but I think it's time we started talking seriously about divorce. This *situation,* as you call it, is just too stressful for all of us. And now . . . well, now, I've got to hang up and get some sleep."

She clicked off and stared bleakly around her bedroom, knowing she had no chance of falling asleep. She might have sounded strong and self-assured on the phone, but she was terrified that if Neil fought for custody of the children, he would win hands down. Unless, of course, she brought up the business of Gil Hoffeld, which impugned her as much as him. And what about Petra? Had her carelessness that night with Dennis cost her the love of her child?

Suddenly, for the first time in a long time, she wanted a drink. It wasn't just a passing whim, but a real hard-core need, a craving that started right in the gut. Her mouth actually watered for the taste of scotch. Unable to control herself, she began to think of where the nearest bar was—she could easily hail a cab and go someplace local. Imagining the rows of bottles, the smell of liquor, the happy ambience, she climbed out of bed and raced to the closet to find something to wear. But as she was pulling on a pair of slacks, a voice in her head reminded her that she had nine months of sobriety in AA, that she was building a new life—a life that included her children and this big wonderful house and interesting friends, and that she would lose it all if she went out and drank. "Jesus," she whispered aloud in the silent room. Her whole body shook as she crept back to the bed and sat down. She had heard people in AA talk about their fear of being "struck drunk," and now she knew what they meant.

Still shaking, she pulled on a thick sweater and slowly started downstairs to make herself a cup of coffee. Coffee was a poor substitute for the scotch she had craved so badly a few moments ago, but taken black and strong it would give her system a jolt, and perhaps go a little way toward removing the depression that had begun to settle over her.

She had two cups and then went to the living room, where she stood looking gloomily into the dead fire. She needed desperately to talk to someone. But who? Felicity was in New Orleans, where she and Michael had gone for Thanksgiving, Musette was in L.A., and Gwen always turned her phone off at night. Feeling frightened, she gave a loud, anxious sigh. In AA they were always told to use the phone when there was trouble, and here she was, at one of the most distressed moments of her life, without a single soul to talk to. She thought about that a moment, a cold wave of panic rising in her. Then she grabbed the phone and dialed Musette's number on the chance that she might have come back early.

A sleepy voice said, "Hello, who is it?"

Charlie gulped and said, "It's me. God, you're back. I'm so glad to hear your voice."

"Charlie? Jesus, what time is it? Is something wrong?"

Charlie imagined her feeling around for the light switch and foggily looking at her bedside clock, still in full makeup and satin, looking as much the old-time movie star as ever. "I'm sorry to wake you," she said. "It's around one-thirty in the morning, and I'm calling you like a good member of AA because I feel like shit."

"You do?" breathed Musette. "Listen, let me just, uh, turn on the light here, and . . . can you hold on a minute?"

"Sure."

"I need to wash my face. Don't go away."

Charlie nervously twisted the cord of the phone around her finger. A minute later Musette was back, sounding much fresher. "All right," she said. "Now tell me what's wrong. Why you feel like shit."

"It's a long story," said Charlie. "You have to promise to be discreet."

"I'm always discreet."

Charlie lit a cigarette and looked down at her naked toes. Their winter-white color disturbed her, and she shifted her gaze to the Gary Green painting, which she had finally hung to the left of the fireplace. "About a month ago," she said, "I started an affair."

"Jesus. With who?"

"My art teacher."

"You mean the one who's in AA?"

"Yes, him."

"Why didn't you tell me sooner?"

"You've been away so much. I didn't even think you'd be there tonight."

"I got in around dinnertime. I think I'm going to go crazy

flying back and forth like this. But tell me about the affair. How did it start?"

"That's sort of beside the point. The thing is . . . Neil's found out about it."

"Jesus, how?"

Charlie held her cigarette sideways, examining it before tossing it into the fireplace. "Petra told him." She repeated the conversation she had had with Neil, ending in a sob. "I'm afraid he's going to take the children from me."

"I don't see how he could do that," said Musette. "You have the children, you're the mother. Don't they always decide in favor of the mother?"

"Not if she's a proven alcoholic."

"You're in recovery, Charlie. That should count for something. Listen, are you in love with this guy?"

"I'm not sure. Sexually, yes. And I think he's a really talented painter."

"Would you leave Neil for him?"

Charlie gazed at the bright reds of the canvas in front of her. "Not specifically for him. The funny thing is, I've gotten really friendly with Neil over the past few months. I can't see us ever going to court. And I know too many incriminating things about him. I could ruin him politically if I wanted."

"In which case he wouldn't"—Musette gave a dry cough—"risk locking horns with you, would he?"

"No," said Charlie. "He wouldn't."

"Then I don't see what you're so afraid of. Look at things in their truest light: you have two darling children, one of whom will certainly need some psychotherapy. You have a husband who, from the sound of it, will dance to any tune you care to play. And you have a deliciously sexy and talented lover. What more could you want?"

"Peace of mind."

"For that," laughed Musette, "you either need to die or move to a hilltop in Tibet, and in your case I don't think either would be too practical. Now listen, darling, what I want you to do is get in bed and say the Serenity Prayer over and over instead of counting sheep. In the morning, when you open your eyes, call me."

Like an obedient child, Charlie went upstairs and climbed back into her warm, comfortable bed. She didn't feel particularly reassured or happy, but at least she knew she wouldn't drink.

Now, for the next hour, it was Musette's turn to sit up deliberating in the middle of the night. The conversation with Charlie had excited her, and she needed time to think and plan. She remembered the artist, Dennis MacLeish, a thin-faced, ratty sort of guy. How the hell could Charlie prefer him to Neil?

But it didn't really matter, she thought, smiling contentedly as she removed a Valium from the pillbox on her bedside table. Let Charlie screw around with whoever she pleased, as long as the marriage was over. The important thing now was for her to talk to Neil. She had hardly seen him in the past month because she had been spending so much time in L.A., but on Monday morning she would call him and make a date. Then, when they were together, lying happily on this very bed, she would casually bring up the subject of Charlie's lover. "Charlie's having a great time with this new man of hers," she would say, making it sound as if *everyone* knew about the affair. Everyone but poor, cuckolded Neil. Once he got over being upset and embarrassed, he would see that Charlie was the cheap one, playing around with some crummy guy, and that she—sleek, glamorous Musette—was the better choice for a partner. It would take some time, but he would be hers in the end—she was sure of that now.

With a happy sigh, she reached over and flicked out the light. Sweet dreams, kid, she told herself, sliding down the sheets and enjoying the satiny feel of her nightgown on her skin. In a few days Neil would be lying here beside her, whispering love words into her hair and telling her how much he had missed her. Perhaps, now that he knew about Charlie, he would even stay the night. She rolled onto her side, grabbing a pillow and hugging it to her, pretending it was Neil. Things were definitely going her way, she thought as she drifted into a deep, drug-induced sleep. The movie and Neil—she would be a huge success in both ventures.

On the Monday after Thanksgiving Gwen was at her desk, feeling slyly proud of herself. She had just finished a short piece entitled *What to Do when Your Parents Forsake You for the Islands,* and was now reading the pages over, smiling because there were one or two really funny lines. The piece sounded different from anything she had written before. Clipped. Punchy. Unsentimental. *Perfect.* She had written it with a specific purpose in mind: to send as the first of several articles to the *West Indian Voice,* where she intended to become a regular columnist. Or rather, not she, but Raymond W. Taylor, which was the name she had chosen to write under. She sat back in her chair, imagining Raymond. He was about forty. Married, three children, with a job as an English teacher in one of the city high schools. He didn't earn much money, but enough to get by on, and with his wife's income (she was a nurse in the emergency room at Saint Luke's), the couple did pretty well. And now Raymond had decided to try to bring in a little extra by writing the odd magazine article. It seemed he had a way with words...

She had gotten the idea for Raymond at Thanksgiving. Her mother, who was leaving for a short stay in Jamaica the following day, had dragged Gwen along to celebrate at the home of a friend of hers from church. For Gwen the holiday was a painful reminder of the passage of time, and the fact that, from here on in, she would be seeing very little of her mother, who intended to move to Jamaica for good early in the new year. Almost everyone at the party was old. Sarah's friend, a robust, thick-armed widow of about seventy, shouted orders from her armchair. Her three daughters rushed in and out of the kitchen, while the rest of the company dozed in front of the TV. And everyone fawned over Dr. Mitchum, the pastor, a thin, yellowing man who sat forever perched on the edge of the couch with a plate or a cup of tea on his lap. There was a good deal of excitement about Sarah's proposed move to Jamaica. Most of the women seemed to envy her, and everyone had a relative who had gone back there to retire. Gwen, thinking of previous Thanksgivings, grew very quiet. Her sadness must have shown on her face, for one of the daughters came up to her and said, "Hey girl, let's go in the other room for a smoke."

The other room was a spare bedroom, and two of the daughters' husbands, and a third unidentified man, were hanging out there with a bottle of rum. Delphine, the youngest and prettiest daughter, sat on the floor, playing with a baby. When Gwen came in, she looked up and raised an inquisitive eyebrow. "Old folks gettin' to you, huh?" she said.

"They're going on about Jamaica," said her sister, Cecily.

"Oh yeah, Jesus, gimme a break. I hate that when they get started on the barrels of clothing to be sent down there for all those poor needy Jamaican children."

"Cousins of ours," one of the men reminded her.

"Yeah, cousins, who cares? I got my own needy children."

"Gwen's mama's gonna retire there," said Cecily, lowering herself to the bed. She was a large, solid-fleshed woman, and the mattress sagged deeply beneath her weight.

"Really?" said Delphine. "You feeling bad about that? I remember when my husband Arthur's mama moved down there. He went around blue for days. Didn't want to admit it, but he was like a lost little boy for a while."

"How old was he?" asked Gwen, refusing with a calm shake of her head the bottle that was held out to her.

"Arthur? He must have been twenty-five, twenty-six at the

time." She laughed huskily, and Gwen wondered where Arthur was now. Had he been replaced by the silent young man holding a can of beer loosely in his fingers? "No, seriously," said Delphine. "It shook him up at the roots, if you know what I mean. He was used to his home being here in New York City, and now he had to change his way of thinking and get himself used to Kingston."

"You don't mean he wanted to move down there?" said Gwen. Everything these people said she silently recorded for her fiction.

"No, not that. He just didn't know where he belonged. Like most of us from the islands—told to be proud of our Jamaican ancestry, told to get down on our knees and praise the Lord for letting us be born in the USA, told to watch out for the meanness and violence of our American brothers, told so much shit we don't know what the hell's going on."

"He still don't know where he belongs," said Cecily. Gwen looked confused, and she added, "Arthur, I mean."

"Ain't that the truth," said Delphine, scooping up her baby and rising lightly to her feet. "Well, I gotta change this one's diaper and I'm outta here," she said.

Later Gwen asked her mother if Arthur, absent from the festivities, had run off with another woman. "Heavens no," said Sarah, throwing up her hands as if this was one of the funniest things she had ever heard. "Can't imagine a steadier, better boy than Arthur."

"Then where was he?" asked Gwen.

"He's a chauffeur. He had to drive some people clear out to the end of Long Island and wait to bring 'em back again."

"Oh," said Gwen.

"Fact, he gonna drive me out to Kennedy tomorrow. It's his day off, but he'll get all dressed up in that smart uniform of his, and he and Delphine's mama and Dr. Mitchum gonna drive me out there. You can come too if you like."

"Sure, Mama," said Gwen. "I wouldn't miss it for anything in the world."

And it was then that the idea for the article about parents moving back to Jamaica had begun to stir in her brain. She already had plenty of material, and when she met Arthur, quiet, heavyish, serious beneath his visored cap, she immediately trans-

271

posed him to Raymond W. Taylor, schoolteacher, would-be writer. The idea was delicious, and she sucked and chewed on it like the best-tasting candy. At the airport she was so distracted that Sarah said, "Hey, baby, stop acting like you're someplace else, and give your old mama a hug." She did, but as her mother went through the security check and disappeared in a swarm of people on the other side, she was already mentally back at her desk in Manhattan. She remembered John Sinclair's words, "Lady, hell's gonna freeze over before I ever publish anything you write," and her pulse quickened, and her feet, in low black cowboy boots, tapped the floor with excitement. "I'm going to show you, shithead," she muttered to herself. "Oh boy, am I ever going to show you." She knew, too, that writing the article—and eventually also the novel—was the only way she could keep her mother present in her life.

And now it was Monday morning, and the article was ready to go. She wrote a brief accompanying letter—*Dear Mr. Sinclair, I hope the enclosed will be of interest to you. It is the first piece I have ever submitted for publication, and if you enjoy it, or think it has merit, please let me know as I have plenty of other ideas. Sincerely...* She signed the name *Raymond W. Taylor* with a flourish, slid the pages into a large brown envelope, and went and got her coat. Of course Sinclair might reject the thing, but she doubted it. She also doubted that he would realize that she and Raymond, who had the same address, were one and the same person. It was very unlikely that Sinclair had the faintest idea where she lived.

Musette was just about to call Neil that same Monday morning when the phone rang shrilly at her elbow. She grabbed it, a warm rush of blood suffusing her cheeks when she heard his voice. "Hello," he said. "How was California?"

"Great. Despite all our differences of the past, Miroslav signed contracts last week, so I'm relieved about that. How are *you?*"

"All right," he said quietly. "I'll be in New York Wednesday, and I was wondering if we could have dinner."

"I think so. Let me check my book." She glanced at her desk calendar. She had a dinner engagement with someone flying in from California, which she'd have to cancel. "Wednesday looks fine," she said.

"Good. Why don't we meet at L'Hirondelle on East Fifty-third Street. It's small and quiet and the food's decent. Ever been there?"

"No. I can't believe you're taking me to a restaurant. What happened? I thought you wanted to keep a low profile."

"I do, but no one'll bother us there. And I thought we could use a change. Here's the address."

After Neil rang off, she swallowed half a Valium—not much, just enough to steady her—and called Charlie. "Have you decided what you're going to do?" she asked, wanting an update so she would know how to proceed with Charlie's soon-to-be-ex-husband.

Charlie sounded much more composed than she had two nights ago. "Nothing for the time being. I mean that literally. I'm going to cool it with Dennis, and concentrate on taking care of my children."

"And Neil?"

"Don't know. Haven't decided. But I sure as hell don't want him for an enemy. I like him too much."

"So you're not going to end the marriage?" Musette couldn't keep the urgency entirely out of her voice.

"What is this, Musette? Some kind of interrogation?"

"I just think it's so great that you're having an affair."

"Well, that's all it is—an affair. Anyway, I think Dennis's paintings are more important to me than his, for want of a better word, cock."

As Musette was about to leave the apartment Wednesday night, Neil called to say he would be late. "Sorry, Maggie, I seem to have gotten held up. I'm still in New Jersey, but I'll meet you in about forty-five minutes."

At least he didn't cancel the whole goddamn evening, she told herself. An hour later she took a cab to L'Hirondelle. She was wearing a dark red Chanel suit, a pearl choker, and an elegant little cocktail hat with a smoky veil, which she pulled down over her golden eyes. If he wants to keep our affair secret, I'll really play the part, she thought, a smile twitching on her lips.

When she arrived at the restaurant, the maître d' came bustling forward, asking if she had a reservation. She stared coldly at him from behind her veil, and said she believed Mr. Gallagher had called. Then she indicated that she wished for him to remove her mink, which he did with a small click of the heels. As he led her to a table at the far end of the room, the whole restaurant was watching. They may not have recognized Musette from behind her veil, but, she told herself, they knew a star when they saw one.

She ordered a ginger ale and sat back, looking around. It was a murky place, filled with businessmen staying late in town, tired-looking couples who seemed to have very little to say to one another, and one or two younger women smiling into the faces of their much older companions. The red carpeting, dim lights, and red-flocked wallpaper reminded her of a bordello, but the menu was intricate and the food looked as if it was extremely well prepared. Neil arrived a moment after the waiter brought her ginger ale. "Sorry I'm late," he said, putting down his briefcase. "I can't believe the traffic in this town."

"Yeah, it's bad, but L.A. is worse," said Musette, studying him from behind her veil. His face had a drawn, hard-bitten look of weariness to it that had been missing a month ago. "What were you doing in New Jersey?"

"Just business." The waiter placed a scotch in front of him, and he took a quick sip. "You don't mind my drinking?" he said to Musette.

"Not at all. What sort of business?"

"Nothing very interesting. I'm on a committee that allocates funds to certain labs and research facilities. Every so often I check up on them to see that we're getting our money's worth."

"Which committee is that?" asked Musette.

"Health and Science." He smiled at her as he lifted his drink. "You see, my education in biology didn't go entirely wasted."

"In other words, you award grants to private institutions for study purposes. What was this one for?"

"AIDS research. It went to a small pharmaceutical company out in Morris Plains."

"Not, by any chance, Peter Salzman's firm?" she asked, narrowing her eyes.

"Yes, how'd you know?"

"Belle mentioned a grant of some sort when I was there. Is that legal—allocating funds to people you know?"

"Sure, why not? As long as there's no conflict of interest,

which in this case, believe me, there isn't. Like another ginger ale?"

Musette ate very little, and waited with irritation for Neil to hurry up and finish his *boeuf bourgignon* so she could light a cigarette. Smoking during meals bothered him. She fiddled with her pearls, and chatted about California. He was in a terrible mood, and she couldn't seem to get him to relax and laugh at the things she said, which made her feel stupid and girlish, the way she'd felt with Neil so long ago. When she stared into his eyes, there was nothing there, no answering spark—just a vague look of worry and unhappiness. And he was so distant from her, his shoulders hunched like an old man's. Finally she couldn't stand it anymore. "Look, Neil," she burst out, "why'd you invite me here? You haven't seen me in a month and you act like I'm a complete stranger."

"I'm sorry, Maggie. I guess I'm a little upset. Believe me, it has nothing to do with you." He had finished eating, and he gestured to the waiter to bring them coffee.

"Why don't you tell me what's wrong," she coaxed.

He drummed his fingers on the tablecloth. "All right," he said. "I will. Have you ever heard of a guy named Dennis MacLeish?"

She had removed a cigarette from her thin gold case, and she waited for him to light it before answering. How nice: he had brought up the affair himself. She should have guessed.

"Is that why you asked me here? To find out about Dennis MacLeish?"

"It's one reason."

"Don't you think it's kind of weird to be asking your mistress about your wife's lover?"

He smiled at her. "I hate that word—'mistress.' But you're the only person I *can* ask. And I've got to find out about this, or I'll go crazy."

She sighed and leaned forward, placing her elbows on the table, cupping her chin in the vee of her palms. "All right," she said. "I'll tell you what I know about Dennis MacLeish." She hesitated a moment. His face had the shrinking look of a man who knew he was about to receive bad news. "Your wife is in love with him."

"Well, that's telling me straight, isn't it," he said angrily.

"You asked," she said with a shrug. She reached for the ashtray and scratched out her cigarette. This was a difficult role to play; she had to be factual, subtle. She had to suppress her glee. "Now I'll tell you the rest. He's about forty, handsome in a jaded sort of way, and an excellent painter."

"Is he in love with *her?*" Neil interrupted.

"I don't know. I think so." She watched him through drooping, half-lowered lids. "Charlie says he is. One sees them everywhere together."

"I'm amazed the press hasn't gotten hold of this."

"Why would they? When I say they're seen together, I mean at AA meetings. The occasional art gallery downtown. Otherwise Charlie's pretty careful. I don't think she'd want to hurt you or the kids."

"Well, she's done a pretty thorough job of that already," Neil said bitterly. "Did she tell you about how Petra heard them going at it the other night?"

"Yes," said Musette.

"Boy, you know everything, don't you? That's pretty ironic, isn't it, my wife confiding in my...mistress."

"Come on, Neil. It's not as if you've been such a good boy yourself. Here you are getting all hurt and angry, and look at what *you've* been doing the past six months."

"Don't start lecturing me, Maggie." With an abrupt motion, he signaled for the check. His face was hard and angry, the mouth bitten down to a thin, ugly line. When he had paid the check, he stood up and walked quickly to the vestibule. "Where are we going?" she asked, following him.

"I'm putting you in a cab, and then I'm going to the airport."

"So you're not coming home with me?" she inquired anxiously, placing her gloved hands on his shoulders, trying to force him to look into her eyes. He shook her off, and gave the coat check girl a dollar.

Enraged, she fisted her hands, wanting to hit him, but knowing better. "Neil?"

He helped her into her coat, his eyes so full of grief he didn't seem to see her. "I've got to be alone, Maggie. All right? I've got to be alone."

* * *

Fifteen minutes later, back in her apartment, she took a Valium, had a long drink of water, and called Theo Hammond. "Musette!" cried the ebullient little man. "So good to hear from you. Is everything okay? How's the film business?" She sensed he had company and was speaking loudly so that the person he was with wouldn't be threatened by her call—would in fact be impressed.

"I need some information, Theo," she said quickly.

"Yes? What sort?"

"I need the name of a good detective. Someone I can trust absolutely. Do you know of anyone like that?"

"Yes," he said, still talking loudly. "I think so. Let me just go to the other room to get my book." He put the phone down, and she heard him say, "Hang up when I tell you, Eric." A moment later, as he got on another extension, there was a click. "There, that's better," he said in his normal voice. "Now let's see...I don't suppose I can ask you what this is about? I mean is it marital, or financial, or what? Some of these people specialize."

"It's a little of both," said Musette. "I want to get some information on a person I'm thinking of hiring for the film."

"I see," said Theo. "And of course you're willing to pay any amount of money?"

"Well, yes—within reason."

"And this person is here, not in Los Angeles?"

"Here. On the East Coast."

"All right. Well, there's a man named Frank Stiller over on East Thirty-second Street who's very good. He does criminal investigations as well as checking people's backgrounds and that sort of thing, and I'm sure you'll be pleased with him."

"You've used him yourself?"

"Yes."

"And there's no danger of his leaking anything to the press?"

"None whatsoever."

"All right. Give me his number."

The time had come to take matters into her own hands and investigate the death of Gil Hoffeld. The more she thought about it, the more she was convinced his drowning was no accident. There was Neil's connection with Peter Salzman—favors owed since boyhood, a relationship as close, as tangled, as any bound by blood. There was his dying marriage... What had Charlie said on the phone the other night? That she knew enough about him to ruin him politically if she wanted. There was his ambitiousness, his thirst for power, influence, recognition. And there was something else, something Musette had been forced to look at tonight, and that was his love for his wife.

Seeing how grief-struck Neil was because of Charlie's infidelity, she had begun to wonder for the first time—and the thought chilled her right to the bone—if he loved his wife enough to commit murder because of her.

Musette thought so. The jealousy and rage she had seen in his face tonight must have been there a year ago when Charlie was sleeping with Gil Hoffeld. It was so easy to piece together. She could imagine Neil controlling his fury long enough to set up a meeting with Gil, talking him into going for a sail, getting behind him on the boat, pushing him over, and then making it all appear accidental, using Peter Salzman as a cover-up. Peter Salzman who didn't drink in the daytime, and who wasn't a sailor, but who was later paid back with a big juicy government grant.

It all fit. It was nasty, but it fit. And now, in absolute secrecy, she would check out her suspicions, and if it was what she thought it was, she would be at the red-hot center of a drama with Neil—passionate Neil, Neil who could love enough to kill his rival, who played a deadly game of subterfuge, who was the sexiest and most ambitious man she had ever met.

At five o'clock the next afternoon she went to see Frank Stiller in his office on East Thirty-second Street. She was the only client waiting in the shabby little anteroom and he took her almost immediately, showing her into a larger room that had extremely modern telephone equipment, floor-to-ceiling shelves filled with thick looseleaf folders, and a battered old desk on which was a framed photograph of Stiller with another man at a baseball game. Their interview was brief. She told him merely that she was suspicious of Gil Hoffeld's death, and that she wished, for private reasons, to have the whole thing investigated.

"Why don't you stop right there, Mrs. Vlk," said Stiller. "If I agree to take this case, you're going to have to be a little more specific. What makes you think the guy's death was anything but an accident?"

She gave Stiller a level stare. He was a large, open-faced, friendly-looking man with a droopy walrus mustache. His white shirt looked wilted, and his heavy body was stuffed into a cheap blue suit frayed at the seams. But his eyes were intelligent, and she decided she trusted him. He knew his business. He could know hers. "Gil Hoffeld was having a love affair with a woman named Charlie Gallagher. Do you know who she is?"

"Rings a bell," said Stiller. "Isn't she some sort of society lady?"

"Yes. And she's married to Neil Gallagher who's a congressman from Pennsylvania."

"All right. I'm with you. Keep going." He leaned back in his chair, folding big beefy arms behind his head, staring at her. Behind him was an uncurtained window, and she could see the reflection of his bulky body in the dark glass, and behind that the wavering, glittery lights of the city.

"She denies having had an affair with Gil, although a friend of mine spotted them together up on the cape a week or so before he died. That's one piece of information."

"Uh-hunh, what's the other?"

She lit a cigarette, and blew out the smoke harshly. Her hands were sweating, and she wiped them on her skirt. "There are two other pieces of information," she said. "One is that Peter Salzman, the man who supposedly was on the boat with Gil when he drowned, claims that he and Gil had been drinking all afternoon. However, to my certain knowledge, Peter never drinks during the day. He can't unless he wants to be violently ill." She paused and dragged on her cigarette. "The other is that Peter Salzman and Charlie's husband, Neil, are extremely close friends. So close, in fact, that Peter's firm was just awarded a large government grant."

"I see," said Stiller, bringing his chair forward with a thud and resting his arms on the desk. "So you think Gallagher, jealous of his wife, may have bumped off the lover and had his friend conveniently cover up for him?"

"Yes," said Musette. It sounded even more plausible when Stiller repeated it back to her.

"What's the status of the marriage now?"

"Charlie Gallagher moved to New York soon after Gil's death. She and Neil are separated, and she has the children."

Stiller opened a drawer and removed some papers. "You've left out one vital piece of information, haven't you, Mrs. Vlk?" he said.

"Have I? What's that?"

"Your interest in the case."

Musette regarded him thoughtfully. His eyes stared back at her, unblinking, an open innocent blue. "All right," she said. "I'll tell you. I'm having an affair with Neil Gallagher."

"Ah," said Stiller, his steady eyes registering neither surprise nor disapproval.

"Will you take the case?" she asked crisply.

"Yes."

"How long will it take?"

"A week to ten days. The retainer fee will be two thousand dollars. Payable now."

Musette took out her checkbook.

*I*n the week after Thanksgiving Charlie refused to see Dennis, although they spoke on the phone.

"I really want to get together with you," said Dennis in one of his frequent calls. "A lot's happened—I've started painting again, and . . . well, I physically can't stand being away from you."

"You've started painting, Dennis? That's great. Maybe you should concentrate on that, and not me for a few days."

Petra's discovery of them had horrified her, and she now wanted to play the whole thing down, to bring her household back to normal as quickly as possible. She tried to speak to Petra about what had happened. On the evening of Petra's return from Swarthmore, she said, "I think we should talk. It must have been so horrible and lonely for you, hearing what you did."

"I just don't see how you could have done it," said Petra, eyes brimming.

"I have attractions to people just as you do," said Charlie quietly. "It may seem wrong because I'm your mother, and that sort of thing isn't supposed to happen, but the harsh truth is that it does." She attempted a laugh. "Sometimes anyway."

"But what about Daddy? I mean you're still married and everything." She covered her face with her hands. "I can't stand the way you're hurting him," she said in a lost voice.

"I know how hard it is," said Charlie. She ached to put her arms around Petra, but it was the wrong moment—the girl would push her away. "It's confusing for all of us, and it may stay that way for a while. Daddy and I . . . well, we have a lot to figure out, and we don't know what's going to happen, but the main thing is that we both love you, and we always have, and we always will, and whatever else happens is pale next to that."

"But you don't love each other," said Petra reproachfully.

"That's not true," said Charlie. "We do love each other. It's just in a different way now." And as she said them the words seemed true, not just comforting.

For the next week she and Petra were guarded with one another, a thin rime of frost killing off their conversations. Charlie was sure that her daughter despised her. If she smiled at Petra, she got a hard-eyed ugly stare. If she asked her about school, or what she thought she might like for Christmas, the answer was a shrug and the same hard-eyed stare and silence. It was a relief when the weekend arrived, and both children left for Washington to be with their father.

Although it made her uncomfortable after what had happened, she spent Saturday night of that weekend at her house with Dennis. She would have preferred to go to his loft, but he refused. "I've got to get out of here, Charlie. I've been painting like a maniac all week, and I really need a change."

Apparently his trip to the mountains had inspired him. For the first time in three years he was working with his old restless energy, and he promised her that when he finished his new canvas, she would be the first to see it. In the meantime, on that Saturday night, they made love like two people who couldn't have enough of one another. His body bristled with energy, was thin and tense from overwork, and needed the release of deep, urgent sex. He was so turned on by her that she felt herself respond with the same urgency, growing weak, begging him to hurry up and enter her just at the slightest brush of his fingers on her clitoris. "Oh Jesus, baby, we're great together," he said each time, words that even in her excited state struck her as a little cheap and easy. But she didn't care; sexually, they *were* great.

He was ready for her to see his painting the following Wednesday. Leaving the house early that afternoon, she checked to make sure the hallway lights were on. The housekeeper, whose day off normally was on Thursday, had had to fly down to South Carolina for a funeral, and that meant that Petra would be alone for a few hours and would have to fix her own dinner. Although she felt bad about that, Charlie hadn't wanted to cancel Dennis at the last minute. She lied to Petra, telling her she was going to a gallery opening in Soho and might be back quite late. As for Colin, he would be staying with a friend.

She felt a little uneasy riding the old creaky elevator up to Dennis's loft. What if she didn't like the painting? That was crazy; of course she would. She had loved his earlier work before she had come to love his body and his company. But as the elevator, with excruciating slowness, drew closer to his floor, she felt the tension in her mount. And then the old cage rattled to a halt, and there he was, pushing the heavy door open for her, grinning because he saw her slight motion of recoil at the sight of his dog.

When they were inside the loft, he locked the dog away and came and put his arms around her. "Now I can really say hello," he murmured. They stood that way, holding on to each other, for a long time. Charlie didn't want the moment to end, afraid that whatever she might have to say about his new painting would complicate all that was simple and carnal about them. Finally, in a thick voice, Dennis said, "Maybe we should go upstairs first."

"All right," said Charlie, relieved.

His disheveled bed had never looked so welcoming, and for once she didn't mind the windowlessness of the little room, or the choking sense that bad dreams had been dreamed here, and that Dennis—the old drunk Dennis—had lain forlornly for long periods of time staring up at the ceiling. They threw off their clothes quickly and lay down. "Gonna keep these on?" Dennis asked, leaning on an elbow, touching her earrings.

"No," said Charlie, unhooking the complicated lengths of silver, placing them on the floor. She stretched her nude body out under him, and for a while she was happy, for a while she forgot all about her troubles with Petra and with Neil, her guilt at being with the man who was now moving so deliciously inside her.

When they were finished, she lay back against the pillows and smoked a cigarette, feeling very much like a film noir wanton woman, no longer Charlie the society lady, or Charlie the mother. "Want to take a shower?" he asked.

"No," she said, thinking of the scummy enamel of his tub.

"Then why don't we get dressed," he said.

She looked at him through the gray wisps of cigarette smoke. "You're in a hurry, aren't you?" Even in bed he had not lingered.

"No one's seen my painting yet, Charlie. I really need feedback."

She reached for her lingerie. "Okay. Just give me a few minutes to get my clothes on."

Downstairs, he handed her a cup of instant coffee and pointed at the lumpy couch. "Sit there, and I'll wheel the easel over to you. I want you to be comfortable."

His solicitousness made her nervous, but she did as he said, lowering herself to the thin, dog-smelling cushions, and crossing her legs at the ankle. The loft looked as gloomy and dirty as ever. She kept her eyes straight ahead of her, concentrating on the bitter taste of the coffee, and the soulful voice of Alberta Hunter emanating from a record he had just put on. When Dennis came toward her with the painting, she felt a moment's pity for him. He looked so vulnerable, like a sick little boy, pressing his thin weight against the easel, his face a pinched white mask.

"All right, here goes," he said tensely, turning the easel around.

"Like it?" he asked almost before she had a chance to look.

She glanced from the painting to him. Beneath the arms his shirt was soaked with sweat. "Why don't you go stand somewhere else for a minute," she said. "I can't possibly study this with you hovering over me."

"You should be able to tell right away if you like it or not," he said. "I need an immediate response, Vassar. Something from the gut. Not poststructuralist criticism."

"All right, I like it," snapped Charlie. "Now go away, please."

Breaking into a pout, he wandered off toward the kitchen,

and then he must have gone out into the hall because she heard the big metal door of the loft close with a bang. Relieved, she turned back to the painting. It was dark and murky, a black sky against a brown earth, and rising sharply and improbably between the two, a gaunt green mountain, up and down the sides of which trudged hundreds of tiny antlike people. Charlie hated it. It was flat and dull and filled with stupid symbolism. So that's why he worked so hard, she thought. All those ugly little people must have taken hours and hours to draw. She wondered what to say to him. Technically it wasn't a bad painting—in fact, it was probably very good—but in the final analysis, she hated it.

For a few minutes she stood there gazing at it. Then she picked up her coffee cup and went to the kitchen. When he came back into the loft, she was standing by the sink, trying to figure out what to say that would be loving and fair, but that wouldn't just leave her in the role of a supportive helpmate without opinions. "Well?" he said.

She decided to be direct. "Technically I think it's excellent."

"But?"

"But it's not my taste. Look Dennis, you've got the wrong person to criticize this particular painting. It's good, yes, there's no doubt about that, but I just don't go for that kind of surrealism."

"You mean you prefer the famous Gary Green?"

"That's unfair. That's like comparing apples and oranges."

"Sure is, baby, and guess who comes out all mush, like applesauce? Gary fucking Green."

He said this in a shaking voice. His fingers, trying to light a cigarette, were unsteady.

"I don't see why you're so obsessed with Gary Green," said Charlie. "The two of you paint so differently. Anyway, I didn't say there was anything wrong with your painting."

"No. You just wouldn't want it on your living room wall. Isn't that so, Charlie? It just wouldn't fit in with all that empty, boring, overpriced crap you've got there. And the reason I harp on Green is because he's a lousy painter, and you, who think you're so smart, don't have the sense to know that."

Charlie went cold with anger and disappointment. "Then why do you value my opinion?"

He picked up her coffee cup and hurled it against the wall. "Because I want you to like my work, goddamnit! It's important to me."

"How nice it's so important to you," said Charlie. "I'd better go."

He didn't stop her, although with every foot the elevator dropped she half hoped he would. Down in the street she climbed wearily into her car, thinking that it was his problem, not hers, if he was so goddamn sensitive to criticism. Carefully, she edged the car out into the trash-strewn street, drawing her breath in sharply as she saw a rat scurry across the beam of her headlights, gunning the engine as she approached the hill that led up and out of his dismal neighborhood. It wasn't until she had reached her garage and was backing the car into its allotted space that she missed the silvery flutter of her earrings against her cheeks, and realized with a pang where they were—next to a coil of dust on the floor by Dennis's bed. Shit, that means I have to see him again, she thought. But then she had a vision of him looking as forlorn as a little boy in the debris of his loft, and she wasn't entirely displeased.

"What if your mother comes home?" said Petra's good friend Heather Barnes, a blond, softly voluptuous girl of sixteen who, at five o'clock that afternoon, sat perched on the cushioned stool of Petra's vanity table, exploring the many small bottles of nail polish and perfume.

"She's not going to," said Petra, sucking deeply on a tightly rolled joint. Her voice, coming from the middle of her chest, sounded as hollow and forced as a ventriloquist's. She let out some smoke and added: "She and a friend went to some sort of art opening in the city. She won't be back till around ten or eleven or maybe even later."

"You're sure?" said Eliza Dunlap, Petra's other good friend, a pretty redheaded girl who lay on her back, bicycling her legs on one of Petra's twin beds.

"Of course I'm sure," said Petra, handing the joint to Jakey Heller, Eliza's current boyfriend, who was seated on the floor.

"I mean you never know," said Heather, opening a bottle of perfume and sniffing at it. She made a face and closed the bottle. "Adults are fucking crazy, especially parent-type adults. Not that mine really give a shit what I do." She opened another bottle. This time the scent pleased her, and she sprayed some on her wrist and into the vee of her white cashmere sweater, and then reached a pudgy hand backward, impatiently wriggling the fingers. "Hey, Jakey, quit bogarting that joint!"

The boy, who was sixteen and had short dark hair and a heavily muscled body, grinned up at her as he took another pull on the joint. "Don't talk to me about bogarting," he said, raspy-voiced, holding the smoke in his lungs. "When it comes to bogarting, you're a fucking champion!"

"Now, now, kids," said Eliza from her position on the bed. Lowering her legs and rolling onto her stomach, she dangled an arm lazily over the edge of the bed and began playing with Jakey's short, brush-cut hair. Jakey handed the joint to Heather, and moved over slightly so that he was out of her reach. "What's the matter?" crooned Eliza, extending her arm out farther and grabbing at his shirt collar. "Too uptight for a little public display of affection?"

"Come on, Eliza, lay off, will you?" said Jakey, his thick face, with its misshapen adolescent features, flushing darkly.

"Hey man, why don't you give her what she wants?" giggled Wash Davis, the fifth person in the room, a large, rangy, and extremely handsome black boy of fifteen. The others shifted their attention to him, and there was a brief silence, broken by Heather, who cleared her throat and said, "Petra, where'd you put that bottle of vodka we bought the other day?"

"Oh," said Petra foggily. "It's in the back of my closet some-where."

"Well, what are you waiting for, girl? Go find it."

While Petra was looking for the vodka, Eliza slid down onto the floor, landing with a giggle beside Jakey, who this time held very still as she playfully ran her fingers through his hair. In fact, now he seemed happy to have her touching him. He pressed his thigh hard against hers, and after a moment, as if by mutual agreement, they turned their faces toward each other and began to kiss. Their kisses were noisy and intense, and by the time Petra had found the vodka, they had wriggled down flat onto the floor, and Eliza was making little moaning sounds as Jakey, who lay on top of her, ground his pelvis meaningfully into the crotch of her jeans.

"Hey you two," said Heather sharply. "Don't you think you'd better go somewhere else for that sort of thing? I mean there *are* other people in the room."

"Like where?" muttered Jakey, looking up, blinking.

"You could go into my brother's room," suggested Petra. "There's plenty of privacy there if you don't mind the goddamn fish in his tank. It's right across the hall."

"Okay, thanks," muttered Jakey, climbing to his feet with some difficulty, and grabbing for Eliza's hand.

"Well, I sure hope he carries rubbers in his wallet," said Heather as soon as the door was closed. "Oh good, you found the vodka. What are we waiting for, children? Let's pass it around."

Charlie arrived home at five-thirty. The hallway lights were on, just as she had left them, but the rest of the downstairs was in darkness. On the floor by the hall table lay a heap of coats and backpacks. So Petra had some friends over. That hadn't really been their agreement, but she could understand the girl not wanting to be alone at night in the large empty house.

From upstairs came the *thump thump* of rock music, a sign that all was well, and everyone was alive and happy and as annoying as usual. Tiredly she went up to her bathroom where she washed her face and hands and ran a brush through her thick hair. The face that looked back at her from the mirror was old-looking. Perhaps it was the absence of earrings. Or the unhappy mouth from which all the lipstick had been eaten off by Dennis's kisses. She splashed some more water into her face. From upstairs came a peal of laughter. Petra must have opened her door because suddenly the music was much louder, and above it Charlie heard a boy shout, "Hey Petra, you got any towels?"

Jesus, thought Charlie, catching her own look of alarm in the mirror. What in hell is going on up there? She ran out onto the landing and up the stairs—and then stopped, stunned. A boy of about sixteen—but already with a burly-shouldered man's body—stood there barefoot and naked to the waist. Facing him, in the open door of her room, was Petra. The whole place stank of marijuana.

"Towels," the boy repeated, shouting to make himself heard above the music.

"Oh," said Petra. "Of course." But her eyes wore a dazed, dreamy, self-absorbed look, and it was clear that she hadn't understood him. Charlie, standing only a few feet away, realized with a shiver down her spine that her daughter hadn't noticed her. Behind Petra a second face appeared in the door, the blond, thick, sensuous face of Heather Barnes. "What's the matter, Jakey?" shouted the girl. "Things get so hot and heavy you messed up the bed?"

The boy said something that Charlie couldn't hear. But it didn't matter. Heather had caught sight of Charlie over the boy's chunky shoulder, and her face, which seconds ago had been suffused with a sly, jesting humor, was now rigid with fear. "Holy shit!" she whispered. She stood stock-still, unable to move, the color draining from her face, as the boy swung around. "Jeez," he said, pulling at his belt buckle, the realization of who Charlie was dawning in his eyes. Fumbling with the buckle, he turned and ducked across the hall into Colin's room, slamming the door behind him.

Charlie raced after him, thanking God she had refused to have the door fitted with a lock, placing her hand on the knob, twisting it open. Oh, the innocence of that room. The pictures of baseball players, the shelves of boys' games, the steady gurgling of the tank in which swam the precious multicolored tropical fish Colin had saved up his dollars to buy. But Charlie's eyes went straight to the lower bunk of the bed, and there, on sheets decorated with pictures of spaceships, lay a naked girl. A girl she knew, Eliza Dunlap, whose red hair was spread over the pillow, and whose clothes had been dumped on the floor along with a mess of transformers and comic books. The boy, Jakey, his belt buckled now, was struggling into his T-shirt, and his voice was muffled as he said, "For Christ's sake, Eliza, *get dressed,* she's out there."

She, thought Charlie grimly. Behind her Heather was saying, but way too late, "I wouldn't go in there if I were you, Mrs. Gallagher."

Charlie turned on her. "Don't tell me what to do. Not in this house. And get that sly ugly smile off your face. And for God's sake turn off that music!" She turned back to the girl on the bed, who was now sitting up, her cheeks stained a wild, uneven scarlet, her small copper-colored eyes bright with fear as she attempted to hide her breasts behind the sheet. "I give you exactly one minute to get dressed, young lady," said Charlie. "Then I want you out of here. And you," she flung at the shamefaced Jakey, who stood with his hands hanging at his sides like heavy, useless rocks, "strip the bed."

She knew that they had been drinking. Heather smelled of the stuff, and so did Petra, and so did Wash Davis, the good-looking black boy who, when Charlie entered Petra's room, was standing with his hands in his pockets, whistling to himself and staring out the window. The open window was evidence enough that moments ago there must have been a thick wall of smoke in the room. And so was the heavy, cloying smell of incense, which, despite its sweetness, didn't manage to disguise the underlying smells of tobacco and marijuana. And so was the look of fear in their eyes.

She decided that the smartest move would be to make a little speech, and then get rid of them all. But when she opened her mouth she found she was far too breathless and angry for speech, at least for sustained, intelligent speech, and that her words came out singly, with a fierce impact that reminded her of pebbles being thrown one by one at a glass window. "You," she said, pointing at Heather, "where's the bottle?"

"What bottle?"

"Don't be an ass. You know what I mean. Get it."

Heather glanced at Wash, who shrugged and walked slowly over to Petra's bureau, where he crouched down and removed a fifth of vodka, half-full, from the lowest drawer. He held it out to Charlie, his fingers shaking.

"Who bought it?" said Charlie, ignoring his outstretched hand. When none of them answered, she asked again, through clenched teeth, but slowly, as if they were very young children: "I asked, who bought it?"

"Petra and I did," said Heather.

Charlie studied the tall, heavily built girl with her fleshy face and sulky, down-turned lips. "Then *you* take it to the bathroom and pour it out."

"What about Petra?" the girl asked sullenly.

"What about her?"

"She was with me."

"Maybe. But right now Petra doesn't know her ass from her elbow."

This wasn't entirely true. Petra, seated stiffly on the bed, watching her mother, her eyes blinking rapidly, seemed to have returned to earth, and was now looking as frightened and embarrassed as any of the others. Heather snatched the bottle from Wash's hand and went with it to the bathroom. When she came back, she slammed the bottle down on the bureau defiantly.

"In the basket," said Charlie quietly.

"What?" The girl stared at her with hate in her eyes.

"You heard me."

When Heather had deposited the bottle in the wastebasket, Charlie said, "All right, now we'll do the same thing with the marijuana and cigarettes. Only this time"—she swung around and fixed her eyes on Petra—"it's your turn. Get the stuff and flush it down the toilet."

The whole procedure took ten minutes. When they were finished, Charlie looked at each of them, studying with great sadness their young, bright, embarrassed faces, and said, "I'm not going to tell you what this stuff can do. You know that already. All I'm going to say is if you want to mess yourselves up, don't do it here. I don't ever want to see this shit in my house again. And if any of you ever comes here again, and you're not one hundred percent sober, I'll call the police. And the school. As it is, I have to call your parents. Now get out!"

"Are you really going to call their parents?" asked Petra half an hour later, huddled on the living room sofa. She watched as her mother tried to get a fire started in the sooty, wood-stacked grate.

Charlie bent and lit a match to a piece of rolled-up newspaper, and then sat back on her heels, watching as the newspaper burst into flame, and the flames leapt up, spreading quickly in long tongues of orange and yellow and gold until the whole rough underside of a log had been ignited. "Yes, of course I am," she said simply.

"But you can't do that! You can't!" exclaimed Petra, jerking her head so that her brown hair flew into her eyes. "They'll all hate me. Anyway it's my fault! Why should they get in trouble because of me?"

"It's everyone's fault," said Charlie. "Not just yours. But since we're talking about blame, you might as well tell me whose idea it was. Did they try to pressure you into it, or did you invite them over, or what?" She turned from her squatting position and looked at her daughter.

"I invited them over," mumbled Petra. "Actually I invited just Eliza. I don't know, it's sort of confusing. I guess one thing led to another."

"Unh-hunh," said Charlie. "So you see it's everyone's fault. But it's your fault particularly since, A: it was your house, and B: you know exactly what alcohol and drugs can do. That's not the first time you've bought a bottle of something, is it?"

"No," said Petra. "I did it once before. That is, Heather and I did it."

"Heather," burst out Charlie scornfully. "She makes a lousy friend. I can't force you, but I think you should stay away from her. I don't want her coming here again. Is that understood?"

Petra nodded, but Charlie could see from the look in her eyes that she didn't mean it.

"If I catch you with booze on your breath, that's the end of your allowance. If I catch you smelling of marijuana, or sneaking in from doing something stupid with some boy, that's the end of your allowance. And in the meantime, all privileges are off, you are totally and one hundred percent grounded for the next month. Oh, and while I'm at it, I intend to search your room from now on."

"Oh, Mom," wailed Petra, "you can't! That's not fair! That's an invasion of privacy!"

"Call it anything you want," said Charlie, rising to her feet and dusting her palms off on the soft wool of her skirt. "Act like a jerk and you'll be treated like a jerk. And now, you know what? I'm hungry. I haven't eaten in hours, and you probably haven't either. How about some Chinese food? We could order in."

"Yuk, no!" said Petra. "I don't see how you can think of food at a time like this."

"Why not?" said Charlie. "I'm not the one with a guilty conscience."

"Well, *you* were a few weeks ago. When you were with that guy," she added sullenly, as if Charlie might have missed the point.

Charlie gave her a look that said, Don't try my patience, and went to her desk at the other end of the living room. As she was rummaging through the drawer where she kept checkbooks and small amounts of extra cash, Petra, in a low, fearful voice, said: "Are you going to tell Daddy about this?"

"I don't know. Probably."

"I wish you wouldn't. I'll be really good from now on if you don't tell him. I promise. I swear I will."

"You should always be good," said Charlie with a sigh. But she was no longer concentrating on Petra. Money was missing from the drawer. She was almost certain of it. A week ago she had placed three hundred dollars, in twenties, beneath a stack of receipted bills, and now, counting the twenties, she saw that only a hundred remained. She did a quick reckoning—in the past few days she had taken approximately one hundred dollars from the drawer, no more than that. She counted again to be sure, and then glanced at Petra and said, "Did you by any chance borrow some money from me?"

"No."

"Do you think one of your friends might have?"

"Shit," said Petra. "Now you're accusing me of stealing."

"I'm not accusing you of anything. And watch your language. It's just that quite a large amount of money is missing from this drawer."

"Well, I certainly didn't take it, and I'm sure none of my friends did either. We were all upstairs the whole time. Maybe it was Gloria."

"Gloria's not a thief, you know that."

"Well, then maybe you thought you had more money than you really did."

"Maybe," said Charlie dubiously. She stared down into the open drawer as if something there, some tiny change in the placement of paper clips or stamps, would tell her what had happened.

"Please Mom," said Petra, breaking in on her thoughts. "You've got to say you won't tell him."

"Tell who?"

"Daddy. About what happened. All that stuff with Eliza. It's too embarrassing."

Charlie removed a twenty-dollar bill from the drawer and slammed it shut. One thing was sure: Petra hadn't taken the money. Those large brown beseeching eyes of hers carried none of the nervousness of a thief. "I don't see why I should promise you anything," she said, reaching for the phone book to look up the number of the Chinese restaurant. "Not after what happened this afternoon."

"But you have to!"

"Why?"

"Just because you do."

"Oh, come on, Petra. You're hardly in a position to start telling me what to do."

"Please. Oh please."

Charlie looked at Petra, who stared back at her tearfully. "All right," sighed Charlie. "All right, I'll think about it. But in the meantime I don't want to hear any more of your adolescent bullshit, okay?"

She didn't want to add that since she and Neil were just managing to be civil to each other on the phone, Petra could have dispensed with her hand-wringing and tears. A long time would pass before Neil learned anything about this afternoon's disastrous events. If he ever did. She phoned the restaurant and placed an order, and then went upstairs, wanting to be alone for a few minutes. The scene with Petra and her friends—and before that, the fight she had had with Dennis—had utterly worn her out. This was the first time she had had to discipline Petra without Neil's strong presence to back her up, and she felt like an actress who had just played a difficult and demanding role, a role that did not come naturally, and who now needed to run off to her dressing room to recuperate. An actress would receive applause, flowers, fan mail, Charlie reflected bitterly; a mother received nothing palpable for her efforts—only the thinnest sense that possibly she had helped her child, taught her something.

Kicking off her moccasins and stretching out on the bed, she thought fleetingly of the empty bottle of Smirnoff's in the waste-basket upstairs. If Petra had inherited her disease of alcoholism it would be a great pity, but at least she, Charlie—unlike her own mother—would know what to do about it: gently try to persuade her to attend meetings, and show her by example how wonderful it was to lead a full, useful, sober life. The thought that she had AA to back her up suddenly filled her with gratitude; Neil may not have been here to support her in this crisis, but at least she had a place to go, a loving group of people to talk to, and a twelve-step program that could guide her through *anything*.

The doorbell rang, and in a somewhat lighter mood she got up off the bed and hurried downstairs to pay for their dinner. This business of raising children on one's own was tough, she thought, taking the warm, spicy-smelling bag of food into her arms. Even with AA, she missed the reassurance of knowing Neil was standing in the wings, ready to catch her if she fell, applaud her, hold her, just be a friend. But he wasn't a friend now, she thought, closing the door and heading for the kitchen. He wasn't a friend, and she'd just have to learn to live without him.

*a*fter their dinner at L'Hirondelle, the dinner that ended so disastrously, Musette didn't hear from Neil. She tried for nearly a week to reach him on the phone, leaving messages and calling repeatedly—and when there was nothing but silence, she began to feel desperate. Her immediate reaction was to take increasingly larger doses of Valium. In her view she needed the tranquilizer to keep from falling apart—it was alcohol that was the killer, and as long as she didn't touch that, she was all right.

But underneath, without wanting to admit it to herself, she knew that Valium had an effect on her that wasn't always positive: her speech slowed, was sometimes even slurry; her vision lost its sharpness—everything seemed slightly gray; and her energy diminished to the point where she just wanted to lie around. Even Felicity commented on it one night at a meeting, narrowing her eyes and studying Musette with an intensity that made the actress uncomfortable. "Are you on something?" she asked, bringing her face close to Musette's, as if she wished to smell her breath.

"Just antihistamines," Musette said quickly. "I've had a damn cold for weeks and I've had to resort to this over-the-counter stuff to get rid of it."

"Well, you'd better go easy. People like us can get awfully dependent on antihistamines. And from there it's an easy slide to stronger stuff."

"Oh," laughed Musette, taking out a tissue and blowing her nose as if she really did have a cold. "Believe me, this stuff makes me too sleepy to be habit-forming."

After that little interchange she avoided Felicity. On the following Saturday, however, her sponsor was giving a tree-trimming party, and Musette knew that even though she felt like an emotional wreck she would have to go. She continued to try to reach Neil; two nights before the party he actually picked up the phone, and she was so surprised to hear his voice that she didn't know what to say.

"Yes—who is it?" he asked a few times before she finally got any words out.

"It's me, Neil. I've been trying to reach you for days. Why didn't you answer any of my messages?"

"Oh, Maggie." He gave a little cough. "Yes, I apologize. Please don't be hurt by this, but I've needed time to think."

She was speaking into a cordless phone, pacing up and down her living room in a peach silk kimono that rustled with every step; now she stopped to remove a cigarette from a silver dish on an end table. "Think? You mean about what I told you about Charlie and Dennis?"

"That's right."

"You weren't very nice to me that night, Neil." She heard an accusatory note in her voice, and quickly bit down on her lip. Now was not the time to antagonize him.

"I'm sorry," Neil said mildly. "Believe me, it wasn't intentional."

She sucked at her cigarette, fighting to make her voice sound normal as she blew out smoke. "Anyway, I don't see what that whole thing has to do with us."

"You don't?"

"No, I don't."

"She's my wife, Maggie."

"Yes, but you're not sleeping with her. *I'm* the one you sleep with. You haven't slept with *her* in over a year and a half."

"You don't have to remind me of that."

There was a long silence. From the street Musette heard the

screech of police sirens, and nervously pushed aside a thick velvet curtain and glanced out into the darkness over Park Avenue. "When are you coming up to New York?" she asked, letting the curtain fall back into place.

"I don't know."

"Charlie has the children this weekend, which means you're free."

Neil gave an ironic laugh. "What else do you know about Charlie?"

"Only what I told you the other night. I'll be seeing her at a tree-trimming party Saturday. I'd love it if you met me afterward..."

"Oh, Maggie, I'm not sure I could make it."

"Why not? What are you doing that's better? You know how happy I always make you feel."

"Just work—I've got a lot to finish before the Christmas recess."

She stubbed out her cigarette. "Well, you know what? Screw work. Come and have dinner with me instead. Say at about seven-thirty. That'd be a hell of a lot more fun than a bunch of dreary papers."

"Yeah, I agree. But I'd hate to make a promise I couldn't keep."

"You don't have to promise," she said softly. "You just have to do your best. Come on, Neil. For me."

She got him to agree, and even to chuckle at one of her jokes, before hanging up the phone.

Guests were invited to Felicity's party from two o'clock on. Gwen arrived at about four, and was led into the living room by Felicity's little daughter, Bessie, who for once was wearing a dress instead of only panties. "Oh, there you are, Gwen!" cried Felicity, rushing over to her from the tree, which stood, immense and shaggy, in one of the tall front windows. She held a brightly painted wooden ornament in one hand, and a glass of something bubbly in the other, and her face was radiant as she leaned toward Gwen and gave her an awkward hug. "I'm so glad to see you. I was kind of afraid you wouldn't show up."

"Why would I do that?" asked Gwen in an aggravated tone.

"I don't know. You've been so remote lately."

"Well, I've been awfully busy."

"Writing, I hope."

"Writing, yes; among other things."

Felicity looked at her curiously. "Well, whatever you've been doing, it suits you. You look skinny and happy and gorgeous. And I love you in that dress." Gwen was wearing an orange sheath whose subtle yolky color was as exotic against all the dark winter clothing as a mango in a bowl of turnips.

"Yes, well, I am very happy," said Gwen, her dark eyes gleaming. She bunched her strong full lips together, and for a moment it seemed as if she would say something, explain her happiness to Felicity. But instead her lips flattened out into a smile and she said, "I sure am thirsty though. What have you got here for a gratefully recovering alcoholic to drink?"

The reason she was so happy was that she had heard that morning from the *West Indian Voice*. When she had gone down to the lobby to check her mail, a thick white envelope had been among the letters and bills, and she had known immediately who it was from and what sort of news it contained. He wanted her! Certain of that, she tore open the envelope and read:

Dear Mr. Taylor:

I was very happy to receive your piece about West Indians returning to their roots after many years. You show a strong talent, and I would be pleased if you phoned me at the office so we could discuss other projects. Enclosed is a form for you to sign, upon return of which we'll send you a check for $100. Your piece will appear in the paper on December 21st.

  Sincerely,

John Hopeton Sinclair

His signature was an illegible scrawl. She grinned down at it, thinking, Dumb bastard, I sure as shit got you this time, didn't I! She felt as good as if her agent had called to say he had wangled a million-dollar advance for her next novel. Tucking the rest of the mail under her arm and hurrying to the elevator, she decided she would play cat and mouse with him, sending him one or two articles a month, until he had published enough for her to really do some crowing.

In Felicity's dining room a feast had been laid out on the long polished mahogany table—cheeses, breads, salads, a gorgeous pink ham, Christmas cookies, Bavarian cream pie, chocolate mousse, several delectable-looking fruit tarts. Gwen heaped her plate high. She'd forget the damn diet today and enjoy herself. Across the room, Musette also seemed to be eating what she pleased. On her plate was a huge slab of chocolate mousse, and she spooned this eagerly into her beautiful mouth, pinky finger curled, which Gwen had always been taught was a sign of poor breeding. The two women waved at one another, and then Musette shifted position so her back was to Gwen. For a moment Gwen tried to keep her in sight. The actress looked sexy as hell in a tight black dress cut so low in the back that most of her sinewy spine was exposed. But the room was crowded and people kept getting in the way. In a corner, enthroned on a tall brocaded chair, sat an elderly lady who Gwen supposed must be Felicity's mother. In another corner, Norman Shultis, managing editor of Colonial Press, sipped at a large glass of eggnog while Theo Hammond talked exuberantly into his ear. Perched on top of a ladder, Margot Sibley, Gwen's sponsor, leaned over with willowy grace and hung a magnificent white angel on one of the uppermost boughs of the tree.

And then there were shades of last year, of a party Gwen didn't want to remember. The flesh rose on the back of her neck as she turned and saw little Joey Herman, the radio personality, hunched over the keys of the living room piano. He was trying to pick out Christmas tunes against the background hum of conversation, people shrieking hello, babies crying, the rattle of cutlery and glasses, and she remembered he had been doing just that a year ago at the Teasdales' tree-trimming party, that his music had been a background to her growing mood of despair. She had left that party early, terribly depressed; had gone home and gotten drunk, and then, too bleary to think it through, had tipped a bottle of sleeping pills into her palm. Oh, the unhappiness of those times! And now, a year later, here she was: full of energy, working on a new novel, a film about to go into production, sober, living on her own, and happy—yes, gloriously happy! She stared at Joey Herman a moment longer, and then abruptly turned away. Shit, I hope the guy doesn't bring me bad luck, she thought.

"It was amazing," Charlie said. "Not one of those parents wanted to believe their child was involved."

"But you were there!" Felicity cried. "You saw them."

The two women had stolen away from the party, and were having a sponsor-sponsee conversation in Felicity's tiny study on the third floor.

Charlie sighed and reached into her pocket for her cigarettes. "You know, much as I hate to admit it, the whole goddamn incident makes me feel lonely for Neil. At least in the child-rearing department. Last night the phone rang, and there was a moment of dead silence before the person at the other end hung up. And I knew, I just knew, it was Heather Barnes wanting to persuade Petra to sneak out of the house once I'd gone to sleep. At that moment I kind of wished like hell Neil were there for me to lean on."

Someone out in the hall gave a soft cough and both women looked up. It was Musette who stood in the doorway, looking beautiful, cheeks flushed, eyes a dark, mysterious amber, as she said, "Oh, I hope I'm not interrupting anything. I just wanted to say good-bye, Felicity. It's been a lovely party."

"You're not leaving!" cried Felicity, glancing at her watch. "It's only six-thirty."

"I'm afraid I have to. I have a dinner engagement."

"Someone exciting, I hope," said Charlie, always curious about the actress's love life.

"Oh yes," said Musette, smiling brilliantly at her. "Someone very exciting."

"Well, for God's sake, tell us who it is. As your sponsor I should know these things," said Felicity.

But Musette only laughed and put her fingers to her lips, blowing a kiss at the two women. "Sorry, but I've really got to run," she said as she retreated down the hall.

"Lord," said Felicity, staring after her, "that woman is so secretive. She'll talk about money and the movie business and tell all sorts of stories about her ex-husband, but when it comes to anything current or really personal she clams right up. I shouldn't say this, but it's almost impossible to sponsor her. She just doesn't take AA very seriously."

"Whereas I do?"

Felicity smiled at Charlie. "I think you do. There's an old AA saying, 'You're as sick as your secrets.' Musette's full of sly little secrets, which in the end, unless she talks about them, will be her undoing." She stood up from her chair and stretched. "We'd better get back to the party. Everyone'll be wondering where I am."

Charlie thought about that, *Sick as your secrets*. She had heard the expression before, but now, in Felicity's small study, it gave her a nasty jolt. What about her own secret, the one that defined her, that had eaten its way like an acid deep into her bones? If she was as sick as the secret of Gil Hoffeld's death, she was very sick indeed.

So now she wants Neil back, thought Musette, rushing down the stairs. No, that wasn't what Charlie had said. What she had said was, she wished like hell she had Neil to lean on. Musette stopped off in Felicity's bedroom for her coat, pausing in front of the mirror to brush her hair and put on some lipstick. Too bad she hadn't heard the whole conversation, Charlie and Felicity closeted in that dark little room, whispering their secrets like cliquish schoolgirls.

She put her lipstick away, slipped into her coat, and continued down the stairs. She was in a hurry now. It was a quarter to seven and Neil would be at her house at seven-thirty. She needed time to fix her hair, freshen her makeup, and see that the dinner had been prepared according to her wishes. And the drive back to the city took at least twenty minutes.

In the downstairs hall, Norman Shultis, looking a little red in the face, stood in the door to the living room with Gwen. He had his arms around the writer and was giving her a big sloppy kiss, but when he saw Musette, he opened his arms, drawing her into the embrace. "Under the mistletoe," he explained.

"Ah," said Musette, trying to extricate herself.

The publisher had a smear of eggnog on his upper lip and smelled strongly of bourbon. He gave her a sticky kiss, and then, beaming at the two of them, he said: "Now that I've got you both together, I want you to tell me the thing I've been dying to know for weeks. And that is, who's got the role of Winnie in *Homegirl*?"

"Bethany Hunt," Musette said automatically. "But look, I've got to go—I'm in the most awful rush." And she pulled herself out of his embrace and hurried to the door, waving good-bye as she went, not turning to look at Norman, whose face wore an expression of pleased satisfaction, or at Gwen, whose face wore an expression of horror and disgust.

As soon as she could get away from Norman, Gwen ran to find her sponsor, Margot Sibley, grabbing her by the sleeve of her ivory cashmere sweater and saying, "I've got to talk to you."

"What's happened?" said Margot, looking concerned. She took off her huge black-framed glasses and peered into Gwen's face. "You look as if you've seen a ghost."

"I feel that way too," said Gwen. "Do you know what I just found out? That Bethany Hunt is going to play the role of Winnie in *Homegirl*."

"Well, what's wrong with that? She's a wonderful actress."

"Oh no, she isn't. And she's far too pretty for the part. Winnie's supposed to be plain, black, and ugly, not a graceful beauty with yellow skin. People are supposed to feel sorry for her. I can't tell you how upset I am."

"But didn't Musette need your approval before signing her on?"

"She sure did," said Gwen. "As associate producer I have total veto power."

"Well then," said Margot, "it's very simple, isn't it? Either she takes Bethany Hunt out of the picture, or she's got a lawsuit on her hands." She smiled at Gwen. "Does that shock you?"

"A little."

"Listen my dear, if you go into such a competitive dog-eat-dog business as films, you've got to be tough. You've got to look out for yourself, know what I mean? That's show biz."

Musette arrived home very tense and nervous, ran to the living room to check the flowers and put on some music, and then quickly went to her bedroom to change into black silk lounging pajamas. She was about to take another Valium, but decided against it—she wanted to be alert, not slow and groggy. And she wanted to look so sexy that Neil would feel a surge of desire for her the minute he walked in the door.

She busied herself with her hair and makeup, glancing occasionally at her watch; when ten minutes passed, and no Neil, she felt a slight queasiness in her stomach. She gave him another ten minutes and then walked briskly into her office to see if she had any messages. A red light was flashing on the machine. Musette pressed the button, and heard Neil's voice.

"Sorry Maggie, but I've decided to stay in Washington. I'm really not great company at the moment. I'll call you in a few days."

"You bastard!" she shouted. "What am I supposed to do now?" White in the face, she realized she hadn't yet heard from Frank Stiller, the detective, which meant she still didn't have a hold on Neil. As she was standing there, seething, the phone rang. In no mood to answer it, she let the machine take the call.

It was Gwen, a clipped, angry Gwen who insisted that Musette call her first thing in the morning. "Bethany Hunt was not my choice for Winnie, and I refuse to have her."

"Tough shit, bitch!" snapped Musette. "You should have thought of that weeks ago." As the machine clicked off, she gave it a shove that sent it clattering to the floor. Then she ran sobbing from the room. If she had had any liquor in the apartment she would certainly have picked it up that minute; instead she took two Valiums, grabbed the Siamese cat Theo Hammond had given her as a gift a few weeks ago and flung it across the room (the thing had taken to sleeping on her bed, which irritated her), throwing herself down on the pillows and weeping uncontrollably. She cried for what seemed like hours, her fist shoved into her mouth, her beautifully applied makeup running in blurry tracks down her face, her silk pajamas twisted around her curled-up body; she had no idea when she fell asleep, but when she awoke the next day it was already past noon and she had a terrible hangover.

Once Musette's head had cleared and she'd had some coffee, she leaned against her satin pillows and called her entertainment attorney in Los Angeles. It took all afternoon to reach him; when she finally tracked him down and he assured her that she "had nothing to worry about, baby," she put in a call to Gwen. "Hi," she said pleasantly. "This is Musette. How are you?"

"I know who this is, so let's cut the crap. I don't want Bethany in my film."

"Not your film, Gwen. Mine. I own it."

"It's my story."

"Yes, it's your story. But for the time being I own the rights to it—remember?"

Gwen ignored that. "You never consulted me about Bethany Hunt," she said.

"And you never asked. Every time I tried to contact you, you were busy. Look Gwen, let's face it—once you finished the script, you lost all interest in it. Musette-knows-best, that was your attitude. Well, you were right: I do know best, and that's why Miroslav and I chose Bethany for the part."

"Well then, you're both stupider than I thought," said Gwen.

"Bethany's too shallow to play Winnie. She doesn't even look the part."

"She will when we get through with her."

"And she can't act her way out of a paper bag. Don't you see? She'll destroy the whole goddamn film with that phony Hollywood look of hers."

"She's not going to destroy anything," said Musette quietly. "Now listen to me. I've got as much riding on this as you do, if not more. Because if the film's a bust, people are not going to say Gwen Thomas is a lousy writer. Oh no. They're going to say Musette took an excellent script and made a mess of it. That's why I have to choose top talent like Bethany Hunt. You may not like her, Gwen, but other people do. Most of the country loves staring at that beautiful face of hers, so we're going to have to tap in on public opinion."

"Screw public opinion," said Gwen. "I don't give a—"

"No," said Musette. "Public opinion is what puts dollars in the bank. We signed a contract with Bethany weeks ago, so we can't get rid of her. We'd lose all our backing, and we'd have a lawsuit on our hands. Is that what you want?"

Gwen was silent.

"I'm supposed to get a check for half a million dollars from Belle Salzman in the next few days. Remove Bethany from the film, and you can forget about it."

"All right, all right," said Gwen. "But from now on I want you to tell me exactly what you're doing. Even if I've been hard to reach these past few weeks, you've certainly violated our contract by not informing me of every decision and step you've made. All you had to do was put it in writing. And I still don't like the idea of Bethany appearing in my film. I'll have to think about it some more."

Musette kept being put off by Frank Stiller, who said a key witness in the case had disappeared. She forced herself to stay away from the phone, although it was hell being out of touch with Neil. And in the middle of the week she learned that her older sister had to have a breast removed, and flew up to Pittsburgh to be with her. She returned late on Friday, and went straight to the phone to call Neil. "What's going on, baby?" she crooned. "I can't stand not seeing you like this."

"Yeah, I know. I'm sorry. Things are pretty hectic here." In the background Musette could hear busy Washington voices—his aides, a secretary with something for him to sign, a lobbyist bursting into his office. Neil was an impossibly public man—except with his emotions.

"You feeling better?" she asked quickly.

"Some."

"Then why don't you come up to New York? I'll give you one of my great back rubs, famous throughout Hollywood."

"Yeah, I'll bet," he laughed.

"Or I could come down there."

"I've got the children this weekend."

"Well then, how about next week? It's almost Christmas. I've got this terrific present for you. It's wrapped in satin right now, and when you unwrap it it will squirm and wriggle any way you want. Can you guess what your present is?"

He laughed nervously, which was not the reaction Musette had intended. "Look Maggie, we'll be in touch on the phone. I just don't know how to plan things at the moment."

It took every ounce of self-control for Musette not to slam the receiver down in her lover's ear.

Once she heard about Bethany Hunt's being cast in the role of Winnie, Gwen's luck seemed to turn. On the Monday after Felicity's party she received a note in the mail from Walter, reminding her that it would soon be a year since she had attempted suicide. "We should spend that day together, Gwennie." The man's nuts, thought Gwen, in no mood to deal with her ex-husband, who was always trying to find reasons to see her. On Wednesday her little cat, Miss Fish, whom she had had for years, collapsed and was dead within twenty-four hours of kidney failure. And then, on Saturday, just as she was leaving the house for an AA meeting, she received a call from her mother in Jamaica. "Hello, Gwen baby, that you?"

"I don't know who else it would be. How you doing, Ma?"

"Fine. Just fine. Sure is beautiful here. Living in New York you forget what it's like breathing fresh air. And the flowers! Goodness, how they light up the soul."

Gwen, who had heard all this before, interrupted her. "I'm

sort of in a hurry, Ma. Was there something specific you wanted? Otherwise we could talk next Wednesday when you get home."

"That's why I'm calling you, baby. I ain't coming home next Wednesday. Your aunt Shirley's asked me to stay on and celebrate Christmas with her and Harold and the grandkids."

"Oh?"

"You don't mind, do you? I figured with all your parties and fancy friends, you'd be plenty occupied."

Gwen's heart sank to her boots. "I do mind," she said, feeling a little as if she had just been orphaned.

"What's that?"

"Nothing. Forget it. Give Aunt Shirley a kiss for me."

"All right. She sends you one too."

"And Ma?"

"Yes, baby?"

"Drink up some of that fresh air for me, will you?"

Hanging up the phone, she realized she was crying. First Walter and his misguided solicitousness, then the cat, and now this. And she had ordered a turkey for the two of them, had planned a wonderful Christmas meal. She had even been in touch with Dr. Mitchum at the church, asking if he and some of the ladies would like to join them. Instead her mother was abandoning her.

Filled with self-pity, with rage, she slammed out of the apartment and headed uptown to the Harlem Meeting. If she could just find Audrey, big comforting Audrey, everything would be all right. Audrey would put her arms around her and rock her better than her own mother ever had, whispering, "There, there, baby; there, there," until Gwen was calm and steady again. Just the thought of her made tears of gratitude well up in Gwen's eyes.

But Audrey wasn't at the meeting.

Her usual seat in the front row was empty. She wasn't in the back chatting with friends, and she wasn't in the ladies room or in the kitchen either. "Anyone see Audrey?" Gwen asked, but no one had. The meeting started, and after a while Gwen relaxed a little, and began to let the energy of all the people gathered in the room seep into her. The speaker said something about the worst day sober being better than the best day drunk. Ha—that was appropriate. When he had finished, she did exactly what Audrey would have counseled her to do: got her hand up in the air. She was the first person to be called on.

"I feel pretty shitty," she said. In a trembling voice, she let it all come pouring out: her mother's defection to Jamaica, her cat's death, her suicide attempt a year ago, her despair at the idea of being alone on Christmas.

"You got a sponsor?" asked the speaker.

"Yes," said Gwen, her mind jumping to Audrey. "But she's not here tonight."

"Well, you call her when you get home. And remember, it's normal for an alcoholic to get depressed at Christmastime. There's all that booze around; everywhere you look people are drinking and partying and having a blast. Consequently, those of us who can't drink feel left out and punished. But remember, it passes. And the rooms of AA are always open. On Christmas we celebrate together, right here in this space. You'll see—it's a great time: lots of food and music and all your friends. So you don't have to be alone, hear?"

She nodded and tried to look happy, although the idea of celebrating Christmas in a drafty church hall among strangers, however friendly, wasn't exactly appealing. When the meeting was over, she went right home. The apartment seemed empty without Miss Fish, and she turned on all the lights and started rummaging through a pile of papers, looking for Audrey's number. She was desperate to speak to the woman, to hear her low, raspy, humorous voice. But she couldn't find it, and as she didn't know Audrey's last name she was stuck. Deciding she'd call Charlie or Felicity instead, she went into the kitchen to brew a pot of tea. While she was waiting for the water to boil, the buzzer rang from downstairs.

"Yes, who is it?" she asked, glancing automatically at her watch. It was ten-thirty.

"John S.," a voice said, drawing out the S so that it made a hissing sound.

"John who?" she said, her mind not immediately taking in the information.

"John Hopeton Sinclair. Your favorite editor and critic."

"Jesus," she said. And she pressed the button to let him in.

He was dressed in jeans and a soft, glossy, dark brown leather jacket with a fur collar, and around his neck was wrapped a lemony yellow scarf. He wore no hat, and when eventually he removed his jacket she saw that he had on a thin blue T-shirt and nothing else, no sweater, as if the cold and rainy weather outside were something that this small black man could ignore. The shirt clung like a second skin to his muscular upper body, his rounded biceps, but she didn't notice that right away. What she noticed was his face: the hooded look of self-satisfaction and worry in his eyes, the quivering width of his nostrils, the way his mouth and chin bunched together and moved as one unit when he talked. He was carrying a brown paper bag, which he held up to her as soon as he walked through the door.

"What is it—a peace offering?" She wondered for a second if it was alcohol.

"Ice cream," he answered in a guarded voice. "I couldn't bring wine or whiskey, so..." He shrugged his shoulders. She took the ice cream from him and gestured numbly that he should follow her into the kitchen, which was the room she felt most comfortable in. Whatever he had to say could be said in there.

"I was just making myself a cup of tea," she said warily. "Want one?" Seeing this man here was wrong, all wrong.

"All right. Black, three sugars." He grinned, showing those alarming gap teeth of his. "My one weakness."

"Ah—only one?"

He ignored the comment and sat down without being asked, glancing briefly around her small kitchen and pulling a pack of menthol cigarettes from his jacket pocket.

"Do you want ice cream too?" she asked, groping for small talk. Even the most banal words would be better than anything bigger he might want to say.

"What?"

"Ice cream. The stuff you brought. Do you want some with your tea?"

"Just the tea will be fine." He lit a cigarette, drawing on it with a harsh sound and letting the smoke escape in slow gusts from his nostrils. When she put the tea down in front of him he nodded a curt thank-you and went on smoking for a moment in silence. Then he said, "I suppose you're wondering why I'm here."

"You suppose right, brother." She leaned against the counter, watching him through narrowed, assessing eyes.

"I was at the meeting," he said, picking up his tea and blowing on it. "Way in the back, where you couldn't see me. You're going through some pretty rough trials and tribulations, aren't you, baby?" He sipped at his tea and stared at her, his smile bitter and false.

"Get to the point, Sinclair."

"You left the meeting awfully fast. Girl, you were like some kind of bullet whizzing out of there, that black cap of yours pulled down tight over your head, and I thought to myself: she's in trouble if she goes home alone. A girl like that with all sorts of ghosts haunting her."

Gwen snorted. "Your sudden interest is very touching, Sinclair. Whad'you do? Follow me down Broadway?"

"Didn't have to. I had this." He pulled a thick envelope out of his jacket pocket. "A few weeks ago a fellow named Raymond Taylor sent me this article about parents returning to the islands. Well, when I heard you speak at the meeting tonight, bells went off in my head. I closed my eyes and it could have been Raymond

W. Taylor talking about his mama instead of Gwen Thomas. So, since I had the galleys with me I decided to do a little research, and lo and behold the two of you have the same address!"

"What are you going to do about it, Sinclair? Not publish the article?"

"That would be pretty stupid of me, wouldn't it?"

"Well then, why are you here? Why do you hate me so much?"

"I'm here, as I said before, because I didn't think you should be alone feeling as miserable as you do. Now if you wouldn't mind throwing this shit out and making me a cup of coffee in that Melitta you've got there, I'll tell you the reason I hate you so much."

His story was long and complicated and took the better part of two hours to tell, and by the time he had finished it, Gwen was sitting at the kitchen table, her eyes slitted against the smoke of both their cigarettes, her head nodding frequently, as if what he had to say was old and familiar news to her. He had grown up in her neighborhood, one of the boys who used to yell taunts at her as she tripped home from school in her knee-highs and pleated gray skirts. "I thought you were so goddamn stuck-up," he said. "All I really wanted to do was *talk* to you, and you'd walk right by with your nose in the air and this supercilious goddamn smile on your face, as if you and I, baby, were two different flavors, chocolate and vanilla, and you can guess which one of us was which—"

"But I didn't even know—"

"Yes, yes, that's my point. You didn't *know* I existed. And yet there I was, most every afternoon, hanging out on that particular corner of that particular street, admiring the look of you in your smart white-girl's school clothes, that book bag you used to carry slapping against your hip and the sun glinting off the pennies in your loafers."

Like the Thomases, his parents had emigrated to New York from Jamaica, but as soon as the Sinclairs were installed in a tiny two-bedroom apartment on West 147th Street, John's father moved out, leaving his wife, Lorna, on her own to cope with three small children. "We were hell to bring up," Sinclair told Gwen. "She couldn't keep track of us. Anyway, what with working two jobs she herself was hardly ever home, and it seemed some days it was just us and the cockroaches."

Lorna had the same sorts of jobs Gwen's mother had, cleaning houses, taking care of other people's children, but she lacked the strong will of Sarah Thomas, and it wasn't long before her daughter and two young sons were running wild in the streets. John and his older brother, Edgar Charles, only eleven months apart and in the same grade, were free-basing cocaine before they were out of elementary school. Their sister, Rowena, had a baby of her own almost as soon as she got her period at the age of fourteen. And so it went, no restrictions placed on the young Sinclairs, unless those of the building superintendent who would raise a hopeless fist at them, or those of teachers, the best of whom could see the smarts the boys had, but couldn't compete with the draw of the street. Along with the drugs went all sorts of crimes: mugging elderly ladies, breaking into cars, pickpocketing, grabbing merchandise off shelves and making an exhilarating run for it. Eventually they moved on to bigger game, robbing a stationery store on Ninety-sixth Street of $530. In this incident they were with another boy, and they managed to get away before the police came.

"How old were you?" asked Gwen.

"Twenty. My brother was twenty-one and that was the age he stayed, because two nights later he died of a drug overdose."

"Jesus," said Gwen.

John nodded. "All that damn money right up his arm. I watched it happen too. We were in the little bedroom we shared, and I kept slapping him in the face and yelling at him. I tried to make him walk around like you're supposed to do, but it was no use. Anyway I was in pretty bad shape myself. And I couldn't call for an ambulance 'cause with the ambulance would've come the police, and with the police, a shitload of trouble."

"Yes of course. So you stayed with him. What happened then?"

John looked at her and laughed. "A shitload of trouble."

Although he hadn't been carrying a gun, the other boy had, and eventually both of them were picked up by the police and charged with armed robbery. It wasn't John's first encounter with the law, but it was his first serious offense, and he was sentenced to five years in prison upstate. "I didn't do all five years," he told Gwen. "I only did three, and I have to say, looking back on it, they were the three most important years of my life. Why? Because I had time to meditate, to get a hold of myself."

He discovered he had a love of books and learning, that he enjoyed using his mind, puzzling over things, writing his thoughts down in a journal. He had dropped out of school in the ninth grade, but now, in prison, he got his high school diploma and started taking college-level courses in literature and political science. "But what I liked to do best," he said pointedly, "was write. This young white chick used to come in once a week, and I guess she thought I had talent because she encouraged me to work at essays and poetry. Well, I'd spend all night on that stuff, and man it made me feel free and powerful, know what I mean? As if I wasn't behind those prison bars at all, but somewhere way up high in the heavens where I could look down and see the entire world spinning." He laughed. "That sounds crazy, doesn't it?"

Gwen shook her head. "Not to me it doesn't."

"Anyway, it got to the point where I was producing book-loads, and the girl—her name was Nora Addison—said maybe she could help me get some of it published. She said I was good. She'd take me aside and say, 'John, don't ever forget that this is what you really are: a writer.' And I believed her, too. I thought she was terrific, coming in for practically no money and trying to get us guys all fired up about our own culture. Ralph Ellison, James Baldwin, people like that. She'd sit on a chair in front of us, dressed in shapeless clothes, big sweaters, jeans, just about as sexy as a nun. The other guys were always making jokes about her, but I liked her, she was my friend. And then one day, not too long before I was due to go up for parole, she gave me her address. None of the other teachers had done that, and I took it entirely the wrong way."

He wrote Nora's address down in his journal, and went to see her about a month after he was released from prison. She lived in a tiny upstate town called Palenville, but there was no listing for her with the phone company, and he didn't write or call ahead. In a mood of euphoria, he boarded a Trailways bus that took him to within four miles of where he was going. From there he walked, sweating because it was a hot day and he was wearing a suit and had a large cardboard folder of poems and essays tucked under his arm.

The house he was directed to was in the woods, an old stone house surrounded by brambles and neglected rosebushes. It had dark green shutters and he remembered thinking of Hansel and Gretel, and feeling a cold wave of apprehension as he pressed the doorbell. From somewhere in the interior he heard her voice calling, "Come on in, it's open." He heard violin music, and without saying who he was, he followed the music into the kitchen where she stood, dressed only in shorts and halter top, mixing something in a bowl. She was much thinner and straighter than he would have imagined from those big baggy clothes of hers. The long dark indentation of her spine made him lick nervously at his lips. "Miss Addison?" he said, not daring to call her Nora as he always had in prison. "Miss—"

She dropped the spoon and sprang around, wary as a cat. "Jesus, not you!" she exclaimed. "How'd you get here?" Her face went very white, and he could see that she was holding her breath, and that the muscles of her neck were corded with fear.

"The bus."

"What? What? Who said you could come here? Who invited you?"

"I . . . you gave me your address. You said—"

"I didn't say anything. Now get out of here. Get—" She grabbed a paring knife up from the counter and aimed it at him, holding it close to her chest.

"Hey, there's no need—"

"I said get out of here! Get out or I'll call the police!"

"But I only wanted to show you my writing." He held the big awkward folder out toward her. "That's why—"

"I don't care about your writing! I don't want to have anything to do with it! Now get out! I give you ten seconds before I start screaming."

He got out of there fast, not needing to hear more. All the way back to the bus stop he kept turning and looking over his shoulder, sure the police were after him. He was afraid to go home, afraid his parole officer would be waiting for him in his apartment back in the city. For weeks he went around scared of his own shadow, but nothing happened; his visit to the girl in the upstate town seemed to have had no repercussions other than putting a big nasty dent in his ego. For a while he stopped writing. Her words haunted him, and it was a long time before he could bring himself to reread his poetry. And even then, when he took the old folder out one night and dumped all the pages on his bed, he wasn't sure any of it was any good.

"So whad'you do?" asked Gwen.

He stretched, arching his strong upper body so that the ribs stood out in a fluid line like the pleats of an accordion. "What would you have done? I remembered that brother of mine, dead from drugs, and I knew that was one road to happiness and oblivion that was closed to me. And I remembered the joy I'd had staying up nights writing, but I wasn't so sure I could take that road either. Somewhere along the line, though, I got this idea I should go into the newspaper business. I was working in a print shop by then, earning fairly good money, but you know what? Without a college education I was still just a dumb-ass nigger, so I started going to school nights. Didn't finish till I was thirty-four, and then I discovered I had a bachelor's degree in horseshit."

"What do you mean?" asked Gwen.

"I mean that no one was willing to hire me as a journalist. I'd studied English, I'd studied history and sociology and poli-sci, I could write like a sonofabitch, but there wasn't one fucking paper in this town that wanted me once they found out I was black. That was around the time you came out with your first book, and it made me very bitter. Very bitter. There you were, writing about a black experience you'd never had, and there I was with a prison record and a college degree and no future, unless it was shoveling shit."

He grinned at her, showing his funny gap teeth. "Maybe you can see why I started hating you. Anyway, I was all hopped up, mad as hell, and I started drinking more and more. I'd go on these long binges and end up in some damned place with some damn person I didn't know anything about. Years passed that way." He grinned at her again, his face filled with sly amusement.

"And?"

"I was just thinking of all the little Sinclairs I might have fathered screwing around like that. Sometimes when a kid comes up to me in the street saying, 'Mister, do you got any change?' I wonder if maybe he's mine and I don't know it. Gives me a queer chilly feeling."

"How'd you get sober?" she asked, reaching for his cigarettes even though she hated menthol.

"Yeah, well, that's another story." He lit a cigarette for himself, and with the smoke drifting from his nostrils, said, "I was a periodic drinker. That means months would pass with me staying stone-cold sober, and during those months I'd chase after my dream of being a writer. Eventually I got smart about it. If the big important papers wouldn't publish me, the little advertising rags that no one ever heard of would. All I wanted was my name in print, so I chose a shopper's gazette up in Harlem and wrote about shit going on in the neighborhood. Pretty soon the editor got interested in me, and—well, to make a long story short, I ended up with my own column, made a lot of strong connections, and eventually took over."

"That doesn't tell me how you got sober," said Gwen.

He crushed out his cigarette and looked at her. "I couldn't publish a newspaper and be a drunk," he said. "It was as simple as that. Now listen to me, baby, I've done a whole lot of talking, and my mouth is as parched as an African desert, and it seems like we still got a number of things to discuss. How 'bout another cup of coffee?"

"What things do we have to discuss?" asked Gwen, eyeing him suspiciously.

But the small black man only laughed and held up his hard yellow palms and said, "All in good time, all in good time."

C H A P T E R   3 2

C harlie awoke to the drumming of rain on her windows. For a moment she was disoriented. Her body felt used and sticky, and she had a sense of tremendous weariness as if in her dreams she had been forced to run across an endless plain toward a city that never quite materialized. With a deep sigh she pulled the quilt up over her chest. And then she remembered: Dennis had spent the night.

It was not quite seven. Gray light, filmy and subaqueous because of the rain, streamed in from beneath the curtains, and she could see various objects scattered around the room: Dennis's shoes, bits and pieces of clothing, a book hastily tossed off the bed, a plate of half-eaten sandwiches. The bedroom door was closed. She got out of bed, pulling on her robe, and tiptoed into the hall. The house, on this early Sunday morning, could have been empty. Quietly she descended the stairs, stopping every so often to listen, feeling like a prowler in her own home. She knew where all the creaky places were and she avoided them, wondering why she was being so cautious, but also enjoying herself, as if this were a weird game of hide-and-seek, and in the end, with a happy cry, she would find Dennis and throw her arms around him.

Although their relationship had changed, and she wasn't so sure how happy she would be. She thought about this as she came to the last step and paused a moment, her hand on the banister. Dennis had come over the night before to return her earrings. It was the first time they had seen each other since they had quarreled about his painting, and the atmosphere between them had been strained and difficult. Avoiding the subject of art, they had had very little else to say, which was probably why they had been in such a hurry to race upstairs to her bedroom to have sex. And the sex, she thought, smiling at the mystery of it, had been the best they had had in the month or so they had been together—hot, raw, charged with violence. She quivered slightly at the memory of it. Anger had made them passionate, and they had undressed and lain down on the sheets, struggling against one another, kissing fiercely, biting, scratching; and when he held her down and thrust his body into her, it was with such quick-moving hunger and need that she had come almost the instant he was inside her. And that's why I'm so strange and tired this morning, she decided as she descended the final step.

Walking swiftly into the living room, she saw Dennis at the far end of the room, his back to her, his buttocks lanky and pink in the early morning light. In horror, she watched from the doorway as he opened her desk drawer, took out some bills, yanked his old cracked leather jacket from a nearby chair, and stuffed the money into it. Then he must have sensed her presence, for he turned abruptly around, instinctively placing his hands over his penis.

For a moment neither of them said anything. Charlie was the first to speak.

"Take the money out of the goddamn jacket and put it on the desk," she said through stiffened lips.

He did as he was told, his face bland, expressionless.

"And now," said Charlie, aware of how small her voice sounded in the vast room, "go upstairs, get your things, and leave my house."

She shrank back as he passed her in the doorway, not wanting to be touched by him. But she followed him up the stairs and into her bedroom.

"You don't have to watch me," he said, pulling on his shirt.

"Apparently I do."

"You're just a stupid rich bitch."

"Fine. I don't care what you think."

He zipped his pants. "That's a lie. It's important to you what people like me think."

She didn't answer. A moment later he was dressed, and they went back down the stairs in silence. In the hallway, he said, "Well, it's been real," and he held his hand up and gave her the finger, before picking up his jacket and sauntering out the door.

Musette's bedside phone rang and she grabbed it on the second ring, hoping it was Neil.

"Well, I've finally got some results for you, Mrs. Vlk."

It was the detective, Frank Stiller.

"Do you always call people at the crack of dawn on Sunday, Mr. Stiller?"

"I call them when I have what they want. Can you meet me this afternoon at my office?"

"Yes. Tell me, is it what I thought?"

"I'd rather not talk on the phone. I'll see you at three." He hung up without saying good-bye.

That afternoon, punctually at three, she presented herself at Stiller's shabby office on East Thirty-second Street. He opened the door for her, leading her through the small reception area to his inner office, where he gestured her to a seat.

"Don't you want to take off your coat?" he asked, sitting down with a grunt.

"No," said Musette. "I just want to get this over with."

"Okay," said Stiller, pulling a manila folder from a red plastic tray on the corner of his desk and placing it neatly in front of him. "What I learned is that Mr. Gallagher was not responsible for Hoffeld's death, although he certainly was heavily involved."

"What does that mean?" Musette didn't know whether to be relieved or disappointed.

"It means that Gallagher was in Pennsylvania at the time of the drowning. But he knew what had happened, and immediately saw to it that the whole thing was hushed up."

"I'm afraid I don't understand what you're saying. Who was on the boat with Hoffeld? Was he murdered or not?"

"He wasn't murdered. At least, it doesn't look that way, which is why the police dropped the case as quickly as they did. But if they'd dug into it a little deeper, they'd have found out that Mrs. Gallagher was on the boat with Hoffeld when he drowned. Not Peter Salzman."

"Charlie?"

"Yes, Charlie." He jabbed at the manila folder with his thumb. "It's all here, fully documented, in the report."

"You mean Charlie killed him?" She leaned forward in her chair, breathless with excitement.

"No. Charlie wouldn't have had the strength to administer a heavy blow like that. Look, there's really no way this could have been murder. The sea was rough, and Hoffeld had been drinking. So, by the way, had Charlie; heavily. Hoffeld's judgment was off. He probably could barely see, poor bastard, and when he stood up, the boom smashed right into the base of his skull."

"What happened then?"

He shrugged. "She got back to the shore somehow, and immediately put in a call to her husband, who was at their house in Swarthmore. We know that because we managed to get our hands on that day's phone records. And then Neil—Mr. Gallagher—called his old buddy, Peter Salzman, who, as luck would have it, was up on the cape with his wife that weekend, closing up their house for the winter. The Salzmans immediately drove over to Hoffeld's place, just a few minutes away, and after they'd packed up Charlie's personal belongings, Peter put in emergency calls to the Coast Guard and the police. Meanwhile Belle, his wife, drove Charlie to their house to get her sobered up, and then drove her down to New York. From there Charlie caught a plane to Philly."

"How do you know all this?"

He smiled at her. "For a small sum, Eileen Fitzgibbons, Mrs. Salzman's maid, was willing to talk. She'd been with them that weekend, closing the house. And so from her we know that Charlie reeked of liquor and was in a state of shock when Mrs. Salzman brought her home, and also that Peter and Belle had had lunch together that day, and were outside examining their garden at the time of the accident."

Still staring at him, Musette lit a cigarette and sat back in her chair. "I don't understand why the police wouldn't have dug all this out," she said.

"The case seemed perfectly straightforward."

"But the fact that Peter Salzman doesn't drink—doesn't that suggest something?"

"It would if he hadn't had liquor on his breath when the police got there." He regarded her for a moment, and then pushed the manila folder across the desk. "I trust you're going to put this information to good use, Mrs. Vlk?"

"Yes, of course."

"Of course," he said in a voice heavily laden with sarcasm. "Well, you can count on me to be discreet. But I want you to know that if Gallagher does run for president—and I understand he's a hot contender—I'll be looking for you there at his side."

Musette laughed her gay tinkling laugh. But all she said was, "How much do I owe you, Mr. Stiller?"

That night Charlie went to a meeting in her old neighborhood on the Upper East Side. She knew she had to talk about Dennis, and didn't want to risk running into him or any of his arty friends. As she entered the church someone grabbed her arm and said, "Charlie! I'm so glad to see you!"

It was Tanya Hendricks, back from her slip.

"Good lord," said Charlie. She peered at her old friend. "How *are* you?"

"Fine," laughed Tanya. "Really. I've been in rehab for the past four months. You didn't know that, did you? I got out last Friday."

"No, I didn't know that," said Charlie.

"I guess I owe you an apology. I remember vaguely—very vaguely—your coming to my apartment to help me. I must have given you a pretty tough time."

"You did, but that's all right," said Charlie. "It was my first feeble attempt at a Twelfth Step."

"Well, as you can see, it didn't utterly fail."

They found seats together, and Tanya was the first to raise her hand when the speaker had finished. "My name is Tanya," she said. "I'm an alcoholic. What I want to say in this room tonight is very difficult because there are so many familiar faces, and I feel ashamed. But I know that by talking I'll help myself and maybe one or two of you, and so..."

She launched into the story of her slip. Charlie was fascinated. It seemed that Tanya had taken up with people outside of AA, had stopped going to meetings, had become infatuated with an active alcoholic. "I mean who else would I choose?" she said with a sharp laugh.

She described being confronted by her brother, who forced her, for the second time in two years, to go into a rehab. "I really hated him for that. I was a baby who wanted her bottle. But I was also a baby who wanted to grow up, and it didn't take very long before I was glad as hell to be there. And I'm glad to be here tonight. Most of us don't make it back. Most of us end up dead of a dozen different things, illness, suicide, car accidents, fire, all of them connected to the use and abuse of alcohol. And so, if there's anyone in this room considering going out there tonight, think of me. I already did it for you, and I can tell you it wasn't worth it."

"That was very brave," whispered Charlie, squeezing Tanya's shoulder. She raised her own hand, regretting it the instant the speaker called on her. She felt stupid talking about Dennis after the drama of Tanya's story, and so all she said was she'd gotten close to someone in the program who'd taken advantage of her. "He was on a dry drunk, angry and full of rage," she said, aware of all the eyes in the room turned on her. "I should have known better. I should have taken my sponsor's advice about not getting involved with someone in the first year. Now I feel violated."

"Who was he?" whispered Tanya when she'd finished and the next person was sharing.

"Oh, no one you know. No one important."

Musette, gorgeous in a new sable coat, was sitting with Theo in the back of the room. She made a beeline for Charlie when the meeting was over. "Was that Dennis MacLeish you were talking about?" she asked.

"Yes," said Charlie. "Lamentably."

"What happened? Did he borrow money and disappear into the woodwork?"

"Something like that."

"Well, what?"

Charlie sighed. "I caught him taking cash from my desk drawer."

"Jesus."

"Yeah."

"You must feel awful."

"I do."

"Want to come and have an espresso with Theo and me?"

"I can't. The children should be back from Georgetown by now. Some other time, all right?"

"All right," said Musette, her eyes narrowing with concern as Charlie picked up her gloves, scarf, and handbag, and strode from the meeting hall.

The concern Musette felt wasn't for Charlie, but for herself. She backed out of coffee with Theo on the pretext of a headache, and went straight home, where she spent a few minutes glancing through her appointment book. The following week was busy: several Christmas parties, a theater benefit, a private screening of a new film of Bethany's, a fund-raiser for dancers and actors with AIDS. On Friday, only a few days before Christmas, she was scheduled to fly out to Los Angeles.

With a sigh, she closed the book and lit a cigarette. Her mind was working rapidly. Over the holidays Charlie and Neil would naturally be thrown together. There would be family events, formal dinners, attendance at midnight mass, the opening of presents; and without Dennis to think of, Charlie would focus on Neil, the husband who was always there in a pinch. Musette could see it all so clearly. She got up and began to pace the room, her brow creased with worry. If she was going to act, the time was now, she decided. Crushing out her cigarette, she went to the phone, a pulse beating in her throat as she dialed the familiar number.

"Hello—Neil?" she said.

"Oh . . . hello."

His voice was dull. She knew instantly he didn't want to speak to her.

"You were supposed to call me. What happened?"

"I have another life, Maggie. Work. Children."

"I'm not disputing that. It's just that you said you'd be in touch."

He was silent for a moment. Then: "Don't tell me you've been waiting by the phone."

She laughed shrilly. She had practically been sitting on top of the phone, hoping it was Neil each time it rang, but she would never let him know that. "Of course not. Look, let's not fight about this."

"Who's fighting?"

"Well, you don't sound exactly friendly."

He let out a long sigh. "I've got a lot on my mind, Maggie. I'm sorry if I don't sound the way you want me to."

"Maybe I could help you," she said softly.

"What?"

"With those things on your mind . . . maybe I could help you." Musette ran a hand down her throat, pretending the hand was Neil's.

"I don't think so." She heard a rustling sound as he switched the receiver from one ear to the other.

"Why not?" Her voice was plaintive.

He gave another sigh. "Maggie, this discussion isn't leading anywhere."

"That's not my fault. Look, why don't we set aside some time to be together. We always do better tête-à-tête."

"I can't, Maggie. I just can't."

There was a moment's silence. All of a sudden she really did feel a headache coming on.

"Maggie"—Neil's voice was strained to the cracking point—"maybe this is as good a time to tell you as any. I can't see you anymore. I'm sorry. Really sorry. You're a great girl and all that, but—"

"You mean a great lay," she said.

"What?"

"A great lay." Her voice hardened, a layer of ice over a well of tears. "I don't understand this, Neil. For months now you've been in my bed with your mouth all over me. You couldn't have enough of me. And now you're telling me the thing between us is over. Who made you change your mind?"

"No one did. I just don't have time—"

"Oh, yes you do!" she shouted. "If you value your life as a

politician, you'll *make* the time." She gave a forced throaty laugh. "Meet me for lunch tomorrow. An hour is all I need. Believe me, you won't regret it."

"And if I don't?"

"I swear I'll turn your life into the kind of Hollywood scandal miniseries are made of."

"All right," he said, his voice even more strained than before. "But I want this on my turf. Meet me at—let me think a minute—all right, Peter's Grill on G Street in downtown Washington. I'll be there at one."

"Anywhere you want," said Musette. "Just be there."

"Tell me true now, am I the first black man you ever slept with?"

It was late Sunday night, and John Sinclair was lying naked in Gwen's bed, eating potato chips and blowing smoke rings toward the ceiling. Gwen had discovered in the past twenty-four hours that he was a man who *had* to have regular doses of junk food to get through the day. Devil Dogs, jelly doughnuts, cheese puffs, and an endless stream of Coca-Cola had assembled themselves on her kitchen counter. But she didn't mind. From the moment she had found herself in his toughened arms, she had been entranced with the man. To her the stories he told about his life were among the best she had heard in a lifetime of collecting stories. She was reminded of Glady Johnson, whose ramblings about her southern girlhood had been such an inspiration. John, in spirit, could have been Glady's brother, the one who had managed to escape, enduring decades of hardship, to end up here, with her.

The worst story he told was about his sister Rowena. "Poor baby, she took up with this awful guy, this low-down dirty scumbag creep who used to inflict all his unhappiness on his lady friends, know what I mean? Rowena always appeared with bruises on her face, shit like that, but there wasn't a goddamn thing I could do about it, 'cause she always knew better, and this guy cared about her, he was the love of her life. Ha! One night he went into a real solid rage. With her children standing there, peeping through their fingers, he beat her till . . . well, till you wouldn't know that the body lying there on the floor was Rowena. I was the one called in to identify her, so I know, I saw." He paused for a moment and then said hoarsely, "The room it happened in looked like a fucking abattoir. That was back in 'eighty-nine—a couple of months before you won that award."

Gwen could understand now where John's digs at her were coming from. "And the guy—where's he?"

"Still doing time," said John.

"And her children?"

"Foster homes. They're all right, I keep an eye on them. I'd take them in myself if I had a better setup."

It was after that story, very early Sunday morning, that he took her to bed. She didn't object for the simple reason that she felt she owed it to him.

In the next few hours she discovered that his small, strong, mahogany-colored body suited her just fine. Cupping her hand over his bald spot and feeling the springy fuzz of hair around it was a pleasure. Having him lie on top of her, with the glorious dark root of his penis dug in deep, centered her in a way she had never been centered before, even with Walter. And so, when he asked was he the first black man she had ever been with, she answered truthfully. "Not the first," she said. "The second."

"The second? Shit, and how old are you? Forty-four? Who was the first?"

"A guy back at the University of Michigan. When I was a graduate student. And yes, I know, that's a pretty sad statement, but I'm going to ask you not to make fun of me."

"I'm not making fun of you," said Sinclair. "I'm just filled with wonderment, is all." He popped a potato chip into his mouth, and chewed reflectively. "How come you quit after that one guy?"

She shrugged. "Lack of opportunity, I guess. From Michigan I went to teach at a college in Nebraska, and black men—that is, *adult* black men—were few and far between. And then when I was at Tulsa, I sort of got turned off sex and didn't want to *be* with anybody. And then," she sighed, "I came to New York and met Walter."

"What made you interested in him?"

She reached over him for a potato chip. "He was smart. Jewish. I'd always liked Jewish men 'cause they were liberal minded, and because . . . well, I had this thing about the suffering

Jew being close in spirit to the oppressed black. You know...
our people were sold as slaves, but theirs, hell, theirs weren't
valued for anything but the gold in their teeth. And Walter had
so much sorrow in his face. I was a sucker for that right away."

"So you married him. How long before you realized it was
a mistake?"

"Long. Look, John, I was used to a white world. That was
what my mama groomed me for, and that was what your mama
might have done to you, too, if things had been different. I was
her one precious child, remember, and she wanted me to be
safe. And safe, for her, meant I was to rise up in the world and
ignore my color." She laughed softly.

"What are you laughing at?"

"The irony of it. The fact that I'm this big important writer
who doesn't know who the fuck she is." She turned to him,
stroking the hard muscles of his abdomen. "Why'd you ask if
you were my first black lover, anyway?"

"I don't know. Just a feeling. Listen, Gwen, what you doing
Christmas?" He laid his hand atop her hand on his belly. There
was a slight tremble in his fingers—a quiver she could appreciate.

She grinned. "At the moment the day is regrettably empty."

"Good. Then keep it that way. There's one or two people I
want you to meet. And now"—he put the bowl of potato chips
down on the floor—"supposing you get some more experience
making love to one of us nasty ole, dangerous ole colored boys."

*P*eter's Grill was a sleek oasis in an area of Washington unremarkable except for its seediness, its air of once having seen better days. Musette, her smart mink coat shimmering in the sunlight, stepped out of a cab and walked quickly inside. The place was dimly lit, with high-backed booths, thick red carpeting that softened conversation, and an oak bar where half a dozen men in business suits had already started celebrating the holidays. Musette looked around for Neil, and saw him in a booth way at the back.

"Hello," she said, approaching him with her usual long sexy stride.

He gave her a tight-lipped smile of welcome, watching as she slipped out of her coat and sat down. "I hope you don't mind, but I went ahead and ordered for us both. I've got to be back at the office by two-thirty."

"That doesn't give us much time," said Musette. "What did you order?"

"Prime rib. It's the only thing good they've got here. You'll be happy."

She shrugged her shoulders in a gesture of indifference. "This place certainly isn't in the best neighborhood."

"No," he agreed. "But you can't beat it if you want a quiet meal where no one's going to poke their nose in your business."

She lit a cigarette and stared at him. "Did you mean what you said on the phone last night?"

"About our not seeing each other anymore? Yes."

"Why? I want a reason, Neil. I want an explanation."

The waiter arrived with their order. When he had finished unloading the plates, Neil said, "It has to do with Charlie. She's changed since she stopped drinking. She's gotten more interesting. Stronger, with an independence and drive that I admire. And I love seeing her with the children; I love going to her house in Brooklyn and being together as a family. When I found out she was having an affair, it made me crazy. It was as if a light went on in my brain. I knew I couldn't be with anyone else."

"But she doesn't love you," Musette said, fighting to keep her voice matter-of-fact. "She's happy with Dennis. They have the same interests, the same passion for art. Can't you see that?"

He gave her a gloomy smile. "I can't help it," he said. "I want her back. I *need* her."

"You need me," Musette said, keeping her tone steady. This was a negotiation, and Neil had to know the basic selling points. She tensed herself and then relaxed, reassured by the feel of the Valium coursing through her, calming her. "I've got looks, brains, money. In bed I excite you more than any other woman you've ever been with. Certainly more than your wife. Am I right? Neil?"

"Maybe."

"Maybe nothing. I can stare into your eyes and make your groin swell. I can love you with more force and passion than any other woman could love you. I can keep your lifeblood going. And in days to come, when you go for the White House, I can get you more votes by smiling once into the camera than your campaign organizers can get arranging dozens and dozens of boring, costly appearances all over the country. The public adores me. I'd make a perfect president's wife. And at night, when you come back from the Oval Office, I can make your world right again." Musette's voice had grown fervent with advocacy.

"You're suggesting I should divorce Charlie and marry you?" He gave a harsh laugh. "That's exactly the kind of scandal I don't need. You're living with a delusion, Maggie. Weren't you supposed to give up delusions when you gave up alcohol?"

She felt her stomach knot sharply. "What are you trying to say, Neil?"

"That somehow you've gotten this whole thing confused—just like you did years ago."

"What do you mean confused? What are you talking about?"

He made a little sound of exasperation in his throat. "We've had a love affair, Maggie. That's all we've had. A simple ordinary love affair."

"You call what we had simple and ordinary?" Outraged, she leaned across the table, bringing her face close to his. "How dare you, Neil! How dare you come to my house and lie in my bed and then say something like that!"

"Because it's true, Maggie." He pulled his head back, glancing around, clearly worried that someone would hear them. "Look, you're a little upset, I can see that. But you've got to understand that our time together is not going to lead to marriage. It can't. I don't love you that way."

"You love me plenty when you're in my arms."

"Maggie," he said firmly, "listen to me. I don't love you enough to marry you. I never will. You've got to accept that."

"All right." Musette felt her heart shriveling, growing smaller and smaller until it turned to a tiny piece of ice. "I hoped it wouldn't come to this. You talked about scandal a minute ago. Well, I'll tell you about a real scandal." Their plates lay untouched on the table. She pushed them aside, scraping out her cigarette and lighting another. Her tone was hard, even. "I know about what happened up in Cape Cod the October before last. I know that Charlie was having an affair with Gil Hoffeld and that she was on that boat with him when he drowned. I know that you took great pains to cover the whole thing up."

Neil looked at her, shocked, the color draining rapidly from his cheeks. "How do you know that?" he whispered.

"Just by keeping my ears open and asking a few smart questions."

"Charlie must have told you."

"No, she didn't."

"Well, if it wasn't Charlie, it was Belle. That was it, wasn't it? Belle opened that big fat mouth of hers."

"It wasn't either of them," said Musette. "I just happened to hear a few things when I was up on the cape last summer, and I got suspicious, that's all."

"But no one knew. No one knew."

Musette smiled at him. "My agent saw Charlie coming out of a deli with Gil the Sunday before he died. They had the look, he said, of two people who had spent the night together. Well, I thought about that, and I thought about a lot of other things, small clues that other people might not have noticed, and eventually I hired a detective." She gave him another dazzling smile. "Now I have all the proof I need."

"I want to see that proof!" he exclaimed.

"Certainly. I have it right here with me." She drew an envelope from her handbag and pushed it across the table to him. While he was reading the detective's report, she said, "That's only a copy, of course. What I do with the original is up to you. I can either deposit it in my bank vault where it won't see the light of day for a long, long time—if ever. Or, if you persist in this idea of breaking up with me, I can pass it along to a journalist friend, who, as you can imagine, would be only too happy to spread the word. As I said, the choice is up to you."

"What in hell kind of a marriage do you think we would have based on blackmail?"

"Neil, I'm doing what's best for you as well as for me. We belong together. Charlie doesn't want you. You're a fool if you think she does. With me, over time, you could have everything. As I said," she repeated, "the choice is up to you."

He stared furiously at her, his eyes small and icy in a face that was deathly pale. "I'll need a few days to think about it," he said.

"I'll give you twenty-four hours," said Musette. "I've found that too much thought is like cheese...it gets riper and riper until it passes the point of perfection and starts to stink." She put on her coat and gloves and rose from the table. "Good-bye, Neil. If I don't hear from you by this time tomorrow afternoon, I'll call my friend."

He opened his mouth to tell her how ridiculous, how impossible, how out of the question all this was, but she had turned her back on him and was sailing out of the restaurant with a sexy swing of the hips that even the thick fur of her coat couldn't hide. Every man in the place was staring at her, she knew that, just as she knew, deep in her frozen heart, that as soon as he got over his anger, Neil would give in and do as she wanted. He had to. Charlie would never be the right woman for him, would never know how to soothe or arouse him, take care of him, keep the world at bay; in the end, when he looked at things in their truest and most logical light, he would choose her, Musette. Smiling to herself, she left the restaurant, stepping out to the curb to hail a cab. No matter what Neil said, he loved her with a passion that neither time nor money nor politics— and certainly no other woman—could ever destroy.

At two in the afternoon, Charlie, who had been putting the finishing touches on the immensely tall tree her children had talked her into buying, received a cryptic phone call from Neil. "Honey," he said in an anguished voice, "please don't ask a lot of questions, but I need to see you tonight. Can you break any plans you have, and meet me for dinner?"

"I could if you told me what this is about."

"Not on the phone," said Neil in a warning voice.

Charlie knew that voice. "All right, but this had better be good. I was supposed to go to a big reception in Soho for Dick Norris. They're showing his most recent stuff, and there's a painting I'm interested in."

"Skip the reception and meet me at Cafe Jofka at seven-thirty."

"All right," said Charlie. Then she giggled. "You'll recognize me. I'll be the girl in the red dress with the flower in her hair." When he didn't laugh, she said, "Joke," and hung up.

She wore a clingy red dress that showed to advantage the roundness and fullness of her beautiful big breasts, and to be funny she put a sprig of holly in her hair. She arrived at the restaurant before Neil, and was seated at an out-of-the-way table. "Monsieur Gallagher," said the maître d', whom both she and Neil had known for years, "asked to be very private. What would madame like to drink?" Charlie saw a look of apprehension enter his eyes, and realized she hadn't been to Cafe Jofka since getting sober. "A ginger ale," she said, smiling.

As she waited for Neil, she looked around the restaurant,

which was decorated in soft pinks and grays, with mirrors and glass chandeliers and gilt-framed paintings of turn-of-the-century Paris that gave the place an elegant, old-world touch. Tonight, because of the approaching holiday, there was a feeling of excitement in the air. When she saw Neil enter the room, her heart gave a little start of happiness. "Hello," he said, coming up to her. "I'd never have recognized you without those damn berries in your hair."

"It's been a long time, hasn't it?" she said. Neil looked good to her, his shoulders solid, his suit well cut, his eyes crinkled with the pleasure of seeing her.

"Almost exactly a month."

"Well, we've gone without seeing each other for longer than that."

"True. But at least there was phone contact."

The waiter approached, and Neil ordered a scotch and soda. Charlie fiddled with the gloves she had placed beneath her handbag on the table. "Neil, I know you have something to tell me. Well, I have something to tell you, too, so it's a question of which of us is going to go first."

"You go first," said Neil. "You're the lady."

"Let's order dinner and get that out of the way."

"All right."

They studied their menus, though each knew the selections by heart. The waiter recited the specials, and Charlie said, "I'll have the *paillard de veau* with a small green salad to start."

"I'll have the same," said Neil, snapping closed his menu.

Charlie glanced at him sharply. Usually he was more elaborate in his choices. "That was quick," she said. Then she drew a pack of cigarettes from her bag and said, "I sense this is going to be a difficult meal, and so I warn you: I intend to smoke whenever I goddamn feel like it."

"That's fair," said Neil. "After all, I have this." He pointed at his scotch.

Charlie nodded. There was something tender in his tone that she appreciated. She leaned forward so he could light her cigarette, averting her head as she blew out a stream of smoke. "What I wanted to tell you is this. I've broken up with Dennis MacLeish. In fact, the whole thing is a closed chapter, and I never want to talk about it again."

"Ah," Neil said. He regarded her curiously. "Well, that does sort of leave me wondering."

"Oh, there's nothing to wonder about," Charlie said hotly. "The guy was a prick who saw me as his meal ticket. It took me a while to catch on to his little game, but when I did, I sent him packing."

"How interesting," said Neil. Then he laughed robustly. "Well, that makes two of us."

"I beg your pardon?" said Charlie.

"That makes two of us," repeated Neil. "Because you see, I also have a little story." His hands were shaking as he put down his drink. He took two deep breaths and nervously began to tell her about his relationship with Musette, starting at the beginning, seventeen years ago, when she had been a leggy teenager working as a clerk-typist in Allentown, Pennsylvania, and continuing right up to the previous spring, when he had allowed the love affair with her to be rekindled. Choosing his words carefully, he told Charlie about the news clipping Musette had sent him, and her appearance at the NOW lunch, and her continual efforts from that time afterward to form strong and loving ties with him.

"But why?" Charlie exclaimed in a burst of fury. "I thought she was my friend! I can't believe she'd go against me this way. We told each other everything. We were close."

"Oh, she's no one's friend, believe me. She's nothing but a crazy, power-hungry bitch. As to why—that's simple. She used you to get at me. She had an old score to settle from years ago, and so she pretended to be palsy-walsy to get information. When she found out I was lonely and jealous because you'd moved up to New York, she saw her chance and she took it."

Charlie looked closely at Neil. "Did you have an affair with her to get back at me?"

"Sort of. Look, I want to be very clear about this. I didn't love her. What we had was sex in the most base and animal sense. The whole time I really wanted you. It took your affair with Dennis MacLeish to make me see that."

"And now?"

"Now," sighed Neil. "Now is where we run into trouble. She's on a real dry drunk. I swear, if I didn't know better I'd think she was taking something because her moods change so

335

quickly. One minute it's euphoria, the next it's rage." He shook his head. "It's really frightening. She called last night, pissed because she hadn't heard from me. When I told her I didn't want to see her anymore, she got nasty and said I'd better meet her for lunch today, or else." He sipped at his scotch.

"Or else what?"

"Or else there'd be a tremendous scandal."

"And so you met her?"

"Yes, she flew down to Washington."

"And? For Christ's sake Neil, don't keep me in suspense!"

"She knows about Cape Cod, Charlie."

"What?" Charlie could feel the blood draining from her face.

"I said she knows about Cape Cod. Everything there is to know. All of it."

"I don't understand. You mean you told her?"

"No. *I* didn't tell her. That guy, that friend of hers, Harry Langhart, you know the one I mean, her agent... well, *he* told her he'd seen you and Gil on the cape together the Sunday before the accident, and for some reason that one little piece of information sparked her interest. I suppose she wanted to dig up something—some sort of scandal—she could use against me—and you—if necessary. After that, she started asking a lot of questions, and finally ended up hiring a detective. Here, look at this." He handed her the detective report Musette had given him in Washington.

"Oh God," said Charlie, scanning the pages. She felt herself growing dizzy with a panic she knew she had to fight to control. "What does this mean? What does she want from us?"

He gave a shrill laugh. "She doesn't want anything from *us*. It's *me* she wants. Her desire, her insane wish, is that I divorce you and marry her. If I do that, she'll bury the report in her vault with instructions that it should never see the light of day. If I don't, she'll give the story to the press. We've got twenty-four hours, less than that actually, to decide."

A lump of horror rose in Charlie's throat. She swallowed painfully and whispered, "I don't believe this. It's my fault. My ... fucking ... fault."

"Forget it, Charlie. We just don't have time for a lot of re-criminations. We've both been stupid—let's agree to that, and move on. Now how do you suggest we handle this?"

"*I?*" She put her hands to her chest in a gesture of incredulity. "Isn't it really your decision? You're the one whose entire future, whose entire life, is at stake here. I mean if the press gets hold of this..." She shook her head hard to keep back the tears she felt coming. "If the press gets hold of this, you're finished, it's all over for you, everything you've wanted and dreamed of, your whole career, everything, all of it down the tubes..." She stopped, took a deep breath, and began to rummage in her bag for a tissue.

"It affects you, too," he reminded her gently.

"Yes, but that doesn't matter, it's not the same thing."

"And the children, what about them?"

She gave up looking for a tissue, and dabbed at her eyes with the flat of her hand. "The children would go through hell. Absolute hell. Look Neil, if you want to do this thing, marry her, I won't stand in the way."

"How very noble of you."

"Don't be sarcastic!" She was crying more heavily now, and the sprig of holly fell from her chestnut hair onto the white damask tablecloth. She stared unseeingly at it through a blur of tears.

"I'm not being sarcastic," said Neil. "I have no desire to leave you, not to save my political skin or anything else. I don't love Musette. I was alone, and you were away getting your life back together, and I was weak. I never loved her. I was just so alone."

"Look Neil, can you give me your goddamn handker-chief?"

"Yes, sorry—here." He removed the white handkerchief from his breast pocket and gave it to her. When she had dried her tears, he said: "I want us to stay together, Charlie. I want to fight this thing with you and the children at my side. 'For better or worse,' remember? Well, we've seen the worst. Now maybe we're ready to move on to the better part."

"Now it's my turn to say 'how noble,'" said Charlie, waving off the waiter who had approached the table, wanting to know if everything was all right. Neither of them had touched their food. She clenched the handkerchief and looked into Neil's blue eyes.

"Well," said Neil. "What's it going to be... will you come back to me or not?"

"If I said no, would you go off with Musette?"

"Never! Jesus, I have more self-respect than that."

"Then I'll come back to you. You might as well know I always intended to. It was just a matter of time."

$\mathcal{T}$he next morning, at about ten o'clock, Charlie went to see Felicity, who was working at home rather than at the office that day. Neil had not stayed with her the night before; as they were leaving the restaurant, he had announced that he was going to the Salzmans' apartment. He and Peter had made plans to talk. *"Now?"* exclaimed Charlie. "Isn't it a bit late?"

"If he could have seen me earlier, he would have. They had that Christmas party they give out in New Jersey every year."

"Oh." She wrapped her coat more tightly around herself. "Well, don't you think I should come with you? If you're going to come up with some sort of solution to this mess we're in, I want to know what it is."

"Who knows if we'll come up with a solution?" Neil muttered. "Anyway, don't be offended, but Peter and I are better off when it's just the two of us, brainstorming."

"I'm not offended," said Charlie. "I know how it is." There on the sidewalk she took Neil's hands in her own and put them around her neck. They hugged hard for a long time, Neil's head on her shoulder. It felt so good, so simple somehow, to feel him against her. And she realized, with an odd surge of strength, that Neil needed her—now and always—even more than she needed him.

She hardly slept that night. Half a dozen times she sat up, looked at her clock, put out her hand to call Neil at the Salzmans, and then changed her mind. And when she finally did call him in the morning, he had already left for Washington. That was at eight-thirty. The maid told her that Mr. Salzman was on his way to the office, and Mrs. Salzman was unavailable. Putting down the phone, she thought she would go crazy. Petra and Colin came in to kiss her good-bye—it was their last day of school before the holidays—but all she could think of was how much they had been through in the past year, and how much more they might have to endure. And all because of Musette! She wanted to wring the bitch's neck. When they were gone, she dressed quickly and went to the garage for her car. Felicity had said to come over right away, and if Charlie had ever needed her, it was now.

"Jesus, you look awful," said Felicity, taking Charlie's coat. "What's the matter?"

Charlie glanced at the other woman. Felicity's thin cheeks were glowing, and her eyes had a sparkle she had never seen in them before. She exuded an almost palpable excitement, and for a moment Charlie regretted her decision to come and talk to her. "I might look awful, but you look great. Have you fallen in love or something?"

Felicity laughed. "Funny you should put it that way, because that's kind of how I feel. Come on, let's go into the dining room, and I'll tell you about it."

When Charlie was at the table with a cup of coffee in front of her, Felicity said, "Remember my telling you that when I was nineteen I had a child, a little girl, whom I gave up for adoption?"

"Yes, I remember," said Charlie, helping herself to a croissant from a basket on the table. She wasn't hungry, but wanted something to do with her hands.

"Well, I heard from her."

"What?" Charlie put down the croissant, and stared at Felicity.

"Her name's Diane Abernathy, and she wrote me a letter saying she wanted to meet me. Isn't that amazing?"

"Oh my God, Felicity. Where is she?"

"Rochester. That's not where she grew up. She's from out in the Midwest, Des Moines, but right now she's studying at the University of Rochester. Piano. She's a musician, which is totally bizarre since I'm tone deaf."

"But how wonderful," cried Charlie. "Gosh, that makes me want to weep. Have you spoken to her?"

"Yes, last night. As soon as I heard from her, I sent her my number asking her to call me collect. And listen to this," said Felicity, staring at Charlie with glowing eyes. "She'd like to spend Christmas with us. Or at least part of it. When she heard about Bessie—that she had a sister—she wanted to get on the next plane."

"So it's definite? She's going to come here?"

"Pretty definite. She just has to hash things out with her adoptive parents."

"Jesus," said Charlie. "You must feel fantastic."

"As if I'm up in the clouds. It's a dream, I tell you. I never expected this to happen. Never." She stared at Charlie with unseeing eyes, her mind already fixed on a picture of herself and her unknown daughter meeting for the first time, embracing each other. She smiled dreamily, and leaned forward to scratch at the soil of a poinsettia plant to see if it needed water. Then she said, "But you didn't come here to talk about me. You said you had a problem. Why don't you tell me what it is."

Charlie shook her head. "It's nothing, really."

"If it's nothing, why are you shredding that poor croissant to bits?"

Charlie looked down at the white tablecloth, and saw that there were golden flakes of pastry everywhere. She laughed. "All right," she said. "But I don't know where to begin."

"The beginning's always a good place," offered Felicity.

"Yes, right, but . . . look Felicity, can you keep a secret? I mean if any of this . . . this thing that I'm about to tell you got around, it would be a disaster for me and several other people."

"I'm your sponsor."

"Yes, so?"

"That's kind of like being a priest."

"You mean just you and me and God in heaven will hear the words I have to say."

Felicity nodded.

"Okay. You know how you once said that a drunk is as 'sick as his secrets'? Something happened a little over a year ago that I've never told anyone, and that's been . . . well, like a big boa constrictor hanging around my neck. And now it looks as if this thing is ready to strangle me, and if it does, my whole family stands to be flattened like these poor little crumbs here." She pointed at the tablecloth, and then looked helplessly at Felicity.

"Why don't you just tell me what it is," said Felicity quietly.

"All right." She drew a ragged breath and launched into the story of her love affair with Gil Hoffeld. When she was finished she sat in silence for a moment, toying with a lump of sugar. "That's only the first part of the problem," she said finally.

"Jesus—there's more?"

"Unfortunately. It has to do with Musette. Did you know that she's been screwing my husband?"

"No."

"Well, she has. She's a scheming, blackmailing bitch, and it seems that she's been very, very busy over the past few months."

She told the next part of the story quickly, watching Felicity closely to see how she was taking it. "Well, what do you think?" she asked when she had finished.

Felicity sighed, and took Charlie's long tapered hand in her own. "I think there isn't a goddamn thing you can do, except admit your powerlessness over the situation."

Withdrawing her hand, Charlie lit a cigarette. "That helps a lot," she said sarcastically.

"Well, it's the best piece of advice I can give. Once you've accepted the fact of your powerlessness, you'll understand that things have a mysterious way of working themselves out on their own. In the meantime, I suggest you don't drink and go to meetings."

"That old cliché," said Charlie.

"Yes, that old cliché. But for people like us, it's the only thing that works."

At one-thirty that afternoon, Musette was sitting in the bedroom of her apartment, the big glamorous white-on-white room with its silken pillows and mirrored walls where she had spent so many passionate hours with Neil. She hadn't been out yet that day. She was wearing a blush-pink caftan and her hair was tied back from her strained white face with a ribbon. In her trembling hand was a cigarette, the fifth she had smoked in the past hour. Despite the calming tide of Valium on which she floated, her thoughts seemed to be sliding around in all directions. She knew that any minute now she would hear from the man whose words would change her life forever.

With her eyes on the phone, she stubbed out the cigarette and immediately lit another. If only, for these last few moments, she could be as still and quiet as an athlete gathering strength before a big race. One thing in her favor was that Neil knew she was a person who never backed down. Almost seventeen years ago he had gotten rid of her by writing a check, but this time she had the power to have him at her side for good. If she couldn't have him, she would drag his family through the darkest mud. She had already made up her mind about that. He would never practice law again, his children would stare at him with contempt in their eyes, and his wife, eventually, would leave him.

Glancing at herself in one of the gold-flecked antiqued mirrors, she thought he would never risk those things. He was too ambitious, too much of a politician. He would return to her— he had no other choice. It might be with reluctance and fury, but in time he would be glad for what he had done. Lying in her arms, enjoying the passion that animated them both, he would understand that the blackmail had been necessary—a cement that had served to bond them together.

Reaching into the pocket of her caftan for another Valium, she felt very calm and sure. Neil was hers, inevitably.

At five minutes past two the phone rang. Musette waited three rings before picking it up. "Well Neil, I hope you slept last night," she said.

"Very funny."

"No, I mean it. I understand how difficult this is for you. I can only say it's worth it, and it *will* get easier. So will you accept my little proposition?"

"I'd say it was an ultimatum, not a proposition, wouldn't you?"

"Whatever. I'm not interested in semantics, just in results. So ...have you thought about it?"

"Yes, I've thought. Let's get this straight. The deal is either

I divorce my wife, leave my children, and marry you, *or*"—he put a heavy stress on the "or"—"you'll take the report of that private investigator you hired to the newspapers and ruin me for good? Is that it?"

"You got it. But you knew that already, Neil. You're stalling."

"I'm not stalling. I'm just hoping this is a bad dream, and you'll change your mind."

"I won't change my mind, and it's a *good* dream, Neil." She smiled into the phone. "I do worry about Charlie, though—the wrath of a woman scorned."

"Don't worry about Charlie, Maggie. Worry about yourself. You're threatening me with blackmail. Cheap common blackmail."

"You can call it whatever you like. It happens to be what's best for you."

She heard his snort of laughter. "Best? Jesus! What kind of a marriage can we have based on blackmail?"

"You asked me that yesterday."

"Well I'm asking again."

"A perfectly good one. We'll be excellent business partners, far better than you and Charlie. I'll be a gorgeous First Lady, I don't have to tell you that. And in bed . . . well, you're always singing praises to that wet, hot cunt of mine . . . Your words, darling. Remember?"

"Sure I remember. Pillow talk. I never promised you any-thing."

"*I never promised you anything.*" Her voice was mocking. "That's what you said years ago when I was pregnant and you tried to get out of marrying me. Isn't it odd how history repeats itself?"

"This isn't history repeating itself. This is you, a crazy, des-perate, and, I might add, *dangerous* woman, trying to coerce me, through criminal means, into doing something I don't want to do. And let me remind you, that was no innocent little preg-nancy back in 'seventy-five. You'd stopped taking the pill, re-member, and you hoped I'd be fool enough to fall for your bullshit."

Neil was being too forceful for a man in his position. She tried to control her anger. "In nineteen seventy-five," she said slowly, "I was just a silly little girl who didn't know anything, and who didn't have anything, and who fell head-over-heels in love with a handsome guy who meant the world to her. And don't tell me about an innocent little pregnancy. The abortion you made me have—"

"I didn't *make* you have an abortion. It was your choice."

"—*made* me have, caused me to be sterile forever. You hear that, Neil? Sterile, goddamnit!" She paused, fumbling to light a cigarette. "This time it's different, Neil. This time I've got the goods on you, and you'd better believe that I'll use them if I have to."

"I believe you," Neil said. He gave a soft laugh. "You drive a hard bargain, don't you? How do you think your various business partners would feel if they knew you used blackmail and chicanery in managing your affairs?"

"Oh, but they'll never know," Musette said.

"Oh, but they will, because you see"—Neil's voice grew louder, harder—"I've taped this entire conversation, and I intend to send a copy to every single person who's put so much as a dime into that precious movie of yours. Think of it, Maggie. Both of us ruined in our respective fields. Won't that be something?"

His voice cut through her ragged drug haze. "You suck!" she screamed.

"Yes. That makes two of us. And now listen . . . if you try to drag me through the mud, I will do exactly the same to you. Exactly. And that means that not only will Gwen and your backers take away *Homegirl*, but you'll never ever be accepted in movie circles again. You'll lose your power, your position, your authority. Your days as the glorious Musette will be over—"

"Shut up!" she screamed. She could hear her own breath coming fast into the receiver. Her whole body was throbbing with anger. But Neil had her. She would lose everything if he did what he threatened to do; she'd have no Neil, no film, no backing, no fame. And his would be no Hollywood rumor; he had hard evidence. Taping the call—how could she have fallen for such a simple scheme? She tried to push her fury down. "All right, you shit, you're off the hook. But I'll tell you something. Try and run for president. Just try it. Because if you do, I'll publish this thing about Gil Hoffeld so fast you won't know what hit you. And by then I won't care about producing movies anymore. My one sole purpose in life will be to keep you and your goddamn family out of the White House. Get it, asshole?"

"Yeah," he said dryly. "I get it. Now *you* get the hell out of my life."

Musette heard a deliberate click as he switched off the tape recorder and then hung up. For a moment she sat quite still. Then she picked up her phone and hurled it across the room at one of the antiqued mirrors, watching dry-eyed as the gilded glass shattered, forming dozens and dozens of jagged hairline cracks. "I'm gonna get you, bastard!" she screamed. "I'm gonna get you, and when I'm done your life is gonna look just as crazy as that mirror!"

CHAPTER 3 5

Five days later it was Christmas. All communications between Neil and Musette had stopped. Musette flew out to California and spent the day with friends in Bel Air. She was, as always, stunning to look at, beautifully dressed, and no one would have known from her radiantly smiling face that she had just lost, for the second time and for good, the most important man in her life.

That same day Gwen went with her new lover, John Sinclair, to an all-black party in Harlem. The party was given in a renovated brownstone, and the twenty or so people gathered there were very rich and very influential. Gwen knew some of them by sight. A local politician. A judge. A singer. A big-name lawyer. A real estate tycoon who described himself as "Harlem's answer to Donald Trump." John made sure she spoke to everyone, and when they left the party late in the afternoon he whispered to her, "Well, baby, *now* do you know who you are?" Gwen knew. In the course of the afternoon she had come to realize she belonged here, just as she belonged to the less affluent people at the Harlem Meeting, to her mother and relatives at home in Jamaica, and to the man at her side, John Sinclair.

Charlie and Neil and their children spent Christmas, as they always did, at Helene Vandermark's large, stuffy Fifth Avenue apartment. An hour after lunch, they were driving along the chemical wasteland of the New Jersey Turnpike toward Pennsylvania. "Quit worrying," said Neil in a low voice, as Charlie lit her third cigarette in a row. "She won't do anything. Not as long as I've got that tape."

But Charlie wasn't convinced. They spent the rest of the holiday at her mother's farm—Helene, with Theo as a companion, had flown off to Aruba, and so they had the place to themselves—and she tried to calm herself by taking long walks and going to AA meetings in nearby towns. After nearly a year of separation, she felt as if she had to get to know Neil all over again. She had been drunk for so much of her marriage that now he seemed like a stranger to her. Sex was different, too, and in the mornings they would linger in bed, enjoying themselves. In the afternoons Charlie would go looking for him, her body drunk with need. It thrilled her to know that another woman had found her husband so desirable that she would stoop to blackmail to get him. Watching Neil, she could well understand why. In the past year he had stared loss in the face, had risked everything—politics, ambition, family, wife—and the experience had made him a softer, gentler, more liberated man. She couldn't have enough of him.

"Jesus," said Petra in one of many surreptitious phone calls to her friend, Heather Barnes, in New York. "My parents are really going at it these days. It's positively disgusting."

But the family was filled with joy at being together again. For a man whose career had been derailed, possibly for good, Neil seemed remarkably happy. "Don't you mind?" asked Charlie one night when they were in bed talking.

"Of course I mind."

"I mean a lot."

"I suppose a lot. Though in another way it's kind of a relief. Having to always think of the impression you're making is such a goddamn drag after a while." He took her cigarette from her and put it out. "You know, I haven't felt this relaxed in years. As if an enormous burden's been lifted, and that really tells me something."

"Tells you what?"

He kissed her, taking his time, exploring her mouth with his tongue. When he had finished he said, "That I should have been concentrating on you and my life, my personal life, rather than being a politician to the exclusion of all else. That I'd like to go a little bit more slowly than I've been going all these years. That maybe the time's come to do one or two of the things I've always dreamed of doing."

"I thought your big dream—your *only* dream—was to move us all into the White House."

He laughed. "Yes, I must have made it seem that way. But part of me always envied Peter for being able to mess around in a lab the way he does."

"You mean you want to become a scientist?" asked Charlie.

"No, no, I don't mean that. I mean I'd like to do more in the area of science and law. Medical ethics. That sort of thing."

"Oh." Charlie gave her husband a long, curious look. She would have asked him more, but he began gently, and then with mounting passion, to take her into his mouth, and she leaned her head back so her chestnut hair fanned out over the pillow, and moaned with pleasure.

They stayed on in the country even though this meant they had to forgo their usual round of holiday parties. Just after New Year's a snowstorm left them without electricity for a few hours, and in all the whiteness and silence it was easy to forget that they had a serious enemy who would destroy them if she could. Having candles and tinned food in the house seemed more important than whatever Musette could do. But when the excitement of the storm was over, Charlie called Gwen on the pretext of wishing her a happy New Year. She hadn't spoken to any of her AA friends since they had come down to Pennsylvania, and she was desperate to find out what she could about Musette.

"So how are you, darling?" she asked Gwen. "What's going on?" She figured that Gwen, who worked with Musette, was the one person who would know of the actress's movements.

"Oh God, so much is going on I don't know where to start. When are you coming back here, anyway? I love the way you go off and bury yourself in the country without telling anyone."

"I did try to tell you. It's just that I can't bear speaking to that damn machine of yours. Anyway, it was a spur-of-the-moment thing. Neil and I decided to spend a few quiet days together."

"Whew," said Gwen. "That's news. You mean this is a marriage that might actually stay intact?"

"*Is* intact," said Charlie. "Time seems to have done its thing, healed our wounds, et cetera, et cetera. We're both pretty delighted about it. And the children are changed creatures."

"I'll bet. Does this mean you're moving back to Washington?"

"Not till the school year's over," said Charlie. "But enough about me. Tell me your news. You said a lot was going on."

"Yeah," said Gwen.

"Like what?"

"Like I have a new man friend."

"Well, that's pretty major. Who is he?"

"His name's John Hopeton Sinclair. Has a good ring to it, doesn't it? He's Jamaican, the editor of a newspaper, and girl, I feel like I never *lived* till I met this man."

"Isn't he someone you were having trouble with at that uptown meeting you sometimes go to?"

"Yeah, but all that's changed. My whole life's changed."

"What about the movie, what's happening with that?"

"Well, that's one of the things that's changed. And to the better. You see, John, when he heard that Bethany Hunt had the part of Winnie, nearly went through the roof. He felt just as I did, that we needed a homely, squinty-faced type of girl for the role. So on Christmas he introduced me to some people he knows in Harlem, and the upshot is we're taking the film away from Musette."

"What!" exploded Charlie.

"You heard me, girl. We're going to turn this into a totally black production. Black director, black producer, black backers, black everything."

"But is that legal? I mean you and Musette had a contract. She raised those huge sums of money, and signed on actors and ... Jesus, can't you get yourself into a lot of trouble doing that?"

Gwen chuckled. "I could, but one of my lawyers found a big gaping loophole in the contract. Namely the fact that she only had a six-month option. That, combined with the fact that she made casting decisions without my approval, puts her out of the picture. As for the money, it was in escrow. Not a penny of it's been spent, thank God."

"And Musette? Does she know about this? She must be furious."

"Who gives a shit? She tried to screw me over royally with this film, so she's got it coming to her. Now let's talk about pleasanter things."

As soon as she hung up with Gwen, Charlie ran frantically through the house looking for Neil. When she couldn't find him, she threw on a coat and raced outside, and there he was, standing on the porch, staring at the snow, which was still coming down in fine tiny flakes. "Neil," she called out, "I'm afraid we've got a problem."

"What is it?" he said, turning and looking at her, his cheeks ruddy from the cold.

"Gwen's taken the film away from Musette!"

"What?"

"Yes, I just talked to her. Her lawyer found a loophole in the contract, and they've decided to make it into an entirely black production. Musette's out on her ass."

"Shit!" said Neil, his face slowly draining of color. "Does she know?"

"If she doesn't, she will soon. Gwen's lawyer just sent her lawyer some sort of termination notice. What are we going to do?"

"I don't know. Jesus, let me think for a minute."

She could see his breath coming out in quick white puffs on the cold air. "Well, you'd better think fast," she said. "I don't trust the bitch. Once she finds out about this, there's no reason for her not to give our story to the press."

"There's one absolute way to stop her," Neil said.

"Murder?"

Neil smiled. "A little less extreme than that."

Charlie shuddered in the cold. "Neil, you don't have to do it. You can—"

"I *want* to do it," Neil said. "Agreed?"

Charlie just looked at him. He was shivering, but he was smiling too. "I'm glad you're back," she said simply.

* * *

The following day a brief statement appeared in the front section of the *New York Times*. "Neil Byers Gallagher," it read,

> Democratic congressman from Swarthmore, Pennsylvania, held a telephone conference yesterday, announcing his plans to resign from office.
> Mr. Gallagher, who has represented the nineteenth district since 1982, and is the senior member of the Committee on Health and Science, has been known for his strong views in favor of abortion and women's rights. Recently he put forward a bill that would, if passed, require all employers with five or more employees to provide health insurance benefits for their workers. Employers choosing not to buy into a plan would be required to pay a payroll tax of seven percent to a government-sponsored universal health insurance fund.
> Although it is rumored that internal pressures and the unpopularity of some of his views are behind his decision to step down, Mr. Gallagher, whose resignation will take effect immediately, has stated simply that he is "disaffected with his role as a politician" . . .

That morning the phone did not stop ringing. Colleagues of Neil's, members of the press, friends and sympathizers from all over the country, distant relatives, concerned neighbors, even Charlie's hairdresser from Manhattan. The one person who did not call, who did not respond in any way, was Musette. "What if she doesn't know?" asked Charlie, strapping closed a suitcase. The snow had stopped, and the roads were finally clear enough for them to travel up to New York.

"I'll make sure she gets a copy of the article in the *New York Times*."

"You should send her all the articles. The one in the *Washington Post*, the ones in the Philadelphia and Swarthmore papers."

"I'll send her a whole damn press package. The question is, will any of this stop her?"

"Let's hope so," said Charlie. "Though that thing about being "disaffected with politics" may just be like a big red flag to a bull. What politician ever gets tired of politics?"

"You mean she'll want to set the record straight?"

"*Want?* I think she'll have a burning desire. That may have been a tactical error, Neil."

"Well, what else could I have said? I had to say something, and 'for family reasons' was just too vague."

"But it would have been just as true. I wish you'd talked to me before plunging ahead with that press conference."

"I did talk to you."

"Yes, but in more detail."

"Look, anything is going to be a red flag to this woman. I could go off and grow potatoes out in Long Island, and that would be a red flag. There's not a goddamn thing that isn't a red flag except, maybe, my jumping out a window, or dropping dead of a heart attack."

"And even that's a red flag," smiled Charlie.

"Yes, even that. So we're just going to have to learn to live with it."

But over the next few weeks there was not a word, not a single sign of life from Musette. Neil finished up his affairs in Washington, and he and Charlie went about the sad business of closing their Georgetown house. Neil had made up his mind that now that he was out of politics—"for the time being, anyway"—he and the family would stay in New York rather than return to their home in Swarthmore. He wasn't sure yet how he would spend his time. Everything seemed temporary, on hold, until he knew what was going on with Musette. There had been no response to the packet of news clippings he had had delivered to her Park Avenue apartment. When he had called, wanting to talk to her, the secretary told him to leave his name and number.

"But is she there?" asked Neil. "Is she in New York?"

"I'm afraid I can't give out that information. You'll just have to wait till she calls you."

No one seemed to know where the actress was. Gwen told Charlie that all matters pertaining to the film were being handled by lawyers. When Musette's option ran out in April, she and John would be taking over with an entirely new crew. "I'd love to find Glady and have her star in it," said Gwen. Harry Lang-hart, who desperately tried to avoid Neil at a party, had no comment whatsoever to make about his protégée. Felicity, who had not spoken to Musette since her Christmas party early in

December, advised Charlie to go to meetings, meetings, meetings. "You're doing beautifully," she said. "You'll see. Keep it up, and things will work out better than you ever in your wildest dreams anticipated."

Charlie didn't share her optimism. She couldn't believe that one morning her eyes wouldn't be assaulted by the headlines, GALLAGHER PULLS A TEDDY KENNEDY... GALLAGHER AND PAL DEVISE COVER-UP SCHEME... CONGRESSMAN LIES TO PROTECT DRUNKEN WIFE. At night her hands shook when she switched on the TV to watch the evening news. In her mind she knew that no matter how many meetings she attended, no matter how hard or how often she prayed to a God she wasn't sure existed, it was only a matter of time before the other shoe dropped, and their evil secret would be served along with breakfast or dinner to every household in the nation.

But the weeks passed, and the news was the same bland news, and the gossip at dinner parties was the same trivial gossip. Theo Hammond broke his hip walking across the terrace of a friend's house in Aruba and had to be flown back to New York and carried off the plane on a stretcher. Neil started doing research for a book on medicine and the law, and Charlie began to have serious discussions with the art dealer, Edith Pike, about putting money into her gallery on Wooster Street, and becoming partners. As for Musette, it was as if she had dropped off the edge of the world, as if the storm that had buried the Pennsylvania farm in all that whiteness and silence at New Year's had come along and buried her, too. But the silence was more alarming by far than the voice of the actual woman, and Charlie and Neil, their bodies tangled together in a frail sleep at night, did not dream peacefully.

C H A P T E R   3 6

*C*an I buy you a drink?" said the man with the brown slicked-back hair. He had been watching her for the past fifteen minutes, and now he came over and took the stool next to hers.

"Sure, why not?" Her voice was husky and thick.

He waited until the bartender had filled her glass, and then asked her her name.

"You can call me Maggie."

"Hello, Maggie. I'm Joe."

"'Lo Joe," she said, laughing as if this were hysterically funny.

He laughed too. Even drunk, there was something extremely sexy about this woman. Her cigarettes were smeared red at the filter from the thick lipstick she wore, and he liked that. He also liked the look of her long legs dangling from the barstool. "Want another?" he asked as she tipped back her head, finishing off her wine in several quick swallows.

She nodded, licking her tongue across her lips. She was growing cozier with him now, telling him little things about her life, laughing a lot. When she leaned forward, a lock of thick blond curly hair brushed against his cheek, and he thought the hair between her thighs would look like that too. He felt like putting

355

her hand on his crotch, but it was too soon for that. After two more drinks, he kissed her, and she gave a little purring sound, like a kitten. After three, he said, "Look, I have this great idea. How about coming back to my hotel with me?"

She glanced vaguely at him, squinting her golden eyes. "Sure," she said. "That's a great idea."

In the morning she awoke without any knowledge of where she was. Running her hand down her aching body, she discovered that she was partially clad in a pair of men's pajamas, that her pubic hair was matted and stiff, and that she was alone in a huge bed. In the past few weeks she had had a lot of bad moments, but this, she decided, had to be one of the worst. Pushing herself to a half-sitting position, she nearly cried out from the pain in her head. Somehow she managed to find the bedside lamp, and then, blinking her eyes against the light, she saw that she was in a hotel. Whoever she had been with was gone.

Getting up slowly, she went to the bathroom, praying that the guy, whoever he was, had left behind some aspirin. Avoiding her face in the mirror, she searched the cabinets, grunting happily when her fingers came in contact with a tin of Bayers on the top shelf. When she had taken two of those, she rubbed at her teeth with a washcloth, and took a scalding hot shower. She still didn't remember much about the night before. Drying herself in a daze, she wandered back into the bedroom and began to look around. She was at the Marriott—that was the first shock. The room was on a different floor than the one she had stayed in with Neil, and its windows looked out over Broadway rather than an airshaft, but the impersonal gray luxury of the place was the same. As she fought back memories of herself and Neil writhing around on a hotel bed, she had another shock. The man from the night before had packed up all his belongings and departed, but on the bureau were a pair of Ray-Bans, which he had presumably forgotten, and an envelope addressed to her. Quickly she slit open the envelope, and was horrified to discover three crisp hundred-dollar bills inside. There was also a note that read: *Sorry I couldn't be there when you woke up. Buy yourself something nice. Love, Joe.*

Joe? Who the fuck was Joe?

A jerk, she thought, staring at the money. Angrily she flung the bills to the floor, and then sat down and pulled on her panties, stockings, skirt, and shoes. She was beginning to remember a little bit about last night, the loneliness that had sent her out to a bar, the youngish blurry face of a man who had bought her drinks and kissed her.

When she was dressed, she phoned room service. "I'd like coffee, juice, and Alka Seltzer if you have it," she said, risking a quick glance at herself in the mirror, noting with pain the deep, tired circles under her eyes, the reddened puffy skin at her cheeks.

"That room is already checked out, ma'am," said the operator.

"It may be checked out, but I'm still here, and I'd like some breakfast. Send up what I ordered and I'll pay in cash."

She hated thinking about the past few months. Perhaps that was why she almost welcomed what had become habitual: waking to a stabbing headache, to a mind so fuzzy and thick that it was virtually impossible to examine with any clarity the disturbing images that floated through it. Pictures of herself alone in her apartment, wandering from room to room with a glass in one hand and a bottle in the other. Memories of lighting a cigarette and then immediately forgetting where she had put it and lighting another, until pretty soon she had several cigarettes going in several ashtrays. One night, to her horror, she started a small fire in her bed, which the super luckily was able to put out with a fire extinguisher.

The incident had been hushed up. But she began to hate going downstairs to the lobby of her building, hate the doorman's supercilious stare as he tipped his hat to her, hate the darting glances of her oh-so-respectable fellow residents, hate the coldness, the expensiveness of Park Avenue, hate the buzz buzz of the radio station the maid listened to while she was cooking— hate, above all, the ringing of the phone. She told Patsy Shroeder, her secretary, she was not at home to anybody on any account. She asked Patsy to open her mail and pay her bills and send anything that looked important to her accountant or lawyer. She asked the maid to take care of all details of housekeeping, and to please please please leave her alone. And she stopped going out. Liquor was ordered easily enough over the phone, and when she needed fresh air she waited until dark when no one would notice a tall, puff-faced blonde gliding down Park or Madison in a head scarf and a thick quilted coat.

That was how she had lived until last night.

There was a swift tap at the door. Room service with her coffee. She gave the waiter ten dollars, told him to keep the change, drank the first cup quickly, and decided to wait a minute before trying the Alka Seltzer. Her hands shook as she poured another cup of coffee. At least she wasn't on Valium anymore, she reflected, wandering over to the window and staring down at the busy traffic and antlike people twenty floors below. She had started back on the booze in California when her lawyer had phoned with the sickening news that her rights to *Homegirl* would be terminated as of April. Her instinctive reaction had been to go out and buy a bottle of scotch, and the first sip had led her exactly to where she knew it would: peace, forgetfulness, a sense that she was home again.

She left California after the first few days. Too many people knew her there, and it was humiliating to be around Miroslav, who had loved the idea of doing *Homegirl* as much as she had, and blamed her for the loophole in the contract. She went back to New York, thinking that in a week or two she'd go to Europe or the Caribbean. But instead she stayed in her apartment drinking. At first there were constant phone calls. Theo Hammond, Miroslav, Harry Langhart, Neil Gallagher. She refused to take any of them, and when Harry, who had a key to her apartment, showed up unannounced one morning, she told him furiously to get the hell out.

"You've been drinking, Maggie."

"Aren't you perceptive."

"I can't help you if you're drinking. I've told you that before. I've warned you."

She laughed at him. "I don't want your help. I just want you to get the fuck out of here."

"All right, I will. But I think you're a fool, Maggie, to throw it all away because of a little disappointment."

"Losing *Homegirl* is not, as you so callously put it, a 'little disappointment.'"

"Whatever it is, it's sure as hell not worth getting drunk over. Nothing is worth getting drunk over."

She didn't agree with that. She thought there were plenty of things to get drunk over—her aging face with all the little crow's feet at the corners of her eyes, her failure as an actress and producer, the fact that she had allowed the great love of her life, Neil Gallagher, to slip through her fingers. When Patsy, against instructions, showed her a package of press clippings about Neil's resignation from office, she jubilantly poured herself a drink. She'd ruined him! But after a few days that one little triumph wasn't enough for her—not after what she'd been through—and she decided to hand over Frank Stiller's report to the press.

And what had happened?

The report was in her bank vault, and she'd been too goddamned drunk to ever go and get it.

Reluctantly, she turned from the window and went back to the tray of coffee. Time for Alka Seltzer, she thought, gritting her teeth. She drank the medicine quickly, found her coat in the closet, and left the room, ignoring the three crisp bills that lay on the floor. In the elevator, she closed her eyes as the glassed-in cage descended with sickening speed to the lobby. When she was outside, she put on Joe's sunglasses—since she didn't have her own, they would come in handy—and hailed a cab. "I want to go to Seventy-fourth and Second," she said, slamming the door and lighting her first cigarette of the day. It was twelve-thirty. She'd be a little late, but at least she'd get there.

Charlie was nervous about celebrating her anniversary. She couldn't believe that a little over a year ago, on a bitterly cold January day, Tanya Hendricks had dragged her into this same crowded room with its assortment of ill-matched chairs, its fogged-up windows, its steamy smells of coffee and cigarettes, its many happy faces. How sick she had felt! She remembered squinting at the charts on the walls, and wondering what the hell they meant. Twelve steps to recovery. Felicity had been the speaker that day, but she had hardly listened to her because of the headache pounding fiercely at her temples.

Looking around the room today, she felt as if she were surrounded by love. Neil sat across from her, his hair a little longer now, a big bunch of roses on his lap. At the table at the back, slicing up pieces of anniversary cake, was Tanya, who looked up at her and grinned. Felicity, who had come in late, sat cross-legged on the floor, her small pretty face shining with pride. And there was Margot Sibley with her knitting, and Theo Hammond, who had to walk with a cane now because of his fractured hip. Gwen was today's speaker. It was traditional in New York for celebrants to choose a cherished AA friend to speak at their anniversary, and Charlie had asked Gwen because of all they had been through together in the past year. But she had done so with her heart in her mouth: until today the writer had never told her story at a meeting.

The crowded room was hushed as Gwen began to speak. In solemn tones she talked about her Harlem childhood, her privileged education, her sense of alienation from her own people. "For a while there, my sense of identity came from the bottle. Alcohol helped me forget how scared and shy I was. It loosened me up at parties, made me feel like a witty, okay person, and when I started writing—which for me was a frightening process—it relaxed me to the point where I could let the words flow. What I'm saying is that for a while the booze worked for me. But then, sadly, there came a time when it let me down." With a clouded face, she talked about her suicide attempt fourteen months earlier. "I nearly died because of alcohol. But you know what? It led me here, to the rooms of AA, where I've come to know who I truly am...not only Gwen Thomas, daughter, friend, writer, lover, but also Gwen T.—a gratefully recovering alcoholic."

As she said those words, Charlie felt her eyes mist over. She bit down hard on her lip. For her whole life she would cherish this moment.

Just then, bangles snapping together, Gwen pointed a finger at her and said, "This girl here has come a long, long way." She talked for a moment about the shaky, willful Charlie she had met a year ago, and the happily composed woman who sat beside her now, the woman who had a strong, sound marriage, and children whose growing-up she could watch with clear eyes—a woman who knew what she wanted from her life. "It takes a little bit of faith, and a shitload of going to meetings, for everything to work out the way it's supposed to. Charlie and I have both had to learn that the hard way, but the point is, we learned it—we've survived!"

There was a burst of applause. To her embarrassment, Charlie felt a tear slide down her cheek, and quickly grabbed her bag and began to search for a Kleenex. People kept on clapping and clapping. "All right, all right," said Gwen. "Before the cake's served, how about some day counts?"

A hand slowly went up in the back of the room. It was a beautiful slender hand that wore no nail polish, but did sport a flashing diamond ring. A mink sleeve surrounded it as it wobbled in the air.

"Yeah, you," Gwen said coolly.

A shaky voice said, "My name is Maggie. I'm an alcoholic and this is my first day back."

"My God!" exclaimed Charlie beneath her breath. "I don't believe it!" Her eyes sought out Neil's. His face had gone dead white.

Gwen, beside her, grabbed her hand and squeezed hard. "Hey, baby," she muttered. "Don't let her worry you. Just let go, let God, and get ahead with your business. You hear?"

"Yeah, I hear," said Charlie. "I hear loud and clear."

The bedraggled blonde at the back of the room stared at the two of them, a brave smile on her lips. She looked pretty pathetic. Charlie tried to avert her eyes. But she couldn't help seeing Neil rise from his chair and walk slowly toward Musette, the roses still in his arms. When he was almost there, the actress held up a hand and began to speak again. "I . . . I want to say publicly that I've made a mess of things. I got pretty crazy and resentful, and that made me wrong the people I wanted to love. Drugs had a little bit to do with it. When I couldn't cope with my problems I started taking Valium, and then when things got really bad, I drank. But I'm back now. I know there are some people who may not be happy to see me, but I've earned my seat in this room. I've got to try again, and I need your help."

She looked appealingly around the room, and fell silent. The person next to her—a girl in blue jeans—gave her a hug, and there was a smattering of applause. It was time for the break. People stood up and began wandering around the room, most of them heading for the coffee urn and the cake, which had been laid out on white paper plates. Charlie, still in her chair, watched with mounting anxiety as Neil took Musette by the elbow and led her from the room. She would have given every one of her beloved paintings to get up and follow them, but just at that moment someone handed her a piece of anniversary cake, and started congratulating her on her first year.

Out in the hallway a tense Neil said, "Did you get those clippings I sent you?"

Musette faced him mutely. Her head throbbed, and it was difficult to look at him, to meet his eyes. She was horrified that he should see her without makeup. "Yes," she muttered.

"Well?"

She was aware of the stale liquor on her breath, and flushed darkly. "You don't have to worry," she said.

"What?" It was hard to hear above the laughter and sounds of conversation coming from the meeting room.

"I said you don't have to worry. You're out of politics, and I've lost my career. I guess we're even."

"You mean you won't publish the report?"

"As long as you stay away from the presidency, no one will ever see it."

He looked at her dubiously. "How can I be sure of that?" he asked.

Her once beautiful golden eyes, now puffy and dull, stared sadly into his. "I guess you'll just have to have some of the same faith the people in there have," she said, gesturing toward the meeting room with a shrug of the shoulder. "Now if you'll excuse me, I'm going to go and get a cup of coffee."

She turned, nearly tripping on one of her heels, and walked slowly back into the room, pulling big black sunglasses down over her eyes.

In the meeting room Charlie, surrounded by a crowd of well-wishers, was talking to Theo Hammond and nervously watching the door. When she saw Musette, she clenched her hands into tight fists. The actress's face was pale and set, and she was hugging her coat around herself as if she were cold. Following just behind her, the roses still in his arms, was Neil. He pushed his way through the knot of people waiting to congratulate Charlie, his blue eyes lighting up as he handed her the flowers. "Here, my darling, these are for you," he said tenderly. "You've earned them."

"We both have," said Charlie, opening her arms to him.